THE PRIVATE LIFE OF SPIES

· AND ·

THE EXQUISITE ART OF GETTING EVEN

THE PRIVATE LIFE
OF SPIES

── · AND · ──

THE EXQUISITE ART
OF GETTING EVEN

Alexander McCall Smith

Pantheon Books, New York

All rights reserved. Published in the United States by Pantheon Books,
a division of Penguin Random House LLC, New York. Originally published in
hardcover in two volumes in Great Britain as *The Exquisite Art of Getting Even* by
Polygon Books, an imprint of Birlinn Limited, Edinburgh, in 2022, and
The Private Life of Shadows by Abacus, an imprint of Little, Brown Book Group,
a Hachette U.K. company, London, in 2023.

Pantheon Books and colophon are registered trademarks of
Penguin Random House LLC.

Library of Congress Cataloging-in-Publication Data
Name: McCall Smith, Alexander, [date] author.
Title: The private life of spies ; and The exquisite art of getting even : stories /
Alexander McCall Smith.
Description: First American edition. | New York : Pantheon Books, 2023
Identifiers: LCCN 2022052431 (print). LCCN 2022052432 (ebook).
ISBN 9780593700693 (hardcover). ISBN 9780593700709 (ebook).
Subjects: LCGFT: Spy fiction. Short stories.
Classification: LCC PR6063.C326 P75 2023 (print) |
LCC PR6063.C326 (ebook) | DDC 823/.914—dc23/eng/20221122
LC record available at https://lccn.loc.gov/2022052431
LC ebook record available at https://lccn.loc.gov/2022052432

www.pantheonbooks.com

Jacket illustration by Iain McIntosh

Printed in the United States of America
First American Edition
2 4 6 8 9 7 5 3 1

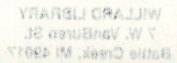

Contents

THE
PRIVATE LIFE
OF
SPIES

Author's Note

These stories are part fiction and part non-fiction. In *Nuns and Spies*, one of the common legends of World War II—that German spies were dropped into England dressed as nuns—is explored. For further discussion of this widespread belief, see James Hayward, *Myths and Legends of the Second World War. Donald and Yevgeni* is based on the life of several historical characters, including Archie Clark Kerr, a British ambassador, and Donald Maclean, a British spy. There is a very informative biography of Clark Kerr: Donald Gillies, *Radical Diplomat*. This biography addresses the question of the unlikely Russian valet, Yevgeni Yost. For further details of the career of Donald Maclean, reference may be made to Roland Phillip's excellent *A Spy Called Orphan*. Finally, on the Vatican Secret Service, see the exhaustive treatment of the topic in *The Entity* by Eric Frattini. There is an immense literature on the *filioque* controversy. The history of this remarkable issue is discussed in A. Edward Siecienski's scholarly *The Filioque: History of a Doctrinal Controversy* (Oxford Studies in Historical Theology).

Nuns and Spies

CONRADIN MULLER WAS AN UNUSUAL SPY. HE WAS RECRUITED IN Hamburg in June 1943, much against his will, and sent on his first, and only, mission in late September that year. He failed to send a single report back to Germany, and when the war came to an end in May 1945, he fell to his knees and wept with relief.

"I never wanted any part of this," he said to his friend, Sister Cecilia. "This whole awful, disastrous mess. Never."

She knew what he meant, and she believed him. "There, there," she said, patting his wrist, as she often did when things became too much for him. "There, there, dear Conradin. All over now. The Lord works in mysterious ways—few can doubt that—but He usually achieves the results He wants. Of that, there can be no doubt whatsoever."

"I have much to thank the Lord for," he said to Sister Cecilia. "For this place. For you and the others. For everything that happened to me. I am constantly grateful."

And he was. His gratitude, in fact, knew no bounds, and he reminded himself each morning of his great good fortune. He had been a spy in wartime, and had it not been for the kindness of Cecilia and all the other sisters he would have met the grim fate that such spies meet. He owed them his life. He owed them everything, in fact, and one day, he hoped, he might be able to repay them. They were kind English people, and he would not hear a word against the English. Not one word.

Until that fateful day in 1943, Conradin had lived a blameless, if somewhat dull life. He was the only son of Gustav Muller, the owner of a small printing business, and his wife, Monika, a piano teacher and an invalid. Gustav was an alcoholic, and unreliable; Monika could walk, but could do so only with difficulty; she relied on Conradin to do the shopping and the housework. When not helping at home, Conradin, who was naturally gifted when it came to foreign languages, had a part-time job teaching English to science students at the university. He also taught occasional classes in Spanish and French, although English was his main subject. He had studied for three years at King's College, London, before the war, and before returning to Germany had taught for two years at a boys' boarding school in Devon, a place of bizarre traditions and minimum academic standards that went bankrupt when Conradin was on the staff. These five years in England meant that he felt perfectly confident in the language, a fact that unfortunately caught the attention of a local Abwehr colonel, whose brother-in-law was a professor of physics at the same university at which Conradin taught.

On the outbreak of the war, of which the Muller family thoroughly disapproved, Conradin was thirty-eight years old. Men of that age were being taken for military service, and Conradin was interviewed by the local recruiting office. The interview, however, was conducted by a retired army officer whose wife was distantly related to Conradin's mother. This relative had explained to her husband that Conradin was the most dutiful of sons and that if he were to be taken by the army, Gustav would be unable to look after Monika. Gustav's own health was shaky—his drinking had eventually taken its toll—and he, like his wife, relied on Conradin's help. The officer himself was sceptical, but he dared not contradict his wife, and Conradin, to his considerable relief, was duly exempted from enlistment.

This exemption was to prove short-lived: when the colonel discovered that Conradin spoke perfect, idiomatic English, he summoned him to his office and informed him that he was happy to report that his offer to work for German Intelligence had been accepted.

"But there must be some misunderstanding, Colonel," protested Conradin. "I have not offered to do anything."

The colonel fixed him with a steely gaze. "It would be very unwise to contradict my recollection of events," he said. "I take it that you understand me?"

Conradin swallowed hard. He had understood only too well. "What do you want me to do?"

"You are to be trained as a field agent," said the colonel. "You will undertake a three-month course, during which you will be shown how to behave like an Englishman." The colonel laughed. "You have to be able to drink tea in a special way if you are to avoid detection in England. In a very effeminate way. Like this." The colonel lifted a cup with his little finger extended, in a mockery of affectation. "See?"

Conradin nodded dumbly. This was the end. He would be captured and that would be the end of him. He had no future now—none.

"And you will be thoroughly trained in the operation of radio," continued the colonel. "Have you ever operated a short-wave radio?"

Conradin shook his head.

"It is most important that operators should understand how these things work," said the colonel. "Not only are there issues of radio wave propagation, there are matters connected with antennae. The correct length is vital for a functioning antenna, you know. There is mathematics involved in that."

Conradin swallowed again. Was it best to be blindfolded when you faced a firing squad? Or could you simply close your eyes?

"So," said the colonel. "That's settled, then. The orderly has prepared the papers."

He clicked his fingers and a uniformed orderly appeared. "Sign here," he said. "And then here. And here."

Conradin noticed the orderly's fingernails. They had been bitten back to the quick. He shuddered.

"You are now enrolled in the Abwehr," the orderly said in a low voice. "Congratulations." His accent, Conradin noticed, was Bavarian. There was a faint whiff of beer. They were like that down there, he thought. They liked their beer-halls. Brutes.

ALTHOUGH HE WAS FAR from being a volunteer, Conradin found some parts of the course stimulating. There were lessons in the geography of Britain, in history—German agents were capable of listing all English monarchs, in order, since Richard III (a "very fine king" said the instructor)—and in the right way of addressing a duke, an earl, or a baronet. They were also given rudimentary training in Morris dancing and in the various types of English beer. At times, the attention to detail in their instruction was impressive, as when the prospective agents were obliged to sit through an hour-long lecture on the correct way of entering a post office, greeting the postmistress, and purchasing a stamp.

"Do not compliment her on her dress," said the lecturer. "Do not address her as *gnädige Frau*, or anything of that sort. Do not talk about anything except the weather. Have you got that?"

There were nods of assent, although many of the recruits were secretly puzzled. How much could anyone say about the weather? Did the English really have nothing else to talk about?

But their lecturer had more to say on the subject. "And when it comes to talking about the weather, always say that it is fine, even if it isn't. The difference between English and German is that while German is a rational language, in which what is said is what is meant, English is the opposite. In English, if something is large, you say it is small; if a problem is a major one, it is described as being a 'little difficulty.' And so on. There are many examples—too many to enumerate. Also, remember that the English do not comment on bad conditions, except when it is raining very heavily. Then you must say, 'Nice weather for ducks.' Do not say anything else. That is very important."

The instructor thought of something. "Everything I have been saying applies only to the English. Do not forget that there are also Scotsmen. They are different. If something is bad, then they will say that it is very bad. If it is good, they will usually say nothing, just in case it *becomes* bad. That is also very important, but you need not worry too much about that, as we are not going to drop you in Scotland—unless there is a navigational error."

This was a joke, and there was laughter.

The instructor grinned briefly, and then continued, "If the French are mentioned in conversation—let's say you're in a pub and somebody mentions them—then you must roll your eyes and say, '*Mon Dieu!*' That will be quite sufficient.

"If Germans are spoken of, then you must be very careful. Just say, 'So much for Jerry,' and leave it at that. If British forces are mentioned, then say, 'Good for our boys.'"

The instructor surveyed them. "Is that crystal clear?" he asked.

"*Jawohl*," they replied in unison.

The instructor sighed. "You must be careful not to say that," he warned. "The English are not stupid. You should say 'jolly good' or 'right-oh.' Understood?"

The instructor looked at them. They were doing well, but there were certain habits that had to be drummed into them time and time again.

"Let me repeat," he said. "If you want to sound like a local, you must use certain words that are very important. *Jolly* is one of them. You can add this to anything—and that is just what they do. So if you are asked how you are, you must reply, 'I am jolly fine.' If you are asked what the time is, you should say, 'It is jolly nearly twelve o'clock,' or whatever. If something unfortunate occurs, then you should say, 'This is a jolly bad show.' You cannot use the word too much."

"Jolly right-oh," they said.

"Jolly good," said the instructor.

Conradin was sceptical about this use of the word "jolly," but he had not been in England for some years and new usages were emerging all the time. It would be best to be receptive to the insights of these instructors, who presumably knew what they were doing.

DURING THE WAR, as in any time of confusion, rumours about German spies abounded in Britain. Officialdom discouraged these, but it was too much to ask that people would not pass on stories that, even if implausible, were not beyond the bounds of possibility. In particular, tales of the disguises affected by German agents were eagerly listened to, embroidered, and then passed on. To some extent, this was the fault of the authorities themselves in encouraging distrust. If people were warned to question the identity of others, then it was not surprising that they might question whether the policeman directing traffic was really a policeman, or whether he was a German agent in police uniform. The Germans, they were told, would stop at nothing in their attempt to infiltrate: the rules of the game, it seemed, had been suspended for the duration.

Historians of wartime myths often cite one particular example of a widespread false belief of the time—that German spies were being parachuted into Britain dressed as nuns. This story was widely circulated, and believed, although it was never backed by any concrete evidence. Like most such legends, the source of the belief is untraceable, although the Dutch Foreign Minister of the time, E. N. van Kleffens, must have helped the rumour on its way when he announced in the early stages of the war that German paratroopers dressed as nuns had been dropped in the Netherlands.

That had not taken place. And yet, with the recent discovery of Conradin Muller's diary in a second-hand book shop in Cambridge, we now have a reliable first-hand account of just such a case. On his first mission in September, 1943, this frightened and unhappy German agent was dropped by a Luftwaffe aircraft over a Suffolk field. He was dressed as a nun, and he carried with him a pouch of maps, a small short-wave radio, a battery, and a Roman Catholic missal. As the drone of the aircraft that had brought him across the North Sea faded away, Conradin looked up past the canopy of his billowing white parachute. He could make out the stars in the night sky—innocent, neutral witnesses of the foolishness of men. It was a strange moment for him. He wanted to cry. He wanted to raise to the heavens a roar of frustration and denial. What had he done to deserve this? He had not asked to be here. History had caught him up in its skirts. And, to top it all, he had to endure the absurdity of this fancy-dress, this nun's habit, complete with elaborate wimple, so ill-suited to the business of falling through the sky towards the unwelcoming earth below. They had told him that it was the best possible disguise; that nobody would suspect a nun; that even the most officious policeman would think twice before challenging a nun and asking her to produce papers. "Nuns are above suspicion," they said.

"That is why you are safest if you dress as one. This is confirmed by all sources."

Conradin disagreed. "Why don't they dress us up as pantomime horses?" he whispered to the man sitting next to him at their final briefing. "Nobody ever asks a horse for his papers."

"It is unpatriotic to joke about these things," his colleague reproached him. "Remember, we Germans do not have a sense of humour."

Preparations for departure went ahead. His nun's habit, when it was delivered, was found to be several sizes too large, but was adjusted by a local seamstress. She carried out the final fitting in her atelier, observed by her young son, who watched wide-eyed as Conradin slipped the habit over his normal civilian clothing.

"*Mutti*," said the young boy, "can I be a nun when I grow up?"

"If the Lord calls you," muttered the seamstress through the pins she was holding between her lips. She winked at Conradin. "Children," she said.

"This was not my idea," muttered Conradin.

Two days later, after a bumpy and frightening flight, with the pilot flying at wave-top height to avoid radar detection, Conradin was bundled out of the aircraft into a cold and rushing darkness. As he dropped down, he thought of his mother. She loved him. Just about every soldier had a mother somewhere, who loved him and who would be hoping for the war to end. Down below, though, in the unlit countryside, were people who did not love him at all, but who wished him dead. He had done nothing to them, but they would happily kill him if they had the chance—nun's outfit or no nun's outfit. How could people hate those whom they had never met? Only too easily, it seemed.

He landed heavily, winding himself badly. As he lay on the ground, his parachute collapsed over him like a white silk tent, Conradin struggled to reflate his lungs. He thought he must have broken something, and was wondering whether it might be a leg. If so, he would have little chance, even of giving himself up, as he would be unable to move very far and would have to wait until ignominious discovery occurred the following morning. And that, he thought, would be the end of that. There would be a summary trial—if he was lucky—and then the imposition and exaction of the ultimate penalty. The fact that he was dressed as a nun would only make matters worse. The English would not approve—he had no doubt of that. It would be different if he were to change, but he would have no chance of finding a German uniform which he might don. Even civilian clothes would be hard enough to get hold of.

He sat up before gingerly rising to his feet. There was no pain, no sudden collapse of his legs once he put his weight on them. He was uninjured, it seemed, and could walk. The discovery cheered him: it could have been far worse.

He looked about him. He had landed in an open field, which was fortunate, as there were woods nearby and he might easily have floated down into those. There were no lights to be seen anywhere—he had been told that the drop area was four miles from the nearest village and that all he was likely to find would be farmhouses and barns. None of these, of course, were lit at three in the morning, which was the time at which he arrived in England.

He bundled up his parachute. Strapped to his radio bag was a small field shovel, and he now used this at the edge of the field to dig a hole in which to bury the parachute. This took almost two hours, as the ground was hard, and full of roots. Eventually, though, he was able to finish the task and to cover the disturbed area with leaves. Then he thrust the spade into a ditch, where it was concealed by mud and water, and started down a small lane that he hoped would lead to the village. He had been told that there were two buses a day that would take him to Ely, from where he could catch a train to Cambridge, where a contact would meet him.

It was summer, and by the time he reached the outskirts of the village, the sun had floated up over the horizon. It was a fine morning, and had he not been dressed as a nun, in enemy territory, he might even have enjoyed the walk along the quiet lane. An inquisitive cow watched him from a field; sheep looked up from their grazing; a bird sang to him from a hedgerow. He wanted to cry. He would readily have changed places with any of these creatures, to be free of this world of conflict and danger that human beings created for themselves.

He had been assured that he would be dropped in exactly the right place and that the very best navigators were chosen for these flights. That was not the case. The navigator allocated to his flight was facing disciplinary proceedings. He was drinking excessively and had received several warnings. His calculations were out by miles, and the village outside which Conradin had been dropped was not the intended one. And it happened that this village was home to a convent of Anglican nuns, the Little Sisters of Charity. These nuns, who followed the Rule of St. Francis, ran a large pig farm, a substantial vegetable garden, and a home for those who, in the language of the time, were known as "fallen women." The fallen women were taken in by the nuns, looked after during their confinement, and then sent back to their families with the baby, if they wished, or after the baby had been put up for adoption, should the mothers opt for that. Unlike many such homes at the time, they did not exert any pressure on the mothers to surrender the baby. Nor did they seek to lecture the women or make them feel guilty. "You are all loved—no matter how bad you have been," was a motto worked on needlepoint kneelers in the chapel.

It was outside this convent that Conradin found himself, turning a corner in the lane, just as a line of nuns emerged from the gate, crossed the road, and began to make their way down towards the pig farm. He stopped in his tracks. To his front was the line of nuns; to his left was a millpond. Above him was a clear, empty sky. It was blue, and free. He looked up. God existed. He must do, or something like this could never have happened. He took his radio bag off his back. He held it for a moment, as if weighing it, and then dropped it into the millpond without making a splash. It floated for a moment, and then sank, disappearing in the murky green water. A duck on the other side of the pond flapped its wings.

The line of nuns was now some distance away, and Conradin had to run in order to catch up with them. But he soon reached them and, as he did, one of the nuns turned and smiled at him.

"I was almost late myself," she said to Conradin. "Sister Angela gave me an awful rocket about it the other day."

Conradin nodded sympathetically. "I overslept," he muttered, keeping his voice as high-pitched as possible.

"Easily done," said the nun. She looked at him curiously. "You're new, aren't you?"

"Jolly new," said Conradin. "Just arrived."

They walked on. There were six of them, Conradin noticed, all wearing a habit that he was pleased to see was very similar, if not identical, to his own. They were of different ages, he saw—some looking young enough to be novices, while others were in their fifties or sixties. But they all looked very well-fed, he noticed; indeed all of them looked as if they might have benefited from a diet.

"What is your name, Sister?" asked his new companion as they approached the gate to the pig farm.

Conradin hesitated. "My name?" he asked.

"Yes, your name."

"Sister Conradin," he stuttered. As he gave his answer, he realised that here was a glaring defect in his masters' preparations. They had given him identity papers under the name he would assume in Cambridge, but they had said nothing about his identity as a nun. If that was their level of incompetence, then it was no wonder that they lost so many agents.

"I'm Sister Cecilia," said the nun. "I'm named after Saint Cecilia, although I'm definitely not musical. My singing is hopeless. I try, but I just can't hold a note."

"We all have our talents," said Conradin. "I'm sure the Lord has sent you other gifts."

They were approaching the pig sheds. "Dreadfully smelly places," said Sister Cecilia. "It's not the pigs' fault, of course, but they are a bit smelly."

"Jolly smelly," agreed Conradin. "But they are all God's creatures."

"Don't overdo it," said Sister Cecilia. "Some are, maybe, others— I'm not so sure. There's a very ill-tempered sow. She's called Arabella, and you have to watch her. She'll give you a nip if she gets the chance—a serious bite, in fact. Don't let her get near you. Use your slap board to fend her off." She paused. "I'm looking forward to eating her, actually. Mother says that we can slaughter her next month and make bacon. It won't come a day too early as far as I'm concerned."

"I love bacon," said Conradin.

"And sausages," said Sister Cecilia. "Mother has a recipe that was given to her by the Bishop of Ely. He loves a good sausage, they say."

They were now at the pig sheds and a senior nun was allocating tasks. Sister Cecilia was instructed to clean the feeders littered about the field and then unblock a ditch that ran alongside one of the sheds.

"I'll help you," Conradin said quickly before he could be singled out by the senior nun.

"You're very kind," said Sister Cecilia, offering him a peppermint. "These are very strong, these mints. They're not on the ration, actually. I exchange them for rashers of bacon down in the village."

"Needs must," said Conradin.

They set to work.

"You're very strong," observed Sister Cecilia halfway through the morning. "I bet you're as strong as any man."

Conradin bit his lip. I should have been more careful, he thought. "I come from a strong family," he said. "My mother was a strong lady in a circus. You know the sort of thing? She tore up telephone directories. Lifted motorcycles, and so on."

"That's amazing," said Sister Cecilia. "You're lucky. Some of the sisters find the farm work just too much for them. Mother will be very pleased to have you if you can do all these hard tasks. She often says it would be so good to have a few men round the place—but all the men are off in the army or are unfit for anything very much. So, it's just us and the girls."

"The girls?" asked Conradin.

Sister Cecilia mopped at her brow with a large white handkerchief. "The fallen women," she said. "Has nobody told you?"

Conradin shook his head.

"We run a home for fallen women," Sister Cecilia said. "They come here when they find out they're going to have a baby and their families kick them out. People are so cruel. But we look after them and help them to get back up on their feet. We usually have about five or six girls at any one time. We give them light duties in the vegetable garden or they do sewing under Sister Agnes. We have a contract to make pyjamas for the air force. We can't produce all that many—twenty pairs a week, most of the time, but it's our contribution—one of them—to the war effort."

Sister Cecilia looked up at the sky. They had almost finished clearing the ditch and it was time, she said, to go back for lunch. The other sisters would come back a bit later.

"Have you met Mother?" Sister Cecilia asked as they walked back towards the main convent building.

Conradin shook his head.

"You'll like her," said Sister Cecilia. "She's strict, but she's really kind at heart. Some consider her to be a bit of a schemer, but then she wouldn't have got where she's got if she was unable to hatch the occasional plot."

"I look forward to meeting her," said Conradin. He was unsure what to do, and had decided he would simply let events flow over him. He had abandoned his mission at the moment that he dropped his radio in the millpond. There was no going back now. He would simply see what happened. If they shot him, they shot him—so be it. For the moment, he would continue to be a nun, which, on balance, was far better, he decided, than being a spy.

SEATED AT HER WALNUT DESK, under a painting of Richeldis de Faverches, the English noblewoman to whom the Virgin had chosen to appear in Walsingham, Mother sighed.

"They keep doing this," she said, a detectable note of irritation in her voice. "Mother House keeps sending us sisters without giving us proper warning. Then, when you complain, they say that they did write to us but the letter must have been destroyed by enemy action. That excuse will work once or twice, but after a while it wears a bit thin."

The Mother Superior looked over her half-moon glasses at Conradin, seated on a hard-backed chair in front of her desk. "I take it you were in Salisbury?"

Conradin nodded. He did not want to lie; he had had enough of that. There were so many lies back home, and now he had no heart for them. But he could hardly start telling the truth now, at this late stage, seated here in this convent, in a nun's habit. "Yes. I was there. Then they sent me here."

Mother shook her head. "They really are the limit, Sister Bernadette and the people in her office. But, not to worry—the important thing is that you're here. I gather that Sister Cecilia has been showing you the ropes. She said you were very useful down at the pig farm."

"I enjoyed working with her," said Conradin.

"That's very satisfactory," said Mother. "Some of the sisters don't like working with pigs."

There was a silence. Conradin noticed that Mother's eyes were on his shoes. "Those are good, stout shoes," she said. "Very useful."

He swallowed, and reflected on the fact that he was bound to be exposed. It was a miracle that he had not been seen through straight away; it was inevitable.

"I wish I could get a substantial pair of shoes myself," said Mother. "Everything on offer these days—even if you have the coupons— seems to be made of very thin leather. Wartime economy, I suppose." She looked at the shoes again. "You take quite a large size, Sister," she said.

"I always have," said Conradin quickly. "At least as an adult." He paused. "When I was young, I took a smaller size."

Mother looked thoughtful. "That's the way of things, I suppose," she said.

She rose from her desk. "Well, Sister Conradin, we are so looking forward to having you among us. Sister Cecilia will show you your room—we don't call them cells any more, although some of the older sisters still use that term. I shall see you, no doubt, at dinner in the refectory. We eat very early here."

He rose too, and inclined his head to Mother in a gesture of obeisance. She smiled back at him. "Blessings, my dear Sister Conradin," she said. "And I am so pleased that you have dropped in."

"Dropped in" . . . The words hung in the air, as if suspended between them. Did Mother know? Was this her way of saying that she knew that he had arrived by parachute, and, if she did, was she now on her way to make a furtive call to the local police? In the chapel tower, a bell was being tolled. Would the next thing he heard be the siren of a police car racing to the convent to arrest him?

Sister Cecilia was waiting for him outside. She drew Conradin aside and whispered into his ear, "Mother likes you. She told me as she came out. She said she feels you have been sent to us by the Lord himself—to help with the pig farm. She is very pleased."

He smiled weakly. He had been thinking of something that he would have to discuss with Sister Cecilia and that could not be put off.

"May I ask you, Sister—what are the bathroom arrangements?"

Sister Cecilia did not seem surprised by the question. "We have bathrooms on each floor. There are more than enough of them."

He waited a moment, and then asked, "And are they nice and . . . private?"

Once again, Sister Cecilia did not think the question inappropriate. "Yes, very private. Our order has always stressed modesty. You need have no fears on that score, Sister Conradin. We have never approved of communal washing facilities."

He felt immensely relieved. Now all he would need to do was to lay his hands on a razor. If the worst came to the worst, he might be able to find a knife in the kitchen that could be sharpened sufficiently to allow him to shave. He would have to do that soon, he thought—no later than tomorrow afternoon. The occasional nun may have a voice as deep as his, but there were very few nuns, he imagined, who had to worry about five-o'clock shadow.

He was exhausted that first night, and sleep came quickly. As he lay in the darkness, in his narrow bed, he felt only relief that he had survived the day. The dread that he had experienced during the flight from Germany, the terror of the parachute drop, the fear of exposure that had attended every moment at the pig farm—all of these seemed to melt away. He was alive, and nobody seemed intent on changing that. He had fallen amongst people whose approach to the world about them was not one of confrontation and anger—as it was back in Germany at present—but of acceptance and love. It was so different, and even he, an intruder, an impostor, felt embraced by that feeling.

Before he had retired, he had participated in the later offices of the day—Vespers and Compline—and had found comfort in the gentle, almost whispered liturgy. Tiredness had caught up with him by Compline, and he found himself drifting off during the reading of one of the psalms, only to be kept awake by a friendly nudge from

Sister Cecilia. Then there had been the confession of sins, and as he uttered the words, he realised that he was truly sorry for the wrongs he had done—not that his sins were numerous. He had never sought to harm anybody; he had never wanted to be a spy; he had never accepted the venom of his times; he had done his best to keep away from that poison. But he was nonetheless engaged in a gross deceit, perpetrated every moment that he wore his nun's habit. He was not entitled to that. He was not entitled to the friendship and charity of these women amongst whom he found himself. But what were his alternatives? Were there any at all, other than the firing squad or the noose or whatever fate awaited a captured spy in wartime? His instructors back in Hamburg had said little about that; they had not spelled out the consequences of discovery. He found himself wondering what God, if he existed, would want him to do. God would understand limited options; God would appreciate that not all of us can be brave. God, he knew, would see through his disguise, because God, of all people, could tell the difference between a real nun and a fake one. You can't fool God, he thought . . . and with that in mind, he drifted off into sleep, to dream of pigs who spoke English to him, and a parachute that disinterred itself and floated slowly up into the sky, and of some of those other things, snatches of memory and association, that make up the landscape of dreams.

SISTER CECILIA HAD PROVIDED him with fresh clothing. She complained about the lack of attention to these matters by the order's headquarters in Salisbury. "They should have given you a suitcase with fresh linen," she said. "They always forget to give people the things they need. Fortunately, we have plenty here, but it really isn't our job to give new arrivals the things they should have been issued with by what's her name . . . Sister . . . Sister . . ."

She looked to him for help, and he thought quickly. "Oh, I know the one you mean. Her."

"Her, yes, her. Sister . . ."

"Oh, I keep forgetting her name. She's so . . ."

Now Sister Cecilia came to the rescue. "So bossy. Not that I should be uncharitable, but sometimes . . ."

"Yes. Bossy. She's jolly bossy."

Sister Cecilia nodded. "You know something? I don't think she can count. No, I'm not making it up. I've seen her using her fingers to add things up. And what's the use, I always say, of having a sister in charge of stores and supplies who can't count for toffee?"

Conradin agreed wholeheartedly. "She's useless," he said.

"Well, it doesn't matter," said Sister Cecilia, pointing to the neat pile of clothing she had delivered to Conradin's room. "Once you've put those things away, we can go and feed the pigs. There are slop buckets outside the kitchens. It's dirty work, and I can't stand it, but we have to carry those down to the farm. It takes hours, and the pigs are so greedy, pushing and shoving to get their snouts in the trough. They really are disgusting."

"I don't mind doing that," said Conradin. He glanced at Sister Cecilia and saw her face light up. Now he insisted. "You really must let me. I love doing that sort of thing."

"Would you mind?" asked Sister Cecilia. "It would free me up to go and have a cup of tea with the girls—the fallen women, you know."

"Of course."

"Personally, I don't like to call them that, but that's just me. Mother uses the term and so do the government people who come round here to check up on them. Even the girls themselves use it. It's such a shame."

"It seems unkind," agreed Conradin. "Lapsed, perhaps? Lapsed women?"

"Like lapsed RCs?" Sister Cecilia shook her head. "I don't think that's any better, really. And it's so unfair. The men who cause the problem in the first place aren't called fallen anything, are they? They get away with it. Do they have to go off to a monastery for nine months? They do not. They just carry on—tra-la-la—getting girls into trouble as if nothing had happened."

Conradin shook his head. "Men are beasts," he said.

"Not all of them," said Sister Cecilia. "Some, not all."

"Of course."

Sister Cecilia thought of something. "When you go to collect the slop buckets, be careful not to take the ones with red handles. Those are scraps for the girls' refectory. Don't take those down to the farm."

Conradin frowned. "You mean that the fall—the girls get slops too?"

"Scraps," said Sister Cecilia. "Not slops. There is a difference. Mother doesn't hold with waste. Things like crusts of toast and bacon rind and so on—those go to the girls. It varies their diet, you see. They are all on the ration. And that can be a bit measly, you know. One egg a week and so on, although they get a bit extra because they're expecting. Still, it's not all that exciting and so we give them the scraps from our table too."

Conradin asked whether the sisters were also on the ration.

"Oh no," said Sister Cecilia. "We have our books, same as everyone else, but we have bags of extra supplies. Mother feels that the rules don't apply to nuns. She's a bit of an historian and she says that goes way back to Plantagenet times."

Conradin had noticed that dinner the previous evening had been a large meal. There had been lamb chops, piles of mashed potato, beans and homemade mint sauce. There had been a starter of smoked trout and a dessert of rhubarb and ice cream. And there had been second helpings all round, with some nuns, including Mother, having three. Breakfast had been slightly less substantial, but had nonetheless involved copious quantities of scrambled egg, rashers of thick bacon, and fried mushrooms.

"We produce it ourselves," explained Sister Cecilia. "So why shouldn't we eat it ourselves?"

Conradin shrugged. "I don't see any reason why not."

Sister Cecilia made a dismissive gesture. "The Ministry of Food sends inspectors from time to time. They snoop around farms to see that you aren't taking any stuff you're not meant to. But those people are no match for Mother. She runs rings round them."

"How does she do that?" asked Conradin.

Sister Cecilia tapped the end of her nose with a forefinger. "Best not to ask. What they call the Rule of Silence in Cistercian circles. Know what I mean?"

Conradin did, and asked no further questions.

.   .   .

OVER THE NEXT FEW DAYS, Conradin settled into a new routine. He found that the ordered nature of convent life—the regular meals, eaten while one of the nuns read aloud from a life of the saints or a book of devotions, the hours of work at the pig farm, the domestic duties of scrubbing and polishing—all of these lent themselves to a sense of stability and calm that was just what he needed. The war seemed a long way away, the only reminders of conflict being RAF activity at the airfield some twenty miles away. Conradin had been trained in the identification of aircraft as part of his education in espionage, and he found himself gazing up at the sky and automatically counting the bombers as they headed off towards the North Sea. Apart from this, it might have been peacetime for all the impact that the war had on the sheltered life of the nuns and their young women. Conradin relished that sense of detachment. He detested the war and all that it meant, and here he could allow himself to pretend it was not actually happening. Of course, there were moments when he suffered pangs of guilt: terrible things were happening in Germany and elsewhere, and he was doing nothing to stop them, and yet, when he gave the matter further thought, he realised that he *had* done something after all. He had effectively deserted, and that was an act of opposition by any standards. He expected no credit, but he did entertain the idea, half-seriously, that there should be medals for deserters. Surely they deserved them even more, perhaps, than those who simply obeyed.

He had very quickly made himself indispensable at the pig farm. Not only did he cheerfully take on dirtier tasks, such as the clearing out of the sties, he had also assumed various maintenance duties that the nuns had ignored in recent years. None of the nuns, he discovered, was prepared to climb a ladder; he did so willingly, tucking the skirts of his habit into the black tights with which Sister Cecilia had issued him. The roof of one of the barns was in a bad way, and Conradin soon worked out how to replace or rehang the slates that had worked free of their nails. Poking about in the dustier corners of a barn, he found supplies of paint, and he used this on the wooden sides of the agricultural machinery store. He excavated ditches long clogged up with weeds; he repaired fences tested and breached by generations of pigs; he cleared away all the clutter and detritus that inevitably accumulates in any farmyard, a task that in most cases is talked about at great length but rarely done.

He found himself getting on well with the pigs. "These are intelligent creatures," he said to Sister Cecilia. "You can see them thinking, can't you?"

"They seem to like you," she said.

"And I like them. Pigs are just themselves. They don't try to be anything else."

"That can't be easy," said Sister Cecilia, looking directly at him. "It can't be easy to be something that you're not."

"They don't try," Conradin remarked.

She looked thoughtful. "Do you think they have souls?"

He was not sure. "They might do. But how would one tell?"

Sister Cecilia thought that you could see a soul if you looked in a creature's eyes. "I've always thought dogs have souls," she said. "You look in their eyes and you see it. You see the longing, the love—the whatever. There's something there, I think. Pigs? I'm not so sure. Perhaps."

"Of course, if they have souls, then should we eat them?"

Sister Cecilia considered this for a moment. Then she said, "I love bacon."

Conradin did not take the matter further, and he noticed, anyway, that Sister Cecilia had fixed him with an intense, slightly unsettling gaze.

"Some animals can see through us, you know," she said. "Dogs certainly can, and I think pigs might be able to do so too. Not all pigs, perhaps, but some."

He said nothing. He tried to meet her gaze, but he found it difficult.

"So, for example," Sister Cecilia continued, "a dog can tell whether somebody's lying."

He pretended disbelief. "Surely not," he said.

"Oh yes," she said, her gaze still on him. "A dog can tell. They look into your eyes and I think they must see something that we might not be able to see."

He shrugged. "Who knows?"

There was a short silence. Then Sister Cecilia said, "I think they may be able to sense fear. I think that might be it. Frightened people always give themselves away. It's something to do with the way their hands shake slightly—ever so slightly. Much of the time you wouldn't see it, but then you look, and you see that their hands are shaking."

He made a supreme effort to control himself. He wanted to shake, but he resisted. He tried to think of something else—something innocent. He thought of the psalm that had been read the previous night at Vespers. He had been struck by the beauty of the words. It sounded so far less beautiful in German. But everything did, he reflected. He would stop speaking German when all this was over. He would deliberately forget his German, if you could do that with a language. He would speak English and perhaps Spanish, which was another language he had learned and loved.

He hardly dared look to see if she was staring at his hands. She was, and he immediately put them behind his back. Her gaze came back to his face.

"You must tell me about your childhood one day," she said. "I'd love to hear a bit about it."

He laughed—a contrived, falsetto laugh. "Oh, there's nothing much to say about that. Nothing, really."

Then she said, "Where did you get your accent? It isn't English, is it?"

He was prepared for this. "Iceland," he said. "I was brought up in Reykjavik. We spoke Icelandic, which is like very old Danish."

"Well, I never," said Sister Cecilia. "That explains that." She paused. "What does it sound like? Could you say something in Icelandic for me?"

He laughed. "Oh, I wouldn't want to confuse you. It's a very tricky language."

"But just say something. Anything. Say, 'My name is Conradin.'"

He was cornered. "All right," he said. He cleared his throat. "*Mi naam Conradin iss.*"

Sister Cecilia clapped her hands together. "But I understood that. It sounds very like English, doesn't it?"

"Some of it," he said. "All these languages are more similar than you'd imagine."

"So what's pig in Icelandic?"

He thought quickly. Then, "No, there's no word for pig in Icelandic. Sorry."

"No word for pig!" Sister Cecilia exclaimed. "There must be."

He immediately regretted his answer, but it was too late. He would have to persist. "There are no pigs in Iceland," he said. "Pigs never got that far."

She frowned. "Didn't people take them with them?"

He shook his head. "They tried. Many centuries ago, they took some pigs from Denmark to Iceland, but the pigs did not do well."

"What happened?"

"They froze. Or that's what we learned in school."

It took her a few moments to digest this. Then she said, "It's so sad. But tell me, what do Icelandic people do when they see a picture of a pig? What do they say if they don't have a word for it?"

"They use the Danish word."

"Which is?"

Again, he had to think quickly. "In Danish pig is *poeg*. It's very like the English word."

"And bacon?" she said.

"The same," said Conradin quickly. "*Bakon*."

"This country used to get most of its bacon from Denmark," said Sister Cecilia. "The war put an end to that."

"The war," sighed Conradin.

Sister Cecilia looked at him as if undecided about something. "It's so sad, isn't it?" she said.

He lowered his head. "I am ashamed," he muttered.

She frowned. "Why? Why should you be ashamed?"

The remark had slipped out. But he recovered by saying, "Ashamed at not doing more for the war effort."

"But you're doing your bit," said Sister Cecilia. "You're working on the land. That's war work."

"Perhaps," said Conradin. "But you know how it is. You never feel that what you're doing is quite enough."

.   .   .

BECAUSE THE FALLEN WOMEN took their meals in their own refectory, and because Conradin had not been allocated any duties in the vegetable garden, where they worked for several hours each day, he had only glimpsed them from time to time. When he took the pails of scraps over to their refectory he left them in the small porch behind the kitchen, and did not even see the cook who would later come out to collect them. In his second week in the convent, though, he found himself delivering scraps at the precise time that the cook, a somewhat discouraged-looking woman in her late forties, was coming out of the kitchen to smoke a cigarette. She lived in the village and was not a member of the order. She seemed keen to speak to Conradin.

"You're new, aren't you?" she said, as she lit her cigarette and exhaled a small cloud of smoke.

Conradin nodded. "I arrived last week," he said.

"From the house in Salisbury?"

"Yes." He was growing in confidence. Lying was so easy, he had discovered, even if it left you feeling uncomfortable.

The cook drew on the cigarette. "I hear you've been doing wonders at the pig farm. Sister Gilbert said something about that. She said you've tarted the place up no end."

"I do my best," said Conradin.

"Like to come in for a cup of tea?" asked the cook. "I've got some brewing." She gave a toss of her head in the direction of the kitchen.

Conradin hesitated. He was wary of any new situation where he might be compromised, but the cook seemed friendly enough and her relaxed manner had put him at his ease.

"I should be getting on with my work," he said, "but . . ."

The cook smiled. "But all work and no play, Sister," she said. "You don't want Jack to be a dull boy."

As they made their way into the kitchen, Conradin saw that there were two young women already there, sitting on chairs in front of a large, wood-burning range. One was conspicuously pregnant, the other less so. The young women looked up from the mugs of tea they were holding. They smiled at Conradin.

"This is Sister . . . Sister . . ." began the cook, looking for help from Conradin.

"Sister Conradin."

"Ah, yes." The cook gestured towards the young women. "And this is Elsie, and her friend Minnie."

Elsie, who was the older of the two, looked at Conradin in a frankly inquisitive way. "Hello, Sister."

Minnie mumbled something that Conradin did not catch.

"Elsie's one of our regulars," said the cook. "How many times have you been here, Else?"

Elsie grinned sheepishly. "Four times, Mrs. Evans."

The cook turned to Conradin. "You hear that, Sister Conradin? Four times. You'd think some people would learn from their mistakes." She smiled. "Not our Else!"

Minnie seemed keen to dissociate herself from this shamelessness. "Not me," she said. "First time—last time."

Conradin was not sure what to say. The whole exchange seemed good-natured—almost jocular—and yet, four times . . .

"I know I shouldn't," said Elsie. "But you know how fellows are." She paused, and looked at Conradin. "Of course, you nuns probably don't. It's hard for girls."

"I'm sure it is," said Conradin.

"A bit of self-control wouldn't go amiss," said the cook.

This drew a response from Minnie. "It's all very well for you," she snapped. "Married. Got a fellow who pulls his weight. Nice place to live. Yes, it's all right for you. Poor Else has none of that."

"I've had to battle," said the cook. "I didn't get everything on a plate, I can tell you."

Conradin was embarrassed, and the cook noticed this. "We don't want to embarrass Sister," she said. "We can talk about these things some other time."

"Yes," said Elsie. "There are lots of other things to talk about. There's the war, for instance."

Conradin was silent.

"They say that careless talk costs lives," said Minnie. "You never know who might be listening."

Elsie laughed. "Are you saying Mother Superior could be a German spy? Is that what you're saying?"

"She could be," said Minnie. "How do you know she isn't?"

The cook intervened. "They say they broke up a spy network in Norfolk the other day. They found ten radios hidden in a barn. All tuned to Berlin—every one of them. That's what they say."

"Highly unlikely," said Elsie. "People exaggerate. The rumour mill, you know."

"And you know what else they're saying," the cook continued. "They say that the Germans are dropping agents in dressed as nuns. I'm not making this up. Mrs. Lewis at the post office told me about it. She said the police had been warning people to be extra vigilant."

There was a sudden, awkward silence. Conradin felt his heart leap. He took a deep breath.

"Why would they do that?" he asked. His voice, he feared, sounded uneven. Would they notice?

"That's another of those rumours," said Elsie. "And it's probably the Germans who make them up. Lord Haw-Haw and the like."

"They'll do anything, them Germans," said Minnie.

Conradin finished the tea that the cook had poured for him. "I have a long list of tasks," he said.

"You nuns are always working," said Minnie, grinning at Elsie. "You don't have to, you know. You could stop and take it easy—like us."

"Or some of us," said Elsie, looking at Minnie with mock disapproval.

Conradin smiled. "I'm sure you're both very busy—in one way or another."

Elsie sighed. "We know you don't think much of us, Sister. You don't have to be polite to us. We can take it."

Conradin protested. "But that's not true. I don't . . ."

Elsie did not let him finish. "We can't all be saints, you see."

"No," said Minnie. "We can't. Remember Mary Magdalene."

Elsie and Minnie looked at Conradin as if challenging him. But he simply said, "Of course, Mary Magdalene."

"She was a fallen woman," said Elsie.

"Yes," Minnie joined in. "She fell."

The cook nodded. She, too, was staring at Conradin. He cleared his throat. "So much happened in the past," he said. "But times have changed."

The cook looked puzzled, but then shrugged. "I have some bread to bake," she said. "And you girls are meant to be helping me."

"We must talk again some time," said Conradin quickly.

Later, as they went into the refectory for dinner that night, Conradin mentioned to Sister Cecilia that he had met Elsie and Minnie. Sister Cecilia rolled her eyes. "Those two," she said. "I don't know much about Minnie—she's only recently arrived. A respectable family, I believe. Somewhere up in Yorkshire. But that Elsie—we know her very well."

"I hear she's a regular," said Conradin.

"Four times!" whispered Sister Cecilia, under her breath. "I don't like to be uncharitable, Sister Conradin, but frankly . . . four times."

"And the babies?"

"They're in homes somewhere. I think they've kept them together. Obviously, adoption is a bit more difficult in wartime. Perhaps they'll place them when all this is over." She paused. "And different men, too. Four different fathers, would you believe it?"

Before he could express a view, Sister Cecilia continued, "Mother is kindness itself, but I'm afraid Elsie has really tested the limits."

Conradin shook his head. "Oh well," he said, "every baby is a gift, I suppose."

Sister Cecilia gave a snort. "Four? Four gifts? No thank you, Sister."

IT WAS THREE WEEKS later that Sister Cecilia asked Conradin whether he would care to accompany her into Cambridge, which was not much more than an hour's drive away.

"Mother has asked me to collect some books from Heffers," she said. She smiled. "Improving literature. Somerset Maugham and E. F. Benson. Mother is a great reader and doesn't care much for the devotional stuff."

Sister Cecilia explained that the convent owned a motorcycle, a BSA Blue Star, that was fitted with a sidecar. This had been on loan to the local vicar, who was now returning it to the convent because he was unable to get the fuel to run it any longer.

"Mother has plenty of coupons," Sister Cecilia explained. "For everything. You name it, Mother has it. She's marvellous. She has plenty of petrol coupons."

Conradin was intrigued. He wondered where Sister Cecilia had learned to ride a motorcycle. He asked her, and after only a few moments' hesitation she replied, "Self-taught, Sister Conradin. That's the best way to learn to do anything. Teach yourself—then you really learn things well."

"You obviously taught yourself well enough to get a licence," observed Conradin.

Sister Cecilia looked shifty. "There's the war, of course," she said. "These things are less important in wartime." She assumed a business-like manner. "We'll leave after Terce and be back in time for Nones, or certainly for Vespers."

Conradin agreed, although not without some misgivings, and duly set off with Sister Cecilia the following morning, with Mother, Sister Gilbert, and Sister Angela waving goodbye at the front gate.

"Safe journey," cried out Sister Angela, a small woman with an inordinately loud voice.

Sister Cecilia sounded the horn and Conradin waved. As they shot off down the road, he looked back over his shoulder at the three nuns standing at the gate, waving, and the thought crossed his mind that he had found a family. He had a family back in Germany, but he had created a family for himself here in England. Perhaps, he thought, that is what we all do in one way or another: create families for ourselves as we go through life.

The rural lanes were empty, apart from the occasional cyclist or a hurrying, preoccupied vehicle from the RAF base. They passed a horse and cart, the horse whinnying nervously at the sound of the motorcycle's engine. They stopped at a crossroads, where a bus bound for Cambridge was boarding a small knot of waiting passengers. One of these passengers pointed at them, and heads turned to take in the sight of two nuns sweeping past on a BSA and attendant sidecar.

In Cambridge they parked the motorcycle near the entrance to one of the colleges. Two undergraduates, fresh-faced, and dressed in white flannels and jerseys, smiled at them as they emerged from a low doorway. One doffed his striped cricketing cap, and was rewarded with a wave from Sister Cecilia and what looked like a mouthed kiss.

"Such sweet boys," she observed, adding, "such a pity."

Conradin was not sure how to interpret this, and did not respond. He looked up at the sky, the wide sky of Cambridgeshire, and said, "I've never been here before."

Sister Cecilia said, "I love the spires. The bridges. Everything."

Conradin looked about him. How could anybody wish to destroy all this?

Sister Cecilia was looking at him. "You look sad," she said. "Thinking of something?"

He hesitated, and then answered, "Yes. I was thinking about the pointlessness of war."

"You mean the evil?"

"Yes, that too."

For a few moments they stood in silence. Then Sister Cecilia said, "We should get along to Heffers. Then we can go and have tea in one of the tea-shops. Perhaps a scone as well. With jam."

Conradin's delight on being in Heffers was such that Sister Cecilia suggested that she might leave him there and meet him later in the tea-room next door. She had one or two other errands to run in town, but she could do these herself while he browsed in the bookshop. He welcomed this suggestion, and they agreed that they would meet again at noon, two hours hence, when the planned tea and scone could become soup and a sandwich.

"Mother has given me some money," said Sister Cecilia. "She said that we can treat ourselves. She is so generous."

"Yes," agreed Conradin. "Mother is very kind."

"Mother is love," Sister Cecilia continued. "It does not matter who we are . . ." And here she gave Conradin a meaningful look. "No, it really doesn't matter who we are—Mother loves us in spite of . . ." She paused, and the intensity of the look increased, ". . . in spite of *everything*."

Conradin studied his fingernails. "You're right," he said. "There are deep wells of love from which Mother draws."

"Very deep," said Sister Cecilia.

Conradin looked away. He had nothing further to say on the

subject of Mother's love. He had said everything he wanted to on that particular subject. And so, too, it seemed, had Sister Cecilia, as she now gave Conradin a little wave and wafted out of Heffers in a flurry of black and white. Conradin returned to his browsing, his eye running along the titles arranged on the shelf before him. There was so much that he wanted to read, so many books that he would dearly love to buy and take back to the convent with him in the BSA sidecar. He sighed.

He picked a book off the shelf. *The Poems of Matthew Arnold*. He held it in both hands before he opened it, remembering that the last time he had held this book was with a group of his students in Hamburg. There had been six of them, four young men and two women, and he wondered now what had become of them. The young men were probably caught up, just as he was, in the swirl of dire events that had consumed their world, pressed into the fight started by those shabby bullies in Berlin. Heaven knew where they would be— in the East, perhaps, facing unimaginable horrors—mired in misery, wherever they were. He wanted to weep for those young people, at the start—and possibly the end—of their lives. He had never done that, but now he wanted to, although he knew he could not—not here in Heffers Bookshop, holding a copy of *The Poems of Matthew Arnold*.

He had read "On Dover Beach" to his students and now, as he held it, the book fell open at that page. Others, perhaps, who had taken this particular volume off the shelf and had considered buying it, had turned to that most familiar of Arnold's poems.

He read it now, glancing about him lest anybody should overhear, whispering each word to himself, realising that whatever the poem had meant to him then, in Germany, it meant so much more now, in this place.

"Ah, love, let us be true
To one another! For the world, which seems
To lie before us like a land of dreams,
So various, so beautiful, so new,
Hath really neither joy, nor love, nor light,
Nor certitude, nor peace, nor help for pain;
And we are here as on a darkling plain

Swept with confused alarms of struggle and flight
Where ignorant armies clash by night."

He replaced the book on the shelf. After the war, he said to himself, I shall come back here and buy this book, the very book. It would probably still be there, he felt, because at a time when nations were locked in conflict, when the world was in flames, there would probably be few people who would think of buying *The Poems of Matthew Arnold*.

He turned round. He was not sure what made him do so, but he felt that he had to turn. And as he did so, he saw the figure on the other side of the shop, completing a purchase at the cash desk. He drew in his breath. His hands clasped tight, as they might in a moment of great danger. He stood stock still.

He could not be mistaken; it was impossible. He could not be mistaken because he remembered so well the way that Johan Schneider had a way of standing, just so, and touching his cheek in that pensive gesture, which was what he was doing at that precise moment as he waited for the change from his purchase. It was him; it was Johan Schneider. It could be nobody but him: Johan Schneider, with whom he had spent those difficult four months of training in Hamburg; who came from a small village outside Cologne; who had been a trainee accountant; who played the trumpet, part-time, and not very well, in a dance band; who had a brother called Ferdi, who was a well-known long-distance runner; that Johan Schneider.

He almost called out. Absurdly, he almost called out across the room, forgetting everything—where he was, who he was—forgetting that he was in a nun's habit and Johan was in a dark, rather ill-cut suit of the sort worn by any number of office clerks. And if he had called out Johan's name, what would have happened? If Johan remembered his training he would pretend not to have heard and would certainly not reply. He might glance furtively across the shop floor, of course, and see a nun, but might not realise who the nun was. Unless he knew, that was; unless he had been told by Hamburg that Conradin Muller had disappeared and that he should look out for him in the area in which he had been dropped because he might be compromised by now. The British turned agents; they threatened them with execution unless they played along and sent misleading information back to Germany. The Abwehr knew all about that, of course, and would be cautious.

He waited. Johan had collected his change now, had thanked the bookseller, and was moving towards the front door. Conradin held back for a few moments, studying the spine of *The Poems of Matthew Arnold* in its place on the shelf. Then, as Johan left the shop he followed him at a discreet distance, out into the street and then down King's Parade, keeping sufficiently far away so that he should not be spotted but at the same time being close enough not to lose him. There were groups of students making their way to lectures; there were women out shopping; there was a file of choristers in the uniform of their calling; there were cyclists. Conradin kept his eye on Johan and remained with him as he went down a side street, along a busier road, down a shrub-lined path, and finally along a line of small terraced houses. Johan never looked back, which he should have done, had he been doing as their instructors had taught them. *Always remember to look behind you from time to time. And if you see the same person each time, then assume that you are being followed. Never walk anywhere without ascertaining whether you are alone.* And, of course, if you looked back and saw a nun trailing you, you should be doubly suspicious.

He sauntered past the house into which Johan had disappeared, making a mental note of the name of the street and the number. Then, retracing his tracks, he made his way back into the centre of the town. He returned to Heffers and stayed there until it was time to meet Sister Cecilia in the tea-room.

"Did you have a good time in Heffers?" Sister Cecilia asked.

Conradin nodded. "There are so many books I'd love to read. So many."

"Yes," said Sister Cecilia. "Perhaps Mother will let you borrow her Somerset Maugham. Have you read any of his novels?"

He shook his head. "I'd like to. People speak highly of him."

The waitress came and took their order. They chose pea soup and cheese sandwiches. Ham sandwiches were available, but were twice the price of the cheese ones. "Mother admires financial restraint," said Sister Cecilia. "And cheese is so nourishing."

The waitress left.

"You spent the whole time in Heffers, then?" asked Sister Cecilia.

"Yes," answered Conradin. "The time flew by."

Sister Cecilia looked up at the ceiling. "I thought I saw you on the Parade."

Conradin swallowed. "Me? You saw me?"

"Well, unless it was another sister." She paused. "I was buying elastic. And a pair of new scissors for the girls to use to make those RAF pyjamas."

For a few moments, neither of them spoke. Then Conradin said, "Oh, that. Of course. Yes, I went for some air. Then I went back into Heffers. Bookshops can be so stuffy. Something to do with the paper, I think."

Sister Cecilia's expression was impassive. Conradin looked away. "I'm hungry," he said.

The waitress appeared at the kitchen door and brought their soup and sandwiches to the table. They ate in silence at first. Conradin went over in his mind what he had said to Sister Cecilia. Had he sounded credible?

"I'd love to live in Cambridge," Sister Cecilia said suddenly. "It's such a vibrant place. Instead of being stuck out in the country, with the pigs and the fallen women, and . . . oh dear."

"Perhaps you will, one day," Conradin offered. "You never know what life has in store."

"It doesn't have much in store for me," said Sister Cecilia. "Just the same thing. Matins. Breakfast. Pigs. Vegetables. Polishing. Vespers. And so on and so on."

"But every life is like that," said Conradin. "Everyone's life has its routine. Mother's life. The Archbishop of Canterbury's life. Look at the king himself. What does he have in his day? Get up. Breakfast. Sign things. Pin medals on people. Afternoon tea. Dinner. That's it."

Sister Cecilia laughed. "You can be very funny, Sister Conradin," she said. "Is that your Icelandic sense of humour?"

"Possibly," said Conradin. He thought of a rocky landscape, punctuated by geysers. He thought of green seas washing against cliffs. He thought of how he might go somewhere, one day, anywhere where he might be free of the haunted dream into which the world had been tipped.

Sister Cecilia stared at him. Her face broke into a smile. Then she looked away, as if she felt she must end a dangerous moment of understanding, of intimacy.

They finished the meal and then, laden with a bag of books for Mother and another shopping bag that Sister Cecilia had filled with haberdashery, they made their way back to their motorcycle. A small group of students, sitting on the grass, watched in astonishment as they climbed onto the machine. Sister Cecilia waved to them gaily, and, embarrassed, they returned the greeting.

Sister Cecilia drove back erratically, narrowly missing a boy on a bicycle, and at several points almost leaving the road when she cornered too fast. Conradin did his best to avert disaster by transferring his weight in the sidecar when he felt it would help, but his relief on arriving back at the convent was palpable. They missed Nones but were in time for Vespers, at which it was Sister Cecilia's turn to read from the psalms, and Conradin listened as she spoke of those who would be like trees planted by the rivers of water. Their leaves would not wither, she said, and all that they did would prosper.

He felt her gaze fall upon him as she said this, and he knew, at that moment, that she knew. He was convinced now, and his conviction was confirmed as he glanced at Mother, who was also looking at him over her half-moon glasses, but who looked away quickly when she saw that he had noticed.

He felt strangely calm. It no longer mattered to him what happened. He was ready to give up. And with that willingness to surrender, there came a feeling of unexpected calm. He had done nothing wrong. He had never spied on anybody. He had never fired a shot in anger. He was a conscript in every sense of the word and it was never the fault of the conscript.

After Vespers the nuns all filed out of the chapel. Some of the fallen women had taken part in the service, as they occasionally did, and Conradin noticed Elsie and Minnie sitting modestly at the back. They smiled at him as he walked past with Sister Cecilia, and he returned their smile.

He returned to his room. Dinner would be served in the refectory an hour later, but Conradin decided that he was not hungry. When the bell announced the meal, he slipped out of his room and made his way to the chapel, which he now had to himself although a couple of candles had been left burning on the altar. English churches and chapels, Conradin had noticed, had a very particular smell—a slight mustiness that one encountered nowhere else. It must be a mixture of the odour of candle wax and ancient plaster and flowers left to wilt in the vase. It was a *quiet* smell, he thought—if smells can be quiet.

He found himself kneeling, his forehead pressed against the back of the pew in front of him. He closed his eyes and waited for something to happen within him, although he was not sure what that would be. In his mind's eye, now, he saw Johan Schneider going through the door of that small terraced house in Cambridge. He tried to rid himself of the image, but it returned, and it brought with it the dilemma that had been at the back of his mind throughout the return journey from Cambridge and had persisted through Vespers, pushing aside all thought of anything else. He knew that there was an active spy in the heart of Cambridge. He knew his address. What should he do?

He did not want Germany to win the war because he had long since come to the realisation that his country was the aggressor. This war was not England's fault, nor America's, nor the fault of any of the others to whom it was causing untold suffering. It was for this reason that Germany had to lose. But Johan Schneider was, like him, just one person caught up in a great conflict. He had never discussed with him whether he had volunteered or been drafted—Johan had never seemed to be interested in that sort of thing. He was just there. So, he might have been every bit as reluctant a spy as he, Conradin, was.

He could notify the authorities anonymously, so that there would be no risk of compromising himself. They would act on the tip—he had been told that they always did, no matter that people were left right and centre falsely accusing their neighbours of being enemy agents. And if they searched that terraced house in Cambridge, he had no doubt but they would find Johan's radio concealed there. Then all would be lost, and Johan would be tried and executed as a spy. That meant that the moment he disclosed what he knew, he would be starting a process that would lead to the death of somebody who, even although for a short time, had been a friend. Did he want to do that? Did he *have* to do that?

What if he did nothing? He imagined that Johan was sending back information on troop movements and the comings and goings at the air-force bases dotted around Cambridge. Every time he did that, he was doing something that could lead to the deaths of Allied servicemen. There was no getting round that brute fact. Johan was part of the war machine that threatened the very people amongst whom he, Conradin, had found sanctuary. He was not an innocent. He was a participant.

And yet he was also a man. He was a man who played the trumpet in a dance band, who had a brother called Ferdi, who doubtlessly was loved by a mother and aunts and a wife or girlfriend; who would not want to die. He was all that too.

He suddenly became aware that he was not alone. He did not move his head, but looked fixedly down at the kneeler below him. Whoever it was would think that he was deep in prayer and would leave him undisturbed. He did not want to engage with anybody.

It was Mother, and she now slipped into the pew beside him. He hardly dared look at her, but he saw her.

She whispered, "I find you in prayer, Sister Conradin."

He moved his lips. No sound came.

"I would normally not disturb a sister in her devotions," Mother continued, her voice barely audible. "But there are times when the presence of another helps the heart to be opened. And somehow, I think this is just such a time."

Conradin said nothing. He heard his own breathing, though.

"You see," Mother went on, "sometimes people know what we think they do not know. Sometimes we believe that we are concealing the truth from others, but that truth has been grasped all along by the very people from whom we are so intent on concealing it."

Conradin tightened his fists. If he were to flee, then this would be the time to do it. He could easily overpower Mother, substantial figure though she was. He could steal the BSA and be miles away by the time the authorities were summoned. He could go to ground. He could even go to that terraced house in Cambridge and join forces with Johan. He could lie about his radio. He could invent a story about having been unable to get in touch with Hamburg. He could save his skin—at least as far as his own side was concerned.

But then he realised that he did not want to do that, because that was not the sort of person he was and because that was not the side he was on. It was as simple as that.

He turned towards Mother.

"Mother," he began, "I am troubled in my heart."

Her reply came quickly. "Of course you are, my child. I can tell that."

He caught his breath.

"I've known that, my dear," Mother continued, her tone that of one explaining something very simple and obvious. "I've been aware of that from the very beginning—from the time you joined us. I've been aware that there is . . ." She paused, and looked at him with such sweetness that he was emboldened to think that he could confess to her at that moment—and get away with it: somehow she would understand.

He was about to speak, but she interrupted him with a hand placed upon his forearm. He noticed the veins on her hand; her skin seemed almost translucent.

"My dear," she said quietly. "We all have our secrets. But there is one thing that has always been clear to me, and that is that the Lord is understanding." She gave him another of her sympathetic looks. "The Lord knows that it is not easy to be what you wish to be. And the Lord knows, too, that there are many good people who are obliged to be one thing when they might wish to be another. There is no harm in that."

He listened. He was not sure that he understood.

Then she said, "I know, you see."

His every muscle tightened. He might have to act without delay. For a moment he thought he might even have to overpower Mother Superior in order to make his escape. But the thought appalled him: he could never hurt anybody, let alone this woman who had been so kind to him.

"And Sister Cecilia?" he asked. It was all he could think of to say.

"Oh, she knows too," said Mother. "She has always known. And Sister Gilbert too, but none of the others. We do not need to trouble the lesser sisters with burdensome knowledge."

She smiled at him, and for a moment or two he wondered whether he had jumped to the wrong conclusion. When she said that she knew, *what* did she know? Perhaps she was thinking of something altogether different.

"I can see that you are surprised," she said. "But I have a good instinct for detecting disguise." She smiled.

He looked at her incredulously. Was this all there was to it? Was that all that she knew?

"You see," she went on, "people make the wrong assumption. They think that somebody like me will not have any experience of the world. But I do, you know. *Nihil humanum mihi alienum est,* so to speak. I have, as one might say, seen it all."

He relaxed. This was not nearly as bad as he imagined.

"Of course," she continued. "While you wear the habit of our order, you must be careful not to draw attention to yourself. Do you understand what I'm saying?"

"Of course, Mother. Of course I understand."

Mother sat back in her pew. Her hands were folded on her lap. She looked utterly serene.

"You see," she explained, "Sister Cecilia followed you from Heffers. She had been observing you all the time, and when she saw you trailing that man, she assumed that you had guessed—as she had—that there was something suspicious about him. She put two and two together. She saw where he went, just as you did, and she informed me before Vespers. I informed the police and I believe that he has since been arrested."

For the first time in this meeting, she looked disapproving. "It was unwise of you to take that risk—no matter how well-intentioned you were. What if the police had become suspicious of you? We would all have been most embarrassed. I want you to reassure me that you will not do anything foolish."

He sunk his head in his hands, and wept with relief. Mother put her arm about his shoulders.

He heard Mother's voice in his ear. "We are all caught up in sad events that are not of our making. But such things should not rob us of our humanity or of the mercy and forgiveness that is our due. I don't want to know what unhappiness you are running away from. You are deserving of mercy, as much as I am, as much as any of our unfortunate young women are. You may stay with us until the end of this dreadful war. Your secret is safe."

He could not speak.

"I think it might be best if you abandoned our habit now," Mother continued. "You may wear it in private, if that makes you happy, but not in public. We have an identity for you. You may become a Polish sailor who has been invalided out of the navy. You may grow a beard and dye your hair. Nobody will know."

He looked at her in astonishment.

"Sister Gilbert has obtained papers from . . . from a friend of ours—from somebody who owes us a favour. You may move into the unoccupied cottage on the farm and be the manager of the piggery. You have been such a godsend to us on the farm—I hope you will continue to run it for us—but as a Polish sailor."

He managed to say, "Of course." And then asked, "And what will become of Sister Conradin?"

"We shall put it about that she has been called back to Salisbury," said Mother. "You will be concealed for a few days while your beard grows, and then you will appear and nobody will be any the wiser."

He nodded.

"And I hope," Mother continued, "that you will be able to do something else for us in due course—should you wish to show any gratitude you may feel."

"Mother," he said. "I shall do anything for you. Believe me—I shall."

She inclined her head. "Thank you," she said. "I shall remember that."

TWO DAYS LATER MOTHER announced at dinner in the refectory that Sister Conradin would be returning to Salisbury the following day. Her presence in the convent would, she said, be sorely missed—particularly by those who had enjoyed relief from farmyard duties. That brought laughter. However, she was pleased to be able to impart the good news that in a couple of weeks they would be obtaining the services of a Polish sailor, invalided out of the navy, who would assume the duties of farm manager and general maintenance man for the convent. His name was Jan and Mother was sure that he would be welcomed by the entire community.

After his period of seclusion in a little-used attic room in the convent, Conradin was pleased to emerge as Jan. Sister Cecilia had obtained clothing for him, including a set of Polish navy blouses that were suitable for work on the farm and an all-weather smock of thornproof tweed. There were two pairs of new boots as well, and a chunky green sweater. She had made an effort, too, to make his farm cottage as comfortable and homely as possible, hanging new curtains that the fallen women made out of RAF pyjama material and exchanging a side of pork in the village for a newish bedroom rug.

Conradin relished his return to a masculine identity. He was happy in his cottage and in his work. He soon transformed the barns and made a start on replastering the chapel. Mother was extremely grateful.

He saw Elsie and Minnie from time to time. Elsie had taken to helping with the pigs, her undoubted maternal instincts being evoked by the large sow that had given birth to twelve piglets. The sow was anxious about people approaching her litter, but seemed to exempt Elsie from that suspicion. Minnie kept away from the pigs, but proved to be adept at mending fences, a task that she described as being not all that different from knitting, which she had always enjoyed.

One evening, Mother knocked at Conradin's door. She was bearing a large dish of apple crumble that she had made, and that she thought Conradin might appreciate. He invited her in, and put on the kettle for tea.

Mother looked about the kitchen. "You have made this very homely," she said.

"I do my best," said Conradin.

She was watching him. Now she said, "Of course, any house or cottage is much improved by a woman's touch, I always feel."

Conradin grinned. "I wouldn't argue with that," he said.

"Perhaps one day you'll find somebody," said Mother. "Would you like that, do you think?"

Conradin hesitated. "That is quite possible," he said at last. "I'm very happy here, you know."

She watched him. "Happiness is usually well-deserved," she said quietly.

He made Mother a cup of tea. She thanked him, and began to sip at it.

"I've always hoped that Elsie would settle down," Mother said. "She's a very nice girl at heart, but she has . . . well, she has her failings—just like the rest of us. What she needs, I think, is a bit of stability. A home. And, most importantly, a man." She paused. The room was silent apart from the ticking of the kitchen clock.

Mother now continued, "Yes, I've seen a lot of these fallen women—not that I approve of that term at all, mind you—but I have had a lot of experience of these young women and their needs. I think that Elsie is one of those girls who has certain urges that need to be met, if you see what I mean. If she had a man, and a place to stay, then I'm convinced she would settle down—as long as the man would be prepared to look after her needs, so to speak."

Mother took another sip of her tea.

"In return," she continued, "the man would get a loving wife, a well-kept home, and, I am sure, plenty of children—if that was what he wanted. I expect there are men who would be quite happy with all that."

She took another sip of tea. "Particularly if Elsie came with a lifetime lease to a cottage—for example—just to name one thing."

Mother stopped. She looked across the kitchen table at Conradin. He looked back at her. She was right—as she usually was. There were men for whom that would be not such a bad prospect at all.

"Of course," Mother went on, "Elsie is almost due. She would come with a baby. But every baby deserves to have a father, if at all possible, don't you agree, Conradin?"

He did.

Then she made a speech that caught him unprepared. It was something that he would think about for a long time, and about which he would never be certain.

"There are occasions," she began, "when we say something that is not entirely true. There are occasions when we do not reveal everything we know—when we know something else, for example, that could be very awkward for somebody, but choose not to say it.

Instead, we say something that they think they understand, but that they have not really grasped." She drew a breath. "And then, of course, rather than make things difficult for somebody, we propose a course of action that will leave things undisturbed. And everybody is happier as a result."

They were both silent for several minutes. She knows, thought Conradin. But then he thought: does she *really* know? No, he decided; she does not, and perhaps it is impossible to tell. But then he remembered something that Sister Cecilia had once said: "Mother Superior is a tough old bird, you know. There's no fooling *her*."

He did a quick calculation. He liked Elsie; he might even love her, if he allowed himself to. And there were worse fates than the one that Mother Superior was so clearly proposing.

"Mother," he said at last. "Do you think you might give me permission to marry Elsie?"

"That's a wonderful idea," said Mother Superior, without hesitation. "What on earth made you think of it? But of course, I—and all the other sisters—would be delighted."

THE WEDDING WAS ATTENDED by all the sisters and by a full complement of the fallen women.

"This was surely destined to happen," said Sister Cecilia, as she congratulated the newly-weds outside the chapel.

"I think it was," said Conradin, glancing at Mother Superior, who smiled back at him with her customary sweetness.

They had three children of their own, and the one that Elsie came with. Shortly after their wedding, Elsie's previous three were reunited with their mother and their half siblings. Mother provided the funds for an extension to the cottage. She was so thoughtful that way.

Syphax and Omar

1

SYPHAX BRAHIMI, ESPION

IMAGINE ALGIERS IN 1924. IMAGINE AN UNFORGIVING NORTH-African sun, with its concomitant short shadows, and its penetrating light. Imagine a working street in this city—a street of small shops, hidden arcades, and corners on which urchins stand, watching the business being conducted about them. There are no banks here, nor offices of any importance; no uniformed concierges, no elegant lines of palm trees. This is not a street on which people may saunter, admiring the clothing of others, discussing the displays in the shop windows. The people in this street, with the exception of the children, are on their way somewhere.

Now imagine two men walking along this street, one behind the other. There is no traffic, and so they are unconcerned at being in the middle of the road. The man in the front is in mid-stride—a powerfully built man whose clothing marks him out as one who earns his living in an office rather than with his hands. He wears a fez at a slightly jaunty angle: this is a man who is aware of how he looks; not vain—just aware. He has a white shirt, a bow tie and a long frock coat. His name is Syphax Brahimi, and he is a spy by profession, although he derives almost half of his income as a *rentier*. Two of his five tenants have difficulty in paying the rent, but Syphax is a generous-spirited man and, unlike most landlords, he allows them time to pay, even when they have built up arrears. In return, his tenants express love for him—"I never resent paying the rent to that man," says one of them. "When I am able to, of course."

About ten paces behind him, wearing a white head-dress, is the figure of Omar Benamara. He, too, is a spy. He is poorer than Syphax, and he has eight children and a wife who will not talk to him, for fear, some say, of further children. Every time he tries to address her, she turns away from him, muttering incomprehensibly under her breath. She comes from a humble background—"Her grandparents on one side were Kabyle from the mountains," explains Omar. "They were very difficult people—very independent, very opposed to the French. Opposed to everybody, actually."

There is a figure standing in the shadows, watching Syphax and Omar. This appears to be a woman, heavily veiled, but is, in fact, a man disguised as a woman. The disguise is generally ineffective, as the man is widely known in that part of the city as "the man who is dressed as a woman but who is really a man." This man is also a spy, thought to be working for the Comintern, but who also, when not dressed in his disguise, works as a receptionist in a small French hotel, *l'Auberge de Lyons*, three streets away. The only indication of his political sympathies is a small red badge that he wears on the lapel of his jacket when seated at the hotel's reception desk.

Syphax Brahimi is looking over his right shoulder. He knows that Omar has been following him, because that is Omar's job—just as his job is to follow Omar. Sometimes Syphax will be in the lead, and sometimes it will be Omar. The order depends on the day: on Mondays, Wednesdays and Thursdays Syphax will be followed by Omar; on Tuesdays, Saturdays and Sundays, Syphax will be trailing Omar. They may not be quite as regular in their street appearances as Immanuel Kant, but they are not far off. In Kant's case, the citizens of Königsberg could set their watches by the stages of the great philosopher's morning walk; the residents of Algiers are concerned only that Syphax and Omar should appear—they are largely indifferent to the timing of that appearance.

And imagine that there are two children in the background, watching the Comintern spy with all the innocent curiosity of the young.

These children are a brother and sister. The sister is the older of the two. She is just seven. Her younger brother—aged three—many years later, in 1959, would be arrested. He had become an active member of the nationalist resistance to French rule. His political involvement put him in danger on several occasions, notably when he was picked up by a group of OAS men, beaten up and dumped in the harbour. They thought he was dead, but he was still breathing, and he floated. After independence he trained in massage and eventually became head masseur of the Algerian national football team. He was proud of what he had done with his life. He had two daughters who made good marriages, and an asthmatic son who went to Marseilles and became a taxi driver, eventually owning a fleet of three taxis.

All of that can be so easily imagined when one thinks of a street in Algiers in 1924. But of course there is much more in the lives of these two spies, Syphax and Omar, who were, in spite of being on opposite sides, great friends. Sides are often arbitrary—the result of historical accident: friendship can be much more important than allegiance and membership, and can, sometimes, outrank other, lesser loyalties. Where you are born, and the flag that flies over your birthplace, may turn out to be far less important than the promptings of the heart within.

2

PANTALÉON DUBOIS, PIED-NOIR

SYPHAX WAS BORN IN 1876, THE ONLY SON OF THE DIRECTOR OF a trading company that exported dates and olives. As a young man, Syphax's father had nursed unfulfilled intellectual ambitions, and had, as a result, spared no expense in his son's education. At the age of seven, Syphax was placed under the care of a tutor named Pantaléon Dubois, an arrogant young French *colon* who resented being employed by an Arab-Algerian, but who needed the generous salary offered by Mr. Brahimi. In spite of his assumptions of social superiority, Pantaléon proved to be an effective tutor. He not only insisted on hours of study of Racine, but he also gave Syphax a grounding in modern Greek. "He might choose to live in Alexandria," he explained to his employer. "You never know, and it could be useful to him to have a knowledge of Greek." Mr. Brahimi nodded enthusiastically. "I want my son to be a citizen of a broader world," he said. "I don't want him to think that the world begins and ends in Algiers. I'd like him to be able to go to Paris and mix with the people there—if he wishes, of course."

Pantaléon said nothing. He resented the opportunities that would open up to Syphax. If anybody had the right to go to Paris and mix with educated circles there, then surely it was him, rather than this local upstart. But he knew that he could not afford to go to Paris and he knew, too, that there were people there who looked down on *pieds-noirs*.

Syphax had a retentive memory and an instinctive grasp of language. His French was near-perfect, and his Greek became passable, even if a bit halting. He enjoyed mathematics, but was not particularly numerate, which suited Pantaléon, for whom anything mathematical was an ordeal.

At the age of nineteen Syphax was summoned for a serious conversation with his father. "I'm proposing to send you to Constantinople," he said. "I have been making enquiries and have found an academy there that specialises in the arts. It is called the Academy of Fine Arts and instruction is in French. They offer courses in art and music and in some of the lesser arts, such as glass-etching. They have informed me that there will be a place for you there in the next session, and I have accepted that—on your behalf."

Syphax was silent.

"You're pleased?" asked his father.

"No," said Syphax. "I will always obey you, Father, as you are the fount of all wisdom. But I would very much prefer to go to Paris. You always talked about my going there—remember? You wanted me to meet intellectuals there. Monsieur Verlaine, for example. And other Symbolists. Remember?"

Mr. Brahimi stared at his son. He shook his head. "I have changed my views," he said. "I do not want my son mixing with Symbolists."

"But Father . . ."

Mr. Brahimi's tone was firm. "No, things are different. I have been told that Paris is now a very degenerate city," he said. "It is full of sexual perverts and women of low morals. It is not a place for a young man like you."

Syphax listened to this denunciation of Paris. For all his father knew, he thought, he could himself be a so-called sexual pervert who enjoyed the company of women of low morals. But he did not say this, of course, and meekly agreed to go to Constantinople as his father wished.

"I shall work very hard at this academy," he said to Mr. Brahimi.

"I'm pleased to hear that," came the reply. "I shall give you a generous allowance and a good set of clothing to take with you. You will write to us once a month, please, and come back twice a year to see your mother."

"I shall do all of that," said Syphax.

3

A RETIRED EUNUCH ENTERTAINS

IN CONSTANTINOPLE HE TOOK LODGINGS IN A HOUSE OWNED BY A middle-ranking official in the Ottoman bureaucracy, being allocated two rooms at the back of the rambling family home that the bureaucrat had inherited from a wealthy uncle. There were four rooms in this part of the house, the other two being occupied by one of the last eunuchs who had served in the Sultan's household. The eunuch was a large man with fleshy hands whose passion in his retirement was cooking elaborate dishes. He entertained friends in his living room, serving them his carefully prepared dishes and exchanging snippets of gossip late into the night. He knew everybody in Constantinople, it seemed, and kept a written record of the misdeeds and peccadillos of senior government servants. This, he said, was for the historical record. "I have never sought to blackmail any of these people," he said to Syphax. "I am a chronicler of our times— that is all." He paused. "I am a chronicler of the weakness of others."

Syphax enrolled at the Academy of Fine Arts and attended two weeks of classes there. The courses he took were *French Classical*

Art of the Eighteenth Century and *Napoleon in Egypt*. The lectures on these subjects were delivered in a small auditorium, and were attended by no more than a handful of students. The lecturers were furtive in their manner, and Syphax was told by one of his fellow students that most of them were wanted by the police. One of them, a man described as the Professor of Aesthetics, never delivered his lectures himself, but sent his servant to deliver them for him. This servant did not actually speak French, but read out phonetically the script given to him by the professor.

After two weeks, Syphax stopped attending lectures. Locating a printing office near the Pera Palace, he instructed the printer to produce stationery at the top of which the academy's name was printed. Underneath this, he had printed the words: *Student Monthly Report*, with a series of columns at the top of which subject headings were printed. At the bottom, there was a box entitled: *Student Conduct and General Disposition*.

Syphax collected this stationery from the printer and showed it to the eunuch. "All I ask of you is that you fill this in for me," he said. "The academy is worthless and I hope to save my poor father the embarrassment of realising that he has made a bad choice."

"You are a very considerate boy," said the eunuch, and agreed to do as he was asked. He was, in fact, an expert forger, and had been trained in the alteration of documents in the department that the Sultan had established for those specific purposes.

At the end of the first month, a completed report was sent to Mr. Brahimi in Algiers. In the box reserved for comments on conduct and disposition, the eunuch had written, in his florid cursive hand, "This young man is a credit to his family. He is diligent in his studies and courteous to his professors. They all speak highly of him and believe that he has a very great future ahead of him. We recommend that he continue with his studies here for a further three years, after which he will be well-equipped to make his way in the world in whatever profession he chooses to follow. We also recommend a slight increase in his stipend to cover the rising cost of studying in this city."

The eunuch read this out and then asked Syphax whether that would do.

"It is exactly what I had in mind," said Syphax, "although it would be helpful if you could change *slight* to *substantial*."

"That will be no trouble at all," said the eunuch, laughing as he applied his skills to the correction.

Syphax was happy in Constantinople. He quickly made a number of new friends whose company he found agreeable. He stayed in bed each day until eleven in the morning, when he would rise and saunter off to his appointment with his barber. Then he would have lunch with his friends and visit his favourite steam bath before returning to his lodgings in the late afternoon. On at least one or two evenings a week, he would be invited by the eunuch to join him and his friends over an elaborate meal and listen, entranced, to the gossip they exchanged. Soon he felt he understood exactly what was going on in the city. His Turkish quickly became fluent, although he was told that his accent verged on the effete. "Charming, though," said the eunuch. "And these days, of course, an effete accent is considered very fashionable."

Three years passed. Syphax never returned to the Academy of Fine Arts, although he continued to send forged progress reports to his father. There were no home visits to Algiers, as he claimed to be working too hard, and his father accepted the excuse. "You can never work too hard," he wrote back. "That's the way to get ahead in life."

Life in Constantinople suited Syphax very well. Nothing much happened, beyond meetings with friends and trips to restaurants and the baths. You could live such a life for ever, he thought, and not get bored with it. And that, he decided, was what he would do.

4

NERCESSIAN, ARMENIAN

IT WAS THROUGH THE EUNUCH THAT SYPHAX FIRST MET A MEMBER of the Ottoman Secret Service. This was a thin-faced Armenian whose walrus moustache was stained yellow with nicotine. He was an old friend of the eunuch, who explained that they had once visited Cairo together. They both enjoyed playing chess, although the eunuch complained that his friend was inclined to cheat if he was not watched closely. "It's his training," he said. "He's a spy, you see. They train them to do things like that and it becomes second nature. Never play any game of chance with those people—they cannot help themselves. They will cheat every time."

The Armenian was called Mr. Nercessian. "I know it sounds like *narcissist*," he said to Syphax. "But I am not a narcissist. I do not like to look in mirrors."

"That's because you have done such dreadful things," joked the eunuch. "Only the innocent can look at themselves in a mirror . . ." He pointed at Syphax, a fond, even complimentary gesture. "Innocents like Syphax here."

Mr. Nercessian smiled, and winked at the eunuch. The eunuch returned the wink but then, when he saw that the exchange had been intercepted by Syphax, assumed a serious expression. Syphax found himself wondering about the nature of the relationship there between the spy and the eunuch. Was it a simple friendship, or was he missing something? The eunuch's friends, as far as he had been able to observe on the occasions on which he had been invited to join them, were conventional in their dress and manner. None of them, he thought, was a eunuch, and most spoke of homes and families that were, from the references they made to them, unexceptional in their ordinariness. Admittedly, one or two of them were unusual— the eunuch was friendly with a dwarf who played in a palm court orchestra and whose life, Syphax suspected, was unconventional. And there was another friend who was, according to a comment made by Mr. Nercessian—in an unguarded aside—a dealer in stolen horses; but he was an exception to the progression of minor bureau- crats constituting the bulk of the eunuch's circle. Perhaps the appeal lay in the kitchen, as the eunuch himself had once suggested: "They like me," he confided, "because I feed them so well when they come round here. It's like feeding stray cats—they like you if you give them something good to eat. That's the basis of friendship, you know, Syphax. Don't delude yourself that it's all about shared interests and noble ideals. It's food. Or money. Money is a wonderful maker of friends. If you have money, you have friends."

Now Mr. Nercessian responded to the eunuch's remark about innocence. "If Syphax is so innocent, then he should consider joining us. Innocence is always a good cover in intelligence work."

Syphax said nothing at first, but then, a few minutes later, when the conversation had moved on to a discussion of Russian intentions, he brought up the subject of espionage. "You said I would make a good spy, Mr. Nercessian. Do you really think so?"

Mr. Nercessian turned to face him. The Armenian was eating a large rosewater cake that the eunuch had made, and he popped the rest of this into his mouth before licking the crumbs off his fingers. "I'm quite sure you would," he said. "Spies are born, not made. I detect in you just the right attitude—the right intuitions." He paused. "I could sound out my superiors, you know. Would you like me to do that?"

Syphax hesitated. He was aware, somewhere deep within him, that the answer he gave to this question would shape the rest of his life. In this respect he was fortunate: it is often the case that when we are placed in such a position, we do not realise the significance of the answer we are about to give, and therefore dictate the shape of our future without being aware of what we are doing.

"Well?" prompted Mr. Nercessian.

Syphax glanced at the eunuch, who shrugged.

"Yes," said Syphax. "I would be most grateful, Mr. Nercessian, if you were to speak to your superiors in those terms."

"You must be getting bored," said the eunuch. "A young man has to do something. You can't spend your time going to the barber and sitting around at the baths."

Syphax looked away in embarrassment. "I am very willing to work," he muttered. "I am not lazy. I haven't been doing much over the last few years because I have been busy thinking about what I should do in the future. You shouldn't rush these decisions."

Mr. Nercessian lit a cigarette. "I'm sure you're not lazy," he said. "And I'm sure you will do very well in my profession. There are many opportunities."

"My profession was far safer," said the eunuch. "But alas, there are few openings in it these days." He looked sad. "It used to be different, of course. We were very influential."

"Everything is changing," said Mr. Nercessian. "All this talk of freedom. All this undermining of the empire. First the Greeks, and now, heaven knows who will be next."

The eunuch sighed. "I shall now serve a very special course," he said. "This is lamb cooked for two days in a sauce for which only I and one or two other people know the recipe. There are twenty-two spices involved, some of them being unavailable to the general public. You will like it very much."

Mr. Nercessian now turned to Syphax. "I take it you will be prepared to study? You will need to attend our special college for at least a year. All your expenses will be met, of course."

Syphax answered that he would be happy to do this.

"In that case," said Mr. Nercessian, "my conversation with my superiors will be not much more than a formality. You may take it that you will be accepted."

"You see," said the eunuch. "That's the way to do things."

SYPHAX BEGAN HIS STUDIES at the Ottoman Secret Service College two weeks later. The cadets, as the students were called, wore blue uniforms with silver rings on the sleeves and the words *Secret Service* emblazoned on the chest of their tunics. Syphax thought it rather strange that what should be secret should be so openly proclaimed, and he raised the matter—courteously—with the college principal. The principal listened to what he had to say and then simply put a finger to his lips and said, "Hush." Nothing more was said, and Syphax left the office. Mentioning this later to Mr. Nercessian, the spy laughed and said, "That's all he ever says. I remember, he was on the staff when I was at the college a long time ago. He did exactly the same thing then. Anything you said to him was greeted with a finger to the lips and the word *'Hush.'*"

Syphax completed the course with distinction. At the end of the year he was fully trained in techniques of shadowing, in communicating using dropped messages, and in the art of interrogation. He also learned how to don a disguise, how to assess psychological weakness in others, and how to use invisible ink. At the end of the course, Syphax was placed third in the list of graduates, a position that resulted in his beginning his first attachment on the third rung of the salary scale. He was very pleased, and wrote to his father to tell him that he had completed his course at the Academy of Fine Arts in record time and was now taking up employment in the Ottoman Civil Service. The eunuch forged a graduation certificate from the Academy of Arts and this was sent to Mr. Brahimi, who framed it and displayed it proudly in his office. "That's not worth the paper it's printed on," said Pantaléon scathingly when he came to visit the house. "It's rubbish."

"You're envious," said Mr. Brahimi. "Get out of my house immediately." Then he added, "One day my people will rise up and shoot all of your people. That's one hundred per cent certain, you know."

5

ARISTOTLE, AGENT

SYPHAX STARTED HIS CAREER AS AN OTTOMAN SPY SHORTLY BEFORE the turn of the century. He was then twenty-three, having spent three years pretending to be a student at the Academy of Fine Arts and a further nine months learning his trade of espionage. For the first year of his service, he was allocated to a department that filed reports—a job he found mind-numbingly boring. After a month of doing this, and feeling desperate, he revealed his dissatisfaction and frustration to Mr. Nercessian, when he met him for dinner one evening in the eunuch's rooms.

"The worst thing," he complained, "is trying to file reports that have been written in invisible ink."

"Operational reasons," interrupted Mr. Nercessian. "Some agents have to use invisible ink because of their situation."

"I know that," said Syphax. "But when they get to me, what do I do with them? How can I tell what they're about?"

"Have you ironed them properly?" asked Mr. Nercessian. "It's the ironing that reveals the writing."

"Yes, I always iron them," said Syphax. "But it doesn't seem to work."

"Then file them under *miscellaneous*," said Mr. Nercessian. "That's what I used to do." He paused. "But you're really unhappy? Is that correct?"

Syphax nodded. "I can't face years of this. They told me I might be in that department for five years. I can't face that."

"And you've done a month so far?"

Syphax nodded. "Of course, I've taken eight or nine days off," he said. "I had to go to the barber, you see. And I had an ingrowing toenail."

Mr. Nercessian winced. "Painful. Entirely justified. You can't work with an ingrowing toenail." He paused. "There is a solution, you know."

Syphax waited. He noticed that Mr. Nercessian had lowered his voice—a habit of his when saying anything remotely important.

"Many people take what I might call a pragmatic view of this sort of thing."

Syphax raised an eyebrow. "Yes?"

"Yes. They employ somebody to do their job for them. You pay—and it needn't be very much—for some poor fellow to pretend to be you. He goes in and does your work for you, and nobody's any the wiser."

Syphax remembered the professor who had detailed his servant to deliver his lectures for him. He told Mr. Nercessian about this, and the older man nodded. "That's widespread in colleges and universities. Also, in some hospitals, I'm afraid, which is a bit more concerning. There are some very successful surgeons who never have to operate on patients—because they employ actors to do the job for them. They claim to give them a bit of training that serves them for most simple procedures. For more serious ones, they employ medical students keen to make a bit of money."

"Could you arrange for somebody to do my job?" asked Syphax.

Mr. Nercessian thought for a few moments. "I have just the man," he said. "He even looks a bit like you, which is helpful. He has debts and he'll be pleased to earn the money. You could take him on for a year or two."

Syphax expressed his gratitude. "That will be a great help," he said.

"And in the meantime," Mr. Nercessian continued, "I've been thinking of offering you a job myself."

Syphax was interested. "Doing what, Mr. Nercessian?"

"My job," he replied. "I want a bit of a break. You could do my job, which consists of following people. That would enable me to pursue my private interests a bit more. I'll pay you well enough. And it'll enable you to get out and about more often."

Syphax smiled. "That would suit me very well."

Mr. Nercessian hesitated. "There's something I should add," he said, lowering his voice yet further. "Most of the suspects I follow . . . Well, they don't actually exist. I've found it simpler to invent them, if you see what I mean."

"You make them up? Entirely?"

Mr. Nercessian smiled. "Well, some of them are based on real people—but people who have died. It's safer that way. Others are figments of my imagination—but very credible characters, I must say. The point is filing reports, you see. What they—the powers that be—want is lots of reports. What difference if the reports are about people who don't actually exist? The important point is that the authorities are confident they have the situation under control. And if the authorities feel they have the situation under control, then everybody can get on with the rest of their business in peace."

"Which leads to happiness all round?"

"Precisely. All you have to do is to file reports. One in ten of them will be read by somebody more senior, and so you have to do it credibly. But as long as you do that, you'll be all right."

Mr. Nercessian lit a cigarette, using a gold lighter that Syphax had noticed bore the initials of another. Those of a victim? But the Armenian was too cultivated, too courteous to do anything crude. Perhaps he had found it somewhere and had decided to hold on to it: even a spy might hesitate to have unduly close contact with the police, even with their lost-property department.

"Of course," Mr. Nercessian continued, "you don't want to keep your suspects going for too long. Give them a couple of years and then report that they've gone into exile. That usually pleases the authorities. And it enables you to start again."

"Very satisfactory," said Syphax.

"Yes," said Mr. Nercessian. "The best of all possible worlds, as our friend Dr. Pangloss might say." He smiled. "One of my suspects is actually called Pangloss. I gave him the name. It suits him." He paused. "He's just gone into exile, actually. I've replaced him with a Mr. Aristotle, who's meant to be a Greek agent." He grinned. "And you know what those idiots in Head Office said? They said, 'Watch this Greek, this Aristotle. We think he might be trouble. We've heard the name somewhere.' "

The eunuch, who had been listening to this conversation with amusement, shrieked with laughter.

"Rich!" he exclaimed. "If ever there was an empire destined to fall, it's this one."

TIME, LANGUID EVEN IN those mellow, shaky years of the Ottoman Empire, passed agreeably slowly. Syphax spent the period between 1900 and 1904 in Constantinople, employed by the Ottoman Secret Service, doing Mr. Nercessian's job between daily visits to the coffee houses and baths, and occasional lunch parties on the shores of the Bosphorus. The eunuch gave him regular cookery lessons, and in 1903 Syphax helped him to establish a small cookery school for the daughters of wealthy officials. Even traditional parents were happy to allow these young women to be tutored by a eunuch, and his courses were soon over-subscribed. "One day," he remarked to Syphax, "it might be possible to teach young men how to cook. That will not be for many years—probably not in our lifetimes—but it will happen, I think."

In 1904 Mr. Nercessian was informed that he was to be sent on service abroad. This brought consternation, as he had developed business interests in Constantinople that would suffer if he were to leave them in the hands of unreliable managers. "I must ask you to re-pay the favour I did you," he said to Syphax. "I must ask you to take this assignment in my place. I can arrange for a forger to delete my name from the relevant departmental minute and insert yours in its stead. That is all that will be required. It's a very common procedure."

Syphax realised that he would have to comply. Favours were a serious business in the Ottoman Empire, and by any standards he was heavily indebted to Mr. Nercessian.

"Where is this posting?" he asked. "I'm not saying I won't do it, but I would just like to know where I am to be sent."

"You're in luck," said Mr. Nercessian brightly. "It is to Algiers. Can you believe that? This is something sent by the Almighty. It is clearly meant to be."

Syphax sighed. It was bound to happen, and he would simply have to reconcile himself to it. Sooner or later, the place where you are destined to be will come and claim you. It always does. You may think you've escaped, but you never have: like gravity, such places pull you back, assert their control of your life. You won't get away from us that easily, say these places. We are your place; this is where you are destined to die, however long your life may prove to be. Don't fight it; submit, and in your acceptance you may find peace and contentment. Many do.

6

THEY FOLLOWED

S YPHAX WAS WELCOMED BACK INTO THE BOSOM OF HIS FAMILY BY his father, who embraced him warmly, tears streaming down his face.

"I knew you would return," he sobbed. "I knew you would never abandon us."

"Such a thought never crossed my mind, Father. Not once."

"And all those years of studying," Mr. Brahimi went on. "Now you are an educated man—capable, I'm sure, of holding your own in the presence of anybody Paris can come up with. Anybody." He paused. "But what do you actually do, Syphax? What's this job of yours with the Ottomans?"

Syphax hesitated, but then, holding himself erect, he said, "I'm a spy, Father. I'm an Ottoman spy."

Mr. Brahimi's eyes widened, but only momentarily. Then he let

out a guffaw of laughter. "Of course. Of course, you're a spy. That's
the best cover for being something else. I understand. You say you're
a spy, but in fact you're an official in the Ministry of Supply, or in
some such post. It's very cunning."

Syphax shook his head. "No, Father, you have it wrong. People
have mundane-sounding jobs as cover for their real jobs as spies. You
have it the wrong way round."

Again, Mr. Brahimi laughed. "You're not going to fool me that
easily," he said. "You can't hoodwink your own father."

Syphax abandoned any attempt to explain the situation to his
father, and settled into his new posting. His instructions were to open
an office in Algiers and to observe the doings of the various exiles—
republican dissidents and reformers who had sought sanctuary there.
He was given a generous budget for the payment of informers, an
entertainment fund, and an allowance for the purchase of clothing.

Syphax had no interest in pestering the exiles, for whom he had
considerable sympathy. Indeed, he went even further than simply
abstaining from bothering them—he sent in false reports to Constantinople detailing the imagined demise of various opponents of
the regime: two were reported drowned at sea, another was said to
have been attacked by a rabid dog and have succumbed to hydrophobia, and several were poisoned. The exiles were real, and remained
alive and well, but Constantinople was delighted to hear of their trials
and tribulations. In respect of the exile reported to have been bitten
by a rabid dog and to have developed hydrophobia, Headquarters
in Constantinople sent a coded telegram to Syphax asking him to
confirm that the poor man had suffered an agonising death. "Can
confirm death very agonising," Syphax replied.

The false reports on the death of the exiles had the effect of reliev-
ing them of anxiety. Since they were now officially dead, and their
names removed from the list of those of interest to the regime, the
exiles could relax their vigilance. Although Syphax never spoke to
them directly, the exiles became aware of just who it was who had
done them the favour of killing them off, and responded by establishing a credit balance for his benefit at Syphax's regular restaurant, *la
Maison de St. Julien*.

But reports had to be written, and so Syphax decided that he would devote his time to what he described as his "counter-intelligence" initiative. This involved following the prominent spy, *bon viveur,* and chess champion, Omar Benamara. Omar, who was roughly Syphax's age, was a spy for the Italian government, which although not directly involved in Algerian affairs was interested in what was happening there on the grounds that Algeria was adjacent to its claimed zone of influence in Libya. Omar had been recruited to keep an eye on any agents of other powers who might have an interest in Italian ambitions. This meant that Syphax, as a spy for the Ottomans, who were the current rulers of Libya, was of interest. In a dispatch to Rome, Omar warned them that Syphax needed to be watched constantly as he was in regular touch with the Ottoman authorities in Tripoli and could be expected to do whatever he could to flout Italian claims to be the stabilising power in Libya itself.

The result of this was that Syphax and Omar came to spend every day following one another, moving from café to café, waiting to see exactly whom the other was meeting. They soon became aware of each other, and although they did not speak in the earlier days of this arrangement, they acknowledged one another's presence with a courteous nod of the head.

In 1923, with the emergence of the Republic of Turkey, Syphax was assumed as an employee of the new government. He and Omar continued to trail one another, noting down each other's movements and sending reports back to Rome and Istanbul. They now exchanged a few friendly words in the cafés they frequented, although they still maintained separate tables. The one exception to that rule was on the birthday of either of them, when a single table allowed them to share the birthday cake that the proprietors of the cafés would bake for them. As he sampled these cakes, Syphax invariably cast his mind back to the eunuch and the rosewater cakes he made in Constantinople. "I once knew a eunuch who made delicious cakes," Syphax said to Omar. "That was long ago, though, in a world that seems to have passed . . ."

"Oh," said Omar.

Syphax retired in June, 1935, shortly before his sixtieth birthday. Omar retired two months later. Neither could bear the thought of abandoning their routine, and so they continued to follow one another, as they always had done, through the streets of Algiers, keeping a short distance behind whoever was in front, employing all the usual tricks of disguise and shrugging off that they had acquired in their early training.

They appreciated one another. "Omar is a true professional," Syphax said. "We shall not see his like again."

"Syphax is a great spy," Omar reciprocated. "In the history of intelligence, there have been few of his calibre."

When Syphax turned sixty-five, Omar gave him a book on the history of Turkish ceramics. The world was then at war. Syphax said, as they sat in a café and read the news from Vichy, "It's so different from our own day, isn't it?"

Omar agreed. "Ours used to be a gentlemanly profession."

"You're right," said Syphax, a note of sadness in his voice.

They finished their coffee. Then Syphax rose to his feet and left the café. Omar followed him.

Ferry Timetable

(SCOTLAND, 1984)

HIS NAME WAS FERGUS ANDREW MACTAVISH AND HE WAS A FARMER in a remote part of Argyll. He went to his grave, unexposed, in 2003. At that simple ceremony of farewell, conducted under a West Highland sky filled with sharp April light, only two of those present were aware of any claim that Fergus might have to be listed in the company of some of the century's best-known spies. And those two would never speak about it. Never.

Mactavish—as he was generally known—had a farm not far from Ardgour, a village on the shores of Loch Linnhe, a long sea loch that led up to Fort William and the Great Glen beyond. Ardgour did not consist of very much—a hotel, well-placed at the top of the ferry slipway, a general shop, and a post office. But that was all that most people needed. For any other purpose there was Fort William a brief ferry ride and drive away, or Oban about an hour or so further south. Above the village there were great sweeps of mountainside down which, after heavy rain, thin waterfalls fell like white threads. It was dramatic scenery by any standards, but taken for granted, as such things always are, by those who lived there. The mountains, though beautiful, supported very few sheep; the waterfalls and lochs were all very well but they led to the general damp that brought the midges in their summer swarms; and the sea loch cut one off from places that would otherwise have been more easily reached. Yet it was clearly far better than Glasgow, where people went off in search of work, only to find that they yearned for everything they had left behind, and from which they often returned, determined not to leave again.

Mactavish's farm was barely two hundred acres, but was large enough to support a small herd of beef cattle and a flock of Blackface sheep. He was a good farmer, and made the most of things, as had his wife, who had died when their daughter, Kirsty, was seventeen. Kirsty remained at home, not entirely out of a sense of duty, but because she saw no reason to go anywhere else. This suited Mactavish, as she was a good housekeeper, but he occasionally wondered what would happen if she were to marry. He hoped that she would do so, of course, as he wanted her to be happy, and he belonged to a generation where to be single was seen as a failure significantly reducing one's chances of happiness. But she showed no signs of looking for a husband, smiling enigmatically whenever he tactfully mentioned the possibility. "You never know," she said. "Maybe I will, maybe I won't. And there aren't all that many decent men around here, if you ask me. So maybe I won't."

In 1980, when Mactavish was fifty-four and Kirsty was twenty-seven, there was a major crisis in their household. This concerned land and came about when the local council declared its intention of slicing off a portion of Mactavish's best field in order to build a new road.

"Nobody needs a new road," Mactavish pointed out in a long and outraged letter to his councillor.

"Probably not," replied the councillor. "I certainly voted against it, but it's the committee, you see. They're the ones who look after roads and things like that. They said we do need a road, and that's that. You'll get your compensation, remember."

That, thought Mactavish, was not the point. He wanted land, not money, and he vigorously protested his case to this effect, even engaging a solicitor in Inverness to write on his behalf to the council. His efforts were to no avail, though, and he concluded that the British state, as represented by its road-making authorities in the Western Highlands, was rotten to the core.

Tossing and turning in his bed one night, filled with resentment at the imminent arrival of the council's bulldozers, it occurred to him that if the authorities could treat a law-abiding farmer in such a way then they had sacrificed any claim they might have to his loyalty. And it was at that point, just as he was about to get up to attend to the livestock, that he decided he would work for the Soviet Union. That would teach them, he thought. That would teach them up in Inverness. That would teach them in Edinburgh and London. They would have only themselves to blame.

The *Oban Times* had reported in considerable detail the exposure of Anthony Blunt, and Mactavish was amongst those readers who had followed the case with some interest. He had read about controllers and meetings in London parks. He had read about the Soviet Union's seemingly insatiable appetite for information about military arrangements; well, he thought, Loch Linnhe was a waterway of some importance: you could take a submarine up as far as Fort William if you really wanted to, and that, in fact, might be just the sort of thing that the Soviet Union might wish to do. The *Oban Times* had once reported Russian submarines being sighted off Skye, and that was not all that far away. If you were prowling around Skye in a submarine, then it might be quite convenient to be able to slip into Loch Linnhe for a day or two and rest while British submarines looked for you in the Sound of Mull. You would have to be careful, though, that you didn't try to cross the route taken by the Corran Ferry, because the loch was not all that deep at that point and the last thing you'd want would be for your conning tower to be clipped by the ferry's propeller.

Mactavish thought about all this, and then, in a sudden moment of decision, he obtained a copy of the Corran Ferry timetable. This he placed in an envelope with a covering note, and, having obtained the address of the Soviet Embassy in London from a telephone directory in the Fort William Public Library, posted it. The covering note said: *I am prepared to work for you. This information could be helpful for submarine activity. Please contact me for further assistance. Yours truly, F. A. Mactavish.*

KIRSTY NOTICED THAT her father seemed somewhat jumpy over the days that followed. He had not mentioned his act of treason to her, of course, and she had no idea why he showed such interest in the arrival of the postmistress in her van.

"Are you expecting something?" she said. "A cheque maybe?"

Mactavish shook his head. "No," he said. "Nothing." Even as he spoke, the thought crossed his mind: How very easy it is to lie. That's what those people did. Philby and the others. They were very good liars.

After a week of waiting, he began to feel anxious. What if the letter had been intercepted by the authorities? What if the intelligence people in London had steamed it open and found the Corran Ferry timetable and his offer to work for the Soviets? He had put his address at the top of his letter and so they would have no difficulty tracing him. Perhaps that was a mistake. Perhaps he should have arranged a meeting at what the *Oban Times* had described as a "drop-off point." He swallowed hard. I'm an amateur, he thought. I've made the most fundamental of mistakes.

The sense of excitement and anticipation that he had felt was now replaced by a gnawing sense of dread. This was compounded by guilt. He had betrayed his country in a fit of anger and now, on more mature reflection, he realised what a terrible thing he had done. His father had served in the Argyll and Sutherland Highlanders, just as his grandfather had done. An uncle had been in the Black Watch and had been commended for his bravery. And here he was, Fergus Mactavish, offering his services to the Soviet Union, about which he knew nothing and which had no claim at all on his loyalty.

He went to see the local Church of Scotland minister. Sitting awkwardly in the minister's study, a cup of tea cooling at his elbow, he confessed what he had done. The minister allowed him to tell the whole story before he said anything.

"You should drink your tea, Mactavish," he said at last. "I can't take cold tea myself—never could."

There was a brief silence. Then the minister continued, "You sent them the ferry timetable, you say?"

Mactavish nodded miserably.

The minister smiled. "I wouldn't worry too much about that, you know. You can get the ferry timetable in the shop."

"But I offered to do more."

The minister raised an eyebrow. "What else could you do? I'm not being rude, but what on earth could you do for the Soviet Union?"

Mactavish stared at the floor. "You don't think it's too bad?"

The minister shook his head. "Come on, man, be sensible! Anybody who heard about this would burst out laughing. Anybody would think it's a great joke. Nobody would take it seriously."

Mactavish left the minister's house feeling as if a great weight had been taken off his shoulders. He returned to the farm, where he made a full confession to his daughter.

"I knew there was something biting you," she said. "But I had no idea it would be so ridiculous."

Mactavish said nothing. He wanted now to forget all about it. It was coming up to the lambing season and he would have his hands more than full with that.

A month later, a letter arrived from the Soviet Embassy. When Mactavish opened it and saw the headed paper, he gave an involuntary gasp. His daughter, who had just come into the room, looked at him with concern.

"Is that about the road?" she asked.

He handed the letter to her. "It's from the Russians," he said. "They're coming to see me."

She frowned as she read it. "So this Mr. Yuri Olevsky is coming next week," she said. "Well, you just go to the police. Speak to Sergeant Cameron."

"I can't do that," Mactavish exclaimed. "I can't go and tell the police that I offered to work for the Soviet Union. Willie Cameron would have to arrest me. I'd be taken off to Inverness Prison before I knew what was happening."

Kirsty thought for a moment. "But they might *turn* you. MI5 or whoever they are might use you as a double agent."

Mactavish dismissed this suggestion. "This is what happens when you do what I did," he said, his voice full of misery. "It's the same as with that fellow, Blunt. You get in too deep and then you can't get out again."

She took her father's hand and held it. He looked at her, lovingly, in gratitude. Family would always forgive; they would forgive wrongs both small and large; meanness, venality, even treason.

"When Mr. Olevsky comes," she said quietly, "we'll give him a cup of tea but we must be firm. We shall tell him that you are no longer prepared to serve the Soviet Union."

"I don't think I ever really began to do that," said Mactavish. "That's what the minister said."

"Well, there you are," said Kirsty. "You can tell him that you're not going to start."

She looked out of the window. A squall had blown in from the south west—a veil of gentle rain, like white mist, moving across the surface of the distant loch. The light behind it had the quality of silver.

YURI OLEVSKY WAS IN his early thirties—rather younger than they had imagined. He had dark, slicked-down hair, which lent him the appearance of a 1930s dance instructor. He had very white teeth, and regular features. He was very handsome.

They drank tea together. He seemed nervous, and after a few minutes of pleasantries, Mactavish thought that he should not delay in revealing his change of heart.

"With all due respect to the Soviet Union," he said, "I have decided that I do not wish to get involved."

Olevsky looked at him. "This place you have here is very beautiful," he said.

Mactavish inclined his head in recognition of the compliment.

Then Olevsky said, "I am ashamed of my country. I, too, no longer wish to serve it."

Mactavish and his daughter stared at him. Neither knew what to say. Treason, it seemed, unknown in Ardgour since the 1745 Jacobite rebellion—and that wasn't real treason, if you were a Jacobite—now seemed endemic.

Eventually Mactavish found his voice. "Oh," he said. And then he added, "Aye."

"I told my superiors that I was following up a lead in Glasgow," Olevsky continued. "They do not know I am here." He paused. "I should therefore like to apply for political asylum."

Mactavish looked at Kirsty. "What do we do?"

Olevsky intercepted the question. "You fetch the authorities," he said.

Mactavish shrugged his shoulders. "We don't have any authorities up here. There's Willie Cameron, I suppose, but he's not based here. He's at the police office in Strontian."

Now Kirsty acted. "Why don't you just stay with us?" she asked. "You could get work in the hotel—the one down by the ferry. And I know somebody who's looking for someone to help him on his fishing boat."

Mactavish opened his mouth to protest. She had not asked him how he would feel about having a Russian staying in the house, but then he stopped himself. He looked at his daughter; she was gazing at Olevsky, who was smiling back at her encouragingly.

Over the three weeks that followed, Olevsky settled into the routine of the Mactavish household. At first, he was cautious about going out, and would only venture forth after he had carefully looked up and down the road to see if there were any unfamiliar cars or any other sign of strangers. It was a quiet corner of Scotland, and there was nothing untoward to be seen. But he remained uneasy and one evening he confessed his concern to Mactavish.

"I fear that they will come after me," he said. "They will be wondering where I am. They wait for a few weeks usually—just in case—and then they decide that there has been a defection."

Mactavish listened. "You'd think they would leave a poor fellow alone," he mused.

Olevsky nodded. "They have long memories," he said. "I only hope they don't have any idea of where to look for me."

"I think you're safe," said Mactavish. "And if they come snooping around here, the dogs will let us know. They're great ones for barking at strangers."

Olevsky smiled. He was growing increasingly fond of the Mactavish family—and of Kirsty in particular—and he did not want anything to imperil that. And yet he knew that the KGB had a long reach, and that the Scottish Highlands were well within their range. And he was right: a few days after this conversation with Mactavish, as he was making his way into the village to pick up his host's copy of the *Oban Times*, he noticed a man standing near the ferry slipway, innocently smoking a cigarette. Olevsky stopped as the smoke drifted over towards him. It had the unmistakable smell of Russian tobacco.

He looked over his shoulder. The man was watching him, and now he approached him, walking purposively. Olevsky froze. If he ran, then the man would almost certainly fire at him—and he was unarmed. This is how it ends, he thought.

The man came up to him and Olevsky gasped. It was his colleague, Topornin. They had trained together and had spent many happy evenings drinking vodka and telling stories of the old days at naval college.

"So," said Topornin. "This is a nice place you've found for yourself, Oleg Vladimirovich. Very nice."

Olevsky took a deep breath. If one had to die, one might as well die in comity.

"Oh, it's a fine place, Ivan Ivanovich. It's quiet. It's beautiful. The people are friendly." He paused. "Would you care to come and meet my new friends?"

Topornin hesitated. Then he said, "I could do with a spot of lunch."

"Then come back with me," said Olevsky. "I caught some mackerel yesterday. They're very tasty fish."

"I love fishing," said Topornin.

"Lots of fish here," said Olevsky. "You row out into the bay and come back with ten, twenty fat mackerel."

"Oh, my goodness," said Topornin.

They walked back to the farm together. There Olevsky introduced Topornin to Mactavish and to Kirsty. Then they had lunch together. Mactavish gave Topornin a large glass of whisky, which the Russian downed in a single swig.

"All Russians like to drink," joked Olevsky.

The party continued into the afternoon. At four o'clock the local postman called in with the mail. He and Topornin talked about fishing. More whisky was consumed.

Kirsty's friend, Heather, called in at six. Kirsty played a Russian record that Olevsky had given her. Then Heather and Topornin danced together until they all sat down to dinner.

"Do you think I could find something here too?" Topornin asked Olevsky as they began the venison stew that Kirsty had made.

"Oh, definitely," said Olevsky. "But what about . . ." He nodded his head in the direction of London—or it could have been Moscow.

Topornin put a finger to his lips. "They don't know where I was heading," he said. "I told them I had a lead, but I didn't give them any details. We're safe here, I think."

"You're a real friend," said Olevsky.

"Are there any formalities, though?" Topornin enquired.

"Not here," said Olevsky. "You don't have to report to anybody. You just . . . get absorbed."

"Wonderful," said Topornin.

OLEVSKY PROVED TO BE very handy on the fishing boat. He was also a rather good plasterer, and gradually started doing more of that in houses throughout Lochaber. He and Kirsty married eight months later, and began work on a bungalow for themselves a few hundred yards from Mactavish's farmhouse, in exactly the spot where the road was to have been built. That plan had been scrapped as the council had experienced a budgetary deficit and had other, more pressing needs to attend to. For Mactavish, that was a victory that gave him immense satisfaction.

Topornin and Heather married a few months after the wedding of Olevsky and Kirsty. They built a house on a plot of land further up the glen and Topornin got a job as a deputy postman. He loved the uniform. Heather was proud of him.

Mactavish had two grandsons over the next four years. Olevsky loved to dress his sons in kilts and shower them with gifts sent over from his aunts in Leningrad. When the Soviet Union fell, these aunts came to Scotland for a holiday and brought even more gifts for the boys. They invited Mactavish to visit them in St. Petersburg, which he did with enthusiasm. The aunts told him about the popularity of Robert Burns in Russian translation. "He speaks to the Russian soul," they said. "He really does."

Olevsky framed a copy of the Corran Ferry timetable and hung it on the wall of their kitchen. People commented on this odd choice of decoration, but he said nothing to divulge the reason behind it. Training in the keeping of secrets often survives a change in one's circumstances.

In the summer, on warm days, he and Kirsty, accompanied by their two sons, would follow a path up to a pool at the bottom of one of the waterfalls. They would swim in the bracing clear water and then, while the boys played at the edge of the pool, the parents would lie back in the heather and look up at the sky, on such days cloudless, a pale blue witness to their happiness.

Donald and Yevgeni

THE MAN WITH THE SCHOLARLY AIR OPENED THE PHOTOGRAPH album. He handled it gently, in the way of a porter in an auction house holding an Old Master drawing. He was not wearing the white gloves that such porters wear, but there was in his expression much the same care and reverence.

"These photographs were passed on to me by my grandfather," he said. "Long deceased. His entire career was in the consular service. He was an indiscriminate photographer. He snapped everything."

The woman nodded. "How useful."

"Yes. He said to me, you know, that he could not understand how people could do without having a photographic record of their lives. It was beyond him."

The woman said that she saw how one might feel that. She was not a photographer herself—apart from the occasional family picture—but she enjoyed looking at other people's photographs. "Although I must confess that sometimes I find them sad."

"Why should they be sad? Particularly if the people in the photograph are smiling—as they usually are? Why sad?"

She looked thoughtful. "I find them sad because when the photographs are older ones, I reflect on the fact that everyone in the picture is likely to be no more. It's to do with the transience of life."

"*Vita brevis est?*"

"Exactly. It is."

He thought of something. "In the past, people in photographs kept their mouths closed—for the most part." He paused. "And you know why?"

She waited for him to explain.

"Because of their teeth. People used to have gaps. It was very common. Gaps or rotten teeth. Dental hygiene in those days was not what it is today."

She winced. Anything to do with teeth or nasal passages made her wince.

"I was looking at a photograph the other day," he went on, "of a group of soldiers going off to France. Some of them boys, or not far off it. 1914."

"How sad."

"Yes, it was. But I don't think they knew what they were in for. They were all very cheerful and smiling. So, we saw their teeth. Most of them, as far as I could see, had lost some. Either that or there were lots of blackened stumps."

They were silent. He pointed to one of the photographs. It was a black-and-white picture taken in an office somewhere. A man sat at a desk, while another stood behind him. In the corner was a third figure, wearing a strange costume. The man in costume was diminutive.

"See?" he said.

She peered at the photograph.

"Washington," he said. "The man sitting down is the British ambassador, a man called Archibald Clark Kerr. A very colourful character, which is putting it mildly. Behind him there, that tall, distinguished-looking man is Donald Maclean. He was at Gresham's School, Norfolk, where I went actually. It's how I became interested in him. Britten was there, too. You can see his name on a board in the school hall—and Maclean's, too. A prize of some sort. Then he went on to King's College, Cambridge. He was a member of the Apostles. You know what that means?"

She nodded. She had a vague idea. "A secret society in Cambridge, wasn't it? John Maynard Keynes—and others."

"That's them. They met to read one another papers and discuss issues of the day. They were self-consciously elitist. A bit precious.

In fact, really precious. Wittgenstein was a member. He didn't like it very much."

"He wouldn't fit in, I imagine."

"No, he was odd. He used to sit in a cinema in Cambridge eating buttered toast. I don't know where I read that and whether it's true. It's one of those things that sticks in the mind. Then he wrote the *Tractatus Logico-Philosophicus*."

"Now, there's a title."

He smiled at that. Pointing at the standing figure in the photograph he continued, "Maclean was very urbane, don't you think? First Secretary in the embassy. The consummate British diplomat. And in the corner there—that's Yevgeni Yost, the ambassador's Russian valet, believe it or not, dressed as a Cossack. A dwarf, as they called such people in those days. And still do, I think, although there may be a new term—it's so difficult to keep up."

She stared at the photograph. "Are you serious?" she said. "Do you mean to say that the British ambassador to Washington had a *Russian* valet?"

"He did. Yes. Given to him by Stalin at the end of his posting to Moscow. Archie Clark Kerr was ambassador there before he went to Washington, and got on very well with Stalin."

"You said: *given?*"

"Yes, that's the sort of thing you could do if you were Stalin. Slavery has had many different faces, remember." He paused. "It's all there in accounts of those times. Look it up."

She searched for words, and decided on, "Good heavens."

He looked at her quizzically. "How many idealists do you see in that photograph? One? Two? Three?" He paused. "And how many spies?"

She shook her head. "Who knows?"

"I do," he said. And then added, "Although, when I look at this picture I find myself asking, *How many people keep tiny Cossacks in their office?*"

She laughed. "Is this really true? It isn't some imaginative spy story?"

"Absolutely," he said. "Every last word of it. Listen."

. . .

THE AMBASSADOR FIRST. Archibald Clark Kerr, Lord Inverchapel as he became. He was actually born in Australia, but he always made a great thing about being Scottish, although he never actually lived there. That happens a lot, of course. Some of the most Scottish people there are actually don't live in Scotland. Identities are interesting, aren't they? We can pick the one we feel best expresses something within us. You can be Catholic, or Jewish, or have a particular sexual identity or whatever while obviously being something else as well. And you can create an identity for yourself that can then become the real you. Then people think that you were always what you claim to be, that you were born to it, so to speak, rather than having made it all yourself. And that can be important in the world of spies. They are accustomed to maintaining one identity while really being something else altogether.

His father was a Scotsman who emigrated. He married into a well-to-do Australian family—his wife was the daughter of the Premier of New South Wales—but he came back to Britain when his son, Archie, was only seven. So the boy spent the rest of his childhood in the United Kingdom and was not to make much of his Australian heritage. When he eventually made it into *Who's Who*, his entry made no mention of where he was born, nor did it reveal where he went to school, which was in Bath. He was sent to a school there that eventually collapsed—it had its aspirations, but it was never very successful. So, Archie described himself in his *Who's Who* entry as having been "privately educated." He also took ten years off his age in that entry, which is an odd thing to do, even in a man who dyed his hair. But then Archie Clark Kerr *was* odd. He would never have made it in the civil service today, let alone in the Foreign Office. But times were different then. There were *characters*, you see, and there wasn't the same expectation of conformity. We think that *they* were stuffy. We think that *we* are free of all that. But the truth of the matter is that we are just as conformist as they were. We delude ourselves if we think we are free—all that has happened is that the nature of the constraints has changed—the diktats are different, and issued by a different set of diktat-issuers. We have a hegemony of attitudes just as they did in the 1920s and '30s. What do they say? *Plus ça change, plus c'est la même chose* . . . Except that I think the French never actually say that. We do, and saying it in French adds something, don't you think? A certain *frisson*, perhaps.

The diplomatic service that Archie entered in 1906 was very different from its modern equivalent. Entry was by competitive examination, but was far from open to all. Not everybody could afford to apply: junior staff were expected to have a private income sufficient for the needs of somebody in their position—an important consideration, bearing in mind that they were not paid at all until they had been promoted to the level of third secretary. Once in post, their duties were mundane—opening letters, deciphering telegrams, and filing. Much of their time was spent in idle pursuits of one sort or another, and although they were not as free from duties as were Trollope's non-resident clergymen, the hours were far from demanding. Further up the ladder, Foreign Office mandarins tended not to start their day's work until after eleven in the morning, which left relatively little time to work before they went off for lunch.

Archie's first posting was to Berlin, a place that failed to inspire him, in spite of its diplomatic importance at the time. Like any young diplomat, he was expected to spend a great deal of time mixing in German high society, and he did this with a degree of success. In the summer there was golf and tennis parties; in the evenings there were full-dress balls with dance cards and gossip. There was no shortage of opportunities for flirtations and affairs, useful in making contact with those who knew what was going on in government. Archie was charming, and women liked to confide in him. He soon developed a close friendship with Princess Sophia, the Kaiser's sister, who was married to the Greek crown prince, Constantine. This relationship, in which he played the role of confidant, was typical of the friendships that Archie was capable of establishing amongst the well-placed.

The Greek royal family, into which Sophia had married, was every bit as colourful as Archie himself. Her brother-in-law was Prince Andrew of Greece, a handsome, monocled figure whose disastrous military career culminated in his arrest, trial, and sentencing to death.

He was eventually rescued through the intervention of George V, who arranged for him to be taken by gunboat from Corfu, where he had a villa. Included in the party of fleeing royalty was Andrew's son, Philip, who was later to emerge as the Duke of Edinburgh. Andrew's wife eventually became a nun in an order of her own creation, although she still continued to smoke heavily and play canasta. Her good works, though, were numerous, and included the sheltering of Jews during the Second World War. Prince Andrew lived in hotels and villas in the south of France and Monaco until his death in 1944. His family was split by conflicting loyalties during the war years. While Prince Philip served with distinction in the Royal Navy, his three sisters, unfortunately, moved in rather different circles, and married German princes of one sort or another.

Archie was to have more involvement with unstable royalty in a subsequent posting, this time at more elevated level, to the British Embassy in Baghdad. Iraq was important to British interests, and his posting, as with his time in Cairo, allowed him scope to exercise his intelligence and his sensitive understanding of political trends. The King of Iraq, King Ghazi, was the son of King Faisal I, the monarch who had been put in place by the British, who controlled Iraq after the dissolution of the Ottoman Empire. Ghazi was educated in England from the age of thirteen and wore western dress. He married and produced an heir, but he also relished the company of the young male servants with whom he surrounded himself. One of these, a favourite to whom he was particularly close, was shot by his own revolver, an incident that was alleged by some to have had something to do with the queen, who took a poor view of her husband's young friends.

Ghazi's behaviour was not approved of by the British authorities. Their spies in the palace reported to Archie on the king's every move and indiscretion. Even he, with his liberal and unconventional attitudes, was surprised by what went on in the palace, which included frequent organised pillow fights between the king and his young male courtiers and servants. The king had picked up an interest in this particular pastime during his boarding school education in England, and never lost his enthusiasm for them. His pillow fights in Baghdad were legendary, and were the subject of ribald comment. In spite of all this, or perhaps because of all this, Archie liked the king, and presumably was upset by his early demise in a highly suspicious car accident—if, indeed, the accident had anything to do with the king's death. One of the five doctors who signed the death certificate confessed decades later that the real cause, in his view, was a blow to the back of the head with an iron bar, suggesting that the accident was a cover-up. The most obvious beneficiaries of the king's death were certain shady commercial figures in Iraq, not that anything was ever proved.

Archie took all this in his stride although his progress up the Foreign Office ladder was not entirely smooth, and there were periods when he felt his career was blighted by official disapproval. He was liberal in his sympathies—the opposite of the stuffed-shirt figures who still influenced British diplomatic thinking at the time. Many of them still harboured imperialist ambitions, believing that they could ride out the enthusiasm for self-determination that now began to challenge the old European empires. In Cairo, Archie understood the feelings of Egyptian nationalists who wanted to overturn the British mandate and pursue the cause of Egyptian independence. British policy, though, was at odds with this current, particularly when it threatened British control of the Sudan. When he appeared to favour policies at odds with London's view, it was not surprising that he should incur official displeasure and consequently be given the impression that his career was stalled.

Although his natural talent and his capacity for hard work was to bring about his rehabilitation—resulting in his appointment to the senior position in the British Embassy in China—this tension between his sympathy for the underdog and the interests of those battling against the odds, was to continue to make it hard for him to implement official policy. This was certainly the case in China, where he had to tread a delicate path between helping the Chinese in the face of Japanese aggression while at the same time avoiding direct involvement in the Sino-Japanese war then in progress. Above all, he needed to avoid Japanese control bringing an end to the British trading concessions in Shanghai and elsewhere in China.

SHANGHAI, 1939, IN THE BRITISH RESIDENCY

H E STOOD BEFORE THE MIRROR, ADJUSTING HIS BOW TIE. ONE could buy ties already made up, with wire in the bow to keep them from dropping, but he would never resort to those. He had overheard somebody calling a tie like that a "cad's tie," which had amused him— not that he was too concerned about how other people dressed. He took care with his own wardrobe, of course, and rather liked dressing up when given the chance. The full diplomatic uniform, with its gold braid, its frogging and its sword, looked good, even if at times it could be unbearably hot. He had donned that when he had presented his credentials to the Kuomintang government, and had been pictured with their officials, clutching his plumed tricorne hat.

Tonight's dinner was not a full-dress affair and so he was wearing a simple dinner jacket and black tie. His two guests, whom everybody was looking forward to meeting, had been told that the invitation was evening dress, and he hoped that they would have managed to find something. They were staying for a few days, and so he could always fix them up if more invitations came their way.

He looked into the mirror at his wife, Tita. She was seated at a dressing table, brushing her hair.

Archie said, "Somebody said that I looked like Noël Coward when I'm in my dinner jacket. Do you agree?"

She looked in her own mirror, and their eyes met somewhere in the complex optics of the two reflections.

"Noël Coward? Maybe. A bit. He can sing, of course. And play the piano."

"I said *look* like—not *sound* like."

"I'm not sure that anybody would want to look like Noël Coward." She paused. "And anyway, who are these two? I'm not sure whether I want them to stay."

He sighed. "Too late. I've invited them."

"I wish you'd ask me."

"They're work."

She looked doubtful. "Are they?"

"You know I have to entertain people who turn up. It goes with all this . . ." He waved a hand about. "It goes with the job."

"But poets? Didn't you say they were poets?"

"One is. The other one is a novelist, and dramatist, I think."

"Which is which?"

He explained. "Auden is the poet. His friend is called Isherwood. Auden's the better-known of the two."

"Where did you pick them up?"

He brushed at his shoulders with a clothes brush. He did not like her choice of phrase. He had not picked these two up, and he was irritated that she should take that approach. After all, he had picked *her* up on a beach in Chile. She had been sitting there and his dog had run across the sand towards her. So if anybody had initiated the picking up, it was the dog. She had been eighteen. He had been forty-seven, a member of the British Embassy staff in Santiago, but he had married her nonetheless. But it was, he supposed, a bit of a pick-up, if one was going to use that term. At least he had made her the wife of the British ambassador to China—and a lady, for that matter. She had rather liked it when he was knighted and she became Lady Kerr.

She looked away. She did not like being in China. She did not enjoy being in Chungking, the seat of Chiang Kai-shek's tottering government, with its mists and its cliffs and its scurrying Chinese officials. She did not like the ever-present threat posed by the Japanese, with their demands and their shelling and their insatiable ambition to devour China and anybody else who threatened their plans for the dominance of Asia. She felt sorry for the Chinese, for the millions who lived in squalor, and for whom distant unconcerned government was the lot to which they had been accustomed for generations. She admired her husband for his stand against the Japanese bullies, even if he had to be careful about what he said. He had to live with a policy of appeasement of the Japanese invaders and was unable to give the Chinese the aid and support that they needed to combat Tokyo's bullying. He hated that, and she was proud of his distaste for the policy dictated to him by his distant political masters. She admired his courage and the decency that lay at the heart of his dealings with people who were weaker than he was; she admired the way he was able to see the viewpoint of others, particularly of the Chinese, who felt so vulnerable and threatened. She wondered where that came from? The other British people she had encountered since she married him often seemed arrogant and condescending, unquestioning of the privileges that came with birth and the right sort of contacts. Archie was different—he could play those others at their own game; he could affect the same attitudes; utter the right shibboleths; but he could draw on wells of sympathy that they never possessed. Perhaps that was something that came from being born Australian. They said that Australia was an egalitarian society, that it did not matter who your parents were or where you went to school— that what counted was your character, what was inside you. Perhaps that had somehow been instilled in him in those few, early years in Australia, and had never left him. It was quite possible, she thought. And yet she did not want to stay here in China. She wanted to escape the heat and the smells and the emptiness of the diplomatic round. Archie could hardly complain: he worked all the time and when he was not working he liked to sunbathe or paint in watercolours or do anything but spend time talking to her. There was a part of him, she felt, she would never understand, never touch.

"I did not pick them up," he said icily. "They were introduced to me. They are here to write about the war."

She shrugged. "What's there to say? What have poets got to say about what's going on here?"

"More than you might imagine," he said. "I happen to have read some of Auden's work. He's highly regarded."

She made a face.

"If you read a bit more widely," he continued, "then you might know what I mean."

She threw him a withering glance, before reaching for her lipstick.

He said, "Why is it that women need to paint their faces? Look at these Chinese women. It's as if they're putting on masks."

"Perhaps women need masks," she replied. "Perhaps men make it necessary for them to have masks."

They were both silent. He adjusted his bow tie. It was too loose—it was as if it had wilted in the heat. Everything wilted in this heat.

"And who else?" she asked.

"Who else what?"

"Who else is coming to dinner?"

He turned round. "One or two. Not many. Gunther, if he can make it, which I think he can."

She sighed. "Your great friend."

"Yes, my great friend. One of my many great friends, as you put it."

Gunther Stein was a journalist. He wrote for everybody, it seemed: *The Christian Science Monitor*, the big English papers, the *Berliner Tageblatt*. He was also a friend of Richard Sorge, a Soviet spy in Tokyo, and had acted as a courier for him.

"Gunther . . ." she mused.

"What about him?"

"Just thinking. I wonder if he likes poetry. Do you think he does?"

"He's a cultivated man. I imagine that he's heard of Auden. They may even have met, for all I know. Auden was in Berlin. And his friend Isherwood was there too."

She stood up from her dressing table. He was fond of her. He loved having her in the house. I am incomplete without her, he thought. Funny, that. Odd how we need others, and that we are unable to be in the world without somebody at our side. At least, that's what most people feel. There were always those lone wolves who seemed happy enough with their own company and who did not need the company of others. He was not like that, and he was grateful to her that she had been with him for so long, in all these trying places with all the intrigue and the danger that they encountered there.

Auden and Isherwood were in a talkative mood at dinner. When Tita asked Isherwood what he thought of war, he replied, "War is ghastly. War is sitting around doing nothing, waiting for terror to engulf you. War is not being able to wash or read a book or make love. War is full of dirt and confusion and tears. And it goes on. Day after day after day it's like that."

She inclined her head. He was right.

She said, "Did you meet Madame Chiang Kai-shek?"

Auden said yes, they had met her. And she had asked him whether poets ate cake. "I replied that they did," said Auden. "She seemed surprised. She said that she had assumed that they might live on spiritual food."

"How strange," said Tita.

· · ·

FROM CHINA, ARCHIE'S NEXT appointment was that of ambassador to the Soviet Union. This was a crucial posting, particularly when, after Hitler launched Operation Barbarossa, the United Kingdom and the USSR found themselves on the same side in the war. He found the Russians to be difficult allies—suspicious and resentful of the way in which they were treated by the United States and Britain. What the Russians wanted was as much materiel aid as possible and the opening of a second front that would engage Hitler in the west. There were stumbling blocks in the way of both of these objectives: losses on convoys to Russia were heavy and Churchill and Roosevelt were wary of committing to a firm date for landings in France. It was not easy for Archie to persuade the Russians that their concerns were being addressed and in this way to keep them on board. Fortunately, he got on well with Stalin, who was not always the easiest of company. They shared an interest in pipes and pipe tobacco; it was a rare, and important, friendship.

IN THE FOREST

THE OFFICIAL DACHA STOOD IN A FOREST CLEARING. MOSCOW WAS not far away, a bumpy ride of barely two hours in any of the diplomatic limousines parked in a circle in front of the dark-green building. Off to one side, a gravelled path led into the trees, its edges marked by stones placed at regular intervals. Only the clearing allowed for light to permeate the arboreal gloom; the city may not have been too distant, but this was the start of another Russia altogether, a Russia of endless, monotonous forests that went on for ever, to frozen tundra somewhere very far off.

Churchill did not like it. He thought of Russia as a gloomy place, with people to match; he felt out of sympathy with their heavy, literal approach, what he thought of as their peasant cunning. He was irritated by Stalin's manner towards him, and at their meeting the previous evening he felt that Stalin had deliberately insulted him.

Diplomatically, the meeting between the two leaders was not going well.

Now, walking ahead of Archie, he stamped along the path as it gradually narrowed. As they went further into the depths of the forest, the trees closed in around them, the needles of the spruce scratching their arms, the upper boughs concealing the sky.

"Wretched trees," said Churchill. "You'd think they might rise to the occasional oak."

"Russia," said Archie. "There are a lot of these trees."

"So I have observed," said Churchill.

Archie focused on the back of the man ahead of him—on the shoulders, slightly hunched when viewed from this angle, and the round head perched on them. Shoulders were a metaphor, of course, for the bearing of a burden—and what burdens this man carried. He and the prime minister had always got on well enough, although in the past he had found himself at odds with Churchill's deeply engrained imperialism. But that, he supposed, was a concomitant of being born on the cusp of great changes: it was understandable that one might suddenly seem out of touch with the world that was emerging about one.

"A very rough figure, our Comrade Stalin," Churchill suddenly muttered. "I don't suppose he ever learned any manners."

Archie found himself addressing the back of the prime minister's neck. People could misjudge Stalin, who was wilier than he might appear—and better educated too.

"You know, of course, that he was training for the Orthodox priesthood. He had a slight change of direction."

Churchill knew that. "He claims to have been expelled from his seminary for revolutionary activities. Do you give that any credence?"

Archie hesitated. "*Cum grano salis.*"

"An embroidering of the truth," mused Churchill. "I suppose we all do that to a greater or lesser extent." He paused. "Even you, Archie—even you must have occasionally . . . how shall we put it, exaggerated?"

Was this some sort of trap? Archie wondered.

"Me, Prime Minister? You aren't suggesting that I . . ."

Churchill chuckled. "Everybody has a secret of one sort or another. Diplomats usually have more than one."

"I assure you, Prime Minister, that what you get with me is what you see."

"A tall man with a broken nose?"

Archie smarted. Churchill might be prime minister but that did not give him the right to pass comments on one's nose.

When Archie said nothing, Churchill turned round to face him. You're one to talk, he thought. What they say about you having a baby face is absolutely true. All babies look like you, Prime Minister—or you look like all babies: one might take one's pick.

Archie plucked up his courage. It was not every day that you were called upon to question the prime minister's judgement. He drew a deep breath. "I think you're being too hard on Stalin." He wondered whether his voice gave away the anxiety he was feeling.

"Too hard? That man crossed a line. I don't have to put up with it. I represent the United Kingdom. I'm not some Kremlin underling."

"He doesn't see you as that, Prime Minister."

Churchill snorted. "He should choose his words more carefully."

For a few moments Archie said nothing. Underfoot, the fallen spruce needles crunched against gravel. A bird sang somewhere in the trees—a lonely song that went unanswered.

"You have such great gifts, Prime Minister. You were born with them."

Churchill slowed down. "What do you mean by that?"

It was too late to go back. The rebuke, if that was what it was to be, now had to be delivered.

"I mean that God has given you immense talents. You can charm the birds out of the trees. You can hold entire nations in the palm of your hands with your words. You know that, as well as I do."

Churchill said nothing.

"And I've seen you use that . . . well, one simply has to call it *charm*; I've seen you use that to get people to see things from your point of view. Or to put people at their ease and make them want to help. I've seen it. And yet here you are with this . . . this rough and ready street fighter—for that's what he is, after all—about to get on your high horse and threaten everything in the process."

"He insulted me."

Archie raised his voice. It was unintentional, but it made Churchill slow down again, even if he did not turn round. "But that's what they're all like, Prime Minister. They don't mince their words. They don't know how to. They think aloud. They don't mean to offend; it's just that they don't seem to understand tact, or subtlety, or whatever you like to call it. They're pretty basic, when all is said and done."

Churchill was listening. Now he snapped, "He can fight his own battles—if that's the way he wants it."

Archie caught his breath. This was a moment of profound danger. If Churchill fell out with Stalin, then the Russians might draw the conclusion that they were on their own. And if they thought that, then there was always a possibility that they would try to negotiate their own peace with Germany. It did not take much imagination to envisage the consequences of that: with his eastern flank secure, Hitler would be free to concentrate on the consolidation of his earlier gains in the west. With that, and with Allied exhaustion, the whole course of the war could be changed. He looked up at the sky, or at such of it as was visible through the branches of the trees. The world was so precious, so beautiful—so fragile. Civilization hung by a thread, and had always done so, perhaps, although it was only occasionally that we realised it.

He bit his lip. If the heart within this familiar, obstinate figure before him were to stop, then that great battle, which Churchill himself had identified in his oratory, would be lost. People would give up. The fight could go out of them. That could happen—it really could. But it was not just on that single beating muscle that everything depended; it depended, too, on what he, Archie, said next. Now it was him upon whom the fulcrum of history rested. Him: Archie Clark Kerr, Australian, Scotsman, Knight Commander of the Order of St. Michael and St. George, who had wandered into history and now had to do what history demanded of him.

"Prime Minister," he said, his voice more controlled now. "Prime Minister, Stalin wants in his own rather clumsy way to patch things up. I saw what happened last night at the dinner. I saw him following you to the door. He wanted to talk. He wanted to say sorry—once again, in his own, unusual way. It would cost you nothing to rise above his social ineptitude. You are a man of standing—you come from a background of distinction and achievement. He comes from nothing. He hasn't had your advantages. You should extend a hand to him. It would make all the difference, believe me."

Churchill stopped, so suddenly that Archie almost bumped into him. Then he turned round and gazed at the ambassador. "That's what you think, is it?"

Archie lowered his eyes. "That's what I think."

"And I suppose you know what you're talking about."

Archie raised his eyes again. Churchill was smiling.

"As do you, sir," said Archie.

Churchill hesitated. "You could be right," he said.

"I hope I am."

Churchill reached into his pocket for a cigar. "You smoke a pipe, don't you?"

"It's my only failing."

Churchill laughed. "Could you get in touch with them? Ask them whether we can have a meeting tonight. Just Stalin and I. No Molotov. Can't stand that fellow and his boot-faced look."

"He's not known for his humour," said Archie.

"Fix it up," said Churchill. "And lay on some champagne for me so that I don't have to stomach his vodka."

They turned, and made their way back to the dacha. Archie thought, I have just been present at a moment which may have decided the fate of western civilization. His heart gave a lurch. He had always wanted to be at the centre of things—to be in on the making of history. But he had never imagined that it would be like this: a matter of a brief exchange between two men on a path through a Russian forest, with the sky now threatening rain, and the smell of the spruce, that green smell, as he thought of it, mingling with the wisp of cigar smoke from a newly lit cigar; while elsewhere, altogether elsewhere, men fought and died over tracts of land, and flags, and promises that would never be kept. That was nothing new, of course.

Churchill asked him a question that he missed because his mind had been elsewhere.

"I asked," Churchill repeated, "whether you think Stalin is well-informed."

Archie took a few moments to think about his answer. Then he said, "Sometimes I think he is. Yes. Sometimes I think he knows more than he lets on."

"Could somebody be telling him things?" asked Churchill.

Archie had no answer.

Then Churchill said, "Could you tell me something amusing about him? About Stalin? Just to amuse me in this God-forsaken place?"

Archie thought for a moment. "He went to Sweden in 1905," he said.

Churchill waited. "And?"

"There was a large party of Bolsheviks and Mensheviks. They were going to a meeting in Stockholm, and Stalin was one of them. They travelled up to Helsinki first to catch a boat across the Baltic. They were an unruly mob, as you can imagine. The Bolsheviks and Mensheviks were always at one another's throats over this, that and the next thing. You know how the Reds love their ideological disputes."

Churchill grinned. "Put two cats in a box and they'll fight."

"Well, they all boarded the boat and discovered that their fellow passengers were an interesting lot. A party of circus clowns, no less, with a whole lot of performing dogs and dancing horses. Quite a passenger list. Anyway, before the ship set off the Bolsheviks and Mensheviks started to argue and a fight broke out. It got worse, and there was a general commotion. The clowns were involved, and, one imagines, the performing dogs. The ship got out of harbour but was shipwrecked a short distance out and everybody had to spend the night on the half-sunk vessel before they were picked up by another boat and taken off to Sweden."

Churchill reached for a handkerchief and blew his nose loudly. "My day improves," he muttered, adding, "markedly."

IN CAMBRIDGE, IN 1933

VERY TALL," SAID GUY BURGESS. "BOURGEOIS AS HELL—BUT AREN'T we all? Rather good-looking, but then again, aren't we all?" He glanced at the man to whom he was talking. Such a pity. Wrong team: paid-up member of the wrong team.

Kim Philby smiled tolerantly. "I'm not interested in such things, Guy, dear chap. As you know, I like women. Perverse of me, yes, I admit it. But there have been plenty of us in history, you know. Great artists and composers. Generals and heroes. Possibly even Shakespeare, if you read the *Sonnets* in a particular way. All men who liked women. And women would like you, I believe—if you gave them the chance. And stopped eating so much garlic."

Burgess waved a careless hand. "I just don't have the time, Kim. With all these delectable boys about. How could I? And Mrs. God, to whom we should all be most grateful, has given me certain talents—I should use those, rather than seeking to diversify."

Philby looked away. Mrs. God! Burgess was deliberately outrageous. He drank on a reckless scale and boasted constantly, and openly, about his sexual conquests. And yet there was something about him that was strangely compelling. He was vivacious, witty company and seemed to draw people into his orbit with little or no effort. *Charisma* was one word to which resort might be made when talking of Burgess, Philby thought; *simpatico* was another.

And you had to forgive him, all the sex and drink and braggadocio, even the garlic, because his heart was in the right place, and that, ultimately, was what counted. He understood injustice, and its place in human affairs. He understood the theft that had been committed—and that was the only word for it—the theft that had been committed by those who took from the working classes the fruits of their labour. A child should be able to understand that—to see it for what it was—but that fundamental fact, that *ur*-crime, had been so overlaid with cant and edifice that it seemed that only a few could see it for what it was. Yet it was so simple, so *obvious*. Capitalism was simply wrong. It was not complicatedly wrong—it was *simply* wrong.

Look at the whole, rotten edifice, Philby thought. Look at it. The House of Windsor, the Archbishop of Canterbury, the pious platitudes, the police and prisons, the hangman, the servitude of the millions in the colonies, the daily grind of the people who actually made things, who grew the food, who cleaned up, who went down the mines in rattling cages and who died because the coal dust blocked their bronchial tubes. Look at that, and ask yourself how could you possibly not feel complete revulsion. How could you *not*?

But now they were discussing Donald Maclean, who was a fellow undergraduate.

"Tell me about him," said Philby.

Burgess reached for his martini glass. He had mixed himself three, and they were lined up to be tackled one after the other. They would not last long. "What's there to say? His father is an awful Calvinist Scotsman—you know the type." He fingered the stem of the glass. "Unbending. A politician. Donald is very different, thank goodness. Sons don't necessarily take after their fathers, Kim, which is fortunate for you, because otherwise what would you be? Living in Beirut or somewhere of the sort; probably marrying and having six children by a Nubian girl, my dear—a Nubian! Delicious. Like an apricot, perhaps. All juicy and sweet."

Philby's father, St. John Philby, was a distinguished Arabist.

"I've never known exactly who the Nubians are," Burgess continued, draining his martini glass. "Are they some sort of exotic Egyptian, do you think? Yet another group of people we've taken under our benevolent imperialist fold? I wonder if they write in hieroglyphics? What do you think, Kim? Do you have a theory about that?"

"Don't be absurd, Guy. Or should I say, don't be more absurd than usual."

Burgess embarked on his second martini. "What does Anthony say?"

"About Maclean?"

"The very same."

Philby thought for a moment. "Anthony, as you know, does not waste his words. He's just like that painter of his, Poussin. Cold and classical. Anthony speaks highly of Donald. He thinks he's serious."

"Which is true, I think. Anthony's right. Donald gives every impression of actually meaning it. You did hear about what he did when he came back for his third year?"

Philby shook his head.

"He sold all his clothes," Burgess went on. "The shirt off his back. Everything." He paused. "Now, as you know, Kim, I'm all in favour of chaps who are prepared to disrobe . . ." The martini was disappearing fast. "However, in this case, Donald was simply getting rid of his good stuff to kit himself out in second-hand things from those shops that sell clothes to the hard up. Or the poor, as we should not be afraid to call them. Enough of euphemisms."

Philby raised an eyebrow. "Rather impressive."

"Indeed. And he let his fingernails become dirty. Just like mine." He held up a hand to show Philby. "Although in my case it's laziness. In his case, I think it's ideological. He said he's planning to live in Russia when he goes down. Seriously. I think he wants to teach English to Russians. Such a noble project."

Philby shrugged. "To each his own way of demonstrating solidarity." He paused. He fixed Burgess with a bemused stare. "Have you and Donald . . . You know . . ."

Burgess put down his glass. "Don't be coy, Kim. But the answer is yes, if you must know. It was a long campaign, though. There are still a lot of defences. His father's fault, of course. John Knox et al. Mind you, he's actually more like you than he is like me, I'm afraid. I don't think he's one of us, or, shall I say, one of me, since you, unfortunately, are so boringly unmusical." He sighed. "I don't think there'll be a repeat show. Some plays run only for one night, you know. No encore."

"I think I shall probably look him up after he leaves Cambridge," said Philby. "It's good to keep in touch, I always say."

"Close touch," said Burgess, reaching for the second glass. "The closer the better, in fact. Chin chin, Kim." He looked at his friend. "It's rather sweet, I think, how chaps like you can look up people like Donald and never be suspected of ulterior motives."

"The joy of being of conventional persuasion," said Philby.

"And wanting only to discuss politics."

Philby nodded. "Politics is all there is, Guy." The levity of the last few minutes disappeared. Now he sounded sombre, even regretful. "There's a major war coming—sooner rather than later." He paused, struck by the triteness of what he had just said. How many times had people said that? It had become the most predictable of clichés, in the mouth of the most naïve of undergraduates. How many times did those words occur in newspaper columns, dispensed as if confidential information were being imparted? But that, he told himself, did not detract from the fact that it was true, and needed to be said.

He looked at Burgess. His friend's mask of insouciance had slipped, and he was pleased. Burgess knew when to be serious, even if there were those who thought him incapable of sobering up sufficiently. Philby continued, "We—you and I—are going to be asked—once again—to die for the established order. Do you propose to go meekly?"

"I don't propose to go at all," said Burgess. "Ours is a different battle. And it's already started." He paused. "Shall we pour ourselves more drinks? What is happening to these martinis, Kim? *Eheu fugaces, labuntur martini.*"

"Very funny, Guy."

"Thank you."

PHILBY INVITED MACLEAN to dinner in his flat.

"Just us," he said. "There's a lot to talk about." He offered his guest a sherry. "I hope this is dry enough. Berry Brothers. You know their place?"

"I do," said Maclean. "I've walked past it. I've never been inside."

Philby handed him the glass. "Seen Guy recently?"

Maclean shook his head. "I've not seen many people. I've been reading a lot. A bit of theatre—not that there's much on at the moment."

"I saw Guy a couple of weeks ago."

"Sober?"

"What do you think?"

Maclean smiled. "When he dies, I hope he donates his liver to medical science."

Philby gestured for Maclean to sit down. He pointed to his bookshelves. "Those are all waiting to be read—every one of them. I'll get round to it one of these days."

"You're working?"

"Yes."

Maclean waited. Then he said, "Anything interesting?"

Philby was guarded. "An international organisation." He looked at Maclean over the rim of his sherry glass. "And you? Your plans?"

Maclean replied immediately. "The Foreign Office. I'm going to do the exams. I'll see."

"You know I had a little difficulty there," Philby said. "My tutor in Cambridge objected to me politically. He said that a radical socialist had no business being a civil servant. His reference put them off. You know what they're like."

"I'll be careful about my referees," said Maclean.

"Very wise. With your connections, you shouldn't have too much difficulty getting somebody who'll impress them."

"Perhaps."

Philby took another sip of his sherry. "Do you think you might work for us?"

Maclean looked at him. "Us being?"

"The cause."

There was a silence. "For the Comintern?"

Philby did not take his eyes off him. "That sort of thing."

"Yes."

Philby was taken aback by the speed of the reply. He folded his hands. He seemed bemused. "That didn't take you long to decide."

"Why should it?" asked Maclean. "The lines are clearly drawn, aren't they? I decided some time ago which side I was on." He paused. "I'd like to ask you something, though. Will I be working for the Soviet Union or for the cause more generally?"

Philby made a gesture that suggested that the boundaries were vague. "It very much amounts to the same thing. The one supports the other, and without the Soviet Union, where would communism be? Nowhere? Exactly."

"I want to," said Maclean.

Philby put down his glass. "I was hoping you'd say that."

"I want to do something useful with my life."

"You'll get no better chance than this. When I decided, you know, to devote my life to . . . to the righting of the great wrong, I felt as if I'd suddenly discovered something that made sense of everything. It was a moment of extraordinary clarity."

Maclean was staring at the floor. Now he lifted his gaze. "Like first looking into Chapman's Homer?"

Philby grinned. "I'm not sure whether Keats quite fits. But yes, as I said, it was an important moment for me." He paused. "It's a commitment, you know. You don't enter upon it lightly."

Maclean said he knew that. "I'm serious about it. I've been think-ing about it for years. Even at school."

"And you're sure you're not doing it just to spite your father—or the memory of your father, should I say."

Maclean blushed. "I don't think so."

"I ask that," said Philby, "because it's important to know one's motives. People act for very different reasons. Sometimes we're locked in old battles with Nanny, you know. Sometimes with Mother. You've read your Freud, I imagine."

Maclean became silent, and for a few moments Philby looked con-cerned. "I don't mean to belittle your conviction, Donald. I'm acting as *advocatus diaboli* here."

Maclean nodded. "I understand."

Philby looked relieved. "I think I can arrange for you to see somebody."

"When?"

"Very soon. In a matter of days."

"Who is it?"

Philby said, "He's called Otto. You'll be told by him what he wants you to do. In the meantime, though, this conversation never took place. Speak to nobody about it. Carry on with your plans to do the F.O. exams. Don't advertise your political opinions. Be what you so obviously are."

"Which is?"

"A typical bourgeois parasite. A privileged member of a privileged caste. None of which would stretch your acting ability excessively, would it?"

They looked at one another. Philby reached out a hand. Maclean shook it.

IN MOSCOW, JANUARY 1946

STALIN WAS PLEASED WITH THE PAINTING THAT HAD BEEN NEWLY hung in his office. His eyes kept moving to it, as if he was willing Archie to make some remark about it. Archie was prepared to oblige, but found that it was taxing his powers of diplomacy to conceal his real reaction. The painting was typical of Soviet Realism, of which school there existed countless examples in the corridors and halls of the Kremlin.

"A very fine painting, this one," Stalin said. "That man is a true artist."

"Yes," said Archie. He searched for something to say. "It is a very good likeness of you, I feel. And that's Comrade Voroshilov, I imagine. It certainly looks like him. Remarkably like him—although not as faithful to the original, so to speak, as is his portrayal of yourself."

"It is indeed," said Stalin. "I see that you are an art critic, Ambassador, amongst your many other talents. And, of course, you paint yourself. I have not forgotten that."

"Amateur daubs," said Archie. "Nothing more than that."

"You are very modest. Unlike Gerasimov, who painted this picture. He likes to remind people that he is a great artist."

In these latitudes, thought Archie, pride *definitely* comes before a fall.

Archie took out his pipe. He had brought a gift of tobacco with him that Stalin had received enthusiastically and a sample of which he was even now offering his visitor. "Well, Gerasimov is very popular, isn't he? And justly so, I'd say. There are many people who get pleasure from looking at his paintings."

Stalin nodded. "But we are not here to discuss art. We are here to say goodbye."

"A very sad duty for me, Marshal."

"We all have to say goodbye sooner or later," said Stalin. "It is part of the human condition, is it not?"

"I'm afraid so. There are many things that we do not like, but that are part of who we are."

Stalin looked sideways at him, seemingly uncertain, for a moment, how to take this. But then he grinned. "Man can change, though, once the material conditions that determine his nature are changed sufficiently."

Archie felt that he did not need this elementary lesson in communist theory, but it was his job to be pleasant, and so he simply smiled, inclining his head in an impossible-to-interpret gesture. Stalin never got beyond the level of the predictable, he thought. For all his wili-ness, his cunning, there was no moral imagination.

"There is one thing I thought I might raise with you," Archie continued. "Since we are parting company."

"Of course. I was about to ask you if I could do anything to help."

It was the invitation that Archie hoped would be extended.

"There is a woman who is employed in the embassy. Local staff."

Stalin watched. *Local staff* was another term for *spy*.

"She is a hard-working woman," said Archie. "She has looked after us well."

"I'm pleased to hear that."

Archie continued quickly. "She has a brother."

Stalin watched him.

"Unfortunately, this brother of hers is in a spot of trouble. He has been accused of desertion. I believe that the army is holding him."

Stalin shrugged. "That sort of thing happens in any army—ours included. There are always troublesome elements."

"I wouldn't doubt that for a moment," said Archie. "This man is undoubtedly in the wrong. He deserves to be punished, I'm sure. Severely. But there are extenuating factors in this case. And I won-dered whether you might be able to show the mercy that I know you have exercised so generously in so many other deserving cases."

In diplomacy, thought Archie, you can *never* underestimate the power of flattery, even, or perhaps especially, when it was ill-deserved.

Stalin allowed a smile to cross his face. The eyes, though, were still watchful. "And what are these factors?" he asked.

"He is a dwarf."

For a few moments Stalin did not react. Then he laughed. "Oh, that's very funny," he said. "So, the problem's a small one."

Archie made much of the joke. "You could certainly say that, Chairman."

"And you want me to let him off?"

"His sister would be very grateful. She is a good Soviet citi-zen. She . . ."

Stalin interrupted him. "A good Soviet citizen with a bad brother?"

"Well, I think he may have been under pressure. They're from the Volga, you see, and recent events, as you can imagine . . ."

Stalin waved a hand airily. "That's all over now. There's a new world emerging. Those people are not an issue."

People have never been an issue for you, thought Archie. "Precisely."

Stalin thought for a moment. He looked out of the window. Then he turned and said to Archie, "Why don't you take him as your servant? I am very happy to give him to you."

Archie gave a start. "Give him to me?"

"Yes. In the circumstances he's very fortunate, I would have thought. It is quite in order for my government to redirect his labour. He can work for you now. You take him with you. He can be . . ." He waved a hand again. "He can be your house servant. Your valet. You are always very smart, Excellency, and you will need somebody who can iron your trousers and polish your shoes. A very short man will be good at keeping your shoes well-polished." Stalin laughed. "Other small jobs like that. He's yours. Give the details to my aides and they will take care of everything."

Archie was almost too astonished to speak, but he realised that he had just saved a man's life. So he thanked Stalin effusively, and Stalin accepted the thanks as no more than his due. Then they filled their pipes with the new tobacco and Archie told Stalin something about where it was from. "There's a place called Virginia," he said.

"And another place called Georgia," said Stalin, and laughed again.

DINNER IN NEW YORK

I KNOW IT'S NOT IDEAL," SAID DONALD MACLEAN TO HIS WIFE, Melinda. "But is there ever anything that's unequivocally right?" He stabbed a spear of asparagus with his fork. "Is there?"

She looked at him across the table of their restaurant on 52nd Street. It was a place she knew well—a French restaurant run by a temperamental Lyonnais; she had been a regular customer, with her parents, before she went to Paris. It had changed little over the years, and it seemed that the arguments between chef and *patron*, conducted *con brio* in the kitchen but audible in the dining room itself, were very much the same.

"No," she said in answer to his question. "Perhaps not. But there are varying degrees of unsuitability, and this arrangement is fairly high on the scale."

"There's nowhere in Washington," he said. "Not just yet. H.E. is going to put in for an increase in my living expenses allowance. Once—if—that gets the nod from London, then we could afford somewhere convenient in Washington. But it's a small town, and there isn't much choice."

He looked at her fondly. He could not reveal that there was another reason for her staying with her parents in New York while he spent the week in Washington. His controller was in New York and that was where the information was sent from when it went over to Russia. Maclean needed a reason to make weekly trips to New York, and having his wife there provided a pretext that would be above reproach.

"I'm sorry your mother dislikes me," said Maclean, filling his glass of wine, and then, seeing that her glass was half empty, doing the same for Melinda.

"She doesn't dislike you. I don't know where you got that idea."

"From her manner. From the way she looks at me. From the way her lip curls."

"Mother's lip doesn't curl."

Maclean shrugged. "Would that be because it might give too much away?"

Melinda ignored the barb. So Maclean continued, "However she does it, she leaves me in no doubt about what she thinks."

"Of you?"

"Yes, of me." He stared at her, daring her to contradict what to him had been only too obvious.

Melinda took a sip of her wine. She peered at the menu. "Snails," she said. "There have been world shortages of everything—but never snails. Strange, that."

She watched him as he refilled his glass. That was almost the whole bottle of white wine gone, and they had not yet even ordered the food. She did not say anything, but his drinking worried her. He was nowhere near as bad as Guy, of course—nobody was—but he was still drinking too heavily. That may have been possible in London, particularly when the bombs were raining down and people were relieved just to be alive, but it was much more obvious here in the United States. Of course, if she broached the subject with him, if she pointed out that his drinking was less acceptable in their new surroundings, then he would simply respond that America was strait-laced and hypocritical and that people didn't drink so much because they simply didn't have the imagination to do that—ridiculous, offensive arguments. She knew that he despised her country; that he thought Americans were dangerous, but the truth of the matter was that it was America that was pulling his exhausted, almost bankrupt country out of its fiscal quagmire, and that if it weren't for America then he wouldn't even have the freedom to express his offensive, bigoted views.

"Has your mother revealed the nature of her objection to me?" Donald asked.

She glanced up at him, and then quickly looked away. Her mother had done that, but she had not intended to say anything to Donald. Her mother found him condescending. She did not like his superior manner. She did not like his teeth. She had said, "He's typical of a certain sort of Englishman, darling. Not the sort I have too much time for, I'm afraid."

"You should give him a chance," she protested. "You've only known him for two days."

"Sometimes one can tell these things fairly quickly," said her mother. "Immediately, in fact. You develop experience in judging character as you go through life. You can sum things up."

She felt resentful. "His teeth are not his fault." She could have said much more, but she did not want to pick a fight with her mother, who was fighting enough with her father as it was.

Her mother looked at her. "You say that bad teeth are not one's fault? Is that what you say?"

"Yes."

"Well, you're wrong, my dear. You're wrong. You've been in Europe too long. You've picked up their thinking about teeth. Or lack of thinking about teeth, I should say. Donald can get his seen to now that he's in America."

She looked at her mother. She did not understand; she did not even begin to understand Donald, and his complexity, his secret. She could not because she was too convinced of her view of the world and its rightness. There were other visions of the world, though, and Donald had one of them. For her it was all about teeth and smiles and style. Donald hated all of that, and she could understand how he felt. The America of cheerleaders and farm-boys and glib salesmen—that was what Donald disliked so much; more, perhaps, than he disliked the world of British smugness and its concomitant bone-deep assumptions of superiority. He wanted something better for humanity and was prepared to take risks to help those who wanted to bring that about. She admired him for that. She admired him for the love he had for the weak and the voiceless: the people who had been so brutalised in Spain, the multitudes displaced or killed by European fascism, the people who worked in menial, degrading jobs and who would forever be at the bottom of the heap if it weren't for people like Donald, who saw their plight and tried to do something about it.

DINNER IN WASHINGTON

NO SNAILS," SHE SAID. "NOT A SNAIL IN SIGHT."

He took the menu from her and glanced at it before putting it down on the table. "This is, in my view, an Italian restaurant with a French name." He tapped the table. "Run by Americans."

"At least they try. Some places don't even pretend to be French."

He caught the eye of a passing waiter. He tapped his glass. "Another martini for me please . . . and for my wife . . ." He looked at Melinda enquiringly.

"*Pour moi aussi*," Melinda said.

"Excuse me, Ma'am?"

"Another martini for her too," said Donald. And then, to Melinda, he said, "See what I mean?"

They both laughed.

Melinda leaned across the table. "Tell me about him," she said. "I can't wait to meet him, but first I'd like to hear what you think."

"I've only just met him."

"But your judgement's always bang on."

"He arrived yesterday," said Donald. "He was in his office from noon. We were all brought in to pay our respects. Not that much was said—and I heard even less."

She looked puzzled.

"He speaks very quietly."

She seemed to find that amusing. "That's not a bad thing, surely. In this town at least. There are enough loud voices."

"And he's got a very dry sense of humour."

"Nothing wrong with that."

Donald looked thoughtful. "Possibly. Possibly not."

"What does that mean?"

He chose his words carefully. He knew that she was uncomfortable when he criticised her country. "It's just that I'm not sure whether you people do irony in quite the same way as the English."

She pointed out that he had said that the ambassador was a Scotsman. Or even an Australian.

"Paper Scotsman. Australian-born. He lived in England from the age of seven." Donald paused. "But the point about irony holds. It can be completely misunderstood on this side of the Atlantic. That's no criticism, by the way—just an observation."

She bit her tongue. This was to be a relaxed dinner, and if Donald became anxious or morose, he would drink even more than usual. She would keep it light.

"Oh well," she said. "Tell me about him."

"He likes to be called Archie," said Donald. "And the jury is out—as it always is when there's a new head of mission. They take time to show their hand. However . . ." He left the sentence unfinished, and Melinda waited.

He took a sip of his martini, and grimaced. "Not dirty enough."

"Archie?"

"He's got off to a flying start." He grinned. "He gave a press conference in New York when his ship docked. He didn't take long to raise hackles."

She asked for details. Lord Halifax, the previous ambassador, had been perfect for the role. Was this new man going to be different?

"Well, the ship he was on was full of GI brides," said Donald. "Two thousand, apparently. And all their babies."

Melinda burst out laughing.

"Yes," Donald went on. "All those GIs hadn't hung around over in England. And Archie made a comment about how ugly British babies were."

Melinda gasped. "You can't say that," she exclaimed.

"You can, apparently. And he did. Then he made some remark about baseball, which you *never* do, unless you intend to say how much you like the game and how wrong people are to say it's boring. And he said neither of these things. And finally he referred to the valet he's brought with him."

"Why would anybody be interested in him?" asked Melinda.

Donald waited for a few moments to give his words greater effect. Then he leaned forward to give his response. "Because he's a Russian dwarf."

Melinda's eyes widened.

"And more than that," Donald continued. "He told people that Stalin had *given* him to him. *Given.* What he actually said was, *Stalin gave me a slave.*" He paused. "I gather that nobody could believe their ears. The journalists broke their pencils they were scribbling so fast. Birds fell from the air. The sun stopped in its path."

"I can't believe it," said Melinda.

"He has a great sense of humour," said Donald. "We'd heard about it, but nobody here imagined it would be wheeled out so quickly—and with such effect. Everybody was left scratching their heads."

"Well, at least he's not dull," observed Melinda.

Donald sighed. "The cousins are at a loss," he said. He sometimes used the term "cousins" for American counterparts—in an ironical way. "I had a call today from somebody I know in the FBI and one from a Chicago congressman. The FBI contact asked me whether it was true that there was a Russian with his knees under the table in the British Embassy. I said that I believed the whole man would fit under the table. He was not amused."

"Have you met him . . . this valet?"

"I saw him," replied Donald. "He goes under the name of Yevgeni Yost. He was fussing about Archie. There's no mistaking him—he dresses as a Cossack."

"This is going to be interesting," said Melinda.

Donald looked grave. "I don't like it at all," he said. "We don't want any controversy. And none of us knows anything about this man. Who is this Yevgeni Yost? Why did Stalin present him to Archie? Who does he report to?"

"If he reports to anybody," said Melinda.

"All Russians report to somebody," said Donald. "No, this worries me. I know it sounds funny, but it worries me."

DONALD TAKES WORK HOME

D ONALD WAS ONE OF THE MOST EFFICIENT AND HARD-WORKING first secretaries in the entire British Diplomatic Service. He had a great talent for condensing complicated documents and explaining them succinctly to the members of the many committees he served. His position papers made complex international negotiations intelligible to participants who might otherwise become hopelessly confused. His advice was always pertinent and time-saving. His superiors were full of praise for an official who did everything asked of him, and whose only flaws were his drinking and tendency to be dismissive of those he considered reactionary or ill-informed. But if he was tactless in some respects; if he could be moody and brooding; if he could show every sign of being haunted by something—regret?—then all of these drawbacks were eclipsed by his competence and sheer intelligence.

And all the while, virtually any important document that came into his possession was scrutinised for possible interest to the Soviet Union, secretly photographed, or at least paraphrased, and then passed on through his Russian handler for transmission to Moscow. Moscow Centre, at the heart of the spiderweb, had a code-name for this most valuable of all agents: Homer. It was through the information that he supplied about British and American intentions that Stalin and Molotov were able to go into every meeting with their western counterparts knowing exactly what the other side's bargaining position was. And importantly, Donald provided regular information on secret aspects of the nuclear weapons programme—at a stage before the Soviet Union had itself built any atomic weaponry.

He regularly took work home in a bulging briefcase that became a symbol for his conscientiousness and habits of hard work. Security was lax, and as First Secretary, and so patently in speech and manner a product of the Establishment, Donald Maclean was above reproach. Yet American suspicions of a significant leak were aroused, and when direct intelligence was obtained from a would-be Soviet defector of there being a high-level spy in the Foreign Office, nothing was done to link these accusations to Donald. The source warned that the spy was Scottish, and that he came from an upper-class background, but before he could reveal anything more substantial, the Russian met a grisly end in a Washington hotel room— a consequence of his impending defection's having been notified to Philby, who was then able to warn the Russians of what was about to happen.

But there were others who were suspicious, and one of these was Archie's Russian valet, Yevgeni. He did not like Donald Maclean, and Donald Maclean did not like him. In fact, Donald had tried, as tactfully as possible, to alert Archie to the consequences of having a Russian valet but had met with amused incredulity.

"I wouldn't make too much of it myself," he said to Archie. "But I thought I might mention that I've heard one or two whispering in the State Department about our internal arrangements here."

Archie frowned. "Our internal arrangements? What do they mean?"

"Staffing matters," said Donald.

"None of their business," snapped Archie.

Donald hesitated. But he knew that Archie liked transparency and would not object to direct speaking.

"Actually, it's about your valet."

Archie fixed a disingenuous gaze on Donald. "Yevgeni? How could anybody object to poor wee Yost?"

Donald smiled. "But they do, I'm afraid. They weren't expecting you to bring a Russian servant. You know what they're like, these people. Positively xenophobic, some of them. It's the Dayton, Ohio, view of the world."

"I still don't think it's any of their business who I have to iron my shirts."

Donald said that he thought it was wider than that. "Security. They think he may see things he shouldn't see."

Archie shook his head. "Yevgeni would never do that sort of thing. I saved his life, you know. He remembers that."

"But these people can be put under pressure. Stalin will do anything. He could take Yost's family hostage in order to get him to co-operate."

Archie remained unconvinced. "I saved his life, you know. I don't mention that to anybody—normally—but since you bring the whole thing up, I should perhaps draw your attention to that fact. He would no more steal secrets from me than fly to the moon. He knows what loyalty means." He paused. "In fact, Donald, I trust him as much as I trust you."

Donald looked away. He was not enjoying this. "I thought I should just tell you what I heard. That's all."

"Well, you've told me—and thank you for speaking about it. But I'll be damned if I'll change my valet just because somebody from Hicksville, Ohio, happens to object to my man being a Russian. And actually, he's a Volga German. They've been in Russia since the eighteenth century, and to all intents and purposes they're Russian, but that's what he is. People have not been very nice to them recently, and I'm not going to add to everything the poor man's been through. He was almost put in front of a firing squad, for heaven's sake."

Donald said no more. There was a trade meeting coming up and he had to brief Archie about that. So he simply said, "I thought I'd mention it. It's nothing much."

"Well, you've mentioned it," said Archie. "Now what about this wretched trade fair in Pittsburgh?"

HE BEGAN TO SEE the valet in places where he had no business to be within the embassy. At first, he thought that Yevgeni was simply trying to find his way around the building and had lost his way in the corridors, but then he began to find him talking to the young women in the typing pool, or making coffee for himself in the kitchen normally reserved for senior staff, or down in the basement, going through boxes of gardening tools left there by the gardeners. He also found him in the embassy library, running his fingers along the spines of the books. Donald was polite, but became increasingly irritated by the apparent ubiquity of this man who, although allowed to be in the building to attend to the ambassador's needs as a sort of constantly-on-duty servant, had no reason to wander into meeting rooms or, even more, into the offices in which correspondence was logged or decoding took place.

Donald raised it with one of the ministers, whom he suspected shared his irritation.

"I know that Archie thinks he's not a security risk," he said, "but that man seems to be everywhere—and I mean everywhere."

"I came across him under a table," said the minister. "*Under* a table. Can you believe it?"

Donald rolled his eyes. "I can, actually. What was his explanation?"

"He said that he was looking for something he had dropped."

The minister snorted. "A likely story." He paused. "This can't go on. I'll have to take this up with Archie myself. But he seems to have a bit of a blind spot when it comes to Yevgeni. He's tickled by the idea of having such an unlikely valet. It amuses him to see everybody's reaction."

"Perhaps we're going about it the wrong way," said Donald. "Perhaps it would be more effective for us to ignore him. If people were indifferent to him, the Boss might agree to get rid of him."

"We could try, I suppose."

They did, but it had no effect. And so further representations were made, the volume of complaints from within and without became steadily larger. Archie seemed impervious to the growing feeling against Yevgeni. "Yost is a simple valet," he insisted. "He's harmless. How many times have I told you people that?"

"Many," said Donald. He was aware he was pressing the boundaries.

Archie threw him a disapproving glance. His tone, which could often be modest to the point of diffidence, now became more authoritative. "Well, I'm telling you again. Subject closed."

A SUMMER AFTERNOON IN WASHINGTON

WASHINGTON IN AUGUST: THE SLOW-MOVING TRAFFIC; THE SKY liquid with humidity; the torpor of a time of year when the working population was at its lowest; the politicians away; the civil servants unresponsive; the courts empty of litigants; the bands playing slow tunes requiring minimum effort; in such conditions Donald was watching the slow movement of the clock's hands. He came off duty at five and would go straight to the swimming pool to cool off, but there were two and a half hours to go before he could do that. Lunch had been a limp and wilting sandwich and a cold beer. Dinner would be a lonely affair, as Melinda was in New York. He might end up in a bar somewhere afterwards, just for the benefit of the cool air, and then there would be a night of fitful sleep and uncomfortable dreams.

He was not in a mood to encounter Yevgeni Yost in an unoccupied office, but the valet was there, dressed in what Donald presumed was his summer version of his Cossack's outfit—a white linen blouse and baggy, off-white trousers.

"What are you doing here?" Donald snapped.

Yevgeni looked up. "I am tidying."

Donald frowned. "Tidying what?"

Yevgeny shrugged. "Lord Inverchapel wants a box." He used Archie's full title—the title he had been given before his arrival in post.

"Why do you think there's a box in this office?"

The dwarf smiled. "There is always a box in an office."

"What a ridiculous thing to say," snapped Donald.

"It is not ridiculous. You are ridiculous. You are very ridiculous."

Donald had not expected this. He rarely spoke to Yevgeni, and their conversation had previously been limited to mundane, passing remarks. Now something within Donald gave way. "Get out of here," he said. "Stay in the Residency. Just get out."

Yevgeni's eyes narrowed. There was a light in them, a hard, sharp light. "I know who you are," he said, his voice low. "I can smell NKVD. I can smell it. You don't think I can, but I can."

Donald froze. "You can what?"

"I said: I can smell NKVD, Mr. Maclean. And you are it."

Donald decided to laugh. "Are you accusing me of something? You? You're daring to accuse me of . . ."

"Of spy," Yevgeni interrupted, losing, briefly, his grip of English grammar. "You of spy. Yes."

"Get out," said Donald.

Yevgeni took a step towards him. Donald noticed his shoes, which were black-and-white two-tone. Co-respondents' shoes, as they were known. They were very small—perhaps designed for a woman's foot, he thought.

"They will catch you one day and kill you," said Yevgeni. "The police in London. They will catch you."

Donald turned round and began to walk out. He stopped. He turned round again. "You call me a spy?" he shouted. "You? If there's a spy round here, it's you. You are a Russian. Remember that." Then he said, "Nobody will believe anything you say. You know that, don't you?"

Yevgeni was staring at him. "I know that," he said. "That is why I cannot say it. I cannot say it because you are Mr. Maclean and I am just Yost. I am nobody. Just Yost. And nobody will believe Yost."

There was silence. Outside somewhere, a car sounded its horn.

"Yost," repeated Yevgeni.

Donald took a deep breath. There was no danger, or at least there was no new danger here, because this was nothing but a sudden outburst from a ridiculous little nobody. It meant nothing—nothing at all.

IN SCOTLAND

ARCHIE EVENTUALLY GAVE WAY. YOST WAS TOLD THAT HE COULD no longer serve as the ambassador's valet and would, instead, be employed by Archie on his farm in Scotland. This role he accepted, as he accepted everything that happened to him after that fateful day on which he had deserted from the Red Army. Archie had saved his life, and he was loyal. Unlikely lives can become intertwined.

When, after a relatively short period in office in Washington,

Archie returned to Britain, he spent much of his time in Scotland, where he had acquired an estate in Argyll. Yevgeni's role now included not only managing this estate, but also acting as driver to Archie and his wife. They had brought back with them a green Pontiac station wagon in which they would travel from Argyll to Glasgow, with the diminutive Russian at the wheel.

When Donald was identified as the Soviet agent Homer, the blow to Archie was visceral. Whatever criticism may be levelled against his style of diplomacy, whatever may be said of his colourful foibles, he had been a conscientious servant of his country's interest. It was for him a matter of almost unbearable shame that he had unwittingly nurtured in his embassy one of the most influential spies of the twentieth century.

Donald narrowly escaped arrest. He was spirited away to Moscow, where he spent the rest of his life leading a life of exile, along with Philby and Burgess. Burgess drank himself to death; Philby went off with Melinda after she had moved to Moscow to be with Donald. There is more than one form of betrayal. Blunt remained in London, promised immunity from prosecution. He directed the Courtauld Institute, devoting himself to the study of the neo-classical artist, Nicolas Poussin. He expressed bitter regret for his involvement in espionage.

Yost disappeared into obscurity in a remote part of Scotland. Green hills; sea lochs; weather: all these can enfold and erase the past. He thought of Donald Maclean from time to time, and shook his head.

One afternoon, Yost parked the green Pontiac station wagon outside a café in the small coastal town of Dunoon. People travelled down the Clyde from Glasgow to have lunch in this café, before getting back on the boat that would take them home. Yost went inside and ordered himself a meal of pie and chips—typical Scottish café fare. There were a few people in the café, but he recognised nobody.

Sitting at his table, waiting for his pie to be warmed up, he noticed that there was a man at a neighbouring table who was staring at him. Because of his diminutive size, Yost was used to the stares of others, although usually they would look away if he returned their gaze. This man did not.

The man broke the silence. "I reckon you have a pretty interesting story," he said, and smiled.

There was something about the man's directness that appealed to Yost.

"Yes," he said. "I have had a very strange life. If I told you about it, you wouldn't believe me."

The man laughed. "Try me," he said.

Yost told him. When he finished, the man sat motionless. "Is that true?" he asked. "Are you making this up?"

"Why would I?" asked Yost.

The man looked thoughtful. "You knew?" he asked. "You knew it was Maclean?"

Yost nodded. "Yes, I did. But they didn't look. They refused to believe that somebody like him could be a traitor. They looked at me, and what did they see? I was a far more likely suspect."

"And do you feel bitter?" asked the man.

Yost looked out of the window. Did he? He was not sure.

"I feel angry for Sir Archie," he said at last. "Maclean betrayed his trust. Sir Archie is a good man. He showed me nothing but kindness."

"I understand," said the man.

"And kindness is so important," said Yost.

"Yes," said the man. "It is. Maybe even the most important thing."

Yost's pie and chips arrived. He smiled at the man to whom he had been talking. "I must have my lunch now," he said.

The man nodded.

After finishing his meal, Yost said goodbye to the man in the café. He went outside, got into the green Pontiac station wagon, and drove off. Into history.

Each of us has a little bit of history—not much perhaps—into which we can drive off.

Filioque

(R O M E , 2 0 2 2)

THE INVITATION WAS COMPLETELY UNEXPECTED. IT ARRIVED IN A typed, formal letter, addressed to Pierre Citroën at the French Pontifical College on the via Santa Chiara, tucked away in his pigeon-hole between a note from his philosophy tutor at the Gregorian and an unsolicited leaflet advertising the merits of *Salvatore's Pizzeria di Napoli*. This was a cheap pizzeria, just round the corner, and popular with students at the college. *Why waste your hard-earned money on expensive ambience*, the leaflet proclaimed, *when you can get Rome's best pizzas in a friendly meeting-place right on your doorstep? Ten per cent reduction for seminarians; cardinals, and above, eat free!*

That cheeky offer went down well with the students.

"You'd never see a cardinal in that place," said Pierre's friend Alain. "Not even a bishop. They like those places where it's all starched linen tablecloths and a fancy wine list."

Pierre agreed. "Well, *chacun à son goût*. We'll probably end up like them in due course."

Alain looked doubtful. "Not me. I've never really seen the point of expensive meals. Food is food, however you cook it. Once you've swallowed it, what's the difference? And what's so special about a linen napkin? Don't paper ones do exactly the same thing? Wipe the same lips?"

Pierre thought about this. His friend was right: the sensation of taste was a passing one. Rich or exotic food might please the palate for a few seconds and then, once chewed and swallowed, it was no different from unbuttered bread or plain potato: the feeling of fullness it provided was indistinguishable. And was it worth paying large amounts for the purely transitory pleasure of sitting in an expensive restaurant, fussed over by attentive waiters? He thought not. There were far better ways of spending one's money: on books, for example, or on good shoes, or on a tube of sandalwood *sapone da barba*, guaranteed to give one a closer and more comfortable shave. The Italians were so good at that sort of thing, Pierre had discovered: they made the best shaving creams and the most invigorating mentholated pre-shaving balms. And the very best coffee, of course. And so many other things that a French seminarian should not be bothering about but that he could not really help himself thinking about from time to time. After all, these things were put on this earth for the enjoyment of mankind and were only sinful if they were given undue weight, which he was far from doing. For he was quite able to take them or leave them, he reminded himself: he had given up coffee for Lent once, and had found it only a slight sacrifice, especially as he had allowed himself to continue drinking tea. There was no essential merit in punishing the flesh, he felt—that had long since been abandoned even by zealots. St. Simeon Stylites may have lived on top of a small pillar for more than thirty years, but there would be few, if any, prepared to do that today. Of course, he had read of a contemporary stylite, a Georgian monk, who had lived for years on top of a pillar. In his case, the pillar was a massive outcrop of rock, large enough to allow for the construction of living quarters surrounded by a small curtilage from which to view the world below.

How different that was from his neat, well-heated bedroom in the Pontifical College, with its bookcase, leather-bound easy chair, and mahogany wardrobe. He was not sure whether it would be easier to get close to God on top of a Georgian pillar, at one with circling birds, on terms with the clouds; as it was, his earth-bound bedroom did not preclude the feeling that he often had of being in touch with something greater than himself, something beyond the noisy world of men, something that, in his view, could only be God, or Spirit, perhaps, if you were one of the many these days to whom it did not come easily to use the name of the Deity. And there it was, he thought wryly: that very reluctance manifesting itself, insidiously, in himself.

Now, as he made his way back to his room after breakfast in the refectory, he looked at the envelope he had picked up from his pigeonhole in the post room. He had always been one of those people who liked to examine a letter from the outside before he opened it. Correspondence, he thought, could reveal itself well before it was opened: the postmark, if legible, could tell you where and when the item was posted; if handwritten, the writing on the envelope could speak volumes as to the temperament of the sender; the envelope itself, cheap or inexpensive, heavy or flimsy, would also speak to the importance of the letter it contained. There was no shortage of clues if you looked for them—and more, of course, might be detected if you held the envelope up to the light, as some people did, fearful, perhaps, that a bill or a final demand lurked within.

The letter had been posted locally. The envelope was firm and obviously expensive; his name and address had been typed, in a tall, rather elegant font, and the name of the college was written out in full. His first thought was that it was from the university, but then he realised it would never use such good stationery, its infrequent communications usually being dispatched in cheap brown envelopes or electronically. He was intrigued, but he decided to wait to open it until he was back in his room. Once there, he sat in his leather armchair and used a blunt table knife to open the envelope.

The first thing he noticed was the cardinal's crest at the head of the writing paper. This was not just printed, but was embossed. Below it a typed letter was topped with the handwritten salutation: *My dear M. Citroën.* He read on: "Please forgive me for writing to you out of the blue. You may recall our meeting last week, brief though it was, when you attended the lecture I gave at the Gregorian. You asked me a very pertinent question and I replied that the issue that you raised was indeed an interesting one and would require some reflection on my part. I have now given your question that thought and would be delighted to give you a few observations on the matter if you would care to meet me for lunch some time next week. If you contact my secretary, Father James Heaney, OSB, at the number above, he will endeavour to find a day that suits both you and me. Until then, I remain, Your servant in Christ, Tommaso di Montalfino."

He stared at the letter, reading it again, and then again after that.

This was the first letter he had ever received from a cardinal, and he found it hard to believe it was intended for him. Yet he remembered the lecture, which had been on a subject in which he had a particular interest—the *filioque* controversy. And he had asked a question, emboldened to do so because nobody else in the audience had seemed willing to do so. And yes, the cardinal had answered him courteously, asking for more time to consider his response. He had expected it to end there, but it had not, and somehow the cardinal had found out who he was, where he lived and was proposing to give him the answer to his question over lunch.

He left his room. Alain's room was a few doors down the corridor, and he made his way there, to find his friend just about to leave for the first lecture of the day.

"Guess who had a letter from a cardinal today?" said Pierre.

"That question suggests its own answer," said Alain, tucking a pen into his pocket. "And I assume that it's you."

Pierre nodded. "Right first time."

"Be careful," said Alain, reaching for the linen satchel in which he carried his lecture notes. "If a cardinal writes to a seminarian, I'd say there's an agenda."

"I wasn't born yesterday," said Pierre. He was twenty-three.

His friend's remark had taken the gloss off Pierre's pleasure, and his disappointment showed.

"I'm sorry," said Alain. "I didn't mean to sound sceptical. It's just that . . ." He shrugged.

"He said that he was going to reply to that question I asked at the lecture. That's all."

Alain nodded. "That's sounds innocent enough. And, yes, I'm excited for you, Pierre. Perhaps he's going to offer you a job. Who knows?"

They were both due to graduate in three months and were thinking of their futures. A letter from a cardinal in such circumstances was promising, to say the least.

"Mention me," said Alain, with a smile. "I need a job too. And I'm not sure that I want to end up in some dreary parish somewhere."

"I'll put in a word," said Pierre, laughing, and added, "if I get the chance."

He was not at all sure how such a chance might present itself. One could hardly say to somebody like a cardinal, "Oh, by the way, I have a friend . . ." and then proceed barefacedly to make some request on that friend's behalf. You would have to be more subtle than that—but how? And how should you make known your own needs? Perhaps it would be enough simply to say that you had not yet decided what to do, and that consequently you were open to offers. Such an approach might then be followed with a careless "Something is bound to turn up," which, if all went well, might lead to a few moments of silence while possibilities of help were assessed.

Or there could be long silences that went nowhere. Pierre and two fellow seminarians had had such a lunch in their first year in Rome, having been invited by a monsignor friend of their bishop to join him for lunch in another pontifical college. After their opening conversational gambits had fallen flat, nobody could think of much to say, and the meal had been consumed in complete silence. He was two years older now, and more confident, but he still felt daunted by the sheer scale of this invitation. This was to be lunch with a *cardinal*, with one who might just as easily be lunching with the Pope himself; and it had all come about because he had happened to ask a question about a theological issue on which he had, by chance, chosen to write his university dissertation. It was all most unlikely—but that, he had come to understand, was how our personal die was cast. A chance remark, an unplanned meeting, might govern the whole course of one's life. People kept pointing that out, and although he could not think of any such incident in his own life, he knew that he might identify one in retrospect. Shape and pattern in our affairs, people said, were often best understood when we looked back at what has happened rather than when we looked forward.

LATER THAT DAY HE contacted Father James Heaney, OSB, as the cardinal's letter had suggested.

"Ah yes," said the Benedictine. "His Eminence mentioned that you might be getting in touch. How's your diary looking?"

Pierre caught his breath. He did not have a diary—his life was too regular and unexciting to merit the keeping of a diary, the pages of which would have been largely virginal, apart from the dates of term, which he knew anyway, and the birthdays of his close family, which he was unlikely to forget.

"My diary?" he said.

"Yes," said Father Heaney. "We need to find a day on which both you and His Eminence will be free." He paused. "We've got a lot of committees in the earlier part of next week, and those meetings have a tendency to go on a bit, but things are looking a bit brighter on Thursday and Friday."

Pierre thought: I have no meetings at all—not a single one. And he might have confessed that, but instead he said, "Let me look."

"What about Friday?" asked Father Heaney. "How does Friday look to you?"

"That would suit me very well," said Pierre. He felt ashamed of himself: he should not have pretended in this way. He should have said, right at the outset, "Look, Father Heaney, I don't even have a diary—let alone anything to put in it." That's what he should have done, and yet he had not.

"Well, that's grand then," said the secretary. "Any dietary preferences?"

Again, the question took Pierre by surprise. Nobody ever bothered to ask him whether he could eat anything—the food was simply placed in front of him and he ate it. He was not particularly fond of root vegetables, but he could eat them, and he did not like anchovies, but once again he could eat them if pressed. So now he simply said, "I'm not fussy."

This seemed to please Father Heaney. "That's a refreshing change," he said. "The number of people these days who give you a long list of their likes and dislikes—it happens virtually every time. I was talking the other day, you know, to an archbishop—and I shan't name him, if you don't mind—who seemed to be able to stomach only lettuce and feta cheese. Quite frankly, I'm surprised he's still with us, but there we are."

They moved on to the location. "His Eminence is particularly fond of a small restaurant called *La Regola*," Father Heaney went on. "You may be familiar with the area. It's off the Campo de' Fiori. In fact, you may know the restaurant itself. It has quite the reputation."

Pierre knew no restaurants at all—apart from *Salvatore's Pizzeria di Napoli*—and so he replied, "I don't think I do."

"Well, it's really very good. I had lunch there last week with some Brazilians. They loved it. Fortunately, they were paying . . ." The Benedictine laughed, and Pierre thought: I assume the cardinal will pay, but what if he said, "Let's go Dutch?" No, that was impossible.

They arranged the time, and then Father Heaney steered the conversation towards its close. "A final thought," he said. "Before you ring off, tell me: when do you graduate?"

Pierre told him. But, even as he did so, he asked himself what had prompted Father Heaney's question. He had hardly dared hope that they were thinking of offering him a job, but why else would they have wanted to know about his graduation date?

"I see," said the secretary, and then, "Well, His Eminence will look forward to seeing you on Friday."

The conversation concluded, Pierre went to the window of his room and gazed out onto the street below. He felt that something had changed. He was not sure what it was, but a few minutes ago he had been unwilling to think about his future after graduation. Unlike Alain, he had not been contemplating becoming a priest, imagining that he would end up as a teacher of some sort, or a scholar, if he were lucky. A university post would suit him very well, he thought—something in a department of theology, perhaps, where he could think about issues of the soul and spirituality without having to pretend to have the answers. Such thoughts as he had entertained about the future were vague: now it seemed to him that something concrete might present itself. Many of the cardinals exercised extensive patronage, being able to nominate candidates for doctoral research programmes or fellowships. Something of that sort might now be in the offing, and the prospect was frankly exciting. Even if he would eventually return to France, he would be more than happy to stay in Rome, which he found more interesting than his native Bordeaux. He spoke fluent Italian now; he knew his way about the city; he had a good circle of friends.

He left his room and made his way downstairs, out into Rome, into the city in which centuries of history had seeped into the very stone that made the bustling streets, the alleyways, the silent courtyards.

He looked up at the windows behind which the people of Rome lived their lives. This was a city of mystery and intrigues, and this mystery into which he was being enticed—this unusual invitation—was one that he now awaited with considerable anticipation. But Friday was a few days off, and he would have to stop thinking about it and concentrate on his work. He had an essay to write for his theology tutor, a critique of Karl Barth's rejection of natural theology. His tutor, a Jesuit, prided himself on his ecumenical openness to Protestant thinking, although, when pushed as to the issue of ultimate truth, he always smiled a wan smile before announcing, "Such a pity that they're all wrong."

On Friday he left for *La Regola* well in advance of the time agreed with Father Heaney, killing time by lingering for fifteen minutes in a nearby bookshop. In the restaurant, the proprietor greeted him with surprising deference. He seemed to know whose guest he was, muttering, "Of course, of course," as he showed him to a table in the window.

"This is where His Eminence always sits," the proprietor said. "It gives a view of what is happening in the street."

This observation was delivered with a knowing look, and with the addition of, "Important, that."

Pierre was uncertain what to say, and so he simply nodded. He sat down, and within a couple of minutes a waiter returned with a bottle of chilled sparkling water. Pierre began his wait, paging through a copy of *Corriere della Sera* that a previous diner had left on a nearby chair. He found it difficult to concentrate on the newspaper, though, which was full of reports on internecine Italian political feuds and dire warnings of impending economic crisis. The government, the paper announced, would more or less certainly fall, possibly by the end of the following week. In France, there were riots pencilled in for next Tuesday, and, if the weather was favourable, for the succeeding two days. There would be a possible meteor strike the week after that. He sighed. The affairs of men were far from simple. The Peaceable Kingdom, the dream of poets and artists, was simply that—a dream.

And then, almost without Pierre noticing his arrival, the cardinal was there, ushered to the table by an obsequious waiter.

Pierre rose to his feet. Unhesitating, as if prompted by ancient custom, he took the proffered hand, bowed slightly, and kissed the band of gold on the cardinal's ring finger.

Tomasso di Montalfino was a tall, well-built man in his fifties, which was young to be a member of the College of Cardinals. His features were aquiline, his eyes suggesting an acute, appraising intelligence. A slight fleshiness provided the only hint of the aura of good living about him. His voice, as he greeted Pierre in Italian, was quiet and controlled. This was a man who spoke succinctly and who normally had no need to repeat himself.

"I am glad you could fit me in," he said as he sat down.

Pierre showed his surprise. "But, Your Eminence, it is you who must be busy."

The cardinal smiled. "I have my busy times," he said. "But then again, there are occasions when time hangs heavy." He nodded to the waiter, who went off obediently towards the kitchen. Fixing Pierre with an inquisitive stare, he asked, "Your name—Citroën . . . I'm sure everybody must ask you the same question."

"They do," said Pierre, adding hurriedly, "but I don't mind."

"I owned a Citroën once," said the cardinal. "A Traction. A lovely car. It was probably the best car I shall ever own." He paused. "I take it there's a connection?"

Pierre felt a stab of disappointment. So this was it: the cardinal had assumed that he was a member of the car-manufacturing dynasty. That would explain the invitation: cardinals were not above simple snobbery.

"I'm sorry to say," Pierre began, "but we're a different branch. In fact, I believe we have nothing at all to do with the car people. We know about them, of course, and there may be some ancient connection—way back—but we're really a different family. I think we all have a Netherlands connection, but it's pretty obscure. We all go back to some early lemon-growers—hence the name."

The cardinal did not seem disappointed. "Ultimately," he said, "we're all cousins anyway, aren't we? Isn't that what the population geneticists tell us? That all of us here in Western Europe are descended from a handful of women?"

"I've heard that," said Pierre.

"And that's rather reassuring, don't you think?" said the cardinal. "The idea of universal brotherhood is being borne out by science. It provides additional authority, I think, for the brotherhood we've been talking about all along."

"And for *agape*," said Pierre.

"Yes," said the cardinal. "And for *agape* too. Is it easier to love those to whom you know you are somehow related, even if rather distantly? I think that possibly it is."

"Perhaps," said Pierre.

The cardinal sat back in his seat. "Of course, the requirement to love others," he said, "is at the heart of our Christian message, isn't it? And if we hadn't had that underpinning our civilization, I wonder whether we would necessarily have gone down the route that we have tried to go down for the last couple of thousand years. It could have been quite different, you know." He paused. "Sometimes I wonder where contemporary proponents of human rights think their values came from. They can be very dismissive of us—of the Christian tradition—but has it occurred to them that the values they are so attached to are a direct result of Christianity's stressing of dignity and love? I think perhaps not."

"Yes," said Pierre, and then added, "Or should I say no. I suspect they don't think of it that way."

"Then their sense of history must be rather defective," said the cardinal. "Mind you, I am never in the slightest bit surprised by ignorance. Look at contemporary fascists. Do they know what happened in the 1930s? I don't think they do. Or some of them don't— hence their willingness to peddle the political poison they espouse."

"No."

"And do people remember what Stalin did? Do they remember the Terror? Do they know how many millions died at the whim of a single paranoid dictator?"

"I think they might not," said Pierre.

The cardinal fixed him with an unnerving gaze. "But you do? Am I correct?"

"I don't know much about Russian history, but I do know about some of it."

For a few moments, the cardinal seemed to toy with the idea of taking the point further, but then he said, "Tell me a bit about your family—your Citroëns."

"I think we were Dutch," said Pierre. "I had an uncle who loved doing family trees. He traced us back to the beginning of the nineteenth century, but didn't come up with anything earlier than that. We went to France in the 1860s. To Clermont-Ferrand, initially."

"And?"

"And set up a shoe factory," said Pierre. "That lasted until the early 1930s. We made boots for the army, including the Foreign Legion. The factory did well."

"I can imagine that," said the cardinal.

"My great-grandfather lost interest in the shoe business," Pierre went on. "He left Clermont-Ferrand and went off to Bordeaux. He became a *négociant* in the wine trade. That is what the family has done since then. My father still runs the business."

"A pity about the shoes," said the cardinal. "Shoes are so interesting. Have you ever come across Belgian shoes?"

Pierre shook his head. "Not as far as I know. I don't ask where my shoes are made. They're not expensive, of course." He paused. "Is there something special about Belgian shoes, Your Eminence?"

"They are very comfortable," said the cardinal. "They're what the Americans call loafers. They're very light and you only wear them inside—unless you have special soles put on them. The original soles are compressed horse-hair covered with soft leather. That makes them remarkably light."

Pierre glanced under the table; he could not stop himself. The cardinal smiled. "I'm not wearing them now," he said. "But I like to wear them in my study. They aid concentration, for some reason. Perhaps it's because you cease to be aware of your feet. If you don't have to think about your feet, then you can think about higher things, so to speak."

The waiter arrived to take their order. He approached the table very slowly, almost tentatively, but was encouraged by the cardinal. "We're ready, Enrico," he said. "Or I am and I'm sure my guest will make up his mind quickly enough. Remind us of today's specials, if you please."

"A special selection of antipasti," intoned the waiter. "Some very fine mozzarella—from the boss's uncle's herd of buffalo. In perfect condition. Some special Parma ham from a small village between Parma and Reggio-Emilia. Only available in five restaurants in the whole of Italy. Exclusive."

"Very good," said the cardinal. "There's nothing wrong with exclusivity . . . ," adding, quickly, "as long as you are prepared to share it with others in a truly Christian spirit."

The waiter nodded his agreement. "Then we have a very nice tagliatelle," he continued, "with a porcini mushroom sauce and Sardinian artichokes."

"Sardinian!" exclaimed the cardinal. "That sounds very interesting." He glanced at Pierre. "Have you ever been to Sardinia, Monsieur Citroën?"

Pierre shook his head.

"Brigands," whispered the cardinal.

The waiter suppressed a smile.

"Enrico here," said the cardinal, "is Sardinian . . . but not a brigand. Is that correct, Enrico?"

"Your Eminence is, as always, correct," said the waiter.

"But not infallible," said the cardinal. "That epithet belongs to another altogether."

The waiter smirked. "Then there is ratatouille," he said. "A very subtle ratatouille."

The cardinal made a gesture intended to say, *Well, there you have it.* He turned to Pierre. "I knew a Monsignor Ratatouille once, believe it or not. He was a senior figure in the Palace of the Holy Office. A charming man. A very considerable philatelist, as I recall. And of course you may have heard of dear Cardinal Casaroli, who became Vatican Secretary of State. He was a most skilful diplomat."

"He was referred to in our course on international affairs," said Pierre. "I took an option on Eastern Europe and the Church. We were told he was highly instrumental in weakening the hold of the Soviet Union over countries behind the Iron Curtain."

The cardinal agreed. "They didn't like him one little bit," he said, smiling at the memory. "He was a real target for KGB spies, and they hate to be outwitted. They were desperate to know what he was up to." He paused. "In fact, poor Casaroli was spied upon for rather a long time. It's an extraordinary tale. Have you heard it?"

Pierre shook his head.

"It's a delicious story," the cardinal went on. "Casaroli was presented with a very fine ceramic statuette of the Virgin Mary—a present from a Czech lady of his acquaintance. He was very pleased to receive the gift, but unfortunately the statue had a small transmitter concealed in it. It was, as you say, bugged."

Pierre's eyes widened. "What a terrible thing to do," he said.

The cardinal seemed pleased that Pierre had reacted in this way. "I wholeheartedly agree," he said. "The gathering of intelligence is important, but there are limits to the means one employs. No cause is dignified by underhand methods."

"Of course not."

"And yet," the cardinal went on, "you cannot make an omelette without breaking at least some eggs."

"Yes, that's true."

The cardinal was now staring up at the ceiling. "And fire, I believe, has to be fought with fire."

"That's also true, Eminence."

The cardinal lowered his gaze from the ceiling. "The world is a difficult place, isn't it? Most of us would like not to get our hands dirty, but if we don't engage with the world, then we can hardly be surprised if the battalions of the wicked gain the upper hand."

Pierre waited. He was unsure where this conversation was going, but the cardinal was an easy conversationalist and there was nothing strained about the exchange.

"Some people like to pretend that evil doesn't exist," the cardinal went on. "I believe that they are fundamentally mistaken. Evil is there, right under our noses sometimes, and it is tangible—and powerful. No amount of wishful thinking can will it out of existence. It is a fact. Evil is a brute fact and it can be seen in action every single day."

"I'm sure you're right," said Pierre.

The cardinal lowered his voice. "So, the question with which we are confronted is this: how should we respond? Should we simply try to defeat evil through example—hoping that our good deeds will shame the perpetrators of evil? That's what the pacifists profess, isn't it? They say that if we simply opt out of the circle of violence and wrongdoing, then the repetitive cycle of such things will be broken. I can appreciate that argument. I understand what they're getting at. But . . ." He broke off. He looked downcast. "But I find myself asking this question: what should we have done when confronted with the extermination camps of the Nazis? Should we have restricted ourselves to words, or should we have used force to liberate the remaining poor victims of that unimaginable cruelty and wickedness?"

He looked at Pierre, as if waiting for an answer. And that answer came quickly, as Pierre had no difficulty with this. "We use all necessary force," he said. "We march up and dispose of the guards unless they surrender immediately, of course. We do anything and everything to stop any further acts of murder."

The cardinal seemed surprised by the strength and speed of Pierre's response. "I see that you have no reservations about that."

"No, I don't."

The cardinal nodded. "I'm glad to hear that. So many, these days, are unprepared to defend the right. Their instinct is to appease, I'm afraid." He paused. "That, of course, is an historical example but there are many instances today, in our own times, where evil probes at our defences and where a robust response might be necessary."

A further thought occurred to the cardinal. "And of course, so many people today are relativists—which means that they seriously think it's impossible to distinguish between values. They take the view there's no such thing as truth—even scientific truth."

"I know," said Pierre. "You hear those opinions all the time."

"But they don't challenge Bernoulli's principle at thirty-six thousand feet," observed the cardinal. He smiled, and continued, "And what, I wonder, would these moral relativists say to some wretched victim of contemporary slavery or trafficking? Would they say there's no distinction to be made between your position and the position of the trafficker?"

"I don't think they would," Pierre ventured.

"Then their relativism is inconsistent," said the cardinal. "They have to acknowledge that evil exists and that its condemnation requires the espousal of certain core values—human dignity, freedom, love of others, and so on."

The waiter returned with the antipasti trolley, and began to help them to a selection.

"So delicious," said the cardinal, spreading the starched linen napkin out across his lap. "Please begin, Pierre—if I may use your Christian name."

"Of course, Your Em—"

The cardinal held up a hand. "Please, don't bother about all that. I'm usually known as C. You may call me that, if you wish. It's a sort of . . . a sort of nickname, one might say."

"Does it stand for anything?" asked Pierre.

"It's an abbreviation. I did once know what it stood for, but I never bother to explain to people. People think it's an initialism for Cardinal. That's a possibility, of course. But the point is, everybody calls me C."

They embarked on the antipasti. After a mouthful of Parma ham, and one of delicate, almost liquid mozzarella, the cardinal dabbed at his lips with his pristine white napkin.

"Now then, Pierre," he began, "your dissertation on the *filioque* matter. I never imagined, when I delivered that lecture at the Gregorian, that I would have in my audience one who appreciated the finer points of that immensely complex issue. And then, at question time, in that dread silence when nobody seems to be willing to ask the first question—or even the second, for that matter—you came up with your very astute question. That certainly deserved a lunch, I thought."

Pierre lowered his eyes modestly. The *filioque* was a minefield—it always had been—and he hoped that the cardinal would not expose the limits of his knowledge of the controversy too quickly. He had become interested in the whole question more or less by accident, having come across references to it in an article he read during his first month of study at the Gregorian. The title of the article had caught his attention for its sensationalist ring: "The phrase that tore the Church asunder—still dynamite today." He had been intrigued; theological writing was seldom vivid, but this article presented the argument in a way that made the whole story of the schism between the Western and Eastern churches seem as if it was all happening no earlier than yesterday. He quickly became familiar with the kernel of the matter: the *filioque* clause, which meant "and from or by the son," had been inserted into the Nicene creed by the Western Church. It referred to the origin of the Holy Spirit—or the Holy Ghost, as it was called by some. Where did the Holy Spirit come from? From the Father (God), from whom everything, after all, must come, or did the Son (Christ) have a role in creating it? The Church divided, with the Western Church adding a role for the Son, expressed in the term *filioque*, while the Eastern Church stuck to what it claimed was the original creed. In Orthodoxy, then, the Holy Spirit came from the Father and that was it. And the Western Church, Orthodoxy argued, had no right to add anything to the creed in this unilateral manner. The result was a schism in Christianity—not a small matter.

Pierre read more about the subject, and was amazed at how much there was. Rivers of ink had been spilled on the subject over the years, and passions were intense. He chose it as the subject of his dissertation, but even then he realised that he had hardly scratched the surface of the subject. And here was the cardinal, who had completed a doctorate on the *filioque:* how long would it take for him to realise, Pierre asked himself, that I know very little about the dispute? Of course, Rome was full of people with doctorates in the most obscure theological and ecclesiastical areas. The previous month he had met somebody with a doctorate in angelology, awarded, he learned, for a thesis on the subject of the various orders of angels and the gradations in their authority. Many PhDs, though, were based on very little, and some, he supposed, were concerned with the minutiae of things that did not exist at all. If he were ever to undertake doctoral studies, he suspected he would add to that vast body of writing that would never be read by anybody other than the examiners. But if so much scholarship was a glass-bead game, then it was a game that kept at least some people happy and harmed nobody. Angelology had never made anybody cry, had never sent anyone to bed hungry, had never come between friends . . . He stopped himself: one had to be careful about making any such proposition about anything that might become an ideology. Millions had died for ideologies of one sort or another; countless people had been put to death because they could not give the right answer to some doctrinal question, or because they had been born in the wrong bed, to the wrong parents, or because they had forgotten the shibboleths that might have saved their lives. If there was one thing that humanity had always been good at, it was finding a reason to distrust or dislike others. The seed of that characteristic was there at the very beginning, implanted deep in our nature, only awaiting the slightest encouragement to flourish. *Them* and *us* began in children's games, and stayed with us until our last breath. Except, he thought; except when we cultivated a love of our fellow man, and that took such effort. Loving humanity in general, without distinction—in other words, acting as if all men were one's brothers—was, he thought, as difficult as being on a strict diet; it required much the same determination, much the same willpower. He wanted to do it; the urge to do so was there, and it was what had prompted him to the study of theology and philosophy in the first place, but he was not sure that he had within him the necessary strength, the necessary will. Alain was different: he sensed in him that current of love that the moral imperative required. That was why he could become a priest; that was why he could give up everything that the world had to offer in order to follow the example of the religious leader who, all those years ago, had spoken about love of others; a religious leader who made claims to divinity that he, Pierre, would love to believe but just could not. Not that his disbelief mattered, he thought; you could pretend to believe in things that you knew were unlikely to be true but that you knew offered hope in a damaged and unhappy world. We had to pretend—all the time we had to act as if certain things were true because we knew that otherwise our lives would be even more blighted than they currently were. It was like believing in Santa Claus when you were young; it was just like that. It was like whistling in the dark to keep your spirits up.

The cardinal made a number of comments on the question Pierre had asked at the lecture. "I agree with you," he said, "that the Bonn Conference in 1874 came as close as we could expect at the time to bringing about a rapprochement between ourselves and our dear, misguided Orthodox brethren. Johann von Döllinger was really on to something when he said that the real issue is the precise meaning of the Latin verb *procedere*. You were right, I think, in saying that the problem was that the Greeks had two verbs doing similar work.

"So," he continued, "when the Latin creed says *who proceeded from the Father and the Son (Filioque)*, it does not mean that the Holy Spirit came *equally* from both. It is perfectly possible, within the meaning of the Latin verb, that the Holy Spirit originated in the Father . . ."

"It must have," said Pierre, "because the Father is the source of all creation. Everything comes from God—it must do, as long as one believes that there is a god."

"Precisely," said the cardinal. "But something that is passed *through* another being can surely be said to *proceed* through that being. That's the point that von Döllinger wanted to stress. And I think it provided us with a real opportunity to put division behind us."

"But it was premature?"

"I think so. I know that the issue had been discussed for a very long time—ever since the days of Origen and Gregory Thaumaturgus in the third century. I know that it was the subject of intense debate between East and West. I know there has been a lot of hurt involved, but these things take time. There is a chance, though, that we might be getting to the point where a compromise might be possible."

"But we would have to drop the *filioque* from the creed? Would the Orthodox brethren accept anything less than that?"

The cardinal sighed. "Some would. Others . . . well, you know what human nature is like. It has become a matter of pride for some. And there's an additional point. There's the issue of whether they acknowledge that we had the right to insert clauses into the creed. They're sticky about that. They don't accept our authority to change the creed in that way."

Pierre agreed that this was a serious stumbling block. "Will the Orthodox churches ever accept the primacy of His Holiness?"

"Once again, there are shades of opinion," said the cardinal. "But no, I don't think they will. They would be prepared to work with us on the basis of equality, I imagine, but what would that entail? I imagine that it would require that any change in the creed be agreed by both ourselves and Orthodoxy. And the point is: we are not equal. We have apostolic succession and will not give that up."

For a short while Pierre said nothing. He felt the eyes of the cardinal upon him, as if his reaction to what was being said was being carefully weighed. He took a sip of his glass of mineral water. Then he said, "It's a great pity, because I'm not sure that it matters terribly much whether the Son had a role in the creation of the Holy Spirit. What matters is the Holy Spirit is there, working in the world to help men to see what might be." As he said this, he thought, How can anyone seriously believe that the Holy Spirit is a person? Yet that is what I seem to be saying.

The cardinal frowned. "I understand why you should feel that way," he said. "But we need to be certain, don't we? We need to be certain as to where the Holy Spirit fits in. The Greeks would say that we are effectively demoting the Holy Spirit to a subsidiary place— the junior position within the Trinity. I don't agree, of course; I feel that there is nothing undignified about proceeding from the Son, who is, after all, *of one nature with the Father*. That's crucial, in my view—absolutely crucial."

They discussed the *filioque* issue for a further twenty minutes or so, until it was time for dessert, a cassata of which the cardinal had two helpings. Then it was time for coffee, by which point they had left the *filioque* and moved on to a discussion of a special exhibition about to open at the Vatican Museum. This was a display of artefacts and documents connected with Jesuit missions in Goa. And that was the subject in which they were still immersed when the cardinal suddenly looked out of the window and saw his car draw up outside the restaurant.

"My driver," he explained to Pierre. "I'm afraid that I'm going to have to dash. I've enjoyed our conversation immensely, Pierre, and I wish you all luck with your future. Perhaps a doctorate on the *filioque*—or something similar. The world is so full of possibilities, isn't it?"

Pierre watched as the cardinal was ushered out of the restaurant by Enrico. Directly outside the restaurant a sleek green car had drawn up, and a driver, clad in simple ministerial garb, was stepping out. He opened the car door for the cardinal, who nodded to him as he stepped inside.

The car was an Aston Martin.

Pierre sat down. He was uncertain what to think. The lunch had been a success, he thought, as the cardinal had gone away in good humour after they finished their wide-ranging discussion. Before he left, though, he had said, "My secretary might be in touch. We'll see."

Who was this *we*? Pierre wondered. And what were they expecting to see? Why, indeed, were they bothering to look in the first place? Pierre was asking himself these questions as he prepared to leave the restaurant a few minutes after the cardinal had made his departure. He was shown out by Enrico, all courtesy and solicitude, who, as he opened the front door for him, slipped a piece of paper into his hand.

"Read that later," he whispered.

Pierre waited until he had gone round the corner before he unfolded the note. It had obviously been hurriedly written, but the words were clear enough. *Be careful,* it said. That was all.

HE HEARD NOTHING FROM the cardinal's office for the next two weeks, and had begun to think that the entire episode was at an end. It was a strange thing to have happened, but in his experience, there were plenty of stranger things that happened in Rome. He wrote to his parents to tell them that he had been invited to lunch by a cardinal, and his mother wrote back to say that she had once met a cardinal who was a distant relative of her godmother. She could not remember his name, she said, nor could she recall anything that he said, but she did remember his scarlet biretta. "I hope you made a good impression," she said. "These chances do not come up very often in this life."

No, he thought, they do not, and he was unlikely to receive another invitation like that. But then, one morning he received a further telephone call from Father Heaney.

"Monsieur Citroën," began the priest, "I know that this is no notice at all, but if you happen to be free this morning, I wonder if we could possibly meet. I won't take up much of your time—an hour or so would be more than enough. There's a matter I should like to discuss with you."

Pierre accepted the invitation. He did so automatically—as he was free that morning—but, even as he did so, he recalled the scribbled note passed to him by the waiter at *La Regola*. But it was too late now to remember a prior engagement.

"Good," said Father Heaney. "I suggest we meet in the Borghese Gardens. Perhaps in front of the Galleria Borghese itself. Are you familiar with the gallery?"

"I have been there," said Pierre. It occurred to him, though, that not having met Father Heaney before he was not sure that he would recognise him. Of course, if he were in clerical dress, it would be easy enough—unless, of course, the Borghese Gardens happened to be teeming with priests at the time—which was always possible in Rome.

"Father, I must ask: how will I know you?" he asked. "We've never actually met, have we?"

The priest did not reply immediately, but then he said, "Don't worry, I shall recognise you."

Pierre wanted to ask how, but before he could say anything, Father Heaney explained, "We have a photograph, you see." This made Pierre catch his breath, but before anything else could be said the priest brought the conversation to an end. Now, Pierre sat at his desk, gazing out of his window at the sun-drenched sky of Rome. He should have asked the priest what it was he wanted to discuss. In fact, he felt it would have been more courteous for Father Heaney to give him some indication of the discussion he had in mind, rather than to assume, rather imperiously, that the invitation would be accepted without question. But then he reminded himself: this was a cardinal's office with which he was dealing, and presumably a cardinal's office could do very much as it wanted when engaging with a lowly student.

He looked at his watch. His meeting with Father Heaney was to be at eleven thirty, and it was now barely nine. It would not take him more than three-quarters of an hour to get to the Villa Borghese by foot, and yet, feeling distracted and slightly on edge, he did not relish the thought of sitting in his room until it was time to set off. He made up his mind: he would take his time walking to the Borghese Gardens and once there he could sit on a bench and watch the world pass by until it was time to meet Father Heaney.

Like all city parks, the vast sprawl of the Borghese Gardens performed a multitude of roles: the elegant landscape was a haven for refugees from the busy streets of the city; a retreat for lovers in search of privacy; an inspiration for visitors seeking a vision of classical order. But it was also, to the practised and suspicious eye, a haven for clandestine encounters ranging from the relatively innocent to the unambiguously sinister. Like any public space in Italy, of course, it was a place for display—for the parade of *la bella figura*—even by dogs, brought here by their owners to the special area known as the Valley of the Dogs, where Roman canines strolled and strutted with a sense of style quite lacking in the dogs of lesser cities.

After a few minutes of walking aimlessly along one of the peripheral paths, Pierre found himself looking out over the lake to the Temple of Asclepius. The water was still, and the temple was reflected in its surface, the building's pillars casting tall white lines across the green surface of the lake. He found a bench under an ancient pine tree, and sat down in the shade the tree provided. Although the morning had not yet reached its hottest point, the air was already heavy and sluggish, needing rain to wash it clean. There was silence, but it was that attenuated silence of a great city, the site of a million conversations, the backdrop to the movement, backwards and forwards, of hundreds of thousands of people earning their living. And there was a bird somewhere, too; a bird singing a pure note against the inescapable hum of the city. Pierre closed his eyes, and thought about what Father Heaney might say to him, and what his response should be. Was he being sucked into something—one of those murky intrigues for which the Vatican was famous, and about which Enrico, the waiter, had so bluntly warned him? Was he being picked up? For all he knew, the cardinal had regular meetings with young men approached on his behalf by his secretary. The Church was no stranger to such matters, which was its own fault, Pierre thought: anybody with the slightest knowledge of human psychology knew that a culture of denial and repression would never subdue the demands of the libido: how could it? Or was he simply being helped in some yet to be identified way by a powerful man who had discovered that an obscure student shared an intellectual interest—the *filioque* controversy—and had wanted to do something to mark his pleasure in this discovery? Influential, successful people took pleasure in helping those at the beginning of their careers—there was nothing sinister in that and no objective grounds for imagining that the cardinal and his secretary might be harbouring some ulterior objective. He took a deep breath: he would put suspicion in its place, keep an open mind and, for the moment at least, assume good faith on the part of the Benedictine and his exalted employer.

It was while he was sitting beside the lake that Pierre became aware of two figures further along the shore. Two men were standing at the water's edge, engaged in conversation while they gazed across the lake at the temple on the other side. Pierre was sufficiently far away from them, and shaded enough by the pine tree, not to be noticed by them, but close enough to catch the occasional word of their exchange.

Discreetly, he threw a glance in their direction, noticing that one of them was tall and bearded, while the other, sleeker and shorter, was dressed in clerical garb and was wearing a black biretta. There was no incongruity in this, of course, even if others in the gardens were less formally dressed: this was Rome, after all, a city in which clerical figures were not at all out of place. But Pierre's conclusion was immediate: the man in the biretta was Father James Heaney, OSB. He could be no other. And what brought him to that conclusion was his overhearing of a single expression, dropped into the morning air of the Borghese Gardens as if by parachute: *filioque*. The two men at the water's edge, believing themselves unobserved, were discussing the *filioque* controversy.

Before he slipped away, sidling off his bench so as not to be noticed, Pierre heard one or two other snippets of the conversation. He heard the word "Nicene" and then "patriarch," and then a couple of unmistakably Greek names, "Angelos Evangelis" and then "Aristomenis Petronannos," neither of which he recognised, but which conveyed the flavour of the discussion. And then, again, the expression *filioque*, clearly enunciated, removing all doubt about what was going on. Or creating exactly that doubt?

Neither of the men seemed to notice Pierre and after following a path for a few minutes, he felt himself safe enough to turn back and look in their direction. They were still there, still apparently deep in conversation, although the priest was now reaching into a pocket and extracting something—an envelope, Pierre thought—which the other man examined briefly, nodded, and then slipped into a thin briefcase he was carrying.

Pierre hesitated; if the conversation was coming to an end, he did not want Father Heaney suddenly to see him staring in his direction. And it was now almost eleven fifteen, and he would need to make his way towards the gallery, outside which he and the secretary were shortly due to meet. As he walked in that direction, he thought of what he had seen. Looked at from one angle, it was nothing special. Father Heaney—and he was convinced that one of the men was him—had simply bumped into a friend in the gardens while on his way to his arranged meeting outside the gallery. There was nothing odd in that: even in a city as big as Rome one might have a chance encounter with a person whom one knew. And if that friend whom one happened to meet was a theologian, or an ecclesiastical historian—of whom there would be so many in a place like Rome— then what could be more natural and unsurprising than that one might have a conversation about the *filioque* and some of the figures involved in the debate? But looked at in a different way, there were features of the situation that might make one stop and think. Firstly, there was the appearance of the taller figure. He was thin-faced and bearded, and he had about him, even when seen from a distance, that characteristic bony appearance of an Orthodox priest. There was no essential reason why Orthodox priests should look the way they did, but that was how it was, at least to Pierre. And the beard, of course, spoke volumes.

Suddenly he stopped. It could not have been a chance encounter that he witnessed. An envelope had been exchanged, an envelope containing money or documents, and one did not exchange an envelope with a friend whom one just happened to meet while out for a walk. No, there was something going on, and Pierre thought that whatever it was had not been intended for other eyes.

He turned a corner and saw the impressive shape of the gallery appear behind the trees. He was now beginning to feel anxious and for a moment or two he considered turning on his heels and leaving. He could contact Father Heaney and give him some excuse for missing their meeting, and if the priest suggested another time or place, he could find some reason for being unable to make it. That should bring an end to the matter, as they—Father Heaney and the cardinal—would be subtle enough to realise that Pierre was discouraging any further approach.

He had almost decided to do that when he heard a voice behind him. It seemed to come from behind a yew hedge, but in fact it was from a path that joined the path on which Pierre had been walking. And there, when Pierre turned round, was the man he had seen beside the lake.

"There you are!" said Father Heaney, extending a hand. "I do hope I'm not late."

They shook hands. Pierre noticed that the priest's palm was warm to the touch—as if he had exerted himself in a brisk walk.

"Such a fine day," Father Heaney continued. "Mind you, just about every day in Rome is fine at this time of year. Not too hot—although it's heating up a bit—but certainly nothing like August. Oh, my goodness, August can be a trial, but I suppose you've always been up in France in August—a much more bearable place at that time of year."

"Yes," said Pierre, giving Father Heaney a shy glance. The priest's expression was an open one, his manner warm and friendly. There was nothing threatening about him, and Pierre found himself regretting his earlier suspicions.

They began to walk towards the gallery. "I thought we might take a look at some of the paintings," said Father Heaney. "I never tire of visiting this gallery. It doesn't matter how many times you see a favourite painting—there's always something new to be noticed." He paused. "Do you have a favourite artist?"

Pierre shrugged. "My tastes are fairly broad. I like the obvious ones. Titian, I suppose. Botticelli, of course. I love the *Primavera*, for instance."

Father Heaney turned to him enthusiastically. "Now there's a case in point. I said that we always seem able to notice fresh things about a familiar painting. *Primavera* has more meaning packed into its details than one might imagine. Into every bit of it. The subjects in Botticelli's paintings *gaze* a great deal, and that particular painting is no exception. Hermes-Mercurius, for instance, is portrayed looking up at a concealed god, somewhere behind the hanging fruit in the painting. He sees what we cannot see, *and yet we know it's there.*"

He paused, and looked at Pierre as if waiting for some sign of agreement.

"I see," said Pierre. "I mean: I see what you mean—I'm not claiming to see what isn't there."

Father Heaney laughed. "I understand," he said. "There's a book you might care to read. It's called *Under the Guise of Spring*, and it's all about the hidden messages in that painting. Just *Primavera*—just that painting." He hesitated before continuing. He cleared his throat. "Of course, not everything is what it seems, is it? The world may seem intelligible enough to us—we may think we understand it—but the real meaning of the phenomena we observe may be quite different from what we think it is."

"I suppose that's right," said Pierre. "And yet we can't go through life assuming that there's a hidden meaning to everything. We'd all end up like those conspiracy theorists who argue that black, whenever we encounter it, is really white, and vice versa."

Father Heaney appeared to weigh this. "That's true," he said at last. "And yet what if there really are conspiracies—as there must be? At least some. If we are excessively sceptical, then wouldn't we discount them all—even the ones that actually exist?"

Pierre agreed. "I'm not suggesting we take everything at face value," he said. "All that I'm saying is that as a general rule, what we see is what there is."

"That depends on how general your rule is," Father Heaney responded. "But look, let's go in and look out the Caravaggio. I take it you like Caravaggio. Of course you do. Who could not like Caravaggio?"

Pierre nodded. He had his reservations, though. Caravaggio in his mind was all about rough trade and violence, really, a world of taverns and knife-fights, and the darkness that always lay behind the light. Botticelli was more to his taste, he felt, with his flowers and seashells and women clad in diaphanous garments. He was altogether lighter, no matter what hidden meanings art historians might read into his every brush stroke.

They strolled through the gallery, that at that hour of the morning was largely empty of other visitors. Father Heaney proved to be a well-informed guide, drawing Pierre's attention to the works of artists whom Pierre had not encountered before, and seeming to know an impressive amount about them. It was to Caravaggio, though, that he seemed most drawn.

Standing before *Boy with a Basket of Fruit*, Father Heaney shook his head in sheer admiration. "Look at the detail on the fruit," he said. "What a delectable offering. Look at the peach—one might reach forward and eat it, don't you think?"

"Possibly," said Pierre.

"And there's another thing," continued Father Heaney. "Some of the fruit is diseased. Caravaggio is so determined to convey the truth of what he sees that he has put traces of blight on one of the apples and there, you'll see, is a vine leaf with fungal spots."

Pierre peered.

"And as for the boy himself," Father Heaney said, "he was one Mario Minniti, who appears in a number of Caravaggio's works. He was a Sicilian and was involved with Caravaggio in the street fight that led to the death of Ranuccio Tommasoni. He was a somewhat unsavoury young man, I suppose, but we all have our little faults—in some cases, not so little, perhaps."

Pierre smiled. "Let he who is without sin cast the first stone," he said.

"Precisely," said Father Heaney. He hesitated, as if uncertain whether to say something, but then he remarked, "Do you believe in the existence of good and evil, Pierre? I mean, not just vague concepts of good and evil, but actual good and evil that you can see and touch?"

Pierre looked away. He did not like probing questions like this. He did not like being asked whether he believed in God, even though he studied theology and was in attendance at a pontifical university. He considered these issues private, although he accepted that in many respects they were very public matters on which a stand might need to be taken. Perhaps I lack courage, he thought.

"I think I do," he said.

"Just think?"

"Yes. It's just that I'm not sure whether the dividing lines are always as clear as all that."

Pierre was aware that the Benedictine was staring at him through narrowed eyes. For a few moments he thought that he had over-stepped the mark—that Father Heaney would take offence at his condescending answer—not that he had intended to condescend, but that was the way it must have sounded. But the cleric relaxed, and then bowed his head in a gesture of assent. "You're right. You're quite right. These things are complex . . . And yet, even if they are nuanced, right and wrong still exist, as I'm sure you will agree."

Pierre seized the opportunity to make amends. "Of course. Yes, I completely agree."

Father Heaney came closer to him. They were alone in one of the rooms of the gallery; alone with Caravaggio and Ghirlandaio, and a few other silent witnesses. He lowered his voice. "Monsieur Citroën, I have been asked by His Eminence to . . ." His voice lowered even further. Now it was not much more than a whisper. ". . . to sound you out about an offer of employment. I believe that you have no firm plans as yet as to what to do after graduation."

Pierre found himself whispering his response. "No, I don't."

"Good. Well, as you may or may not know, we have our own secret service."

Pierre gave an involuntary start.

"No, you should not be surprised. The Holy See is a state. We have international legal personality. We have diplomatic represen-tation and we accredit ambassadors here at the Vatican. We have a police force and the Swiss Guards, who are a militia. We have a railway station and courts and we make treaties. We have observer status at the United Nations. In view of all that, it makes sense that we should have a secret service as well."

For a few moments, Pierre said nothing. Then he whispered, "I understand."

"Our secret service used to be called the Holy Alliance," Father Heaney continued. "Today it is called the Entity. It is one of the oldest, if not *the* oldest secret service in the world. Five centuries is a long history in espionage.

"We are staffed by a mixture of lay and clerical agents. I believe in calling a spade a spade, and so I don't mind using the term "spy." We have spies in all the world's major capitals. We share intelligence with sympathetic agencies. We have worked with Mossad and with MI6. We have pitted our wits against the opposition in the form of the NKVD and KGB, as it was in its earlier incarnations. We know a great deal, Monsieur Citroën, about everything. We are shocked by nothing. *Nihil humanum mihi alienum est,* I always say.

"Of course, we need to recruit, and that is something that we do with great caution. Every agent is vetted personally by C, as His Eminence is known in the service. If he disapproves of a potential recruit, then the matter stops right there. If he approves, then the candidate embarks on a one-year training programme. This includes cryptology, the trade craft of espionage, electronic monitoring techniques, and theology. In your case, you would be exempted from the theological element because you have already studied theology to degree level.

"It is not a career without danger. We have lost good agents in our battle against the forces of evil. There are pitfalls at every turn. The hours are long. It is difficult, sometimes, for our lay agents to have a normal family life, as they may have to travel a great deal. However, we do what we can to ensure that the needs of our staff are met. We have a very good dental care programme.

"Engagement is for a period of five years initially, although people may leave at any time if their conscience dictates it or if they lose their faith in what we are doing. Everybody within the service believes in the rectitude of our mission. We could not operate were it not for that complete dedication."

Father Heaney stopped. "I have given you rather a lot to think about, I suspect. You will no doubt wish to consider what I have said before you give us your answer. His Eminence, though, would appreciate a decision by next Tuesday, if possible." He reached into his pocket and took out a slip of paper, which he passed on to Pierre. "Here is his direct line. I shall drop out of the process after this, as he prefers to deal directly with recruits. You will not hear from me again."

The cleric looked at him, his expression serious at first. Then his face broke into a smile. "I imagine you didn't anticipate this when you agreed to meet me today."

Pierre returned the smile. There was a release of tension now, on both sides. "No, I wasn't sure what to expect. I had thought I might be offered a scholarship or something of that sort—but not a job. And certainly not a job of this nature."

"Nobody ever does," said Father Heaney. "It is my lot in life to surprise people."

They began to make their way out of the gallery. It was warm outside, now—almost too warm to stand in the sun. They stood there and prepared to say goodbye, as they were going off in different directions. Pierre suddenly said, "I saw you earlier on, I think."

Father Heaney looked up. "Me?"

"Yes. I saw you by the lake. I guessed it was you—and I was right."

Somewhere behind them in the gardens a cicada struck up its shrill call.

"You were talking to a friend," Pierre continued.

Father Heaney did not respond. Pierre felt uncomfortable. The congenial atmosphere of their earlier meeting had now been replaced by something very different. Perhaps I should not have said that, thought Pierre.

"I think you were mistaken," said Father Heaney. "There are many people in the gardens. You must have seen somebody else."

Pierre was taken aback by the abrupt denial. Did the secretary seriously expect him to deny the evidence of his own senses? He felt annoyed. He would not be doubted in this way.

"I couldn't help but overhear you," he said. "I think you were discussing the *filioque* issue." That, he thought, would show Father Heaney that he was not imagining things.

The secretary's eyes narrowed. "I think you are compounding your mistake, Monsieur Citroën," he said. "And if I were you, I would say no more about it." He paused. "I take it that you understand me?"

Pierre swallowed. There was a note of icy menace in the other man's voice, and all he wanted now was to be away from him. Enrico was right, he thought. These people are not to be engaged with lightly. "I'm sorry," he said. "Subject closed."

"Good," said Father Heaney, abruptly, and turned on his heel. He did not say goodbye.

THE FOLLOWING MONDAY, Pierre spoke to his ecclesiastical history professor, an American Jesuit, Monsignor Henry Downside. The monsignor was a helpful man whom he had always found approachable, and who seemed to know everything there was to know about the complex history of the Church. He had written a commentary on the history of the papacy, a multi-volume work that ran to over four thousand closely printed pages. And even that generous allocation had obliged him, he confessed, to omit a great deal of detail that he would, in an ideal world, have wished to include.

"Professor," Pierre began, "do you know much about the Vatican secret service?"

The monsignor smiled. "I hope I don't know too much," he said, looking over his shoulder in a theatrical way. "There are some topics about which it is wise not to have too much knowledge—if you get my meaning."

Pierre considered this. Once again, he realised that he was being warned—although the warning on this occasion was a veiled one.

"Having said that," the monsignor continued, "there is a great deal of information about these people that is there in the history books—and much of it is distasteful. Certainly, if one looks at the activities of the Holy Alliance in the past, one is struck by its utter ruthlessness. The seventeenth century, for example, was particularly unedifying. That, as you may recall from my lectures—if you were indeed listening, dear Monsieur Citroën . . ." And here the monsignor smiled in that gentle, accepting way of professors who know that not all their students remain awake throughout their lectures . . . "as I am sure you were, of course, then you will recall that at that point the Vatican was a hotbed of intrigue and deeply involved in power struggles within France and Spain."

The monsignor sighed as he contemplated the labyrinthine complexities of European courts of the age. "However, temporal power, I suppose, inevitably involves a struggle for dominance. And that means that agents of the powerful will be pitted against one another, spying on each other, doing whatever they can to advance their particular cause. Such is human nature."

That observation prompted a further sigh. "I might give you an example," he went on. "Espionage provokes counter-espionage. During the reign of Louis XIV, French spies were particularly active in Rome and they even succeeded in establishing a network within the Vatican's secretariat of state. They had three priests in the Vatican archives department. Their job was to copy documents—which they did. They made extra copies, though, and passed these on to France's representatives in Rome. The Vatican suspected this was going on, having learned that there was a network of spies and that its leader had the code-name of Scipio. That has a modern ring to it, doesn't it? Major spies in our own times have often had classical-sounding code-names. Nothing changes, you see, Monsieur Citroën: very little in human affairs is new. But then, I am an historian, and I suppose people would expect me to say that."

The professor continued his story. "Let us return," he said, "to a fresh spring day in May, 1687—only yesterday, in Church history terms. The head of the Vatican's spy network at the time was one Cardinal Paluzzi, a man of considerable power. He was told by his agents that the document-copying departments always seemed to make one more copy of every confidential document than was required. What happened to these extra copies? Minolta spy cameras did not exist in those days, of course, and a spy could hardly carry a portable camera obscura with him . . ."

Pierre realised that this was a joke, and he smiled, even if so belatedly that Monsignor Downside looked a bit disappointed.

"Anyway," continued the cleric, "Cardinal Paluzzi ordered his toughest agents, the monks of the Black Order, to arrest one of the copyists—a monk himself—and to torture him until he revealed the names of his fellow spies. He was then killed and hung up from beneath a bridge. Attached to the body was a small piece of black cloth with two red stripes on it. That was the calling card of the Black Order."

He paused, and Pierre wondered whether this was to emphasise that he should remember this detail.

"Since then, the methods of the Holy Alliance have become less, how shall I put it, less robust? But they still operate in the murky world of espionage and consort with toughened agents of the secret services of other states. There is nothing you can teach the Holy See about survival, you know. They are not naïve. Nor are they un-worldly. They know where their interest lies and they will pursue that with all the determination of those who are satisfied that right is on their side."

The monsignor paused to draw breath. Suddenly his expression changed, as if a thought had just occurred to him. "Have you been *approached*, Monsieur Citroën?" he asked.

Pierre hesitated. He had not intended to reveal any details of his conversation with Father Heaney, but it seemed that Monsignor Downside had guessed what had prompted his interest. He hesitated, but he was by nature frank and did not want to hide the truth from his professor. "Yes," he replied at last. "They've spoken to me—indirectly, of course, but they made their intentions clear enough."

The monsignor absorbed this information gravely. "And have you responded?"

Pierre shook his head. "I have to let them know by tomorrow."

"They haven't given you much time."

"No. And I find myself uncertain as to what to do. A bit of me is flattered by the invitation. Lots of people would love to be asked to be a spy, wouldn't they?"

The monsignor raised an eyebrow. "It appeals to a certain sort, perhaps. Many spies are misfits. They may be people who have been disappointed by the world. They may be people wanting to settle old scores with a fate that has not given them what they feel they are entitled to in life. They may be locked in battle with a deceased parent or they may be looking for a father. They may think that espionage will give them an importance that they don't have in their ordinary life. They may want approval, and find it in the praise given them by their handler. There may be many factors at play, many of them based on some pathology of the soul."

Pierre was silent. It was obvious to him that Professor Downside considered spying to be a very inferior occupation.

"Of course," the monsignor went on, "the decision must be yours. I would not presume to influence you in any way, but you should be aware of the nature of the choice you are being asked to make. Do you want to spend your life in the shadows? Now there *are* shadows, and it is the lot of some to work within them or, indeed, on their periphery, in their liminal territory. But if you are one who prefers to be in the clear light of day, then perhaps it is best not to dwell in penumbral regions. That's all I am saying—no more than that." He paused. "Do you get the drift of what I'm saying?"

Pierre nodded. "I understand, Professor."

"Good," said Monsignor Downside. "That is all that I could wish for in any of my students' understanding."

THAT EVENING, Pierre knocked on the door of his friend, Alain, further down the corridor in the students' living quarters. He heard his friend's voice reply from within and he entered the room. Alain was at his desk, struggling with a passage of New Testament Greek. He looked up at his friend and smiled. "You know something, Pierre? You're really fortunate you don't have to learn Greek. Never, ever forget that."

"At least it isn't Finnish," said Pierre. "I gather that's a really difficult language."

"That's why there are only five million Finns," said Alain. "If Finnish were easier, then there would be far more of them."

Pierre laughed.

"By the way," said Alain. "Who was your monastic friend?"

Pierre looked puzzled. "Friend?" he asked. "I'm sorry, I don't know what you mean."

"Your visitor, earlier today."

Pierre shook his head. "I didn't have a visitor."

"Well, I saw him coming out of your room," Alain explained. "I was coming back to my room and I saw him coming out of your door. He didn't see me, but I saw him. He disappeared down the corridor."

Pierre's puzzlement deepened. "A monk?"

"Well, he was in monastic garb."

"Did you see his face?" asked Pierre.

"No. I didn't."

Pierre sat down. "I need to tell you about something," he said.

He started with the letter from the cardinal. Then he went on to describe seeing Father Heaney and his furtive meeting beside the lake. Finally, he recounted his conversation with Monsignor Downside. Alain listened without interrupting him. When he had finished, he rose from his seat and went to gaze out of the window. It was from there that he addressed his friend, not turning round as he spoke.

"There's only one conclusion you can draw about this Heaney character," he said. "He's a double agent. You saw him meeting with a contact from the other side. He must have been passing him sensitive documents. It's a classic drop, as they call it in espionage circles."

Pierre wondered what the documents might have been.

"Something to do with the *filioque* controversy," said Alain. "You said you heard them talking about that."

"But . . ." began Pierre.

He was interrupted. "You need to tell C. You have to warn him."

Pierre was about to reply to this when he stopped himself. *How did Alain know about C?* He had said nothing about that being the cardinal's acronym. He was positive about that, which suggested that Alain knew more than he might be owning up to knowing.

He decided to test his supposition. "You mean the cardinal?" he asked.

Alain replied quite naturally. "Yes, him . . ." Then his voice trailed away as he realised that he had fallen into a trap.

Now Pierre was certain. "How do you know about C?" he asked.

Alain opened his mouth to reply, then he closed it. He turned round to face his friend. "Because I'm in the Entity," he said quietly. "I have been one of its agents for over a year now. I'm on a Holy Alliance scholarship here—all my fees are paid—and any dental costs."

That was all the confirmation Pierre needed. He remembered that Father Heaney had said something about the secret service's dental plan. Alain knew about it, and that meant he was telling the truth.

"I don't know what to do," he said weakly. "What if Father Heaney finds out that I've reported him to C as a possible double agent?"

Alain looked sympathetic. "You'll be in danger," he said.

"I don't know what to do," Pierre repeated, his voice cracking with emotion. "I never asked to get caught up in all this *filioque* business."

Alain understood. "I agree, your position is rather sensitive." He thought for a moment. Then he suggested that they go to Pierre's room and check to see if anything had been disturbed. "They may have planted a bug," said Alain. "That's the sort of thing they do."

They went quickly down the corridor and Pierre unlocked his door. Once in his room, Alain raised a finger to his lips to signify the need for silence. Pierre nodded his assent. Then he saw what had happened. He pointed to an open drawer in his desk. Tearing a piece of paper from a notebook he wrote: *My notes on the* filioque *controversy—gone.*

Alain read the note. He looked grave. Then he wrote his reply, *You should get out immediately—like now! Pronto!*

MONSIGNOR DOWNSIDE was both helpful and reassuring. When Pierre went to see him the following day, he listened carefully to what he had to say about the break-in and the removal of his notes on the *filioque* controversy. After he had finished, he shook his head sadly. "Typical of their methods," he said. "Typical."

"I want to go home," said Pierre. "I want to go home to France. I want to return to Bordeaux."

"That sounds very wise," said the monsignor. "You know what my favourite Bordeaux wine is? I'll tell you: Pauillac. I have some 2009 in my cellar. Gorgeous. And I have two cases of 2015 Margaux—a secondary wine from a very good estate and therefore a terrific bargain."

"Will you be able to speak to the college?" asked Pierre. "I've almost finished my course. I could write my final exam in Bordeaux—under supervision, of course."

"I shall make it my business to ensure that you get permission to do just that," said Monsignor Downside. "I also have some rather good Graves, you know. Last time I was in Bordeaux I visited several of the chateaux there. I also went to Sauternes and tried some dry Sauternes. People forget that they make dry Sauternes—and some of it is very fine indeed. Did you know that you can have Sauternes with *pâté de foie gras*? Did you know that? People think that you should only have it with dessert, but they are very wrong, you know."

PIERRE RETURNED TO BORDEAUX two days later. His parents met him at the airport, where his mother flung her arms about him and his father, grinning with pleasure, slapped his shoulder several times. The following week he wrote his final examination under the supervision of the deputy principal of a local technical college. He achieved a distinction in that subject, as well as an overall distinction in his degree results.

"What now?" asked his father.

It was a question that Pierre knew he could answer in such a way as to make his father happy. That answer, though, also reflected what he now knew he wanted himself. "I'd like to be a wine *négociant*, Father. Will you take me into the business?"

"Oh, my dear boy," said his father, struggling to hold back his tears. "My heart is overflowing with joy."

Pierre proved to have all of his father's abilities—and even more. He made astute purchases of parcels of fine wines and found a good market for them. The customers liked him. Sometimes he discussed theology with them, but not very often, which was a relief to the customers.

Two years later he married Annette de Quarante-Cinq, the daughter of a couple who owned a small chateau and a moderately productive vineyard. Their wines were highly regarded and were even served by Air France—in economy class. Pierre was welcomed into the family, as his new father-in-law had blood pressure issues and was keen to retire. After his retirement, le Comte de Quarante-Cinq and his wife went to live in the Auvergne, where they had a house on top of a hill and where his blood pressure tended to come down. It was something to do with altitude, he explained, but Pierre was not sure whether there was any medical basis to the explanation.

Pierre and Annette ran the vineyard. They had two daughters, both of whom were keen dancers. Pierre never thought again of the *filioque* issue, although one evening he had a dream in which he was back in Rome, in the Borghese Gardens, he thought. He came across a man sitting on a bench who turned to him, and said, in the dream, "You know something about the *filioque*? It doesn't matter. It just doesn't matter."

And then he awoke, and he was back in their comfortable small chateau, in the early morning, with the shoots of a creeper tapping at the window, and the sun on the vines and distant hilltops, and the sound of the wind, the gentle wind, which might have been a spirit, perhaps, and possibly was. Who knew?

He got out of bed. It was a big day at the winery: wine that had spent two years in the barrel was bottled. He was pleased with the vintage in question and had high hopes for it, as had several wine writers. They had been enthusiastic, and one of them, the correspondent of a major American wine magazine, was coming for lunch that day. Pierre would present him with a signed bottle in an oak case.

The wine writer arrived shortly before lunch. Pierre met him outside the chateau and showed him into the cellar. "Here," he said, reaching for the bottle they had prepared for their visitor. "Here is our new wine."

The writer looked at the label. "*Filioque?*" he asked. "Nice name for a wine."

"Do you think so?"

The writer nodded. "Yes. Good choice." He paused. He looked puzzled. "What does it mean?"

Pierre smiled. "It's complicated," he said. "And it's time for lunch."

THE
EXQUISITE ART
OF
GETTING EVEN

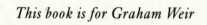
This book is for Graham Weir

Sweet Vengeance

AN INTRODUCTION

A DESIRE FOR REVENGE IS SOMETHING THAT EVERY ONE OF US MUST have felt at one time or another, unless, of course, we are saints—which most of us are not. Somebody wrongs us and, as we nurse our pain and sense of injustice, we imagine the wrongdoer having exactly the same thing done to him or her—or even worse. This is revenge: the biter bit, and it is very satisfactory, a great theme for Elizabethan drama.

Why—and whether—we should feel that way about revenge is a question that has interested students of human nature as much as it has troubled philosophers. The impulse to exact revenge is undoubtedly strong in the human psyche: one only has to observe the behaviour of small children to see how it rears its head at a very early stage. As W. H. Auden observed in his much appreciated (although subsequently suppressed) poem "September 1, 1939": *I and the public know / What all schoolchildren learn / Those to whom evil is done / Do evil in return.* Auden was talking about political pathology, based on international wrongs, but the same observation might be made about our ordinary quotidian experience.

Where does this desire for revenge come from? At its heart, there seems to be some notion of justice and reciprocity. What you do to others, you must expect to be done to you—that seems only fair. If we are to live together in harmony, it might be argued, it is important that the scales be balanced—everyone must understand that those who seek an unfair advantage over others will pay for what they do.

But, strictly speaking, that is not so much revenge as retribution. Revenge is more personal—it is an action performed with a view to satisfying the feelings of one who has been wronged. Revenge has nothing to do with ensuring social peace or correcting any imbalance. It is invoked purely to make the wronged person feel better. Revenge is quite different from dispassionate retribution or correction: it is for this reason that revenge has been described as "wild justice."

Of course, that does not make revenge morally right. In fact, seeking revenge has always made philosophers feel uncomfortable. Exacting revenge adds to the sum total of human suffering, rather than subtracts from it. And, in terms of the recovery of the victim, there is a lot to be said for showing mercy and forgiveness rather than insisting on revenge. Forgiveness is more healing than the infliction of pain: there is ample evidence for that proposition, as any study of conflict resolution will tend to confirm. You don't necessarily get better by making another suffer.

And yet, we remain fascinated by revenge, which still plays a part in our affairs no matter how hard we try to overcome the urge to get even. We should not delude ourselves, though, as to the sterility of revenge. No Sicilian or Appalachian blood feud was ever ended by the taking of revenge, and we would do well to remind ourselves of that. Having said that, I am reminded of the story of the Spanish conquistador who, on his death bed, is asked by his confessor whether he has forgiven his enemies. "Enemies?" he replies. "I have no enemies, Father. I have killed them all."

THE FOUR STORIES THAT follow are all tales of revenge. Each has a particular background in terms of something that I have experienced or thought about. The first story, "Vengeance Is Mine," occurred to me after I had paid a visit to a small Caribbean island some years ago. There was only one town of any consequence on this island, and that was more of a village than a town. Yet, as I walked down the main street there, a very large and extremely ostentatious car made its way down the road. I saw that the driver was a comparatively young man. Now, there are various ways of acquiring such a car, some of them even honest. I had the distinct impression that this car, though, might have been the fruit of less than honest activity. This was just a suspicion, but I'm afraid I thought of drug money. I may have been doing the owner a gross injustice, but it had that feel to me. And that was when the idea for this story occurred to me. What if somebody came back to his island, dripping in money? What if somebody on the island took moral exception to him?

I changed the setting, and it became an island off Scotland's west coast. Yet all islands have something in common: people take a close interest in the affairs of others, and, in some cases at least, there are people who don't like to see others getting away with things they should not get away with. In Scotland, our Calvinist background underlines that. We still believe that people should pay for their transgressions. We still disapprove. We still rather enjoy seeing tall poppies cut down where they stand. All of which might deter a gangster from considering taking up residence on the Hebridean island of Mull.

Vengeance Is Mine

———◆◆◆———

MURDO HAD A FISHING BOAT. AT TWENTY-EIGHT FEET, IT WAS NOT considered a large one, but it was a good sea-keeper, and he could venture out, if he so desired, in all but the most severe weather. Down below was a Ford Dover marine diesel engine, over thirty years old, that had never once declined to start; nor had it ever faltered for a moment in its constant, patient thudding. "The boat's heartbeat," he said of that sound.

He lived on Mull, an island off the west coast of Scotland. To the north lay Skye and its attendant small isles—Rum, Eigg, Canna, and the evocatively named Muck. The small isles were home to a handful of people—fifteen, in the case of Canna, while Muck somehow supported enough to have a tiny school, with a single teacher. Murdo's island was considerably bigger and had a population of several thousand people, living on farms and smallholdings dotted amongst its hills and modest glens. There was one town, Tobermory, and a smattering of villages. Here and there, harbours tucked away on the island's jagged coast were home to a small number of fishing vessels, of which Murdo's boat, the *Iolaire*, was one. *Iolaire* means "eagle" in Gaelic, and Murdo had a sea eagle, wings wide in flight, painted just off the bow, on the port side. The painting was the work of his cousin's son, who fancied himself as an artist but was not very good at portraying birds, or anything else, really. The eagle seemed to have only one eye and its talons were far from aquiline, resembling, some said, the feet of a greylag goose. But Murdo was loyal and would hear no criticism of his nephew's artistic endeavours.

Murdo's house was no more than a stone's throw from the harbour in which he kept the *Iolaire*. The village itself was on the west side of the island, looking out past a cluster of small islets—mostly tidal rocks—towards the Treshnish Isles and then to Coll. Beyond that was the Sea of the Hebrides, the stretch of water known as the Minch, and the final outposts of Scotland, the outer isles of Barra, Mingulay, the Uists, and, as a lonely afterthought, the abandoned isles of St. Kilda. Then there was nothing until Canada, across mile upon mile of empty Atlantic, vast, cold fields on which pelagic fish were hunted.

Murdo was forty-eight and had the strength and robust health of one who spent his life out of doors, earning his living under an open sky. Unlike some of the islanders, whose fondness for whisky was well known, Murdo was temperate in his drinking habits. He liked peaty whiskies from the distilleries of Islay, to the south, but he would never take more than a single dram on any evening, and he always diluted whisky with water, an act of chemistry that he said improved both liquids considerably.

He had been married once but now described himself as a bachelor. It was possible that he was divorced: his wife, Helen, had served him with papers to that effect, but he had tossed them aside unread. He had no time for lawyers and their wiles. It made no difference to him. She had assured him that she would never ask him for money, as she was well provided for by her new partner, the proprietor of a successful fish-and-chip van in Glasgow, and since Murdo had no intention of ever marrying again, his matrimonial status, it seemed to him, was of no significance. It was no business of the government, nor of anybody else, he thought, whether he was married or not.

He had met her at a dance in Tobermory, when he was in his early thirties. She had been working as a barmaid in a hotel, a rambling Victorian building that clung to a clifftop overlooking the Sound of Mull. One day, people said, the hotel would fall into the sea, but they were talking nonsense, as the cliff edge was a good way away and had shown no sign of getting any closer. Helen was six years younger than he was and came from Gourock, a town on the Clyde, not far from Glasgow. She had been given the job at the hotel on the strength of her appearance—she was strikingly good-looking, in a rather blousy way, prompting the hotel manager to whisper to his wife, "Barmaid material, if ever there was. Put her behind the bar, and we're in business."

After they had married and settled back in the village, Helen quickly became bored. Her job now was to drive the day's catch to the other side of the island, where it would be loaded on a boat that plied regularly between Mull and Oban. She did not like this work, which she said should be done by a man. "I'm not designed to howk fish about," she said.

He laughed at that. There were all those old photographs of women carrying fish baskets on their backs uncomplainingly. She must have seen them. "Remember the herring girls? Remember them? They did all that work up and down the coast. No complaint from them, was there?"

She pouted. "Poor women," she said and shook her head.

"Just them?" he challenged. People were always going on about how hard it was for women, but what about men? It was hard for everybody, he thought. "What about the men? They went out in all manner of seas. Swept overboard and drowned. What about them?"

"Poor men," she said.

In spite of Helen's distaste for the work she was expected to do, they somehow got by. Then, one June, on a brilliant summer day, when Ben More, the highest mountain on the island, was sharp against the sky, she packed a suitcase and caught the bus that went over the hill. At Craignure she boarded the ferry to Oban, where she took another bus all the way down to Glasgow. There she stayed for a few days with her younger sister, having left a message for Murdo that she might be back in a few weeks' time, or might not. It was probably best, she said, for him not to expect her.

The sister was a regular at a ballroom called the Palais de Dance, one of the dance halls that injected a bit of glitter into the hard lives of working-class Glaswegians. She took Helen there three nights in a row, and on the third night she met a man called Andy McNiven.

"Andy has a fish-and-chip van," her sister said, on introducing them.

"And pies," said Andy.

"Yes, and pies," the sister confirmed.

"That's great," said Helen.

She and Andy got on well. He offered her a job in the fish-and-chip van because his wife, who had helped him for years, had gone off with a sailor from the nuclear submarine base on the Holy Loch.

After a month, Andy asked Helen to marry him. "I never actually married Maggie," he said. "People thought we were married, but we weren't. Not legally, if you see what I mean."

Helen explained that she thought that she and Murdo were probably still legally married but that she would see a lawyer and change all that. "I think you have some forms to fill in, and then you go and see the sheriff, and that's that," she said.

"Sounds simple enough," said Andy.

SOME YEARS LATER, a friend said to Murdo, "Looking back at it, Murdo, do you regret marrying Helen? Of course, don't answer if you think the question is too personal."

Murdo considered this for a few moments. He did not have to think for long before replying, "Not really. We weren't a brilliant match, but that wasn't her fault. I shouldn't have asked her to marry me. That's down to me. You get what you ask for, you see."

The friend frowned. "You mean—what goes around, comes around? That sort of thing."

"Aye," said Murdo. "You get what you deserve, I think. In general, that is."

The friend looked out of the window. They were in Murdo's kitchen at the time, a pot of strong tea on the table before them. "Do you think so?" he asked.

Murdo nodded. "I think so. Yes. I've always felt that. If you do something wrong, then sooner or later . . ." He shrugged. "Sooner or later, you'll suffer the consequences."

"I'm not so sure," said the friend. "I think that a lot of folk get away with it, especially these days, when everything's gone to the dogs. You know how it is—nobody cares any longer about who does what."

Murdo looked at his friend. He was right, he thought. He shook his head. "You may have a point, Donald," he said. "In the old days—"

Donald interrupted him. He smiled. "When exactly were the old days, Murdo?"

"The day before yesterday," came the answer. "When you and I were young, Donald. In the old days, if you did something you shouldn't do, you knew that you'd pay for it."

"Which is why people were a bit better behaved," mused Donald.

"Perhaps. There were policemen then . . . You saw them in the street. Even in Tobermory. There was that Constable Frazer— remember him, Donald? Big fellow with red hair. You wouldn't cross him, sure enough."

"He gave that Billy Jamieson a clip round the ear," Donald remembered. "Taught him not to help himself to other people's lobster pots."

"That was before human rights," said Murdo. "Human rights stopped that sort of . . . What do they call it? Some fancy name. Community policing?" He sighed. "Changed days. People can do pretty much as they please."

"Looks like it," said Donald. "No avenging angel. No justice. Nothing."

Donald brought the conversation back to Helen and her departure. "You've been by yourself for a long time now," he said. "Ever thought of getting yourself fixed up again?"

Murdo shook his head. "Not really. I'm all right with my own company. I'm comfortable enough." He paused. "And now I'm an elder of the kirk, you know. That keeps me busy."

Donald understood. He had heard about his friend's appointment as a church elder—it had been in the *Oban Times*—but had forgotten to congratulate him.

"That's a very important position," he said.

Murdo nodded. "The new minister is a breath of fresh air," he said. "That last fellow was too . . . How shall I put it? Too wishy-washy. I'm not sure he believed in very much. This new one has very clear ideas. He can't be doing with all this liberal theology stuff."

"This new one believes in judgement?"

"Definitely," said Murdo. "Of other people, of course."

"Of course."

"There's nothing wrong with a day of judgement," Murdo remarked. "People get uneasy these days if you start talking about that sort of thing. But just not mentioning something doesn't mean it isn't there, does it?"

It took Donald a little while to sort that question out. Then he replied, "We'll pay for it, you know. We're creating a hell for ourselves right here—let alone anything down below. People rampage around. They show no respect for anybody else. It's not right, Murdo—it's not right. We need to try to get our sense of justice back. We need to teach people that if you behave badly, you'll get it. It's as simple as that."

"You're right there," agreed Murdo.

Donald looked regretful. "Too late," he said. "Too late for any of that, Murdo. Things have . . . How do they put it these days? Things have *moved on*."

"I haven't moved on," Murdo said meditatively. "And I don't think it's too late, you know."

Donald would remember those words later on. *I don't think it's too late.*

NOR DID THE NEW minister at the church near the harbour think it was too late. He was called the Reverend Lachlan Maclean, and he came from Stornoway, on one of the largest of the outer islands. He had been brought up in a Gaelic-speaking household but was perfectly bilingual and felt as confident—and as convinced—in English as he felt in Gaelic. He was a graduate of New College, the divinity school of the University of Edinburgh and, thanks to a St. Andrew's Society scholarship, of the Union Theological Seminary at Princeton. At Princeton, he had written a thesis on Calvin and won a prestigious prize for an essay on the concept of sin, subsequently published under the title *The Rehabilitation of Sin.* The Reverend Maclean was in no doubt about the existence of sin, and he strongly disputed the notion that wrongdoing was a relative notion, its contours defined by individual preference. "We all know exactly what sin is," he said, with that directness for which he was widely admired. "Sins, you see, are things you shouldn't do, and we all know what those things are. They are the same for all times and all places, and for all men. No problem there, if you ask me. That's about as clear as anything ever can be."

The Reverend Maclean had no time for modernisers. He was particularly appalled by efforts to prune the hymnary of wordings and concepts that might be considered old-fashioned. In the view of some of these modernisers, all references to the Devil should be removed from hymns or liturgy, as there was no real reason to conclude that such a being as the Devil actually existed. "The fools," pronounced the Reverend Maclean. "Saying that the Devil doesn't exist is exactly what he wants you to say. Make no mistake about that. Beelzebub kens these things fine. That's the precise script he'd write for us if he had the time. These people don't realise it, but they are playing right into his sulphurous hands." He paused. "And when they die—those so-called liberal theologians—oh, my goodness, are they going to suffer. It almost makes me feel sympathetic towards them, but then I remind myself—they had it coming to them."

Murdo enjoyed the Reverend Maclean's sermons. He did not mind their length—they lasted, on average, just under an hour—as they were firm in their disapproval of everything that he happened to disapprove of himself: moral relativism, first and foremost, and then, in no particular order, immodest clothing, vulgar television, badly behaved children, London, Roman Catholicism, Sunday football, and a variety of other issues on which the fringes of Scotland were at odds with the zeitgeist. As he sat there and listened to the minister's condemnation of these insidious influences, Murdo found himself imagining what it would be like locally were the dreadful day of judgement to dawn, as clearly promised in the scriptures. He had no doubt but that he and the Reverend Maclean would be spared the divine retribution—not to say revenge—that would be visited on the land, but he had his doubts about some others, including a few of his neighbours. There would certainly be some gnashing of teeth in the bars of Tobermory as the drinkers and wastrels were driven out into the street to face the brimstone awaiting them; and there was that deckhand on the MacBrayne's ferry who was always flirting outrageously with the female passengers—he would have something to answer for on that day. Oh, he would grovel and apologise, but it would be too late, and he would be tipped down into the infernal regions of perpetual fire. It would all be very satisfactory, and it gave Murdo a warm feeling to picture it, even though he knew that it was, unfortunately, rather unlikely to occur in his own lifetime. People had been waiting for the dreadful day of judgement for years now, and it had never arrived. It was most disheartening.

Murdo knew that the local sinners were hardly a patch on some of the sinners you encountered in places like Glasgow and, even more so, London. Paris, too, was another place where sinners were thick on the ground. He had heard that France in general was a dreadful place for sinning, and quite shameless about it. Of course, they were French, and the French had had nobody like John Knox to set them straight. They were hedonists, through and through, sitting about in their cafés, drinking coffee, and talking about the sort of thing that the French like to talk about. They would pay for it eventually, he was sure, but in the meantime he had to admit that they seemed to be having rather a good time.

Murdo felt that although there were undoubtedly some sinners on Mull, there were not all that many, and none of them were really conspicuously evil. One spring day, though, everything changed, and a significant sinner—the real McCoy—arrived on Mull and announced his intention of staying. This was news, and it travelled quickly up and down the island, eventually reaching Murdo as he tied the *Iolaire* to the harbour pier and began to unload his iced and already crated catch.

A farmhouse just outside the village had been on the market for some time. Now, Murdo heard, it had been bought, and the new owner had already been to inspect it before the painters moved in. Donald gave Murdo this news as he watched him hosing down his deck with the harbour hose.

"The new owner is not short of cash," said Donald. "He's from Fort William originally. Name of McCoy. I've heard about him from folk up there. Not good."

Murdo frowned. "Why's he coming here, then? What's wrong with Fort William?"

"I'm told they don't want him there," said Donald. "I'm told that the boys over there didn't want him about the place."

"If the boys don't want you . . ."

"Yes. And these were boys he had been at school with, mind."

Murdo looked thoughtful. "Sometimes people are envious of success. If this boy went off somewhere and made his fortune, they might not like it back home. You know what people are like."

Donald did, but he quickly pointed out that this situation was not at all like that. "He went down south," he explained. "London. Then he was in Miami, I believe. He came back a rich man."

Murdo waited. It was not unheard of for people to go to America and return with a newly minted fortune in their pockets. There was money to be made over there, as Andrew Carnegie was to discover. Now Donald said, "Dirty money. None of it was legally acquired."

Murdo raised an eyebrow. "From?"

"Night clubs. Shady deals. That sort of thing."

"So, he was a gangster?" Murdo asked.

"So I've heard," said Donald.

Murdo grimaced. "Not the sort we want around here."

"No," said Donald. "Definitely not."

Then Murdo asked, "Have you met him yet?"

Donald shook his head. "I saw him when he was going up to take a look at the place. You could hardly miss his car—a muckle red Bentley. Sleekit. Long as your boat."

"Red?"

"Yes. Fire-engine red. It must have cost"—he shrugged before continuing—"hundreds of thousands."

"Not an honest car, then?"

Donald smiled. "Definitely not."

Murdo finished hosing down his deck. He looked up and saw that in the distance, just coming into view, there was a large, red car. "Speak of the Devil," he said.

. . .

ROBERT R. MCCOY, widely known as Rob Roy McCoy, drove his red Bentley Continental along the unpaved road that led to the farmhouse previously known as Tattie Mains but now dignified with the name South Ness House. He noted the bad condition of this road—which he now owned. Potholes, some of them filled with water that disguised their full extent, occurred every few yards, and here and there the rains had completely destroyed the camber. He had already spoken to a contractor, who had agreed to bring over a grader to sort out the problem, but until then the road was a serious threat to his Bentley's suspension.

The car was his pride and joy—a trophy, really, the most tangible sign of his success in life. He had bought it new in Edinburgh and driven it over to Fort William when he went back there to look up some of his old friends. That had not been a successful visit. He had intended to buy a house in the area and then to open a hotel or bar—not that he needed to, but in order to give him something to do. The coolness of his welcome, though, had persuaded him otherwise, and in impulse he had chosen to buy the house and its accompanying three hundred acres on the west coast of Mull.

Now he was here to spend a few months doing the place up and preparing it for when his long-term girlfriend, Kitty, arrived from Florida. She was a native of Belfast but had no desire to live in Ireland. "Scotland I can just about manage, Robbie," she said. "But Ireland, no. Never going back there. Never, but." It was an Ulster habit to add the word "but" to a comment, and Kitty did that frequently.

He had told her about Mull, and she had been lukewarm but came round to his view of things when he explained that they could divide their time between Mull and Marbella. Kitty did not like the heat, and so they would spend the summers in Mull, where it was always cool, and the winters in Marbella, when the temperature would be comfortable and not too extreme.

On this particular trip, Rob was to meet the interior decorator he had chosen to decorate their new home. Kitty was not particularly interested in such matters and had asked only that the living room should feature a bar with stools upholstered in zebra skin, or an artificial fabric representing zebra skin. "I'm not sure if zebras still exist," she had said to Rob. "Are they extinct yet, Robbie?"

Rob was not sure. "Perhaps," he said. "But you can still get zebra skin, I think."

"And the pool," she said, "I'd like that in a sort of conservatory. Make it infinity, like that pool we had in Florida, in the first house. I loved swimming right up to the edge and looking out towards the . . ." She faltered at that. Kitty was geographically challenged and was not quite sure of the name of the sea over which she had looked from her infinity pool.

"Caribbean," supplied Rob. "It's your actual Caribbean over there, Kitty."

"Whatever," said Kitty. "You'll know what I mean, but."

The decorator, who was due to arrive the following day, was called Bambi Trefoil. She lived in London and had decorated the Essex home of one of Rob's contacts, Tommy Jones. Tommy was unfortunately in prison now and unable to enjoy the luxurious surroundings that Bambi had prepared for him, but he took comfort in the knowledge that these were awaiting him on his release.

Rob was not going to interfere too much. Bambi had assured him that she would obtain all the furniture and fabrics needed to transform South Ness House into a suitable home for a man of his status. She would source these, she said—she used the word "source" as a verb a great deal—from a variety of suppliers and was confident that he would approve of what she provided.

Rob was intending to use local contractors as far as was possible, as he felt that it was important to show willingness to support the local economy. Although he was from Fort William, which was on the mainland and not on Mull, he still thought of himself as a local boy in these parts and he would not want people to think he had forgotten that. This plan, though, proved to be difficult to execute, as local contractors, for whatever reason, seemed unwilling to tender for the work.

"Not touching that with a bargepole," said one. "Thanks very much."

"I've put the work out to a whole range of local builders," his architect said. "But not one of them seems interested. Odd, that. You'd think they'd jump at the work."

Rob shrugged. He was indifferent to petty local opposition. Who were these people? Nobody. His car cost as much as their houses—possibly more. They should think about that from time to time. "Bring people in from Glasgow," he'd said. "Put them up at the local hotel. There are plenty of contractors down in Glasgow who'll take this on."

That proved to be the case, and for the last six weeks a variety of contractors—plumbers, plasterers, roofers, and joiners—had been working away to make the house ready for Bambi's finishing touches.

"My blank canvas," said Bambi, as Rob showed her round after her arrival. "The ideas are *flooding* into my head, Rob—flooding."

He had booked her into a hotel a few miles outside the village. He was staying in the house, in the main bedroom, in which there was already a bed and wardrobe, both obtained by Bambi.

"I sourced the wardrobe in the Chilterns," she said. "There's a dear little place there that sells French furniture. I just love it—love it to pieces. And the bed is pure Napoleon—pure Napoleon. *Très* imperial, Rob, as you'll have noticed."

They ate lunch together in the kitchen, on a table that Bambi had sourced in Inverness, with cutlery sourced from an auction in Perth. They had a steak and kidney pie sourced from the supermarket in Tobermory.

"So romantic," enthused Bambi. "*Déjeuner sur l'herbe*, almost. If we were outside, if you see what I mean."

"Cool," said Rob.

"Your name," Bambi said, looking at him over the rim of her wine glass, "wasn't there an earlier Rob Roy? Where have I heard of him?"

"There was," said Rob. "There was Rob Roy MacGregor. He was something of a wild man, but Scotland was pretty wild in those days. Everyone was an outlaw, more or less."

"So romantic," Bambi repeated. "That's what I like about this country. The romance. The mountains. Waterfalls. Sheep. It's all to die for."

On the third day of Bambi Trefoil's visit, Rob decided that he had fallen in love with her.

"As you know," he said, "I'm in a relationship. But I've been reviewing that, and I think it's time for me to come out of that relationship. I need to ask myself where I'm going in life."

This was what Bambi had been hoping to hear. She secretly liked rough, decisive men. And rough, decisive men who were also conspicuously solvent struck her as being particularly attractive. "You mean you need to emerge?" she said.

That was exactly right, thought Rob. "Yes, I need to emerge. And I think I am, you know. I think I am emerging."

Bambi listened. "I feel very much the same. I'm sort of mixed up with Trefoil, as you know, but he and I have got to the end of our mutual journey, I think. We've explored; we've flourished. But now we need to let one another go. We have to. It's a question of space for growth. And I'd be the last person—the very last—to deny him that space. I really mean that, you know."

"Space for growth is very important," agreed Rob. He was a fast learner, and he had acquired a facility with the sort of terminology Bambi liked to use. "You have to be free to fulfil your inner potential."

"You're so perceptive," said Bambi. "We speak the same language, I feel."

"Fate," said Rob. "You know what I get when I look at you and me, Bambi? I get future."

The following day, Rob sent a text message to Kitty. *Don't come after all,* he said. *I need a bit of space. Let's cool things for a while.* This was followed by an emoticon—a smiling face—and an "x."

She phoned him that afternoon. "Okay, Rob, tell me straight: it's Bambi, isn't it?"

He hesitated, but only for a few moments. "Yes," he said.

"So, it's about sex? Right?"

He drew in his breath. "No need to be crude," he said.

There was silence. Rob heard her breathing. Then she said, "If that's the way you want it, then that's the way you want it."

He said, "I'm glad that we can be grown up about it."

Relieved that this was dealt with, he took Bambi out for a drive in the red Bentley Continental.

"Lovely motor," said Bambi appreciatively.

They drove over to Tobermory, where Bambi sourced a scarf and a box of Scottish confectionary known as tablet. They each ate a piece as they sat in the Bentley, the radio tuned to a hard rock station in

Glasgow. People walking past stared at them with disapproval. They knew who Rob was. This was an island, and people knew.

One of the passers-by was the Reverend Lachlan Maclean, who was in Tobermory to do his weekly shop at the supermarket. He slowed down as he walked past the Bentley. He frowned. Rob caught his eye. He knew who the Reverend Maclean was. He smiled, but the minister turned his head away quickly and continued on his way to the supermarket.

"Who's that?" asked Bambi.

"The local minister," said Rob. "They're always like that. Miserable bunch. Sense of fun? Forget it!"

"He gave you a bit of a look," said Bambi. "Did you see it? Maybe he didn't like our music."

"Envy," replied Rob. "I'm used to it." Then he expanded, "You go off and make a bit of money. Then you come back, and what do you get? Envy! That's Scotland for you, Bambi."

Bambi nodded. Then she said, as if thinking of something for the first time, "I don't think I ever asked you, Rob: where did you make your money?"

Rob licked fragments of tablet off his fingers. "My money?"

"Yes." She gestured at the car around her; at the white leather upholstery; at the walnut fascia.

He tapped the side of his nose. "Business."

She looked at him. "But what sort of business?"

"Arranging things," said Rob. "Import, export. Think: deals."

"You were a sort of middleman? You sourced things?"

Rob nodded. That, he thought, would do. "I sometimes sourced things. Yes, I sourced."

"It's very satisfying, isn't it?"

Rob laughed. "Sourcing? Yes, it is. And lucrative."

"Getting people what they want is a real calling," observed Bambi. "That's how I view my own work, you know. I see a need in people—a need for beauty in their surroundings. And I give them what they are . . . what they are yearning for." She paused. "It's all about yearning, isn't it, Rob?"

He agreed.

. . .

TWO MONTHS PASSED. Now it was early August, and an area of high pressure settled over that part of Scotland, bringing long, warm days and a flat sea. Murdo went out fishing three days a week, but on other days he would make himself available for charter to small groups of visitors who wished to visit Fingal's Cave on Staffa, or cruise out to the Treshnish Isles in the hope of spotting basking sharks. There were birdwatchers, too, who were keen to see puffins and the other sea-birds that bred around that part of the coast. Murdo's boat was not ideal for these purposes, as it was slow and smelled permanently of fish, but these drawbacks added to the authenticity of the experience for those visitors who liked to drop a line for mackerel and quiz Murdo on the life of a real fisherman.

These outings were arranged through the nearby hotel, where a small notice informed guests that:

SMALL PARTY SEA TRIPS CAN BE ARRANGED WITH
A LOCAL SKIPPER.
SEE THE MIRACLE OF FINGAL'S CAVE
THAT INSPIRED MENDELSSOHN!
WATCH BASKING SHARKS AS THEY FILTER
PLANKTON THROUGH THEIR GREAT JAWS!
SEE THE COLOURFUL PUFFINS BOB
UP AND DOWN ON WAVES!

And it was on one of these trips that Kitty went after she had arrived at the hotel, having booked herself in for a week.

She was discreet, keeping to herself and taking her meals in the privacy of her room. During the day, she took walks along the shore, picking up and discarding shells and odd bits of driftwood. Her only outing was the booking she made for Murdo's boat, on which she planned to go out to Staffa.

Murdo was used to having at least three or four guests on the boat and found it strange to have just one. At first, there was little conversation, but after an hour or two, when they were well out to sea and the sun had come out from behind a cloud, Kitty began to talk.

"There's somebody living near here," she said. "A man by the name of McCoy. They call him Rob Roy sometimes."

Murdo inclined his head. He was not one to give too much away. "Could be," he said.

"Do you know him?" she asked.

He answered her with a question of his own. "Do you?"

She looked out across the gentle swell of the sea. "I do, as it happens."

He was watching her. "He's from Fort William originally. He hasn't been long in these parts."

She nodded. "I'm not surprised. He's on the run, you know. He's a gangster."

Murdo's eyes widened. This confirmed everything he had thought about Rob. "That car of his . . ." he began.

Her expression was one of disgust. "How do you think he bought that?"

Murdo let out a whistle of surprise. "I see. Well, a car like that couldn't be bought with honest money."

"No."

Murdo looked at her. "How do you know this?" he asked.

"I'm a police officer," lied Kitty.

Murdo's eyes grew wider.

"Our problem, though," Kitty went on, "is that we have no proof. We can't make a case against him. You know how these people are— they cover their tracks." She sighed. "So, I'm going to have to go back down to London empty-handed. That's it."

She watched his reaction. Then she said, in a tone of regret, "I sometimes think it's a great pity that local people can't take things into their own hands. You know—deal with people like that in their own way. You'd think they might be able to come up with some way of showing such people the door."

Murdo said nothing. They could see Staffa now. Off their starboard bow, a large white sea-bird, yellow-beaked, circled higher and higher, until it dropped into the water like a stone.

"Gannet," muttered Murdo. "They enter the water at sixty miles an hour, you know. Sixty."

He was thinking.

THE REVEREND LACHLAN MACLEAN sat in his sparsely furnished study. It was not a comfortable room—there was a desk, a metal filing cabinet, and a large, glass-fronted bookcase. There were three straight-backed chairs—one for the minister, and two for visitors. There were no rugs on the floor. On the wall behind the desk there was a picture of the Mount of Olives.

Murdo had put on a suit to visit the minister. The jacket was ill-fitting, as it had belonged to his father, who was a man of stouter build. The trousers, which had large turn-ups on the legs, were shiny at the knees.

The Reverend Maclean had fixed his cold blue eyes on Murdo. Neither was speaking. Then the minister broke the silence. "How very kind of her," he said.

Murdo nodded. "She has no particular connection with Mull," he said. "But she so appreciated the peacefulness of her stay here."

"And you say she's now gone?"

"Yes, she had to return to London."

"What a pity," said the Reverend Maclean. "I would have liked to have thanked her personally." He paused. "It's a very generous gift. Two thousand pounds is no small amount."

Murdo agreed. "I'm sure that the parish treasurer will find it useful," he said.

"Very," agreed the Reverend Maclean. He looked bemused. "And all this happened as a direct result of a trip out to Staffa?"

"Yes," said Murdo. "Sometimes I find that people are changed by the beauty of the sea. And the quiet, I suppose. It makes them think about their priorities."

"That's something we all need to do," agreed the Reverend Maclean. "We should examine ourselves regularly. We should open ourselves to grace."

"Yes," said Murdo. "We should do that, I think."

They looked at one another.

. . .

MRS. SUMNER, THE WIDOW of the former harbourmaster, and a stalwart of the church, whispered to her friend, Mrs. Brodie, as they waited for the service to begin the following Sunday.

"Have you heard, Bessie? Have you heard the news?"

Mrs. Brodie had not.

"Well, I'll tell you," said Mrs. Sumner. "You know that man with the car—that great big red car? That one?"

"Aye, I ken him. Not a nice piece of work, I hear. A gangster, they say."

"So I've heard. And his past is catching up with him. My daughter cleans the house for him, you know."

Mrs. Brodie waited.

"And you wouldn't believe it, but he found a sheep's head on his pillow. Blood all over the place."

"No!"

"He did. He was terrified, apparently. Packed up immediately. But then his car went on fire. Shot up in flames. Nothing left, apparently—just the chassis."

"No!"

"Yes!"

"And he's gone now?"

"Yes, he hired a car from Tobermory and that's him away. And that woman of his, too."

Mrs. Brodie shook her head. "Well, well . . ."

She was unable to finish what she was saying as the Reverend Maclean was now rising to his feet. He cleared his throat.

"Good people," he said. "My text today is Romans 12:19, where it is written, *Do not avenge yourselves, but rather give place to wrath, for it is written 'Vengeance is mine: I shall repay.'* "

It was a good sermon—one of the Reverend Maclean's best, thought Murdo. After the service, he and two other elders joined the Reverend Maclean and his wife for a Sunday lunch: lamb chops. Sourced by the minister himself.

A Melbourne Story

AN INTRODUCTION

MELBOURNE IS A FAVOURITE CITY OF MINE. THIS STORY IS SET IN Fitzroy North, a suburb of the city, a place of small bungalows with tin roofs, shady verandas, and, in some cases, ornate French ironwork. In such a place I have imagined a drama school, not entirely dissimilar to the dance academy in which I was obliged, as an unwilling teenager, to learn ballroom dancing. There was French chalk there on the wooden floor, and there were sluggish ceiling fans that barely disturbed the air. My teacher used to drag on a cigarette as she taught me the quick step and the cha-cha. She blew the smoke over my shoulder. That was how things were in those days.

The revenge here is sought in the world of actors. Now, actors are no worse nor better morally than the ordinary run of humanity, but they do tend a bit more towards backbiting and petty jealousy than people who follow other callings. Or not (a necessary qualification, to avert howls of protest from my actor friends). Perhaps it would be fairer to say that we are all liable to feel jealousy of those who succeed when we may fail to do so. We may pretend to welcome the success of others, but do we really accept it? Do we prefer failure? As Gore Vidal thought, we might die a little every time a friend succeeds.

Actors, in general, make good friends. They kiss you warmly and without provocation. They use the term "darling" to all, without any attention as to the length of time they have known the other person. Even dogs are called darling. They sign off their letters with the words "Oceans of love." By and large, they mean it.

The Principles of Soap

***

*"Brecht is all very well, but most of us, if we are honest,
will admit that we still take pleasure in a well-crafted soap."*
—George Peters, *Thirty Years of Film and Television*
(I can find no record of this publication, which is
not surprising, as it is entirely made up)

DAVID THOREAU WAS AN ACTOR—NOT A PARTICULARLY GOOD ONE, but not as bad as some. "Look," he said, "I know where I am on the talent spectrum. Some people are up there"—he raised a hand above his head, the realm of the Oliviers, the Streeps—"while some people are down there." And he pointed to the ground, the realm of the pantomime artists, the single-line extras, the members of the chorus line. "I'm somewhere in the middle." And with that he smiled. There is a particular pleasure in knowing exactly where one fits in—and accepting it.

He came from a former gold-mining town in Victoria. The gold had run out a long time ago, but the seams that rippled beneath the undulating Australian countryside had lasted long enough and been sufficiently productive to leave the town with an attractive civic centre, an impressive library, and two well-designed golf courses. Farming became once again the mainstay of the local economy, and the town's annual agricultural show attracted visitors from throughout the state. It was a good place in which to grow up, to raise a family, and then to grow old, playing golf and attending the popular bingo sessions in the country club. It was, however, very dull, and anybody of any imagination or ambition tended to leave the town at the age of eighteen, when they went off to one of the large cities, for work or education. Very few people stayed behind unless they went into a family business or took on a family farm.

David had always wanted to act. It started, his mother later said, when he was chosen to play the role of Joseph in the local kindergarten's nativity play—a role that he threw himself into with considerable vigour. Joseph was never intended to steal Mary's limelight, but that is how David tackled the role, elbowing Mary out of the way in the stable scene and brushing off the Three Wise Men before snatching their gifts. At the end, when applause broke out and the children took a bow, Joseph moved swiftly to the foreground, pushing Mary into the crib and breaking the spindly leg of one of the papier-mâché sheep.

"That boy's going far," muttered a bemused member of the audience.

"Real ambition there," agreed another, adding, "And there's talent too."

And there was—at least at the level of the school drama club. Year after year saw David playing the lead part in the school plays, and so, when the time came for him to choose a career, there was really very little question about what he would do.

"I'm going on the stage," he told his parents. "Professionally, that is. I want to be a famous actor."

His father glanced at his mother before he addressed his son. They both wanted him to be an accountant, which was what his father was, although not a particularly successful one. "The theatre's difficult, son," he said evenly, trying to sound as if he were dispensing dispassionate advice. "A lot of people want to act, but hardly any of them make it. Such a shame, but there we are. Those are the facts. Always look at the facts."

David reeled off five or six household names.

"Oh, yes, they made it all right," said his father. "But how many hundreds of their contemporaries didn't? Thousands, I'd say."

"You know something, David?" chipped in his mother. "They work as waiters."

She looked at him as if she had just imparted a dreadful warning. Now she continued, "Most waiters went to drama college, you know.

Nobody goes to waiting college. It's drama you study if you want to be a waiter."

David closed his eyes. What did his parents know? Nothing. Zilch. Nada.

"How many waiters do you know who are really accountants?" she continued. And then, turning to her husband, she said, "Do you know any accountants, Dick—any—who have to work as waiters?"

"Not off the top of my head, Lil," he replied.

David stared at his parents. They were not bad, as parents went—he could easily have done worse, he thought—but they really had no idea of what was what in the theatre. Of course, he knew that it was a competitive world, but the people who ended up as waiters were the ones with no talent, who should never have tried to go on the stage in the first place. He was different. He did not wish to be boastful, but who had been chosen for the lead role in every single school play for the last six years? He had. And who, after sending an enquiry letter, had received an encouraging response from the Roger Dare Acting Studio in Melbourne informing him that places were available on the one-year full-time acting course starting in February? This course, it was explained, introduced the student to all the skills that were necessary to audition successfully for theatrical and film roles both in Australia and abroad. Many of the school's graduates had gone on to stellar careers in London or Los Angeles. "The sky," the school's brochure claimed, "is the limit when you train with Roger Dare. *Dare to be great!* is our motto. Make it yours: contact us about enrolment today. Please remember to send a (recent) photograph."

David had shown the brochure to his father. "See here, Dad," he said. "See those quotes there—they're from past students who have all got acting jobs. See what they say. Just read it, Dad. That's all I ask."

His father glanced at the glossy brochure. "Why do they ask you to send a photograph?" he asked suspiciously. "You see what it says there? It says, *Please send a photograph*. Why do they need a photograph to decide if you can act?"

David humoured his father. He was so *yesterday*. He had *no idea*.

"They need it because if you want to be an actor you have to be . . .

well, you have to look the part, see. They don't want people who maybe have only one ear, say."

"Why would they have only one ear? Who's only got one ear?"

David was patient. You had to be patient with your parents. "I'm not saying anybody in particular only has one ear," he replied. "I'm not saying that. That was just an example. And maybe there are people who have a really gross nose. There may not be all that many parts for people with really gross noses. It might be better for them to do something else. That's all that the photograph means."

The application duly went off, strongly supported by the drama teacher from the local school. *This young man,* she wrote, *has been the mainstay of our drama programme for the past six years. His performance as King Lear last year is still being talked about, and the leading part he played in our* Tribute to Mime *program was even mentioned in the local newspaper. With the right advice and assistance, I am confident that he will, in due course, mature into an actor of some consequence.*

Seeing this glowing reference, David's father wondered whether he had perhaps been too ready to write off acting as a career for his son. "We may have to eat our words," he confided to Lil. "I'm rarely wrong, but there it is in black and white: *an actor of some consequence.* That means only one thing to me: our David can act."

"Seems like it," said Lil. She looked thoughtful. "Where he gets it from is anybody's guess. None of my family were actors. They were mostly sheep people."

"Strange," mused her husband. "But then I suppose it's often like that with people of talent." He smiled. "Did Mr. and Mrs. da Vinci say to one another, 'Where does our boy get his ability to draw?'"

"Who knows, Dick?" she replied. "They say that when you have children you never know what you're going to get."

"True," he said. "You don't."

"And we've ended up with an actor."

"So it seems, Lil. So it seems."

THAT WAS IN 1996, when David was a month or so short of his eighteenth birthday. That was a bit young, his parents felt, to live entirely independently in Melbourne, and so his mother arranged for him to stay with her cousin, Nell, in Fitzroy North. Nell, a piano teacher and widow of a radio engineer, had a red brick Federation-style bungalow with wide pillars at each end of the veranda. The house had a postage stamp–sized garden in the front, intersected by an uneven paved path. Along the edges of the path there were small cement casts of cockleshells painted white and pink. The gate through which access was gained to this path was of wrought iron, with a fleur-de-lys motif. That, Nell explained, was because the first occupants had been a French couple who owned a lace-importing business. In her view, that fact, along with the fleur-de-lys adornments, gave the house a certain continental sophistication, reflected, should other associations be missed, in its name: Montmartre.

There was more than enough room for a lodger, as some years ago the house had been extended at the back, where the kitchen gave out onto an ill-kept patch of lawn, and from there onto a narrow sanitary lane. A garage had been added to the end of the back garden, and this was occupied by a car belonging to a neighbour—Nell did not drive—and by various garden implements. There was something uncomfortable about this garage—something in its atmosphere— that David picked up immediately when Nell first showed him round.

"I don't like to go in here at night," she said. "There used to be a light, but it doesn't work any longer. I think there is some sort of presence—not that I believe in such things. But I still get an odd feeling when I'm here."

David agreed. "Maybe something happened here," he said. "A long time ago. Something bad that has left its trace. There are places where that happens. Hanging Rock and places like that."

"You don't need to come out here," said Nell. "Jimmy Gordon next door takes his car out from time to time; otherwise nobody sets foot in it. Best ignored, if you ask me."

The house itself had a very different atmosphere. Nell was untidy, and a bit of a hoarder. As it happened, she liked the theatre, and there were shelves of books on theatrical subjects and box after box of old programmes from the Athenaeum Theatre on Collins Street. Nell was a regular frequenter of the Athenaeum shows, especially musicals, of which she knew the words to all the songs. "There is nothing to beat *My Fair Lady*," she said to David as she poured him tea on that first afternoon. "Perhaps you'll be able to study it at the Roger Dare—who knows?" She looked at him fondly. "I don't want to raise anybody's hopes too much, but I wonder when we'll see you, David, on the stage of the Athenaeum? No, don't blush. There's every chance. You must have the talent, or you wouldn't have been accepted by Dare's. They don't take everyone, you know. I've heard of plenty of young people who have tried to get in there, but no luck. Plenty."

"I don't know," said David. "We'll see."

He was confident, though, that the Athenaeum would only be a first step. He was thinking more of the West End of London or Broadway, even of Hollywood. It might take a bit of time, but he was convinced that he had it in him. You could either act or you could not—and he could.

She showed him to his room, which was at the front of the house. It had net curtains, a writing table, and a straight-backed chair. The bed was high and narrow and had the look of a hospital bed. The bed-spread was a thick cotton sheet on which had been printed the words of Kipling's poem "If."

"To inspire you," said Nell, and laughed.

THE FOLLOWING DAY he made his way by tram to the converted fire station that housed the Roger Dare Studio. An introductory session was to be held at ten, after the new intake of students had registered and been given their timetable and coursework materials for the first term. Then, in the main practice hall, they met Roger Dare himself, a dapper figure in his late forties, wearing a striped blazer of the sort favoured by rowing crews. A red silk cravat around his neck, he held in his right hand an ebony cigarette holder in which no cigarette was placed. There were nicotine stains in the small sandy-coloured moustache he had cultivated above his upper lip.

"Today," he said to the assembled group of thirty students, "is a new beginning for each and every one of you. It is the first day of your theatrical careers—a day that some years from now, I imagine, you will remember and ask yourself: did I understand then, on that morning all those years ago when I first signed up at drama school, what a great adventure I was embarking upon? And the answer you will give, I suspect, is that you did not, because nobody knows at your stage of life just what they are letting themselves in for when they set out to become an actor. This is not just any career. This is not the same as being an accountant, or a nurse, or a fireman—as you will have seen, this is an old fire station. This is a *calling*—the equivalent of joining a monastery or going off to an ashram in India. This is *enlisting* in a body of men and women who dedicate their lives to the stage. You give your life to that, you know—you don't give just part of it, you give your whole life. You become an actor in your *soul* as well as in your sinews. Being an actor is what you *are*, not just how you happen to earn your living. And that bit—the earning of a living—is never going to be anything but tough. The theatre may bring great rewards to some—my friend David Niven was one of those who did rather well . . ."

David drew in his breath. He was in the same room as somebody who knew David Niven. The closest he had come to such greatness was the librarian at school whose uncle had met Noël Coward.

". . . and the same might be said of my good friend Peter Finch, who did well enough too. But for most actors, there is no fortune waiting to be made. There may be a living, but it is unlikely to be a very generous one. But does that matter? I don't think it does. What matters is being backstage, waiting to go on, hearing the hum of the audience out there, and then that moment, that glorious moment, when you go out on stage and every eye in the house is on *you*. And that is when I hope you say to yourself, 'Going to the Roger Dare was the best thing I ever did in my life.' Is that too much for me to hope? I don't think so. And why do I say that? I say it because there have been more students than I can remember who have said that exact thing to me. And each time I have heard it, I have felt the same flush of pride as I feel right now, talking to you here this morning, as you are about to begin your course. That is what I feel, ladies and gentlemen—that is what I feel in my heart."

Roger Dare stopped. He looked down at his cigarette holder, which David saw was shaking. He took it from his right hand with his left, and then put it between his lips, still without a cigarette. He looked up at the ceiling, and the lights were upon his nicotine-stained moustache and the shoulders of his striped blazer. One of the students began to clap, tentatively, but was soon joined by the others. There were murmurs of appreciation as well. Roger Dare brought his gaze down from the ceiling and let it move across the faces of his students, as if assessing each one.

David glanced at the young man sitting next to him, who looked back at him and smiled. "Mr. Dare's a great actor," he said.

"No," said David. "I don't think he was acting."

They introduced themselves. The student next to David was called Henry. His father was a grazier. Henry had gone to Geelong Grammar and applied to study drama at the University of Sydney before he had heard of the Roger Dare. "Those university courses are not about acting," he said. "They're about drama. Shakespeare and so on. I want to *act*."

"What in?" asked David.

"Television series," said Henry. "I see myself in a police show. Long-running. And you?"

"Theatre," said David.

"*Hamlet?*"

"Yes, but other roles too. I like *Macbeth*."

"Tragic," said Henry. "She was the one who pushed him into it, you know. I don't think he would have done it if it hadn't been for her."

Roger Dare was now announcing the day's programme. "We're going to start with a limbering-up," he said. "That's how we'll start every day. Physicality, ladies and gentlemen—that's the first thing you need to get on top of. Inhabit your body. Your body is you. Make it a partner in a *unity* of expression and *being*."

They had been instructed to bring loose-fitting exercise clothing. Now they changed into these and then re-assembled in the hall to begin their limbering-up session. Music was played, and they were encouraged to dance. David noticed that Henry was somewhat clumsy. Roger Dare noticed that too. "You're Henry, right?" he said. "Well, Henry, I want you to try to overcome a certain stiffness in your gait. Loosen up. Really loose. Nobody's looking at you, you know."

But David saw that Henry was being watched by one of the young women. They were all wearing name badges, and he could see that she was called Virginia. She had a cruel mouth, he thought, and seemed to be smiling at Henry's awkwardness. When she saw that David was looking at her, Virginia looked away sharply. David thought, She's my enemy. He was surprised to find himself thinking that, because he was naturally affable and did not easily make enemies. But he did not like her. He glanced at Henry, who smiled back at him and continued with his stiff, un-coordinated movements. Perhaps he would loosen up in due course, thought David. And there was more to acting than simply being fluid in one's movements; Henry must have other talents to have been admitted to the Roger Dare. These would no doubt emerge as the course got under way.

Over the next two weeks, they were subjected to a barrage of exercises, workshops, and long sessions before mirrors, exploring facial expressions. "You are the raw material it is our task to shape," said Roger Dare, peering over shoulders into the mirror. "Your faces are the clay with which our potters will work."

David looked at his face. Then he looked at a photograph of Peter Finch. The eyes were different—that was the issue. Peter Finch's eyes were eloquent—that was the word—while David felt that his own eyes . . . Or was it the jaw? Was his jaw strong enough to convey determination—when determination was called for? Or was it more suited to an impression of hesitation, or even weakness?

"You can do special exercises," Henry said, when David spoke to him on the subject. "They develop the chin muscles. Do you know that your chin has muscles? But I wouldn't worry too much—your jaw is pretty average, I'd say, which means that it's well suited to lots of parts."

David looked at Henry. His face was nothing special; in fact, it was one of those faces that was instantly forgettable. If you saw Henry on the street or on the tram, five minutes later you would never be able to recollect what he looked like and give a description. All that you could say, David thought, was "eighteen-ish, average height." Even the colour of his hair was indeterminate. It could be called dark, but then, in a certain light, it looked much fairer. And some of it was short, while in other parts it seemed to be fairly long.

He wondered whether Henry was doing the right thing in hoping to go on stage. And he detected a similar reservation in the way in which Roger Dare and some of the other staff members looked at Henry when he was doing the prescribed exercises. Roger Dare was careful not to single out any one student for praise or criticism, but when he watched Henry he almost always frowned, as if puzzled about something.

"I'm finding this course really tough," Henry confided in David at the end of the first month. "I'm working at it as hard as I can, but I don't seem to get anywhere. Yesterday, in play reading, I stumbled over every line—every single line. I couldn't get it right."

"Nervous?" asked David. "Maybe you're too nervous."

"Maybe. I tell myself not to worry, but . . ." He shrugged.

"Have you tried breathing exercises?" asked David. "You take a deep breath, and then you hold it in. It calms you."

Henry was keen to clutch at any straw. "Does it work?"

"It does for me," replied David. "Sometimes I get a bit jumpy just before I go on. That's when I take a deep breath and hold it in. It works for me."

The following day, the class was divided into small groups to work on short excerpts from well-known plays. Henry and David were both in a group allocated to a scene from *The Importance of Being Earnest*. Virginia was in this group and was revelling in the role of Lady Bracknell.

"Suits her," whispered David.

"Stuck-up tart," Henry whispered back.

But Henry was nervous—David could tell that as he glanced at his friend. His hands were shaking, and his breathing seemed shallow.

"Take a deep breath," David said out of the side of his mouth. "Then hold it in for as long as you can. Really hold it. Your heart rate will go down."

Henry did as David suggested. Inhaling deeply, he closed his eyes and clenched his fists. Virginia noticed this.

"What's with him?" she asked.

David gave her a discouraging scowl.

And then, after a rather short time, Henry fainted, falling heavily to the floor, like a puppet whose strings had suddenly been cut.

"Jeez!" exclaimed Virginia.

Roger Dare was standing nearby, his empty cigarette holder protruding beneath his nicotine-stained moustache. He spun round, saw Henry, and rushed to his side. The cigarette holder fell to the ground and broke in two pieces. Seeing this, Roger seemed to forget for a few moments about Henry and busied himself in retrieving the broken holder. That left it to David to attend to the casualty, who by now had come round and was trying to sit up.

Roger Dare bent down to examine Henry. "You all right, my dear fellow?"

Henry made little of what had happened. "I'm just fine. I passed out, I suppose."

"He was holding his breath to calm his nerves," explained David.

Virginia overheard this. She laughed. David spun round. "What's so funny?" he spat.

"Keep your hair on," said Virginia.

Roger Dare asserted his authority. He glanced disapprovingly at Virginia. "You go and sit down, Henry," he said. "If you need to go home, that's fine. Take the day off."

Henry retired to the side of the hall, from where he watched the others performing Wilde. Afterwards, he and David went for lunch in the café down the road from the drama school.

"I'm sorry I suggested that breathing thing," said David.

"You weren't to know, mate."

"Yes, but still . . ."

Henry sighed. "I shouldn't have fainted. That's another thing I'm going to have to work on—not fainting."

They treated themselves to a large pizza and talked about the lives they had led before coming to Melbourne.

"I've been thinking," said Henry. "Both of us have families who wanted us to be something other than what we wanted. Do you think all families are like that?"

"Not all," said David. "Some, but not all."

Henry sighed. "I don't think I'm ever going to get anywhere with acting. I don't know if I've got the talent."

David was quick to disagree. "You've got heaps of talent, Henry. Heaps. It'll come. All you have to do is loosen up."

"And not faint?"

"That too."

Henry looked wistful. "Do you really think I've got talent?"

David nodded. "Yes, I do."

"And Virginia?" asked Henry.

David had to admit that he thought Virginia would probably be a success. "People like that usually are," he said. "I know it's unjust. I know that it shouldn't happen—but it does."

"So, there's no fairness in life?" said Henry. "Is that what you're saying?"

David lowered his eyes. "Something like that," he said.

AFTER A FEW MONTHS in Melbourne, Henry acquired a girlfriend. He had met her at a party held by a cousin of his, an engineering student at the university. She was called Penny and was the daughter of a successful car salesman, Ern Throwover. The unusual name had become well known in Melbourne from the stickers that his cars bore on the rear window, each proclaiming, *Another Great Car from Throwover Motors.* Penny had recently celebrated her twentieth birthday, being six months older than Henry, whom she called, for some unexplained reason, Hoggy. She had an open, rather optimistic-looking face, with a slightly retroussé nose around which was a scattering of faint freckles. Henry told David that he had counted these freckles, and that the total was thirty-four. "There's one that I'm not sure about," he said, "so I didn't count it. If it becomes more definite, I'll make it thirty-five."

As befitted the daughter of Ern Throwover, Penny had a car of her own, a pastel-coloured French sedan with her father's sticker loyally displayed on the rear window. Most of the students at Roger Dare could not afford cars and were envious of the few who had one. Virginia, in particular, made scathing references within Henry's hearing to the "very odd-looking, vomit-coloured car" from which "somebody"—she did not name him—was occasionally dropped off for classes. This brought amused glances directed towards Henry, who pretended not to have heard but noted these remarks with a mixture of embarrassment and cold anger.

Virginia eventually met Penny in a nearby café where she found her having lunch with Henry. Uninvited, she joined them at their table and took the opportunity to find out more about the other young woman. Henry felt deeply uncomfortable; he could see that Virginia was assessing Penny, trying to elicit her views on a variety of subjects and even asking her about "that lovely car" that she had occasionally seen her in. Unaware of the undercurrent of animosity, Penny spoke freely, telling Virginia about an overseas trip she had taken on the previous year in which she had been to Rome and Venice and also to Copenhagen. "I really liked Sweden," she said.

Virginia smiled. "Yes," she said. "Great place."

"Have you been there?" asked Penny.

Virginia glanced at Henry. She shook her head. "No, but I do know where it is."

Henry swallowed hard. "Copenhagen's . . ."

He left the sentence unfinished. He wanted to correct Penny, but he felt it would only make it worse. He was already imagining what Virginia would say to the others. "She thought Copenhagen was in Sweden—she really did. I'm not making this up. True as God. That girl is really stupid."

He mentioned the encounter to David later that day. "She was leading Penny on," he said. "She was trying to make her look stupid."

David listened gravely. The problem, he thought, was that on this occasion, Virginia was right. Penny was not very bright. There was no way round that brute fact. She knew nothing—or next to nothing—and was slow to pick up on most things. This was not to say that she did not have her good points—she was kind and supportive, and she made Henry feel good about himself. That was more important than anything else.

"Penny's not stupid," said David. "Far from it."

Henry looked at him appreciatively. "She knows quite a lot," he said. "It's just that she doesn't show off—know what I mean?"

"Yes," said David. "Unlike some people. Unlike Her Flaming Highness, Virginia."

They both laughed.

.   .   .

NELL TOOK TO HENRY the first time she met him.

"I like your friend," she said, after David had brought Henry back to the house one Saturday afternoon. "I like people who are straight-forward."

"I like him too," said David. "We seem to be on the same wave-length."

Nell nodded. "Wavelengths are the thing, aren't they? And you know immediately if you're going to be able to communicate with somebody. There are some people who are just . . . well, just impos-sible. Hopeless. No shared values."

David thought of Virginia. She was an example.

"And you think it's pointless trying to get anywhere with people like that?" he asked.

Nell thought about this. "Probably. You may get through a little— I'm not saying that you can say nothing to them, but it's an uphill battle. And most of the time, I think it's hardly worth it." She paused. "Jimmy Gordon next door—his wife, Barbie. You haven't met her yet, but she's an example. She and I are never going to agree about anything. She's National Party—goes to all their meetings. Makes the sandwiches. But while I could forgive her that, she's anti–everything remotely modern. Hates modern art. Sees reds under every bed. Doesn't like artistic men. It's a long list. She's impossible— no two ways about it. She should go and live with the bogans in Dandenong."

She suggested to David that he invite Henry to dinner at the house one Sunday. "You tell me he has a girlfriend," she said. "He could bring her, if he wishes. What's her name?"

"She's called Penny," replied David. "Penny Throwover."

Nell frowned. "The car people?"

"That's her dad."

"They're both invited," said Nell. "I'll get a rack of lamb."

Henry and Penny arrived in the pastel-coloured car. David came out to greet them at the fleur-de-lys gate and brought them in along the shell-lined path.

"Are those real shells?" asked Penny.

"Concrete," David replied.

"Fabulous," said Penny.

Henry pointed to the wooden sign on which the house name was displayed in burned lettering. "Montmartre," he said.

"What's that?" asked Penny.

"It's a part of Paris," David explained. "Artists live there. And there are nightclubs."

Henry put a hand on Penny's shoulder. "Penny's been to Paris."

"I know," said David. "I want to go some day. God, I want to get away."

"From here?" asked Penny. "Don't you like it here? Fitzroy North?"

"From Australia," said David. "Not permanently. Just for a while."

"When you're a famous actor," said Henry, "you'll be living in London. Or even New York. We'll come and see you."

Penny gave Henry a sideways glance. David thought she blushed. "We?" she said.

"You can come too," muttered Henry, embarrassed.

David saw Henry look down at his feet. They had reached the small porch at the front of the house. David felt a rush of affection for him. Not only was he physically clumsy but his friend's awkwardness extended to saying the wrong things, too. David wanted to say to him that it didn't matter; that he was who he was, and that he liked him in spite of it, and that it was obvious that Penny liked him too—and Nell. He was a good bloke. That could compensate for just about anything: that you were a good bloke.

Nell served their dinner, which they ate outside, on a table that she had set out in the back garden. They ate early, and at the beginning, as they sipped at the chilled white wine Nell had brought for the occasion, there was still some sun that shone through the wine glasses, refracting coloured light onto the tablecloth. Then the sun went down, and Nell brought out four candles, which she placed in the middle of the table. Stars swung up in the sky—and the Southern Cross was high above them.

Nell asked Henry whether he had ever acted in a Shakespeare play. "David tells me he played Lear," she said.

Henry replied that he had been the understudy for Richard Gloucester in an abbreviated version of *Richard III* they had performed at school. "Somebody else played Richard," he said. "But they let me be the understudy."

"What's that?" asked Penny.

"It's the guy who learns the part in case the main actor gets crook," explained David. "All the big theatres use understudies. If Hamlet gets run over by a tram on his way to the theatre—"

"Or he loses his voice," interjected Henry. "Then the understudy comes on."

Penny looked disbelieving. "He just sits and waits?"

"Yes," said Henry. "I didn't have to go on stage."

"It must be unusual for a school production to bother with understudies," said Nell.

There was a silence. David knew why Henry had been an understudy. It had been the consolation prize, as he would never have been good enough to take the principal role. He looked away, in case Henry should see that he knew. But Henry now said, "I think they asked me to be the understudy because they didn't think I was good enough to be in the play but they still wanted to give me a part."

"Nonsense," said David. But he said it too quickly.

"Why would they do that?" asked Penny. "You're a great actor, Henry. Everybody says that."

David laughed. "He's better than I am—I can tell you that." And he added, "And I'm not going to get very far, as it happens."

Nell admonished them both. "You boys just need to have confidence. You both have it in you. Of course you do. Why else would you be at drama school?"

"Yes," chimed in Penny. "Why else?"

Nell started to rise from her chair. "I've got Shakespeare in there."

"In the house?" asked David.

"Yes. In my bedroom. All the plays. Ten volumes. They belonged to my mother. I love Shakespeare." She was looking at Henry. "If I get it, would you read something from *Richard III?*"

Henry gave a nervous laugh. "Right now? Me?"

"Yes," said Nell.

She made her way into the house. Penny giggled. She turned to Henry. "I'd like to hear you, Hoggy."

"I'm not very good," protested Henry.

"Nell would like it," said David. "We don't get much Shakespeare round here. Do it for her."

Nell returned, carrying a large, blue-bound book. She had inserted a marker, and now she opened it at the chosen page and handed it to Henry.

"There's a very moving speech there," he said. "Poor Richard. It's where Shakespeare reminds us to feel sorry for him."

"Why?" asked Penny.

"Because he wasn't very nice," said Nell. "I don't know what they teach you in history these days, but I learned about him when I was at school."

David avoided looking at Penny. He doubted if she knew much history.

"He was accused of killing his nephews," Nell continued. "He smothered them with a pillow while they were staying in the Tower of London."

Penny looked surprised. "He was their uncle?"

"Yes," said Nell.

Penny shook her head. "Some uncle," she said. "I don't think I like the sound of him."

"There are those who say that he was innocent," said Nell.

"Then why did he kill them, if he was innocent?" asked Penny. "That doesn't make sense to me."

David looked at her. He had never been sure what Henry saw in her—apart from the obvious. That was the trouble with the obvious—it tended to obscure the not-so-obvious. Nell was also looking at Penny and smiling. "History can be really interesting," she said.

The remark was not addressed to anybody in particular, but it was Penny who replied. "I really like history," she said. "There's so much of it. All that stuff."

Nell pointed to the book. "Go on, Henry," she said. "Give us Richard's speech."

Henry stood up and started to read the speech. David closed his eyes. He was cross with Nell, because he thought she should not be embarrassing Henry in this way. He was her guest, and you did not ask your guest to read excerpts from *Richard III* unless you were confident that they wanted to do it. And poor Henry—look at him—he was so wooden in his delivery.

At the end of the performance, Penny stood up and kissed Henry before he could sit down.

"That's phenomenal," she said.

Henry sat down. He was pleased with how he had done, and now he glanced at David for confirmation.

"That was terrific," David said. "It's a great piece of theatre, that." He paused. "Should we tell Mr. Dare about that? Should we suggest he chooses it for one of our classes?"

Nell remembered something. "I saw Roger Dare in Shakespeare once. I'd forgotten that, but now I remember. He was playing . . . I can't recall, actually, what it was, but it was here in Melbourne. There was a big piece about it in *The Age*. I remember they said it was odd that he should have had a cigarette holder in his mouth when playing Coriolanus."

"Did Coriolanus smoke?" asked Penny.

Henry shook his head.

"Who knows?" said David.

Nell was tactful. "I don't think tobacco existed in those days." She laughed. "It's one of those things most people—including myself—don't really know about, isn't it? When did people start smoking? I'm not sure."

Penny said, "I don't know. Sorry."

David now mentioned that Roger Dare had repaired his cigarette holder with a piece of sticking plaster. "He dropped it when . . ." He stopped himself.

"When what?" asked Penny.

David looked apologetic. "When Henry fell over."

Penny looked concerned. "Did you fall over?"

"I fainted," said Henry. "I was holding my breath, and I fainted. I was out of it for only a couple of seconds."

"You mustn't hold your breath," said Penny. "Okay? Don't hold your breath."

"I won't," said Henry, and he took her hand and pressed it.

"Good," said Nell. "Thanks for reading that, Henry. You did it really well. I felt I was there, right there, watching Richard."

"Did he die in real life?" asked Penny.

"Everybody dies in real life," remarked David, and laughed. Nell looked slightly pained. She gave Penny a protective look; at David, she glanced reproachfully.

They sat outside for half an hour longer. The stars were bright. The sound of laughter drifted across the fence; others were sitting out on this warm night, under the stars. A car went past in the road; a dog barked, briefly, before a shout silenced it. David felt happy. He was with his friends. He was doing what he had always wanted to do—he was in the theatre. He had his life before him. He had no reason to be anything but content.

THE COURSE LASTED a full year. At the end, a small graduation ceremony was held in the practice hall. Students were invited to bring friends and family to listen to Roger Dare making a speech and presenting the graduates with what he called a "certificate of successful completion."

"When you graduate from a university," he said, "you get a few letters after your name. Of course, if you are a successful actor, you don't need anything like that. My friend David Niven used to say that he did very well without the letters B.A. after his name—and I think he was right. What counts is what's in the box, not the label. Peter Finch, a great actor—whom I am proud to be able to call my friend—he says much the same thing. But you people who are graduating today from Roger Dare do have some letters after your name, and I'll tell you what they are: S.U.C.C.E.S.S. For those of you who don't have your dictionary with you, that spells 'success.' Your road to success starts today, as you leave this academy. Put your heart into the theatre, and the theatre will put its heart into you. That's what you need to remember when you leave this place."

David invited his parents and Nell. They sat proudly in the front row, listening appreciatively to Roger Dare's speech.

"So, he knows David Niven," whispered David's mother. "You

heard that? David Niven. The one who was in *Separate Tables*. Remember?"

"It shows," his father replied, *sotto voce*. "This bloke's got class."

At the reception following the ceremony, Roger Dare made a point of chatting to every guest, posing for photographs with parents and family friends, his cigarette holder in hand, a fresh sticking plaster around the break. Nell reminded him that she had seen him as Coriolanus, and he put a hand to his brow in astonishment. "Such a long time ago," he said. "So much water has flowed under the bridge since then."

"I enjoyed it very much," said Nell.

"Darling, you're too kind," said Roger Dare.

Virginia sought out David at the end, just as the guests were leaving.

"I'm going to miss you and Henry," she said. She looked in Henry's direction; he was with his parents and Penny on the other side of the room. There was pity in her glance.

"I'm sure we'll all see one another around," said David.

Virginia nodded. "Poor Henry," she said. "I doubt if he's going to get any work. He's so *sincere,* if you know what I mean, but I don't think he really gets it."

David stiffened. "What's it?" he asked.

"Acting," replied Virginia airily. "You get it. I hope I get it. Most of the others get it. But not Henry, I'm afraid."

She looked at David, as if challenging him to disagree. But he was silent. There was no point in engaging with her, he thought; she would never change. You could say what you liked to her, but it would never make any difference.

"Did I tell you I've got a part?" Virginia asked.

David felt himself grow cold inside. "No, you didn't." He would not ask her what it was; he *would not*.

"Since you ask," Virginia continued, "it's theatre work. A four-week run—minimum, probably more. And the director has promised me something for afterwards, but I'm not sure if I'll take it. I'm interested in production, you know."

David bit his lip. I hate her, he thought. But then he thought, No, I don't. You shouldn't hate other people, Nell said, because it was just too exhausting. If people who hated other people put the same amount of energy into liking them, then they would find out that they didn't hate them at all. David wondered whether that was true. He could start, perhaps, by trying to like Virginia.

"I'm really pleased for you," he said. The words seemed to hurt his throat, and for a moment it seemed to him that he might choke.

"Are you all right?" asked Virginia.

"Yes," said David. And then added, "You must be very pleased. I don't think anybody else has got anything."

"It's early days," said Virginia generously. "Some of you may get something. You know what Roger says: persist. That's his motto, you know. He showed me this shield-thing he has on the wall. It has *Persto* painted on it. That's 'I persist' in Latin, you see."

David managed a thin smile. "*Presto* would be a good motto," he said. "If you were the impatient type, that is."

Virginia looked blank. Then she said, "Be that as it may."

Roger Dare came over to join them. "My star pupils," he said. "You and you. Star quality. Both going far."

He smiled at Virginia. Then he turned to David. "Have you got anything fixed up? Anything short term?"

David shook his head.

"Are you interested in something to keep the wolf from the door? *Pro tem*, of course."

"I'll do anything," said David.

Roger Dare seemed pleased. "That's the spirit. Take a job, I always say, and go to every audition you can. Audition, audition, audition. We all did that, and it's still the way to do it—unless you're lucky, like Virginia here, and walk straight into a major role."

"I owe it all to you," said Virginia.

Roger Dare acknowledged the compliment with a brief movement of his cigarette holder. "I do my best by all of you. It's all part of the Roger Dare ethos." He patted David's forearm, "And you, my dear fellow: I shall see you immediately afterwards—in the office. I'll give you the details."

He went off.

Virginia looked at David. "Creepy," she said.

"They're all like that," said David. "Theatre people are like that. It doesn't mean anything."

Within a short time, the reception was over. Nell was hosting a lunch for David's parents back at Montmartre, and she left with them; David said he would join them after he had spoken to Roger Dare. "He has a job possibility for me," he said. "I don't know what it is, but I'll find out."

"That was quick," said his father.

David was cautious. "We'll see what he says."

He waved goodbye to them and made his way to Roger Dare's office. The door was open, and he was beckoned in.

"Graduations are such bittersweet occasions," Roger Dare said. "They are a beginning, in a sense, but they are also goodbyes to some of the best friends you'll ever make—the very best friends."

"I've enjoyed myself here, Mr. Dare," said David.

"I'm glad. And I've enjoyed teaching you—all of you."

David waited. Then he said, "You said you might need me for a job." David knew he did not want to go back home and thought it might help his cause to appeal to Roger Dare's sympathetic side, so he added, "I like the city. I like living here."

"Of course you do," said Roger Dare. "I come from a small town myself. A long time ago, of course, but . . ." He sighed. "Sometimes in my dreams I'm back there, you know. It's really depressing. I'm back in Mildura. I know it's not so bad these days, but when we lived there . . ."

"Dreams are like that, aren't they?" said David. "I sometimes dream I'm back at school. I have to write an exam and I know nothing about the subject—nothing."

"Too true," said Roger Dare. "Or you're at a party in your pyjamas."

A short silence ensued. Then Roger Dare said, "A friend of mine can give you a job. Not acting, I'm afraid, but it will keep you going. You can get time off for auditions. He's a theatre-goer—you'll find him to be a supportive boss." He paused. "Interested?"

"Could be," said David. And then, more enthusiastically, "In fact, yes, definitely."

"Good," said Roger Dare. "He said he'll train you on the job."

"And the job itself . . . ?" David began.

"Restaurant work," said Roger Dare quickly. "Waitering. The pay's not bad and the tips can be quite good."

David said nothing. It was as if a prophecy had come to pass. It was a Nostradamus moment.

FOR THE NEXT FOUR YEARS, David worked at the George Court, an expensive restaurant in the business quarter. The proprietor, Roger Dare's friend, was called Terence Collins. He had moved to Melbourne from Adelaide after selling the family hotel he ran there. When he first bought it, the George Court was rarely full, having been run down by its former owner. Terence Collins changed that, employing a chef who had built up a considerable reputation in Sydney but who had married into an Italian family in Melbourne and wanted to move closer to an ailing mother-in-law. This chef soon made his mark on Melbourne, and in due course was offered a daytime cooking programme on local television. This programme, *The Secrets of the Kitchen*, proved wildly popular, largely through the fascination the audience developed for the chef's colourful banter with the assistants who appeared with him on the show.

David did not mind being a waiter, and he was, in fact, rather good at the job. To add to the authenticity of the dining experience, he affected a French accent when speaking to the diners and would indulge in lengthy descriptions of the dishes on offer, using his hands to make extravagant and over-stated accompanying gestures. It was not uncommon for reviews of the restaurant to make particular mention of the "amusing and loquacious French waiter" who added considerably to the pleasure of visiting the restaurant. Terence Collins was pleased. "You bring them in, David. No two doubts about that, mate: you bring them in."

As Roger Dare had promised, Terence Collins was prepared to give David time off to attend auditions. These took place every ten days or so and could involve absence for an entire shift. Terence did not dock his pay, but encouraged him, even when audition after audition failed to produce any work.

At least there were occasional appearances in television advertisements, and these were lucrative enough to help David put down the deposit on a small flat not far from Nell's house in Fitzroy North. Nell wanted to help him with this purchase, even though she knew that she would miss him terribly when he moved out. "He's the son I never had," she confided in a friend. "But one has to let go."

"True," remarked the friend. "Plenty of people have let me go in my lifetime."

Nell still had faith in David's acting ability. "Remember," she said, "even if things are slow right now, remember that you played Lear. Don't forget that. And remember what Roger Dare said about you. He said you could be a star. He said that, David. I heard him. Those were his very words."

David shrugged. "Something may turn up. Who knows?"

"You can come round here for meals any time," said Nell. "My door is always open—you know that."

He looked at her fondly. Melbourne was full of people like Nell—decent people, generous people. It might be a bit stuffy at times, but decency trumped stuffiness, he thought, and he had decided that he would not mind too much if he ended up living in Melbourne for the rest of his life. He was realistic now about the chances of ever reaching the West End in London, or Broadway, or anything like that; he would make do with whatever came his way, even if it was only the occasional part in local repertory theatre. And if he could get more television advertisement work, that would help him save towards the overseas trip that he would like to make at some point. He had always wanted to see Paris. He could visit the real Montmartre and send a postcard back to Nell saying, *Recognise the name of this place?* He would try to get to Rome too. As a boy he had been given a book called *Ancient Rome for Boys and Girls* that had a large picture of Christians facing the lions in the Colosseum. At the age of seven that had led to some confusion when he had heard mention on ABC News of the Coliseum Theatre in Sydney. Were there really lions there, and did that sort of thing still happen, right here in Australia? He thought of the local Anglican vicar, who had a scar on his left cheek. Had that been inflicted by a lion? Had the Reverend Jones succeeded in getting away, perhaps by leaping from the stage of the Sydney Coliseum before the lions could pin him down? Now he remembered his quaint childhood misconception, but the thought of seeing the Colosseum, or what remained of it, still appealed.

He moved into his new flat. He was proud of it and chose his furniture carefully. Nell gave him an armchair, an occasional table, and a mattress. Henry gave him a radio, a bathroom cabinet he had been planning to throw out, and a wine-rack capable of holding a dozen bottles.

It was through Henry that David met Annie Harkness. She was a radiographer, and she was friendly with Henry's sister, who worked in the Melbourne children's hospital. David met her at a party that Henry held, and he and Annie took to one another immediately. Six months later they were engaged, and they married four months after that. David's flat was their first matrimonial home, and Annie set out to make it as comfortable as possible. She disposed of Henry's wine-rack and bathroom cabinet, but kept the chair, table, and mattress that Nell had donated. When the batteries in Henry's radio failed, she threw that out too.

Annie was vaguely embarrassed that David made his living as a waiter. "Don't get me wrong," she said, "there's nothing wrong with being a waiter, but don't you think you could get something a bit more . . ." She searched for the word but could not find it.

"Prestigious?" suggested David.

"I wasn't thinking of that," she said. "It's just that you could get something that used your mind a bit more—know what I mean?"

David smiled. "I do use my mind," he said. "Every day. You try remembering what eight people want for their main course. You try remembering that this person can't take vinegar on his salad, or that person wants carrots but no broccoli, and so on. You try remembering what the six specials are and how chef has cooked them."

She apologised. "I didn't mean to be rude, David. Sorry. It's just that . . ."

"And at least being a waiter gives me the time to go to auditions. A lot of auditions are in the morning, and I don't work then—or at least, not before twelve. If I had an office job, I couldn't keep going off for these."

"You're right," she said. "And the important thing is your acting career, David. I know how much that means to you."

"So, I'll just carry on at the restaurant for the time being," he said. "Something may turn up."

"It will," said Annie. "It will, David. I know it will."

Annie was right. It did, and it turned up in the restaurant, one Friday afternoon, when Roger Dare made a reservation for a table for three. David took the telephone booking.

"My dear fellow," said Roger. "How nice to hear your voice. I take it that all is well?"

"Just fine, Mr. Dare. Just fine."

"Splendid. I wonder if you could keep a table for three—one of those nice ones by the window. I'm going to be lunching with an absolutely charming chap who might—just might—have something for you. But enough of that. The lips are sealed—sealed tight—until we see one another at the appointed hour."

David was intrigued, but Friday was a busy day in the restaurant, and he did not have the time to think about what Roger Dare had said. In due course, though, his old tutor arrived, and David took him and his two companions to the best table in the house.

"Just the place," enthused Roger. And then, turning to one of his friends, a mild-looking man wearing horn-rimmed spectacles, he introduced him to David. "This is Tim," he said. "Tim is . . . now, wait for it, roll drums, tra-la, a . . . famous television producer."

Tim looked embarrassed. "Not famous."

"But, my dear fellow," said Roger Dare, "you have such a long list of successes appended to your humble name. You mustn't be so modest."

"I don't know," said Tim, glancing at David as he spoke. "I've got a lot to be modest about."

David smiled. He could tell that the glance Tim had given him was one of appraisal. He hoped that there would be no misunderstandings. He seated them and then went off to fetch the martinis they had ordered. As he left the table, he felt Tim's eyes on him.

He returned and passed them each their martini.

"A martini at lunch on Friday," said Roger Dare, raising his glass in a toast. "How much more sophisticated does it get, I ask myself."

Then Tim reached out to touch David's sleeve.

"Roger says you're one of his graduates."

David nodded. "Yes. I enjoyed the course very much."

Once again, Tim's eyes went up and down him. David felt even more uncomfortable. He was aware now that he was blushing.

Tim now turned to Roger. "You're right," he said. "He's the type."

Then, to David, he said, "Would you mind repeating after me, 'I've had a bad day at work. I can't take any more, Helen. I just can't.'"

David did as he was asked.

"Nice," said Tim. "Now, would you mind saying, 'You say that one more time, Eric, and I'll tell Helen everything you think I don't know. I'm warning you.'"

David caught Roger Dare's eye. Roger nodded his encouragement.

Right, thought David. I shall over-act. The lines were hardly poetry, but David delivered them with all the resonance and power of the Shakespearean stage.

After David had delivered his line, Tim clapped his hands together. "A natural, Roger. You were spot on. This is Bruce, as I live and breathe. Perfect. Right looks, right voice. Everything."

Now he addressed David. "You've just had an audition, David. An unusual one, yes, but an audition nonetheless."

"Tell him," Roger urged.

Tim turned round in his seat so that he was speaking directly to David. "We're about to start filming a new soap right here in Melbourne. Good budget. Six months airing guaranteed, whatever the figures are—although they'll be good, I can tell you." He paused. "I'm casting. And I think you're just right for one of the principal characters. He's called Bruce, and I had in mind somebody who looked just like you and who spoke very much as you speak. Interested?"

FEDERATION STREET PROVED TO BE wildly popular. David's character, Bruce, was not the lead, but was nonetheless important to the story, and appeared in just about every one of the three episodes made and broadcast each week. It was demanding work, even if playing Bruce came naturally to David: the hours were long, and the script could change with very little notice. But the atmosphere on the set was always friendly, and the fees increased as each season attracted a wider and wider audience. David now found himself being smiled at in the street and frequently stopped for his autograph by some die-hard fan. Now he went back to the George Court as a diner, taking members of the cast as his guests, and was fussed over by the waiters—other resting actors—who all knew of the extraordinary stroke of luck that had propelled David from obscurity to soap stardom. They hoped that a similar thing might happen to them, but knew it was unlikely.

"Lightning doesn't strike in the same restaurant twice," said one of the waiters, another Roger Dare graduate. "But you never know."

"No," said David. "The important thing is not to give up hope."

It seemed that *Federation Street* would run indefinitely. David was friendly with the principal screenwriter, a man called Maurice, a television veteran who had another five years to go before retirement. "As far as I'm concerned, Bruce is safe for five years, mate," said Maurice. "I'm not going to write him out. You happy with that?"

"Sure," said David. "Suits me. I like the part."

David had now been in the series for five years, and a further five years would bring his involvement up to a full decade. There were few actors who enjoyed that sort of continuity of employment. "I'm really lucky," he said to Annie. "This has been our big break, you know."

"You're wonderful," she said. "Everybody loves Bruce. You make him so . . . so human."

David smiled. "Long may it last," he said. "And as far as I can see, it will."

DAVID WAS IN THE BATH one morning when the call came in from Roger Dare. As he stood in the corridor, a towel wrapped about him, he could tell immediately from Roger's voice that something serious had happened.

"My dear fellow," Roger began, "I have the most terrible news to give you. Horrible news. Dear Tim has been taken from us."

David waited, his heart suddenly a cold stone within him. He struggled to speak. "What . . . what happened?"

"He and Caroline went up to Queensland on one of these short breaks."

"He mentioned he was going," said David. A plane crash?

"He went up north—the Daintree, I believe. And he went fishing."

David held his breath.

"A beastly crocodile took him," Roger went on. "I don't have all the details, but apparently he was trying to release a trapped line and he fell into the water. The salty was waiting."

David said nothing.

"You there, my dear fellow?"

"Yes. It's . . ."

"It's awful. Indescribably awful."

He and Roger spoke for a few minutes longer before Roger hung up. David went into the kitchen, where Annie was making scrambled eggs. "Tim," he said. "A crocodile got him."

Annie gasped. David sat down. They stared at one another, uncertain what to say or think.

TIM WAS REPLACED by Virginia. Since her graduation from the Roger Dare, her career had taken her to Sydney and, for a period of three years, to London. Now she had returned to Australia and was contacted by a head-hunter to see if she would take over the production of *Federation Street*. She had agreed, provided that she was allowed to do some direction as well. These terms were agreed. She would be principal producer and, at the same time, she would direct half of the episodes.

Virginia addressed the cast and crew on her first day in the job.

"I know how much you people are missing Tim," she said. "He was one of the greats. But I'm sure that he would want us to carry on much as before. That will be his monument—a smooth transition into a new era for *Federation Street*."

Taking David aside, she said to him, "It's great seeing you here, David. Just like the old days at Roger Dare's."

"It's great seeing you, Virginia."

"And tell me, how's Henry?"

David explained that Henry had had a few parts here and there.

"Back half of a pantomime horse?" asked Virginia, and then laughed.

David bit his tongue. He had to work with this woman.

"Poor Henry," said Virginia. "And that girlfriend of his? Miss Einstein? What was her real name?"

"Penny. He married her."

Virginia rolled her eyes. "Oh well," she said. Her tone changed. Now she was sympathetic. "I do hope he's happy. I suppose one comes to terms with . . . with one's lot in life. Poor Henry. Such a pity."

They got down to work and, over the next few months, none of the actors noticed any difference in their working lives. But then at the end of a full day's shooting, Maurice came up to David and whispered, "You and I need to meet in the pub right now."

David asked him if there was anything bothering him, but Maurice seemed unwilling to speak. "In the pub," he said. "Half an hour's time—okay?"

Maurice was already there when David arrived. The screenwriter nodded to him and took a sip of his beer. "Bad news," he said. "We had a storyline meeting this morning. Me, the story editors, and Virginia."

David knew what was coming.

"I'm out?"

Maurice nodded sadly. "Afraid so. I argued against it, but Virginia wasn't listening. She said . . ." He hesitated, but David urged him to continue.

"She said that she thought you had become stale. She said we need new blood."

David was aghast. "Stale? But . . . but look at the audience figures. And the letters we get. Nobody else thinks that."

Maurice shrugged. "She does. And she wants to replace Bruce with a new character, Tony. He's going to be Hazel's ex-lover who's come back from Hong Kong and wants to set up a gym and personal trainer's business. He was in the series back in the day. A really flat storyline, if you ask me. But that's what she wants."

"And me?"

"You're going to be taken by a crocodile on a trip up north."

David stared at Maurice with disbelief. "That's really tactless," he said. "After what happened to poor Tim."

Maurice agreed. "That's what I said, but she just laughed and said that if that sort of thing could happen in real life, then it could happen in a soap." He paused. "And there's more. You remember who played Tony when he was in the story before? He's going to play him again. Same actor. Jack Porter. Yes, him. And you know something else? Who is Virginia's long-term lover, in real life? That's right. Jack Porter. They've been shacked up for years."

It took David a few moments to absorb the full perfidy of the plan. The budget restricted the number of actors who Virginia could employ. If she wanted to give a job to her actor lover, then she would have to get rid of an existing member of the cast—and that, it transpired, was to be him.

"I hate her," David muttered. "I try not to hate people—I really do. But I hate her, I'm afraid."

Maurice nodded. "You're right about hate, Dave. It never helps. But sometimes it's understandable."

David looked down into his beer. He did not feel like drinking.

"When?" he said.

"It's going to be done in stages," replied Maurice. "Jack is going to be introduced next week. We'll be filming with him. Then the following week you go to Queensland and you're out. She'll probably be telling you that tomorrow. She said something about it. She's planning to get rid of Bill as well."

"Bill!" David exclaimed. Bill was the popular and long-serving principal cameraman. Like Maurice, he was getting into his late fifties and might not find it easy to get another job.

"Who's going to take Bill's place?" David asked.

"Jack's cousin," replied Maurice. "He was with ABC up in Darwin. He's left them and is looking for something down here. I heard from one of the technical people that it was all stitched up."

David sat back in his chair. He and Annie had recently bought a new house. The repayments were large. They would manage, but it would be tough.

"Sorry about this, mate," said Maurice. "I thought you should know." He looked at David apologetically. "I'm going to have to write the relevant episodes tomorrow and the day afterwards. We're shooting them on Friday. I'm not looking forward to it."

Later that evening, David and Annie went out to dinner at Henry and Penny's house. David told them about what he had just learned from Maurice. Henry listened with a growing look of disgust on his face.

"Ghastly woman," he said.

"I remember her," said Penny. "She made me feel this small." She made a gap between her thumb and forefinger.

Henry shook his head. "It's so unfair. You're so popular. The viewers love you."

"They do," said Penny. "The woman in the pharmacy told me that you're the reason why she watches *Federation Street*. She said her sister-in-law agrees with her."

"They all love you," said Henry. "Penny's right."

"You need to fight back," said Penny.

David made a despairing gesture. "I don't see how I can. The producer runs the show. Virginia calls the shots—that's just the way it is." David's eyes suddenly widened. "Unless . . ."

They looked at him.

"Unless what?" asked Henry.

"Unless what was meant to happen to Bruce were to happen to Tony—he's the ex who has turned up from Hong Kong."

Henry frowned. "I don't get it."

David explained. "Unless the crocodile gets Tony rather than Bruce."

"It's all the same to crocodiles," interjected Penny. "We all probably taste much the same to them."

Henry smiled. "You'd taste really good," he said to Penny. "I'd be a bit tough."

"No, you wouldn't," Penny replied. "You'd taste just right, Hoggy. No, I'm serious—you would."

Annie steered the conversation back to David's suggestion. "Tell us what you have in mind," she said.

David told them, and they listened carefully. At the end, Henry voiced his doubts. "It all depends on whether the technical people—the people who do the transmission—are prepared to play ball."

"Yes," said David. "It does. But I can tell you something: there are one or two of them who are no friends of Virginia's. It's old business—I don't know what it is, but there's feeling there."

"In that case," said Henry, "you could try. I take it that Maurice would be on board."

David explained that he was confident that Maurice would be only too happy to be involved. "He realises that Virginia is behaving corruptly. There's no other word for it. It's corruption. Maurice is dead straight. He doesn't approve of that sort of thing."

"Good," said Henry. "Then do it."

MAURICE REQUIRED NO PERSUASION.

"Brilliant plan," he said. "But let's just go over it again. I write the episodes that Virginia wants. All as ordered. Yes?"

"Yes. Then in the lunch-hour, when nobody's around, we record an alternative episode. Virginia's always away on a Wednesday afternoon, so she won't find out. In this episode, Tony goes to Queensland and the news comes through that he's been taken by a crocodile. We obviously can't let him in on this, and so it will all be done through reportage. But he'll definitely be written out."

"And you stay in?"

"Yes. Then we give that version—the one we've made ourselves—to the technical people and get them to transmit it instead of the official one, so to speak. It goes out in the evening—in the usual slot—and viewers throughout the country see it. As far as they are concerned, that's Tony out of the story while I remain in."

Maurice chuckled. "And she won't be able to do anything about it, as you can hardly reverse what has already been broadcast."

"Exactly. And at the same time, we go to management and put our cards on the table. We tell them about how she's proposing to replace Bill with Jack's cameraman cousin. They won't like that."

"And I tell them that if nothing is done about it, I'm out of it and they'll not get a replacement in time."

"Yes," said David. "Then we hope they fire her."

"I normally don't like getting people fired," said Maurice. "But there are occasions where it is the only right and proper thing to do."

"We should always behave correctly," said David.

"In life and in drama," agreed Maurice. "Oh, this is very satisfying."

"Revenge can be like that," said David. "As long as it's calibrated correctly."

"And is it? In this case?"

"Absolutely."

IT WORKED BEAUTIFULLY. The unofficial episode was recorded at a time when the only people in the studio were the conspirators. Then it was handed over to the technicians, who took the official recording off the system and substituted the version in which Tony meets with an untimely end in Queensland. That episode was then transmitted.

Virginia called a meeting to establish what had happened. When David saw her, she was shaking with rage. He said, "Your little game's over, I'm afraid."

Her lower lip trembled. There were little flecks of spittle on it. "My little game? What do you mean?"

"We've discussed it with management, Virginia. They were appalled. You're history. Sorry to be so blunt, but there we are. And poor Tony. Such a pity. That's not a nice way to go."

For a few moments, David thought that she might slap him. He saw her hand rising, but then it dropped, and she turned away.

As for *Federation Street*, it continued to prosper. Maurice seemed to acquire a new creative wind, and his plots became even more emotionally engaging and charmingly impossible. Viewer ratings climbed and climbed. Virginia was replaced as producer by Henry. That was David's suggestion, but it was one that was approved of by management, as the CEO of the company was a close friend of Henry's father, having been in the same masonic lodge for years. Penny was given a small part but proved to be so popular that she was promoted to a much more significant role.

The four of them—David, Annie, Henry, and Penny—went to dinner at Nell's house to celebrate the fact that everything had worked out so well. Nell said, "I'm so proud of you, David—I really am."

Nell had barbecued lamb chops. She had made a special potato salad to go with the chops: this involved mustard seeds and chopped chives. They ate outside. There was a suggestion of a breeze, just a suggestion, and it was like gentle breath against their skin, the gentle breath of the one you love. The Southern Cross hung in the sky, its points bright, confident, reassuring.

"I am so happy," muttered David.

"Yes," said Nell. "We all are."

Cavalleria Rusticana

IN WHAT FOLLOWS, THERE IS AN ACT PERFORMED BY ONE OF THE characters that, when looked at afterwards, seems appalling. Its potential effect is dreadful, and its effect on the actor is profound. Yet it is typical of the sort of human act that may be performed without having been thought through beforehand by the actor. Not everything we do is fully intentional. Not everything we do is accomplished after we have considered the consequences. Not everything we do is the result of what is sometimes called "joined-up thinking." We act in the dark, sometimes on impulse, unaware of the ripple effect of what we do. We may act in a particular way because we are responding to internal promptings for which we are not entirely responsible. Much of our action may even be determined by influences and events that occurred before we were born. To recognise that is not to commit oneself to a completely deterministic view of human action; it is simply to recognise the truth of the proposition that who we are and how we view the world may be determined by the bed in which we happen to be born, by the society in which we grow up, and by the beliefs with which we are endowed.

To give an example: the people who burned witches in the seventeenth century did not do so because they were inherently evil people: they did what they did because of where and when they were born, and because of the beliefs they held as a result of those factors.

Judging the past by the standards of the present is facile. Some judgement is possible, but it must be tempered by an understanding of the historical context in which human action takes place. That is not to say that past wrongs should be presented as anything but wrongs: cruelty does not become something other than cruelty simply because it was perpetrated by those who felt they were not being cruel. What it does mean, though, is that we may have to recognise that the perpetrators of acts of cruelty or injustice may not have grasped the objective wrongness of their acts. The judicial torturer of the past may have considered himself an agent of justice, determined to elicit the truth, rather than a torturer. That may limit the usefulness of condemning him for what he did.

Then there is the notion of accident. At one level what happens in this story is simply an accident. That is debateable, and yet we must be very careful to preserve the notion of accident as an exculpatory category. People should not be held responsible for that which they do by accident; only if an accident flows as a direct and foreseeable result of a freely chosen action should an accidental consequence be laid at the door of an actor. If, when approaching a road junction, I genuinely fail to see an approaching car, and if, at the time, I am driving with due care and attention, I do not see how the collision that follows can be seen as a result for which I can be held *morally* accountable. That is the whole point of the word "accident": an accident is an event that is nobody's fault. Unfortunately, we live in days when we are particularly keen to find somebody to blame for any misfortune that occurs. We want scapegoats, even if they are innocent. This is dangerous, as it has the effect of making society retributive and morally undiscriminating. It leads to harsh judgements and the pillorying of those who meant no harm. To live in a world in which morally nuanced assessments of human acts is impossible because the public wants blood . . . That would be a nightmare—but it is a nightmare to which we might be closer than we think.

I feel sorry for everybody in this story. I feel sorry for the person who exacts revenge, because, on balance, revenge is wrong and never helps. I feel sorry for the dog, because he is a dog, and should be judged as a dog. Dogs bark: it's what they do.

Monty, Tiger, Rose, Etc.

ROSE FIRST SAW COLIN AT THE THIRTIETH BIRTHDAY PARTY OF HER vivacious, redhead friend, Vicky. It was a large party, held in Edinburgh, at Vicky's father's golf club. "Vicky has *countless* friends," somebody once said to Rose. "It's something to do with being a redhead. You speak to virtually anybody—*anybody*—and they'll say, 'Oh yes, I know Vicky.' One hundred per cent of the time. Try it."

So, it was not surprising that when Vicky decided to have a party to celebrate her birthday—"Almost a third of a century!" she remarked—there were over sixty people there. And that was just the tip of the iceberg, people said. Those were just the close friends—there were plenty of others who heard about the party and who would have loved to have been there but who were not invited. "You just can't keep everybody happy," Vicky said.

But Rose, who turned thirty the same year, was there because she had been at school with Vicky, and they were like this, she said, crossing two fingers to demonstrate the closeness of their friendship. And because they were so close, Rose felt she could be frank with Vicky about her interest in Colin, as they looked across the crowded room at the well-built man near the window. "I'm going to faint, Vicky. Seriously. Faint. Look at him—I mean, just look at him. Where did you get him? A male-order catalogue?" She paused, then spelled out the word "male."

Vicky laughed. "That's an idea," she said. "They could have one of these catalogues with the models wearing the sports shirts and chinos and so on, but you can't order the clothes—you order the man himself. A great idea."

Rose waited. "So?" she prompted.

"All right," said Vicky. "He's called Colin. Colin Fanshaw. Lovely name, that, don't you think—Fanshaw." She paused, and then continued, "I wouldn't, if I were you."

Rose looked puzzled. "You're warning me off?" It occurred to her that Vicky might be involved with Colin, in which case she would apologise for her tactlessness and bow out—it was Vicky's party, after all.

Vicky lowered her voice. "Colin is good-looking—*very* good-looking, but"—she lowered her voice even further—"he's also very dull."

Rose cast a glance across the room to where Colin was standing in a small group. They were all laughing. He did not look dull to her. "He doesn't look—"

Vicky cut her short. "But he is. He's perfectly nice, but . . . do you want a man to be *that* nice?"

Rose looked thoughtful. Her last boyfriend, Freddie, from whom she had recently parted after two years, had been possessive and demanding. A nice man, she thought, was just what was required. "I've got nothing against nice men," she said.

Vicky shrugged. "Do you want to be introduced?"

Rose hesitated. She could not see any reason why she should not at least meet Colin. If he proved to be as dull as Vicky suggested, then she could easily detach herself and talk to somebody else. There were plenty of ways of getting away from bores at parties. "Yes," she said. "If you don't mind."

Vicky smiled. "Poor Colin," she said. "He means well. He's an accountant, by the way. I think he does tax returns—that sort of thing." She gave Rose a knowing look. She had given her every warning and need not reproach herself. Some women, of course, liked dull men and, for all she knew, Rose was one of them. There was no accounting for taste, she thought, as she led her friend across the room, through the throng of partygoers, her friends, all celebrating her birthday, all well disposed towards her.

Rose whispered to her, "I was just interested in meeting him— that's all."

Vicky laughed. "Your secret's safe with me."

Rose blushed. It had always seemed to her to be most unfair that an overt expression of interest by a woman in a man was taken by some—not all, of course, but certainly by some—to be something to feel apologetic about. It was yet another example of the double standards that people had in these matters. Things were changing, of course, but not fast enough, in her view.

They reached Colin and his two friends. He turned to face them. "The birthday girl," he exclaimed, holding his arms out towards Vicky. "Come and give Colin a big kiss."

THEIR FIRST DATE WAS to a cinema. The film was not one that Rose was keen to see as she had read a very lukewarm review—"What's this film about?" asked the reviewer—but Colin had chosen it and she had gone along with the suggestion. He had called her after she had given him her telephone number at the party. "What about a movie?" he had said. "The Dominion Cinema? Any time that suits you."

She hesitated, but only for a few moments. Vicky had been right, she thought: Colin was not very exciting. But at the same time, there was nothing exactly *wrong* with him. He had been good-looking when seen from over the other side of the room, and he had been even more so when viewed from close-up. But were looks enough to sustain a relationship? Marrying for looks was as pointless, she said to herself, as marrying for money. But then she stopped herself. Was marrying for money pointless, or was it simply *expedient?* There were many people who married for money and never regretted it—not for one sybaritic moment. She knew at least one person who had married a much older man who happened to be extremely wealthy. He had lasted two years and then died. "So considerate of him," another friend had observed. He had left her with two expensive flats, a house in France, and a forty-seven-foot yacht in an Ionian marina. The widow had dyed her hair and started a new life. "She turned quite blonde with grief," observed the same friend.

Colin arranged to meet Rose at the cinema, where he bought two tickets for the large sofa seats at the back. Then he went off for two large tubs of popcorn. She did not like popcorn, but she tackled it nonetheless. Colin said, "This is great, don't you think? Sitting here, eating popcorn. Just great."

She said, "Yes. I like the cinema."

"I'm glad," he said. "I've always liked the cinema—ever since I was a boy. There's something about it, you see—I don't know what it is, but there's something about it."

She thought about this, and then replied, "It's dark, I suppose."

"And there are films."

"Yes, the films are important."

The advertisements began. She glanced at him in the semi-darkness. His profile was really breathtaking, she thought. He was like one of those Greek gods with their straight noses descending like a mountain ridge. And she thought, There's nothing wrong with being handsome. Sometimes, good-looking people could be pleased with themselves; often they could be narcissistic, and arrogant too. But then there were people who had those sorts of looks and yet were modest and unassuming. She felt that Colin was probably one of these, and this realisation made her warm to him.

They went out for dinner later that week. Then he invited her to an office party. "They're mostly tax accountants," he said. "But they're a great crowd, you know."

At the party, one of his colleagues said to her, "So you're the Rose whom Colin's been talking about. He said you were a real stunner. And I see what he means."

She felt flustered. The tone of the remark was intrusive—the colleague was a flirt, she thought—and yet it pleased her to hear that Colin felt that way about her. Her fondness for him increased, and she decided that the following week she would mention him to her mother. She had said nothing yet, as she discouraged her mother's only too obvious desire to interfere in her private life, but now she thought the time was right to say something.

Rose's parents lived in a part of Edinburgh that had views of the Firth of Forth and to Fife on the other side. Rose had been brought up there, and her parents still kept her bedroom exactly the way it had been when she had lived there. It was at the top of the house, under a combed ceiling; and if you craned your neck when you looked out of the window, you could see the islands of the Forth, indistinct blue shapes in the distance.

Her mother, Elaine, chaired four committees. She played bridge to a high standard and was a member of the official government body that supervised the ancient monuments of Scotland. She was tireless in her fundraising for charity and was a regular correspondent in the local newspaper, berating the government for its various failures. Rose was her only daughter, and Elaine was ambitious for her. When Rose was still at school, she had lined up various boys of her age whom she thought would, in due course, be acceptable suitors. Her favourite amongst these was a boy called Lawrence, whose father was a professor of medicine, and who, in Elaine's view, would be an ideal husband—in the fullness of time, of course. Lawrence, however, did not like girls, and he declined to dance with Rose, or anybody else for that matter, at the Edinburgh Teenage Ball at the Highland Show Grounds.

"I don't understand that boy," Elaine complained.

To Rose it was perfectly obvious. "I do," she muttered, keeping her voice down so that her mother would not hear her.

"You'd think he'd like to meet a few girls," Elaine continued.

"No, you wouldn't," said Rose, again *sotto voce*. You'd imagine that mothers would know about that sort of thing, Rose thought, but perhaps they did not.

Rose had gone to university—in Stirling—where she started a degree in business studies. That lasted five months, and then she decided that university was not for her. She accepted a job in Julie's Designs, a wedding dress shop on the south side of Edinburgh. It had its demanding moments, but she found that she enjoyed the work and the contact that it brought with people. She had been there for ten years now and had no desire to move.

"You need to get a qualification," her mother said. "What if you lost your job with these dress people? What would you be able to offer another employer?"

Rose shrugged. "I can do . . . general stuff."

Elaine stared at her. "General stuff? And what, may I ask, is general stuff?"

"It's stuff that needs doing," Rose replied. "That sort of stuff."

"Darling," sighed her mother, "fond though I am of you, at times you can be infuriating. The world is a very competitive place. You can't go through life thinking that 'general stuff,' as you put it, will be there for you. A lot of 'general stuff,' has been outsourced, for a start. There just isn't enough 'general stuff' to go round."

"I'll be all right," said Rose. "There are lots of things I can do."

Elaine struggled to control herself. She wanted to shake her daughter. She wanted to say to her: do you realise just how much you do *not* know about the world? But she knew that would be the wrong thing to do. You could not reason with so many of the young, because they were incapable of realising that they might be wrong. That was no fault of theirs, of course; it was simply the way that people of that age were. Neuroscience was always coming up with new insights into the folly of youth, showing us how the plasticity of the brain persisted until well into the twenties; and that until they reached maturity, people might be hard-wired to think in a particular way, or fail to see things that would be perfectly apparent to those a bit older than they were. One had to be tolerant. Rose would come round to her way of thinking, Elaine told herself; it was just a question of time.

Now, when Rose broached the subject of her new relationship, Elaine listened attentively, but tried not to give the impression of being too anxious about what she was being told. She was aware of her daughter's sensitivity over what she saw as unwarranted parental interference, and Elaine had learned to restrain herself. It did not always work, but at least she tried.

Elaine struggled to keep her voice even. "A new friend?"

"Yes," replied Rose. "He's called Colin."

"Colin?" Once again, Elaine battled to preserve the impression that she would never pass judgement on something as unimportant as a name. "Colin?" she repeated.

Rose pursed her lips before replying. Her mother was a snob: it was as simple as that. What was wrong with being called Colin? Did she think it was common? Throughout her childhood, that word had hovered around in the background. *Don't do that, dear, it's a bit common.* She actually said that sort of thing, Rose reminded herself.

Her mother said that in the twenty-first century. It was ridiculous. The idea that anything could be disapproved of because everybody did it was absurd. We were all common, when it came down to it. We all came from the same stock, ultimately—and nobody was inherently any better than anybody else. Surely everybody realised that by now—but not her mother, apparently.

"Yes," said Rose, engaging in her own struggle to keep the temperature low. Elaine was her mother, after all, and she still loved her, in spite of her attitudes. All mothers had attitudes, she thought, and sighed inwardly. They said things that were completely at odds with the way people felt these days. They were ambitious for their offspring. They thought their own children could do no wrong, even when other people's children were meeting with disapproval for one reason or another. Mothers! What could one do but sigh?

"Yes, Mother. Colin. You'll like him, I think."

Elaine tried to smile. "Oh, I'm sure I shall, Rose." And then she thought about Freddie, who had been the last one, Colin's predecessor. Whatever Colin's drawbacks might be—and they would, no doubt, be revealed in due course—he could hardly be worse than Freddie, with his discoloured teeth, and his going on and on about tennis. And then there was the fact that he had no prospects, or none that she could see, at least. He worked in a camera shop, and it was difficult to see where that would lead. Eventually, though, Rose had seen sense and decided that he was too controlling and possessive. Elaine could have told her that right at the beginning—it was obvious what sort of man Freddie was—but there would have been no point in trying. Everybody knew, Elaine told herself, that if you made your reservations too obvious, then that would simply encourage your son or daughter to dig in. Everybody knew that. So, Elaine had bitten her tongue time and time again, and said nothing.

Now it was different. Freddie had been shown the door and it would be possible to be more honest about how she had felt.

"I must say, Rose, that I'm sure Colin is an improvement. He must be."

Rose said nothing. She watched her mother.

"It's not that I didn't try with Freddie. You know that, I hope.

Anybody you bring home is welcome here—of course they are. It's just that Freddie was a bit . . ."

"Common?"

Elaine affected surprise. "I'd never say that, Rose. Never."

Rose thought, You'd think it, Mother. But she did not say that. She said nothing.

"Freddie had his good points," Elaine continued, trying, as she spoke, to think of them, but concluding that there were none. "It's just that I thought—and Daddy, you know, thought the same, although he never said anything to you—I thought that you could do so much better." She paused. "Did you ever manage to get Freddie to go to see Mr. Macgregor about his teeth?"

Mr. Macgregor was the family dentist. He lived in a village just outside the city with his Polish wife, who bred poodles.

Rose looked resentful. "It wasn't for me, Mother. You don't tell other people to do things about their teeth. Teeth are a private matter."

"Oh, I don't think so, Rose. I don't think teeth are private at all. We all see each other's teeth, surely. And if somebody has halitosis, well . . ."

Rose glared resentfully at her mother. "Freddie did not have bad breath. He had a slight discolouration of his teeth because of . . . because of . . ."

Elaine waited. It was poor dental hygiene, in her mind, but she doubted if her daughter would see it that way.

". . . because of some mineral deficiency when he was a boy. That can cause discolouration in a person's teeth."

Elaine looked sceptical. "Mineral deficiency? In the water? If that were the case, then surely we'd all have discoloured teeth. We all drink the same water, after all."

She waited for her daughter to answer, but Rose was smarting in silence. Now her mother went on, "Of course, Freddie was from Glasgow, wasn't he?"

The silence continued, but now seemed even heavier.

"And they like their Irn-Bru over there, don't they?" Irn-Bru was an orange-coloured, sugary drink, popular in the west of Scotland.

Rose shrugged.

"I imagine it's not terribly good for one's teeth," said Elaine. "But I don't know. I might be wrong about that."

Rose looked out of the window. It was a defence mechanism to which she often resorted when speaking to her mother. She took a deep breath and decided to ignore the comments about Glasgow and Irn-Bru. "I thought that I might bring Colin round," she said.

"That would be wonderful, darling. We'd love to meet him. And . . ."

"Yes?"

"And, Rose, I want you to know that we shall make every effort— every effort—to get on well with him. If you like him—and you must, I imagine—then that's enough for Daddy and me. We'll like him too."

Rose stopped gazing out of the window. "He's an accountant. Daddy can talk to him about that."

The effect of this disclosure was immediate—just as Rose had imagined it would be. "An accountant?"

"Yes, he's a partner in a firm of tax accountants. They have a branch in Glasgow too, and one in Aberdeen."

This was wonderful news—quite wonderful. "My goodness. They must be busy."

"Colin works in the Edinburgh office."

That was *very* acceptable. "Quite right."

"And he went to Watson's." Watson's was a large Edinburgh school of which Elaine approved.

"A very good school. Daddy almost went there, remember?"

Rose nodded. "I remember."

Everything had changed now, as far as Elaine was concerned. "We'd love to meet Colin. Invite him to dinner. Next week, perhaps. Would that suit you? And Colin too, of course. He must be very busy."

"I'll ask him."

Elaine moved towards her daughter. She put an arm on her shoulder. "We want you to be happy, darling. That's the only thing that counts—the only thing. Happiness. And if Colin makes you happy, then that makes Daddy and me happy too. You know that, don't you?"

Rose had to admit to herself that she knew that. And when the meeting took place the following Friday evening, she felt relief that her parents gave every sign of liking Colin. And this continued over the following weeks, when, for one reason or another, she and Colin paid several visits to the parental home.

It was after one of these visits that her father drew her aside.

"A word in your ear, Rose."

She waited.

"This is a slightly delicate matter," he began. "But I thought I might have a word with you about it, nonetheless. Your Colin . . . We do like him, you know. Mummy and I really get on with him, and she tells me that she thinks . . . Well, she thinks you might be serious about one another." He laughed. "I'm not one to pick up on these things, of course. Women's business. But if that's true, and if that means that you and Colin will be joining forces, so to speak, then I want you to know that I would like to transfer some funds to you to help buy a place."

He looked at her and smiled. She returned the smile—instinctively, warmly.

"Six hundred thousand pounds," he said.

She struggled to speak. But then she said, "Six hundred thousand?"

"Yes. I imagine that Colin will have access to the balance of what you'd need for a nice house. Somewhere like Balerno, for instance. Have you thought of Balerno? Or Currie?"

Balerno and Currie were two villages on the edge of Edinburgh. The houses were comfortable—and expensive. They had large gardens and a view of the Pentlands, the hills that rose to the south of Edinburgh. Balerno was aspirational—it was not first home territory. But here was her generous father making it possible.

"Daddy, you're so kind. You're the kindest man in Scotland. You really are." She kissed him. Then she thought, I'll give him six kisses—one for each hundred thousand pounds.

He looked bashful. "Have I read the situation correctly?"

She nodded. She had been intending to tell them, but not just yet. Now, however, it seemed right to break the news. "Colin and I are getting engaged. I was going to tell you. And he wanted to have a word with you too."

Her father nodded. "The formalities, so to speak. And, of course, it has our blessing. I wouldn't be doing this if it didn't."

"I suppose not."

He became business-like. "Talk to Colin. Tell him what we have in mind. Then start looking for a suitable place."

She did as he suggested and spoke to Colin that evening. Colin shook his head in astonishment. "I had no idea your old man would be so generous," he said. "Amazing."

"He said we should start looking."

Colin said that his friend, Gavin, worked for one of the large estate agencies. "He has houses on his books that will be sold off-market. He knows what's out there."

"I can't wait," said Rose. "Our own place." She looked at Colin fondly. I am very lucky, she thought. I have a nice, easy man. He may not set the heather alight—there are certainly more *interesting* men around, but that's not what I want. I don't want to be married to the *Encyclopaedia Britannica*. I want to marry a man who will get on with things quietly; who'll fix things that go wrong in the house; who'll go off to the supermarket for me from time to time—and stick to the list; who'll let me do the things I want to do and not want to be in my hair all day. That sort of man. And Colin, she was sure, was that.

For his part, Colin was proud of Rose. She was attractive, and she did not sit around, as some women did, and expect to be fussed over. She was her own person. And part of that, of course, was her career, that was just about to take off. The owners of Julie's Designs had decided to retire, and they had offered Rose first refusal on the business. The shop was held on a lease, and so the asking price was purely for the goodwill. This proved not to be too expensive, and Colin was easily able to arrange the financing for Rose. He was proud of the fact that his fiancée was a managing director, even if the business of which she was managing director only employed one other person.

Gavin got in touch a few days later about a house that he thought might suit them. "It's in Balerno," he said. "Just off the West Lanark Road. There's a street of houses built about fifteen years ago. They're all high value, although some are a bit smaller than the one I have in mind for you."

Colin asked about the number of bedrooms and garages. Gavin replied that there were four bedrooms and three garages.

"Three garages?" exclaimed Colin. "Now you're talking, Gavin."

"I knew you'd like that," said Gavin. He turned to Rose and smiled. "Men's business, you see. Men like garages."

Rose laughed. "Sad," she said. "Poor men."

"And the garden is fantastic," Gavin went on. "I was looking at it the other day, when I was out there to get the particulars. Two acres, which is pretty good for somewhere so close to town. It needs a bit of work, but—"

Rose interrupted him. "That's fine by me," she said. "I've always wanted to have my own garden. I've been doing an online course in horticulture."

"She's very smart," Colin said to Gavin. "She knows what's what."

"I'm sure she does," said Gavin, inclining his head to Rose. "There are plenty of possibilities with this garden. You wait and see. You'll be thrilled, I suspect."

They went with Gavin to inspect the house. The owners were out, but Gavin had keys, and he led them through each room, pointing out features that he thought might interest them. "Of course, you have to see beyond the present owners' taste," he said, looking askance at a set of curtains in lurid lime-green. "But once you do that, you see the potential."

Rose agreed. She glanced at Colin and sensed that he shared her enthusiasm for the house. While Gavin went off to deal with a phone call, she and Colin conferred privately. They both wanted the house.

Three months later, a matter of days after their wedding, they took possession of their new home. Colin was planning to convert one of the three garages into a workshop, while Rose immediately started work on the re-design of the garden. She ordered a large load of topsoil, with the intention of creating new beds, planting shrubs and trees, and a new rockery in which she would plant alpines. Elaine gave them a generous garden centre voucher, with which they decided to purchase a water feature and two garden benches. "I always thought you'd make a very good gardener," she said to Rose. "I always thought that."

Parts of the garden were already well established. In the vegetable section, there was a large bed of garlic that had been planted in January by the previous owners and was now full of healthy-looking plants. Rose was delighted by this: she loved garlic, and the thought of having her own crop was particularly appealing.

Rose was happy—perhaps happier than she had been for years. She had decided that she loved Colin, even if she had rapidly plumbed whatever depths he had—and these were hardly profound. He was undemanding company and utterly predictable in his attitudes and his habits. The adjective that best described him, she felt, was "inoffensive." And to that, she felt she might add "solid," "decent," and "reliable."

Elaine agreed with her daughter's assessment. Her relief at the wedding was palpable. Until the ring was placed on Rose's finger and the minister uttered the words that declared the couple husband and wife, she had been concerned that something might happen to frustrate the union. Somebody would change his or her mind—it happened, after all, and sometimes at the very last moment, right at the church door or altar. But now any change of mind would be too late: Rose had become Mrs. Colin Fanshaw, and he had, by the same token, become Mr. Rose Fanshaw. It was perfect, as far as Elaine was concerned, and her pleasure in this outcome was enhanced by the thought of what might have been had Rose married Freddie. There was a world of difference between being mother-in-law to a good-looking partner in a firm of accountants and being in the same relationship with a man with stained teeth who worked in a camera shop. The average life was littered with close shaves, she believed, and that was one of them.

"I thank my lucky stars that Rose chose Colin," Elaine confided to a friend. "When you think of what some parents get when it comes to sons-in-law, the blood runs cold."

"Ice cold," agreed her friend. "No known faults?"

Elaine shook her head. "Not as far as I know. He's not the most exciting man in Scotland, but who wants excitement?"

"Not me," said the friend, perhaps a bit wistfully.

·   ·   ·

ROSE AND COLIN'S HOUSE had a name: Pentland View. This was a reference to the Pentland Hills, which rolled out from the southern boundaries of Edinburgh; soft, feminine hills, unlike the higher mountains of northern Scotland. The name was appropriate, as the view from the house was, indeed, of the Pentlands and of the stretch of farmland between the city and the hills.

On either side of Pentland View were houses built at the same time, but of rather different style and, in both cases, slightly smaller. One of these houses was called Waverley, and the other was called Cairnside. Waverley was owned by a retired couple who spent much of their time away, at a country cottage in the Scottish Borders, near Selkirk, not far from Abbotsford, the home of Sir Walter Scott, author of the *Waverley* novels. That provided the key to the house's name. Rose and Colin met this couple on the day they moved in, when the husband brought over a bowl of home-grown strawberries as a welcome gift.

"This is a very friendly community," he said. "We've been happy here, and I'm sure you will be too."

Rose asked about Cairnside, enquiring as to who lived there. Their neighbour hesitated. It was only a brief hesitation, but Rose noticed it.

"They're away at the moment," he said, glancing over the fence in the direction of the other house. "He's an engineer in the oil industry up in Aberdeen. He spends quite a bit of time on the oil rigs, I believe. And she . . ." There was a further hesitation, again a short one, but eloquent for all its brevity. "She calls herself Tiger." This was accompanied by a raised eyebrow. "I have no idea what her real name is. There's a husband called Ray, I believe."

Rose waited. Would more information be forthcoming?

The neighbour looked away. "We don't see a great deal of them," he said. And then he changed the subject. If she wanted help with the garden, he knew a man from Kirkliston who looked after gardens. He could put them in touch, if necessary.

"I'm planning to do the garden myself," said Rose. "But I'll let you know. Thanks."

The neighbour smiled. "It will be good to see this garden properly looked after," he said. "The last people made an effort, but I think they were too busy. His business was taking off and he had to go down to London a lot. She had a sister who wasn't very well and needed a lot of help. They didn't have the time."

"I'm going to do my best," said Rose.

"Good," said the neighbour.

ROSE AND COLIN HAD taken a week off to get everything sorted out in their new house. On the third day after they moved in, their other neighbours, the owners of Cairnside, turned into the drive and stopped in front of their garage door. Rose watched from her kitchen window, standing sufficiently far back so as not to be seen from outside. She had a clear view of the parked car and the people getting out of it.

She smiled as she saw Tiger alight from the passenger's seat. Now she knew why the neighbour had hesitated. Tiger was a brassy blonde. Her hair was piled up in a beehive style, popular in the nineteen sixties and seventies but seen less frequently since then. She wore a tight, hip-hugging dress in pinky-beige. She looked as if she was somewhere in her thirties—not much older than Rose herself.

But it was her husband who was the surprise. He was short and stocky and wearing a T-shirt that displayed the muscled torso beneath. Even from a distance, she could see that his upper arms, knotty with biceps, were heavily tattooed. "Popeye," she muttered, and smiled to herself.

More was to be revealed. Tiger now walked round to the back of the car and opened one of the rear doors. As she did so, a large dog pushed past her, almost knocking her from her feet, and began to career around the lawn. The muscular man shouted at the dog, which ignored him and tore round the side of the house, only to emerge a few moments later from the front, barking loudly. Above the sound of the barking, she heard Tiger shouting out the dog's name. "Monty! Monty!" The dog ignored her too.

Tiger and the man went inside. Rose sat in her kitchen and thought about what she had seen. These were not the neighbours she had imagined for herself in Balerno, which had a reputation for quiet respectability. Tiger did not look the part, and nor did her husband, with his Popeye arms and tattoos. Of course, I shouldn't jump to conclusions, she told herself. I must *not* become my mother. I must *not*. She is the last person I should turn into. And yet, she knew that people often became their parents. It was depressing, yes, but it was often true.

Half an hour later, when Rose was in her garden, surveying a bed where she was planning to plant shrubs, she noticed that her neighbours had emerged from the house. Ray was carrying a suitcase that he loaded into the car before turning to give Tiger a quick kiss on the cheek. Then he got into the car, started the engine, and reversed down the drive. As the car set off, Tiger stayed outside to wave before going back into the house. She did not see Rose watching. Rose wondered whether she should go over to introduce herself but decided against doing so. She would go tomorrow, she thought, as it was a Saturday and Colin would be able to accompany her.

But the meeting took place earlier than she had anticipated. She remained in the garden for fifteen minutes but when rain set in, she took refuge back in the house. It was at that point, though, that she heard a furious barking outside. Looking out of the kitchen window, she saw that the dog she had seen earlier on, Monty, had crossed over from the neighbouring garden and was standing at the foot of a tree in her backyard, barking at a squirrel that had scampered into the branches above.

Rose was not sure what to do. She had nothing against dogs in general, but this dog made her feel uneasy. It was large and clearly aggressive, a Rottweiler, or perhaps a mixture of Rottweiler and some other equally unpleasant breed. Rose shuddered: she had read in the newspaper a few days ago of an unprovoked attack by one of these large, aggressive dogs on a man in Glasgow. The victim had been lucky to escape with his life and had ended up being badly scarred by the mauling. She would certainly feel very uncomfortable if Monty were to make a habit of coming into her garden. There was a fence between the two properties, but it had not been maintained, and she had already noticed that there were several places where it would present no real obstacle to a dog.

Suddenly Monty stopped barking, and Rose saw that Tiger had appeared. She went up to Monty, calling his name while admonishing him volubly. She had a leash with her, and she clipped this onto his collar at the same time as she happened to look up to see Rose staring at her through the kitchen window.

Tiger gave a friendly wave as Rose emerged from the house.

"Sorry about this," Tiger called out. "Monty is a naughty boy sometimes." She looked down at the dog, from whose jaws a tail of viscous saliva was dripping down. "Who's a naughty boy, then? Who ignores Mummy when she tells him not to chase squirrels?"

With Monty having been scolded, Tiger beamed at Rose. "I'm Tiger," she said. "I'm your new neighbour—or you're mine. Same thing, I suppose."

Rose introduced herself. Monty was looking at her, as if sizing her up. The saliva detached itself and fell to the ground.

"He dribbles," said Tiger. "These large breeds often do, don't they?"

Rose dragged her gaze away from Monty. There was something nasty about the dog, she thought. There was something menacing about his eyes.

"I've told him not chase squirrels," Tiger went on. "If you find him going after them, don't hesitate to tell him off. He knows that he shouldn't be doing it."

The two women looked at one another.

"I'm really glad you've moved in," Tiger said. "The previous people were a bit . . . well, not to put too fine a point on it, a bit stuck-up." She put a hand to her mouth and giggled, as if she realised that she had spoken out of turn. "I hope they weren't friends of yours."

Rose shook her head. "We didn't know them."

"Well, they thought of themselves as superior, if you ask me. What's the word? Condescending."

"Possibly," said Rose.

"Anyway," said Tiger. "They're gone, and I'm not going to miss them." She paused. "Was that your husband I saw earlier this morning? Going off in his car?"

Rose nodded. "Yes, Colin."

Tiger grinned. "Dishy," she said.

Rose was uncertain how to react. You did not say things like that about other people's husbands—you just did not. She shrugged. "He's my husband," she said.

"I meant the car," said Tiger, bursting out laughing. "Dishy car."

Rose was flustered. This woman was playing with her. She did not mean the car—it was perfectly obvious that she was referring to Colin. There was no such thing as a dishy car.

"And that was yours driving off earlier on?" asked Rose.

Tiger pulled at Monty's leash, to stop him sniffing at Rose's feet. "Yes," she said. "That's my Ray. He works up in Aberdeen. He often goes out to the North Sea rigs. He's a mud engineer."

"Oh yes?"

"Yes. They're the people in charge of pumping mud into the oil wells to bring the oil out. It's an important part of drilling for oil, but most people don't even know they exist. That's what Ray does."

"Fascinating," said Rose.

"You and Colin should come round for drinks some evening," said Tiger. "When Ray's back. Not that I always know when that will be."

Rose accepted the invitation. "That would be very nice."

Tiger glanced around the garden. "It looks as if you're going to transform this place," she said. "It's become a bit of a dump."

Rose smarted at the insult. She had seen Tiger's garden, admittedly only from her side of the fence, but she had not been impressed. "I hope we make an impression on it," said Rose. "But it can take a long time."

"London wasn't built in a day," said Tiger.

Rose frowned. "Rome," she said.

Tiger looked surprised. "What about Rome?"

"I think that it was Rome that wasn't built in a day."

Tiger pouted. "I didn't say it was."

"Of course not."

There was a brief silence. Then Tiger looked at her watch. "Monty needs his tea. I always feed him at this hour of day. They get used to a routine, you know. And these big dogs have a hearty appetite. You wouldn't believe how much dog food we get through in a week."

"I bet it's a lot."

"Seven kilos," said Tiger. "Seven kilos!"

Rose expressed surprise. What was the point, she wondered, in having an animal like that eating one out of house and home? A West Highland terrier would be a much more manageable proposition and less of a drain on the earth's resources. Of course, some people wanted to have a large, powerful dog. What she had seen of Ray suggested that he might be such a person, with his bulging muscles and tattoos. And Tiger herself, she imagined, would probably want a very masculine dog rather than a simpering lapdog. It all made sense, perhaps.

Tiger suddenly asked, "You don't have a cat, do you?"

Rose replied that they did not. She liked cats, though, and had had a Burmese as a girl.

"Just as well you don't have one now," said Tiger. "It's a bit of a relief, actually, because Monty, I'm afraid, is not good with cats."

Rose looked down at Monty, who looked back up at her, his eyes filled with malevolence.

"Yes," Tiger continued. "The people in your house before you . . . What were their names again? The people who sold you the house?"

"They were called Drummond, I think."

"Yes, Drummond. Well, they had a cat—a very fat cat with one eye. I don't know what happened, but this cat had only one eye. This meant that he couldn't see as well as other cats."

"I can imagine."

"Anyway, he was also rather slow because he was so fat. It was their fault, I'm pretty sure. They fed him too much. He was always eating. And Monty, unfortunately, got him when he was outside and couldn't get to a tree in time. It was awful, but I don't think he felt very much. It was very quick."

Rose looked down at Monty again. It seemed to her that he was grinning with pride now. Impossible. He could not understand what was being said.

"They were really unpleasant about it," Tiger continued. "I didn't order Monty to do it. It's not as if I set him on the cat. The cat should not have been out on the lawn like that, especially since he only had one eye. What did he expect?"

Rose felt that she had to defend the cat. "I'm not sure. It was his garden, after all."

"But animals don't see it that way," protested Tiger. "Animals don't understand about human boundaries. How can they?"

"But animals do understand these things," Rose corrected her. "Animals are very territorial. They have a very clear idea of who owns what."

Tiger did not attempt to refute this, but she looked vaguely sulky.

"Anyway," said Rose, "I mustn't keep Monty from his food."

"No," said Tiger. "Monty can get very cross if we don't feed him on time." She looked down at Monty. "Who can be a very impatient boy? That's right, Monty, it's you that Mummy's talking about. Very impatient."

ROSE RESISTED THE TEMPTATION to call Colin at his office. She could not wait to describe Tiger to him, but she wondered whether she would be able to do her new neighbour justice. *London wasn't built in a day . . . It's you that Mummy's talking about . . .* And the bee-hive hairstyle. Everything. It was all terribly funny. And yet, at the same time, that dog was not at all funny. That was an evil creature, as all those fighting dogs were. It should be illegal to keep dogs like that—in fact, some breeds were already illegal, she thought, although it must be difficult to decide what dogs fitted into which category. Siamese fighting dogs, she thought; no, it was Siamese fighting fish. She smiled at the confusion: perhaps it was illegal to keep piranhas. Pit bull terriers? Was it against the law to keep a pit bull terrier?

When Colin came back from the office, she opened the front door to him with a grin on her face.

"I met our new neighbour," she said.

Colin put down his briefcase. "I need a drink," he said. "I've had a hellish day."

"Poor darling. Did you hear what I said?"

"No. Something about the neighbours." He took off his jacket and tossed it onto a chair. "Oh yes? Which one?"

Rose pointed in the direction of Tiger's house. "That one. And she really is actually called Tiger. Can you believe it?"

Colin smiled. "Is that really her name?"

Rose said that it was the way she had introduced herself. "And it suits her—it really does. She has a beehive hair-do—blonde, of course. Lots of curves. Make-up caked on."

Colin shrugged. "That's what these places are like. Move to Balerno and that's what you get."

Rose shook her head. "I don't think so. She's really . . ." She hesitated. She had no word for it, and she could not use her mother's term. She was not going to say that.

"Common?" said Colin. "That's what your mother would say, isn't it?"

Rose looked reproachful. "Mummy is old-fashioned. She doesn't see anything wrong saying things like that."

"I wasn't criticising her," Colin reassured her. And, he thought, it will take a lot for me to criticise any parents who give us six hundred thousand pounds.

Rose grinned. There was a certain pleasure in being on the side of the fallen angels—or at least on the side of the old-fashioned ones. "Actually, that's exactly what she is. Brassy as Sammy Burns's scrap metal yard."

"Hah!"

"I didn't meet her man," Rose continued. "I saw him. He looks like Popeye the Sailor Man, but a bit rougher. He's called Ray. He's gone off to do his mud engineering up in Aberdeen."

"Mud engineering?"

Rose gave the explanation that Tiger had given her. "They use mud to force the oil up. Apparently, that's what they do."

"Sounds messy," said Colin. "Not for me."

"But I did meet their dog," Rose said. "A horrible creature. A Rottweiler crossed with something nasty—heaven knows what. Evil little eyes. Big jaws. Slobbering all the time."

Colin made a face. "Not very nice."

"No. He came over into our garden and chased a squirrel up a tree. Then she came back and started fussing over him like a mother hen. It was ghastly. Sick-making."

Colin opened the drinks cupboard that they had placed temporarily in the sitting room. He poured himself a whisky.

"I take it that we're not going to be close friends," he said.

"Definitely not," said Rose.

"Should we even try?" asked Colin.

Rose shook her head.

"Oh well," Colin said. "We could plant a hedge. A big one." He looked out of the window, into the garden. "And a fence. With a watchtower, perhaps. What do they say about fences?"

"Good fences make good neighbours."

"Yes. That." He looked at her, smiling wearily. "We don't need this, do we?"

She sighed. "You know what's been worrying me? It's the thought— just a possibility, of course—that the reason why the Drummonds moved is because of . . ." She inclined her head in the direction of Cairnside. "Because of them. Tiger and Ray."

"And the dog . . ."

"Yes, and Monty."

Colin looked thoughtful. "I don't blame the dog. Bad dogs are the way they are because of their owners. Good owners make good dogs."

Rose was not so sure. "Maybe sometimes," she said. "Then you get dogs that are just naturally bad—you know, it's in their genes. A form of canine original sin. Or canine psychopathy. Even if those dogs have good owners, their real nature will come out."

Colin conceded that this was true. But then he said, "Let's not talk about it any longer. Let's go out for dinner."

There was a restaurant just down the road—a place called The Hearth. Colin had suggested trying it when they had driven past it a couple of days earlier. Now he said that it would be a good way of de-stressing, and Rose agreed.

"I'm going to have a shower," he said. "And get out of this suit. One of these days, you know, men are going to revolt against suits. They're going to burn them and—"

His radical declaration got no further, as he was interrupted by a raucous barking from next door. This persisted, in spite of the sound of Tiger shouting, "Monty! Monty! Shut your face, Monty! I'm going to kill you, Monty!"

Colin glanced at Rose. She looked away. It was just too painful.

.   .   .

THEY RETURNED FROM their meal at The Hearth. They had not been disappointed: the cooking was excellent, Rose said, and Colin got on well with the proprietor, Tony, who supported the same football team as he did, Hearts. They had a long chat about football while Colin was paying the bill.

"We're going to have a great season ahead of us with that new striker," Tony said.

"He was expensive," Colin said. "I hope he's worth it."

"Oh, he will be," Tony assured him. "You know what I always say? I say that every penny a team spends on a good player comes back doubled. Yes, that's true. You look at what happened to Celtic when they spent all that money on that Brazilian. Was it worth it? It most certainly was. You saw it with that goal in Amsterdam. Remember that?"

Colin did not. "I don't remember other people's goals," he said. "Just ours."

"Wise policy," said Tony. "Didn't T. S. Eliot say that people cannot bear too much reality?"

Colin looked puzzled. "Perhaps," he said. Then he added, "Not really. I've never heard that, actually."

"Well, he said something of that nature," Tony continued. "It was in one of his poems."

Rose smiled. "Colin doesn't do poetry," she said.

Colin looked at her. His expression was slightly cross—almost wounded. "And you don't either," he muttered.

Tony looked embarrassed. "Oh well, lots of people have said lots of things."

They travelled back in silence. As they neared the house, Rose said, "I'm sorry, Colin. I'm sorry about what I said about you and poetry. I didn't mean to belittle you."

"Fine," muttered Colin.

"It's just that I'm feeling upset about things. My nerves are all frayed."

He slowed down. "About things? What things?"

"The new house. That dog. Is this how it's going to be? Are we going to have that creature barking his head off all day and night. And what if he attacks us?"

Colin attempted to make light of her suggestion. "He's not going to attack us. A lot of those dogs are all bark and no bite."

"I'm not so sure . . ."

They had reached their gateway. They had left it open. "And anyway," Colin said as he drove up the short drive to the house. "And anyway, if he did, we'd go to the police. They put down dogs that attack people."

"All very well when we're already being mauled," Rose said. "Not much comfort there."

"It won't happen," said Colin.

That night they were awoken shortly before midnight by a loud howling. Rose woke first and sat bolt upright in bed, her heart thudding. Then, still half asleep, Colin dragged himself out of bed and took a confused step towards the door. Rose switched on the light.

"That dog," she said. "What's happening?"

Colin crossed the room to the window and peered through the curtains. An outside light had come on next door, and he was able to make out the shape of the dog standing on the kitchen doorstep. The animal was quiet now, but after a few seconds he raised his head and howled again.

"He's shut out," said Colin. "She's put him out."

No sooner had he said this when a light appeared in Tiger's kitchen, and she appeared at the door.

"Bad Monty!" she scolded. "Bad, bad Monty!"

The dog scrambled into the house and the light was soon switched off.

"I don't believe it," said Colin. "She must have put him out deliberately. She must have known he'd make a commotion."

Rose lay back in bed. She reached over to the bedside lamp and switched it off. She could not think of anything to say.

IT WAS NOT ONLY the garden of Pentland View that required attention but the house itself. Although the roof was sound, there were tiles here and there that had loosened, and guttering that had blocked. There was something wrong with the water supply, too—a fault that had not been picked up by the surveyor in his pre-purchase report—and there had also been a call from the local council to say that a trench would have to be dug along one side of the property. And other small jobs needed to be done, with the result that there was a constant stream of tradesmen over the first three weeks of their occupation of the house. Rose took time off from Julie's Designs to deal with all this; she had a competent assistant there who was eager to show that she could run the business single-handed, if necessary.

The workmen from the council arrived that Monday morning. Colin had just left for work when they rang the doorbell and invited Rose to see where they proposed to dig their trench.

"It'll be a wee bit messy," said the foreman apologetically. "The water main here is deeper than elsewhere, but we'll try not to disrupt things too much."

The trench was dug quickly, a large mound of earth appearing on either side of the yawning gap in the earth. Rose took the three workmen a cup of tea at mid-morning and saw that they had excavated to a depth of ten feet or so. They told her that they had already installed the new section of pipe, but, since their mechanical digger had been taken off to another job, they would have to return on another day to fill the trench in.

Once they had gone, she spent several hours working on her new flower-beds and then an hour or two unpacking possessions that were still stored in the removal men's crates. She heard Monty barking from time to time and, on each occasion, she felt anger rise within her. There was no excuse, in her view. A large noisy dog was simply out of place in a suburb; he should be on a farm somewhere, not here where he was a constant irritant to neighbours, not to say a danger.

The next day, Elaine came to visit. She had seen the house briefly shortly after it had been bought but had not been back since Rose and Colin had moved in with their furniture. Now she stood in front of the house and cast her eye about the garden. Turning to Rose, she said, "There's work to be done, isn't there? But it's going to be worth it, I think."

Rose took her round to the back of the house to show her the work she had already done on the incipient vegetable patch. "Artichokes," she said to her mother. "See?"

"Watch them," said Elaine. "They spread."

"And garlic," said Rose. "That bed over there is entirely garlic. We shall be able to keep you and Daddy in garlic too. For the whole year."

"Good," said Elaine. "To have assured supplies of garlic is so . . . so reassuring, I always say."

They left the vegetable garden and began to walk towards the back door. As they did so, the sound of barking came from the other side of the house.

"A dog?" said Elaine.

Rose took a deep breath. "That's next door's. It sounds as if he's come in again."

Elaine looked concerned. "You'll have to nip that in the bud, dear. You can't have a dog running wild."

Rose felt irritated. She knew that. She felt that her mother assumed that she was somehow tolerating Monty. "I'm fully aware of that, Mother," she muttered through clenched teeth. "I haven't been encouraging him."

"You need to throw something at him," said Elaine. "Dogs soon get the message if you throw something at them."

"He's a very large dog," said Rose. "I'm not sure that would be wise."

The barking seemed to get louder, and a few moments later Monty bounded into view round the side of the house. When he saw Rose and Elaine standing stock still, staring at him, he stopped in his tracks. He sniffed at the air and growled.

"Shoo!" hissed Rose. "Go home, Monty. Shoo!"

Monty stood his ground. His growling became, if anything, rather more menacing.

"I'm going to have to call the police," said Rose. "I'm going to go inside and call the police to tell them there's a dangerous dog on the loose."

Elaine shook her head. "The police won't do anything. They're grossly under-resourced. They won't lift a finger for this sort of thing." She paused. "We're going to have to do something ourselves."

And with that, she bent down and picked up a steel garden trowel she spotted in a garden trug near their feet.

"Mother," began Rose, reaching out to restrain Elaine. "Please, don't." But it was too late. Her mother had hurled the trowel at the dog—and had done so with remarkable accuracy. The garden implement hit him squarely on the nose, causing him to emit a yelp of pain.

"Horrid creature," shouted Elaine. "Vile animal."

Monty's reaction to the onslaught was to turn tail and make his way as fast as he could for his own yard, howling in indignation as he did so. His flight was witnessed by Tiger, who had watched the encounter through her kitchen window and now came rushing out to embrace her traumatised pet. Bending down to embrace Monty, she examined his snout for damage. The dog's skin had been broken, and several drops of bright red blood now spattered onto the frilly white blouse she was wearing.

Tiger bundled Monty into the kitchen before striding purposefully across her small patch of lawn to the boundary between the two gardens. From where she stood, she was able to shout out to Rose and Elaine as they stood, paralysed by embarrassment, at the back of Pentland View.

"I saw that," Tiger screamed. "I saw what you did to a defenceless dog."

This was too much for Elaine, who quickly recovered from the shock of being shouted at. "Defenceless?" she shouted back. "Excuse me! That dog's positively dangerous."

This seemed to whip Tiger to new heights of indignation. "Pick on something your own size, you old cow," she screamed.

Elaine opened her mouth as if to say something in response, but the insult was too great. She could not believe it. This was Edinburgh, or almost; this was broad daylight; this was actually happening. Her eyes were wide with shock.

Rose shook a finger in Tiger's direction. "That old cow's my mother," she said. "I'd prefer it if you didn't insult her—if you don't mind."

Elaine looked at her daughter in astonishment. Momentarily confused, Rose said, "No, I didn't mean it that way, Mummy. I didn't mean to say that you're a cow."

Tiger overheard this. She laughed and then turned to go back inside. Rose groaned. "I wish you hadn't done that," she whispered to her mother.

But Elaine was unrepentant. "Did you hear her?" she asked. "Did you hear the language?"

"I know," sighed Rose. "But still . . ."

Once inside, Elaine sat down to recover. "You're going to have to act decisively," she said, her voice faltering. "You're going to have to put up a proper fence—all the way along that side. As high as possible."

Rose nodded glumly. "I know, I know. But it'll cut off the view from that side. We won't see the hills."

"You can't have everything. Hills or . . . or that dreadful woman and that Cerberus."

"Cerberus?"

"He was the dog who guarded the Greek Underworld," Elaine said. "He had three heads."

"Monty has one."

"Metaphor, darling."

They sat for a moment in the silence of the kitchen. Then Elaine said, "Try to think of some deterrent. Don't they make things that scare dogs off? Electronic devices? I seem to recall that Mr. Macgregor said something about having a cat scarer on his lawn."

"Mr. Macgregor the dentist?" asked Rose.

"Yes. They live not far from here, you know." Elaine paused. "Why not ask him?"

Rose shrugged. "I don't really know him that well. And I went to Colin's dentist last time. He knows him from the golf club."

"I could ask Mr. Macgregor," Elaine offered. "I have an appointment next week, as it happens. I could have a word with him. He may even know those dreadful people—or know about them, should I say?"

THEY SAW NOTHING OF Tiger over the next few days. They heard Monty barking, though, and there was a brief incursion during which he ran round their lawn once or twice before retreating onto his own territory. On several occasions, though, they were woken at night by his barking, when some movement in the garden—the sly passage of a fox, perhaps—attracted his attention. These incidents had a bad effect on Colin, who had difficulty in getting back to sleep once he was woken up. And sleep deprivation made him tetchy, which in turn unsettled Rose. Balerno was meant to be peaceful; that was why they had moved there; that was why they had committed all that money—the entire six hundred thousand pounds, topped up by a burdensome mortgage—to purchase something that was proving an elusive dream. It would have been more peaceful to stay in town, Rose thought—right in the middle of the city with all the noise that went with that, rather than to come out here to this . . . Rose searched for the right words, this . . . war zone. No, that was a bit extreme, Rose thought, but that was how it felt at times. The garden was the no-man's land into which forays had to be made under the watchful eyes of the enemy. At any time, Monty might dash out like an enemy tank, every bit as threatening.

And then Monty dug up Rose's garlic. She was back at work now, and was about to drive off to Julie's Designs, when she decided to look at her vegetable garden. And that was when she saw the havoc wrought on her garlic bed, which looked as if a small earth-moving machine had moved through it. And the same thing had happened to a nearby flower-bed, where bulbs and plant stems were strewn in every direction. Rose looked on in utter dismay. There was no doubt in her mind that this was the work of Monty. They had heard him barking the previous night, and she had remarked to Colin that the barking seemed to come from their own garden. But they were half asleep and had done nothing about it—and now this was the result.

She summoned Colin to see the damage. He looked on in dismay. "Oh, darling—all that hard work of yours. All that work. That wretched dog."

Rose wiped at her eyes. "We'll have to get in touch with somebody about that fence," she said. She looked around the garden. It was a mess. Not only was there the damage that Monty had wrought, but the council had yet to return to fill in the trench. She had phoned them twice but had been unable to get beyond a recorded announcement proclaiming that her call was important to them. There had been no action.

Colin agreed about the fence. "I'll try to find a name," he said. "There'll be plenty of fence people."

It was that evening, though, that Mr. Macgregor called round, accompanied by his Polish wife, who bred poodles. He drove up in his blue estate car and knocked on the door while his wife remained in the vehicle.

"Mr. Macgregor," said Rose, as she opened the door. "I didn't expect to see you. This is . . ."

"I was passing by," said the dentist. "We live down at the end of the road, you know. I didn't realise that you had moved in until your mother mentioned it to me."

"Of course. She said she was going to be seeing you."

Mr. Macgregor smiled. Rose noticed that he had very white, regular teeth. "Anna and I thought we should welcome you to the neighbourhood. You must meet Anna." He gestured towards the car.

"Won't you come in?" asked Rose. "Colin isn't back from work yet, but I can offer you coffee, perhaps."

Mr. Macgregor shook his head. "We have to get back. Anna has her dogs, you see. Dinner time coming up."

"Of course. Poodles, somebody said."

Mr. Macgregor nodded. "I call them Anna's nursery. She breeds them. Rather successfully, as it happens. Nice dogs." He lowered his voice. "I hear that you're having problems." He cast an eye in the direction of Cairnside. "Problems with certain people." He looked at Cairnside again.

Rose made a face. "I'm afraid so."

He lowered his voice further. "Dreadful people, I'm afraid. One doesn't like to be uncharitable, but . . ."

"It's their dog," said Rose.

"Oh, I can well believe it," said Mr. Macgregor. "Your mother told me that the dog's been running riot in your garden. He attacked one of Anna's poodles, you know. We were in the village, outside the store, and that woman came along with her brute of a dog on a lead. Anna said that it lunged at her little Celia. It actually bit her around the neck. The vet had to put in six stiches."

They walked towards Mr. Macgregor's car, from which Anna now emerged. The two women shook hands.

"This is a very nice house," said Anna. "You must be very happy to have found it."

"And a fine garden," said Mr. Macgregor. He looked at the trench. "What are you doing over there?"

"The council," said Rose. "They dug it up to fix the water main. They're meant to be coming back to fill it in."

"They take their time," said Anna. "They always do."

Mr. Macgregor smiled. He pointed to the trench. "It's a pity that their dog doesn't fall into the hole," he said. "That would give him a nasty fright. It would teach him a lesson."

Rose laughed. "Nice thought," she said.

"Your mother asked about electronic scarers," said Mr. Macgregor. "You could try one, I suppose. We found that they can keep cats away, but . . ."

"But dogs don't seem to mind them so much," said Anna. "At least, that's been our experience."

"I'll look into it," said Rose.

"You must come and see us," said Anna. "I could ask some of the neighbours for drinks. There are some very nice people round here."

"And some not so nice ones," said Mr. Macgregor, with a grin.

Rose glanced at the trench. They were standing near it now, and it was deep and dark—to all intents and purposes, like a grave. She looked at Mr. Macgregor. He was so reassuring, with his precise diction and his courteous manner. She thought that she should not have gone to Colin's dentist. She would go back to Mr. Macgregor, she decided, because one should stick to a good dentist: loyalty meant something in those relationships. She glanced at the trench again. She remembered what he had said. She turned away.

SHE KNEW THE McADAM pet shop; she had often driven past it on her way to Julie's Designs. It was just on a busy road and had a large sign outside: *All Things for All Our Furred and Feathered Friends: Proprietor, Henry McAdam.* She had never had occasion to enter the shop, but she had found herself wondering about Henry McAdam. What sort of man would he be? She thought of him as a sort of contemporary Dr. Dolittle, able to divine the needs of animals, tirelessly providing all the bits and pieces that ownership of even an undemanding and very ordinary pet seemed to require. Now, as she stood before its front display window, she could make out Henry McAdam behind the counter inside, engaged in conversation with a customer.

As she went inside, her opening of the door triggered an old-fashioned mechanical bell. Henry McAdam looked up from what he was doing and gave her a welcoming smile. "Just a moment," he said.

He finished serving the other customer, who thanked him and went off with her parcel of goods. Henry McAdam rang something up on a till before approaching Rose. Her attention had been attracted by a display cage, in which a family of guinea pigs huddled together in a bed of curling paper shavings.

"Lovely little things, aren't they?" Henry said.

"Yes," said Rose. "Although I never quite know where they fit in. They're not mice or rats, are they? Are they something to do with squirrels?"

"*Caviidae*," said Henry. "Rodents, actually. That's all one needs to bear in mind. These ones were not in very good shape when I got them. They had been kept in a cage with a floor of sawdust. Sawdust produces tiny splinters that irritate their skin, poor things. Well-meaning, but not a good idea. They're much more comfortable now, with paper, as you can see.

Rose shook her head. "I wouldn't have known."

"Are you interested?"

Rose laughed. "No, I wasn't thinking of guinea pigs."

Henry looked expectant.

"Dog treats," said Rose. "I was looking for something that a dog would find irresistible. A treat that no dog can refuse."

Henry stroked his chin. "Big dog or small dog?"

"Big," said Rose. "Massive. A Rottweiler-cross."

Henry's expression was one of distaste. "I imagine that he eats you out of house and home. Those large, thick-set dogs have an awful appetite."

"He's not mine," said Rose quickly. "He belongs to a friend of mine."

"Ah," said Henry. "A present. Well, that's very thoughtful of you. And I think I have just the ticket for you."

He went behind the counter and extracted a packet from a shelf on the wall. "These are called Dogs' Delights," he said. "I don't know what they put in them, but dogs go wild over them. It's the canine equivalent of catnip, I suppose."

"That sounds ideal," said Rose.

"People keep saying that the manufacturers of some of these pet foods put nicotine into them. The idea is that they make the cat or dog into an addict."

Rose looked disapproving. "Nicotine?"

"I think it's one of those urban legends," said Henry, passing her the large packet of Dogs' Delights. "They list the contents, and I see no mention of anything untoward. If animals appear to be addicted, it's probably just because they like the taste."

"And dogs really go for these?" Rose asked.

"Yes," said Henry. "They love them. They're large, bone-shaped biscuits. They're very meaty, which explains the price. They aren't cheap. But as an occasional treat, they're very good value."

"They sound like just what I want," said Rose.

"Good."

Henry put the treats into a paper bag. Rose gave him her credit card, and he completed the transaction.

"Would you like to go on our mailing list?" he asked.

She almost said yes, out of politeness, but stopped herself in time. She realised that she would rather that nobody knew about this transaction, and so she did not want to leave any further evidence of her having been there. Already, by proffering the credit card, she had left an electronic footprint.

"I don't think there's much point," she said. "This is just a one-off present. Thank you anyway."

She left the shop and returned to her car. She noticed that her heart seemed to be beating faster than usual. I have done nothing wrong, she said to herself. I have done nothing wrong yet, that is.

THAT EVENING, COLIN WAS home later than usual, having been obliged, rather against his will, to attend an early evening drinks party organised by a client. He attended such corporate occasions faithfully, but he did not like them. "Small talk depresses me," he said. "And these functions rarely rise above that. Golf, holidays— that sort of chatter gets me down. I feel I want to suddenly shout out something shocking and bring the whole thing down about my ears. But, of course, I never will—don't worry."

"I know you'd never do anything stupid," Rose said. "You're far too intelligent."

"Far too feart," said Colin, using the Scots word for "afraid."

She thought, And me? Will I ever do anything stupid? People who did stupid things—really unwise things—were usually those who were bad at joined-up thinking. They did not link cause and effect. They did not think things through sufficiently to see what would happen. I am not like that, she thought. I will take a risk, where a risk needs to be taken, but I'll be fully aware of what might happen. I'll decide what to do on the basis of what the odds are of any particular result. If you did that, then your actions would be calculated, rather than chaotic, as some people's behaviour was. It was simple common sense, really: don't do anything you may regret. Why anybody should find it hard to follow that rule escaped her.

Because Colin was late home after his drinks party, they did not sit down to dinner until almost nine. Colin liked something simple when he had been out earlier in the evening, and so Rose served the twice-cooked goat cheese soufflé that she knew was one of his favourites. With this, they had a walnut salad and roasted red Romano peppers. Rose poured them each a glass of white wine, which Colin sampled and described as "pleasantly flinty."

He looked at her. "I'm very fortunate," he said.

She watched him across the table. Of course he was fortunate—just look at him.

But that was not what he meant. "You know, I sometimes think of what my life would have been like if we hadn't met one another at Vicky's party. I think about that, and you know something? It can make me break out in a cold sweat, because so much of our life is just chance, isn't it? We may meet the right person at the right time, or we may just miss that person by a hair's breadth—by this much." He held up a thumb and forefinger, separated by the tiniest space. "Yes, by that much. It could happen—in fact, it probably happens all the time."

"Maybe," she said.

"And then we tell ourselves that we were somehow meant to meet the other person—the person we marry, for instance. We convince ourselves that it was all destined to be, that the planets were all lined up just so that we could meet one another, but it doesn't work that way, of course. Our human affairs are nothing when looked at against the background of the planets shooting around in space. Nothing. *We're* nothing. We like to think we're everything, but, in reality, we're nothing."

Rose nodded. Colin was being unusually talkative, which must be the effect of the wine, she thought. He must have had something to drink at the business party earlier in the evening, and now there was the pleasantly flinty wine to further loosen his tongue.

"I said I was fortunate," Colin continued. "What I meant was that I am lucky to have you."

Rose blushed. She did not mind being complimented, but she was surprised by Colin's unaccustomed loquacity. She replied, "I'm the fortunate one. I'm lucky to have you."

He shook his head. "No, it's me—I don't know what I would have done if I hadn't met you."

She made light of this. "You would have found somebody else. I don't think you would have struggled."

"I'm not so sure," he said. He yawned. "I'm really tired."

"I'm not surprised," she said. "A trying day at work, and then being on duty at the party. You must be shattered."

"I'm going to go to bed," he said. "I know it's early . . ."

"I'll stay up a bit," said Rose. "There are one or two things I have to do." One thing in particular, she thought.

They finished the goat cheese soufflé and, although Colin offered to clear up, Rose insisted he go to bed. She loaded the dishwasher and tidied the kitchen. She turned out the downstairs lights but did not go upstairs. Rather, she left the house by a side door and made her way to one of the garages. She had left it unlocked and went inside, closing the door behind her, before she turned on the light. The cardboard box was waiting for her, ready to be cut for its new purpose. It had contained the new fridge that had been delivered the previous week, and she had been intending to cut it into small enough pieces to allow it to be put in the recycling bin. Fortunately, she had not got round to that and was now able to cut the box into wide strips, four or five feet in length. She made six of these, and then, stacking them together, she switched off the garage light and made her way out into the garden.

The cardboard strips were exactly right for the purpose she had envisaged for them. Laid out side by side across the top of the trench in the garden, they completely concealed the void beneath them. A few handfuls of soil scattered across the top served as camouflage, so the fact that there was a deep trench below the cardboard was not readily apparent, especially at night.

She went back into the kitchen, making sure once more not to turn on any lights. She had left the dog treats on the table, and now she took these, opening the bag as she went back into the garden. She sniffed at the air; even the human nose could detect the strong meaty aroma that arose from the bone-shaped biscuits. Henry McAdam had been right: any dog would go wild over a smell like that. She smiled at the prospect that lay ahead. There was no real victory in outwitting a dog, but there was a distinct pleasure in teaching one a much-needed lesson. What she was doing was not cruel: it was simply an obedience lesson, a necessary intervention to bring an ill-behaved dog into line. That was in the dog's interest, surely, every bit as much as it might be in the interests of suffering neighbours.

The moon had gone behind a cloud, but there was still enough light for Rose to make her way safely to the edge of the trench. Bending forward—but being careful not to put any weight on the layer of cardboard she had put in place—Rose tossed a handful of Dogs' Delights into the middle of the trap. Then, just to be on the safe side, she added a few more, scattered closer to the edge this time. If Monty found these, he would then be tempted to go further to wolf down the others. And as he did that, the cardboard would give way under his weight and collapse into the depths of the trench, along with its canine burden. That would teach him. The trench was far too deep for him to be able to climb out of it, and he would spend an uncomfortable night down below, reflecting—if dogs could ever reflect—on the consequences of straying out of his own territory. He would learn a lesson, Rose hoped, but more than that, she would have the satisfaction of paying him back for what he had done. He had destroyed her garlic bed. She had been so excited by the thought of a garlic crop, and he had wrecked it. She hated him for it. She wanted to punish him—and his owner too—and she would do just that. She was not normally vindictive, but this was different; this was special.

She went back into the house, closing the door behind her after hesitating, just for a moment, on the doorstep. Should I really be doing this? she thought. Was it not perhaps even a bit cruel to lure a dog, even an ill-tempered dog like Monty, into a trap? It was not as if she was planning to hurt him—a dog of that size would hardly be damaged by tumbling into an earth pit—but, even so, it might be just a little bit harsh. But then she thought of how else she might make her point to both Monty and Tiger, and she decided that there was no other obvious way. There was no point in trying to talk to Tiger; she must have been only too aware of her neighbour's annoyance. No, she would proceed with her plan—it was just too delicious to abandon. It was very sweet revenge, indeed. It was compensation for the garlic that was never to be. It was about garlic, and yearning, and disappointment, and justice. It was about so many different things.

Colin was asleep when she went into their bedroom. She looked at his head on the pillow and wondered what he dreamed about. He said that he did not remember his dreams, and that he doubted whether he dreamed at all. She told him that everybody dreamed and, if he did not remember what he dreamed about, it was simply because he had never trained himself to commit the dreams to memory. He listened but was unconvinced. "I still think I don't dream," he insisted.

She undressed and slipped into her nightie. She had a magazine on her bedside table and paged through it, but she found that she could not concentrate. She was thinking of Tiger. What was it like to be Tiger, she wondered. What was it like to have hair like that, piled up on top of your head? Was it uncomfortable? Did the beehive move in high winds? Would rain flatten it?

And what was it like to live with somebody like Ray, with his muscles and tattooed arms? What could you talk about with a man like that? If, in fact, he was a man like that—for Rose suddenly realised that she had never actually met him, and she was judging him purely on a fleeting glimpse of him getting out of their car and then driving off to Aberdeen. Yet a mere glimpse could tell a whole story, and she felt that there would be no surprises in store if she ever were to get to know him better. That is not to say I don't have an open mind, she thought. I am not my mother . . . yet.

She drifted off to sleep, thinking of Tiger and Ray and Mr. Macgregor's wife with her poodles, and of the garlic strewn all over the wrecked bed in the vegetable garden. Just after two, she was woken by a noise from outside. She had been in a light sleep, and she was instantly awake. It was not a bark; it was more of a yelp. And then there came another sound—a thud of some sort.

She smiled in the darkness. That was Monty falling for the bait. That was the wretched dog being taught a long overdue lesson. She strained to hear what she thought would follow—the desperate barking that might waken Tiger and bring her out to investigate her dog's misfortune. But there was nothing, and Rose wondered whether she had imagined it. She considered getting up to see if anything had happened, but she decided not to go outside. She would not like to meet Tiger—or Monty, for that matter—in the dark.

She managed to get back to sleep and did not wake up again until Colin brought her a cup of tea at seven the following morning. He was going off to work early, he said, and would skip breakfast. "Take care," he said.

"Of course," she said. And then she asked, "Have you heard any barking from our canine friend?"

He shook his head. Every morning when Monty was let out of the house at about six thirty, he would spend several minutes barking. That had not happened.

"He must be sleeping in." Colin said. "I suppose dogs do that from time to time."

Rose did not reply, but she was wide awake now. She blew Colin a kiss as he left the room and then drank her cup of tea, rather too quickly, slightly scalding her mouth. She heard him leave the house as she got out of bed and began to dress. The day outside, she noticed, was a fine one: the air still and the sky clear of cloud. She would have a leisurely breakfast and then go to Julie's Designs, although her presence there was not really necessary at the moment, such was the competence and enthusiasm of her assistant. If she wanted to spend a few hours in the garden before going into town, that would be perfectly all right. A few hours in the garden . . . She had put the matter out of her mind, deliberately, but now it came back to her. Monty.

She went out into the garden. Walking round the side of the house, she was able to see the trench and the piles of earth beside it. She stopped, straining her ears for some sound. None came. She took a few steps, nonchalantly, as if undecided what to do. She need not have bothered—from that part of the garden she could not be observed from the neighbours on either side. She approached the trench and saw that the cardboard covering had either been removed or fallen into the trap. Her heart gave a leap.

She decided to call Monty's name, and she did so now, softly at first, and then slightly louder. She stopped to listen. There was no response. She knew what she had to do, of course: she would have to approach the trench and peer down into it to see if the dog was still there. She took a step forward and stopped again. She was unable to face it. Monty must be there, but he must be dead. She had killed him. He had fallen into the trap and broken his neck. That explained the silence.

The awful realisation dawned: I have killed my neighbour's dog.

She took a deep breath. This was ridiculous; she should go and look into the trench. The cardboard might have simply given way. There might have been rain, for all she knew, and cardboard loses its stiffness if it gets wet. She took a step forward, but she could not bring herself to go on. She could not face looking down at the corpse of her victim.

She called Monty once more, again with no response. Then, reaching down, she picked up a handful of small stones and tossed these into the mouth of the trench, still refusing to look. She heard the stones fall to the bottom of the trench. Nothing happened.

Now irrational fear took over. Running back towards the garage, in which she kept her gardening tools, Rose fetched a shovel. Returning to the nearest pile of earth, she began to push the soil into the trench, still not daring to look at what she was covering up. She worked furiously, ignoring the sweat that now began to make large damp patches on her blouse. For half an hour she worked without a break, making a significant impact on the piles of earth beside the trench.

Then she stood back and, after a brief moment of hesitation, forced herself to look over the side of the trench. She was surprised to see that she had nearly filled it, and got back to work quickly, completing the task shortly afterwards. By the time an hour was up, there was no more earth to be shovelled and, dropping her shovel where she stood, she began to make her way back to the house. But as she did so, something caught her eye: a bright glint of metal in the grass close to the now filled-in trench. Reaching down, she picked the object up: a small key ring with two keys attached and a silver letter "T," executed in a childish, florid style. She frowned. Was this something dropped by one of the council workmen when they had first come to dig the trench? Surely not. No workman digging a trench would carry something like this.

And then the realisation dawned on her. These were Tiger's keys; they had to be. The initial raised the supposition, and the aesthetics of the "T," provided the confirmation. But what had Tiger been doing in her garden? She froze. Tiger had heard Monty fall into the trench, or she had been woken by his howling for help. Rose herself must have slept through that, but Tiger had heard. And then she had tried to rescue her dog and, in the process, had fallen in. She had broken her neck—it was perfectly possible to do that if you fell in a trench.

And then she had lain there—already dead, perhaps—next to Monty, until the perpetrator of all this had come out and started shovelling soil over them. The thought halted Rose in her tracks, and for a moment she stood quite still as a wave of terror passed over her. She had killed somebody. It was her fault. It was a moment of unfathomable horror, unmitigated in any way. She tried to say to herself, "This is an accident," but it came out as, "This is no accident." She had dug the trap deliberately, hoping that Monty would fall into it. Had she thought for a moment, it should have occurred to her that not only might a dog fall into it, but a person. Of course, she should have thought of that, but she had not, and now that precise disaster had happened.

She felt weak. She wanted to think. She made her way into the house and sat down, not on a chair, but on the floor. She struggled to breathe. She closed her eyes, as if that might eradicate or conceal what had happened, but when she opened them, the world was still there—that world in which she had done this terrible, irreversible thing.

She felt something sharp in her hand and realised that she was still grasping the keys she had picked up. And there came to her the first glimmer of hope. All of this was surmise. She had not seen Monty, and she had not seen Tiger. If only she had looked into the trench, she might have seen that it was empty. Of course, it was empty; of course, it was . . . She now tried to persuade herself that none of this had actually taken place. What really happened was this: Tiger had come outside in the night in response to Monty's howling. In the course of her rescue of the dog—requiring only the sort of ladder that everyone had in their house—she had dropped her keys. That was all. And even while Rose sat there, abject on the floor, Tiger was no doubt enjoying a leisurely cup of coffee in her own kitchen while she watched one of those inane daytime television shows that she must surely like to watch, with Monty, unharmed, sleeping at her feet, already having forgotten—as dogs must do—the unfortunate experiences of the night.

She immediately brightened and picked herself up from the floor. It was now clear what she had to do. She would put out of her mind these ridiculous fantasies and go over to Tiger's house. She would ring the bell and give Tiger the keys, telling her that she had found them in her garden and, by implication, censuring her for trespassing there. It was Tiger who should be feeling guilty, because Monty had no business coming into her garden and falling into her trench.

She left the house and made her way to Tiger's front door, passing the trench on the way but not afraid now to look at it. This was not a grave, after all, not the scene of any crime; it was a perfectly ordinary patch of dug-over ground; it was no more than that.

She reached Tiger's front door. It was slightly ajar.

She took a deep breath. People left their door open for all sorts of reasons. The weather was warm; there had been a high-pressure zone hanging over the country, slow to shift. Of course one might leave one's front door open, to encourage a through-breeze.

She pushed the button of the doorbell and heard it ring within the house. Westminster Chimes, she noted—how typical, she thought; how suburban; how *frilly*. Why not have a simple ring—as she and Colin did? It went with the beehive hairstyle and the key ring with its fancy initial, and having a husband who had tattooed arms, and a dog like Monty, and . . . everything, really.

She waited a few seconds before ringing once more. Again, there was no answer. Now she felt alarm creep up on her again. She pushed the door open gingerly, as a burglar might test a breach of security. The door opened into an entrance hall. There was a table against the wall on one side and pegs on which coats were hung. An umbrella with a plastic canopy lay on the ground, as if dropped there. On the table there was a mobile phone and a yellow plastic ball-point pen.

"Anybody home?" Rose called out, trying to sound confident, but her voice cracking under the strain of the moment.

The house was silent. She called again, stepping into the hall now, and then a third time. There was no response. She swallowed hard. A door off the hall led into the kitchen—she could see the fridge from where she was standing—and she went through that into a large, well-equipped kitchen, gleaming with glass surfaces and shining appliances. She stopped. In the centre of the room was a table with two chairs. On the table was a tea-pot, a cup, and a plate. The plate had a half-eaten piece of toast on it—she could see the teeth-marks where Tiger had taken a bite. The cup was half full of tea.

She stepped back in horror. Her initial fears must be right. This was a house that had been walked out of by somebody who did not come back in. What she had imagined to have happened must have taken place. She had killed Monty. She had killed Tiger.

Rose stumbled her way through the rest of the house, just to be sure. She searched everywhere, except for one room, which was locked. She knocked on the door, but of course there was no reply, and she turned away.

She returned to the hall and went outside, closing the door behind her. She reached for the key ring in her pocket and inserted one of the keys in the lock. It fitted perfectly, just as she imagined it would. Making sure that the door was locked, she then posted the key ring and keys back through the letterbox.

She began to walk back down the garden path. As she did so, she saw somebody coming towards her. She stopped, her heart thumping loudly, her breathing short. She saw that it was the postman, Graham.

She said the first thing that came into her mind. "No reply. She's not in, Graham."

He greeted her and then said, "Doesn't matter. No parcels—just some letters that will fit in the slot. Nothing large."

He was looking at her, smiling. Was there something unusual about his expression? Had he seen her coming out of the house? If he had, then he might be wondering why she should have said that there was no reply. She remembered something her mother had said to her when she young: *Once you start to deceive, there's no stopping.* Deceit built upon deceit until the whole edifice of lies came tumbling down.

The postman carried on to Tiger's front door while Rose returned to her house. Once inside, she stood still for a moment, clasping and unclasping her hands in an agony of regret. The thought that gnaws at the conscience of so many wrongdoers now occupied hers: if only I could turn the clock back to the moment before I did what I did; if only I could do that.

She went into the kitchen and called Colin. He was in a meeting and sounded distracted. "It's not a very convenient time," he told her before she managed to say anything.

She struggled to speak.

"Are you all right?" asked Colin, his tone now one of concern.

"Yes," she said. "I am. But no, not really."

"What's wrong?"

"Something has happened."

Now Colin's anxiety was obvious. "Something? What something?"

"Monty—" she began.

He cut her short. "Has he been in the garden again? Have you spoken to her? To Tiger?"

"Colin," she said, "please come home. I know you're busy at work, but I need you. Right now. Please."

He hesitated for a moment before replying. He would be home within half an hour. In the meantime, she was to sit down and wait for him. "Make yourself tea," he said. "And don't do anything else. Nothing. Do you understand?"

THE EXQUISITE ART OF GETTING EVEN

He rang off, and she sat down, hunched in misery, close to tears, but too shocked, perhaps, to do something as simple and as human as burst out crying. She told herself that she had not meant to harm Monty—that she had only wanted to discourage him. It was not her fault that he must have fallen in an awkward position and suffered serious damage. And it was certainly not her fault that Tiger had come out and fallen into the trench herself. What could she expect if she went out under cover of darkness and began to prowl around her neighbour's garden? She had only herself to blame for that.

But none of that provided more than the briefest moment of respite. The awful truth was that she, Rose, had set the whole thing in motion. She had wound up the clockwork mechanism of events and started it on the course that led ineluctably to this result. She was the cause of what had happened; it was her responsibility alone, and if the truth were ever to come out, then she would serve—quite deservedly—a long prison sentence for . . . What did they call it? Culpable homicide—that was the term. She would be convicted of culpable homicide, if not murder. It would be in the newspapers. Her friends would be appalled. She imagined their reaction, as reported in the press: *We never suspected she was capable of killing somebody— not once . . .* Nobody suspects that of their friends, of course, and then the friends turn out to be capable of the most terrible things, as almost all of us are, if conditions are right; we all have Cain within us, not far from the surface, ready to nudge us into atavism.

COLIN SAT OPPOSITE HER at the kitchen table.

"Take a deep breath," he said. "Just take a breath."

She clenched her teeth. "I am breathing. I never stopped."

He sighed. "It's no use your snapping at me. All I'm suggesting you do is calm down. That's all." He paused. He saw that she was now doing as he suggested and taking a deep breath. That should help, he thought.

"Tell me what happened," he said, trying to sound reassuring but not succeeding entirely. "Things are often not so bad when you spell them out."

But they were; and when she had finished telling him about what happened, his eyes were wide with concern. "You didn't look in the trench?" he asked. "Not at all?"

She shook her head. "Not until it was half filled up."

Colin closed his eyes. Now he took a deep breath. "All right," he said, opening his eyes again. "Let's not panic. I must admit I am a bit put out by what you've told me, but . . ." He raised a finger. "But let's just look at it in a cool and rational manner. Was there any evidence that anybody—dog or human—was in the trench?" He did not wait for her to reply; instead answering his own question. "There was nothing. Not a single bit of evidence."

"And the key?" Rose asked. "What about the key?"

"That could have been dropped at any time. And it's possible that Tiger went out to rescue Monty. She might have dropped it then."

"And then gone back to the house?" asked Rose.

"Precisely."

Rose thought for a moment. "Why was her door open?"

Colin shrugged. "She might have gone out and forgotten to close it. People do that, you know."

Rose was not convinced. "I don't think so," she said.

In attempting to convince his wife that she had nothing to worry about, Colin had succeeded in convincing himself. "There'll be a perfectly innocent explanation," he said. "You have no need to worry. None at all." He paused. "Things like . . . like what you think happened, just don't happen here. Not in Balerno. Nor in Edinburgh, for that matter. They just don't."

Rose stared at him. "Then where do they happen?"

"In fiction," Colin said. "In films. Not in real life. And definitely not in the real life that happens around here."

Rose transferred her gaze to the floor. The she looked up. "Could we go over and check?"

Colin stood up. "Good idea," he said. "We'll go and take a look-round. She may even have come back by now."

"From where?"

"I don't know," said Colin, a bit impatiently. "Really, Rose, this is a big fuss over nothing."

Over murder, she thought.

They went out into the garden, skirting the trench—the scene of the crime, Rose thought—and into Tiger's garden. Colin went up to the front door and pressed the bell, turning to grin at Rose as he did so. He waited a few moments and then rang again. From within the house, they heard a telephone ringing in the hall. Leaning forward to press his ear against the letterbox, Colin listened as the answering machine picking up the call.

"You have reached Tiger and Ray," Tiger's recorded voice announced. "I cannot get to the phone right now . . ."

Or ever again, thought Rose.

". . . so please leave a message after the tone."

It was all very clear, as was the voice that spoke after the tone.

"Tiger? This is Marge. Look, where are you, for heaven's sake? You said we'd meet at the tennis club at eight. I was there, on the dot. Why the no-show? Give me a call and we can book the court for some other time. Don't worry, I'll let you win—as usual."

The voice cut off and the machine became silent. Rose turned and looked at Colin, who had heard the message too. He seemed less confident now.

"See?" said Rose, adding, "You heard that. See?"

Colin stepped back. "Did you try the back door?"

Rose shook her head.

"Then let's."

They went round to the back door. It was locked, and there was no sign of life when they looked through the kitchen window and then through the windows on either side of the house. When they went round to the front once more, Colin said, "Well, I suppose the next thing to do is excavate the trench."

Rose grabbed his arm. "No, Colin," she said. "We can't."

Colin sighed. "Well, how else are we going to establish that what you are worrying about is highly unlikely"—here, he repeated himself to drive home the point—"highly unlikely to have occurred. How else?"

"I can't face it," said Rose. "I just can't. And anyway, what if people saw us digging? You can see the trench from the road. What if somebody saw us?"

"But people often dig in their gardens," Colin pointed out. "It's an entirely innocent activity."

But Rose shook her head. "I want to get away, Colin," she said. "I just want to get away for a few days. I can't face being here right now."

Colin frowned. "You can't run away from things, you know," he said.

Her nerves were frayed, and she snapped back at him, "I'm not running away from anything. I just want to get away for a few days. Can't you just drop everything for forty-eight hours? You're a partner, after all—the firm can't tell you what to do."

"Oh, really, Rose . . ."

She began to sob. "I can't bear it, Colin. I can't bear being here with that"—she gestured towards the trench—"with that reminder."

He moved to put his arm around her. "Darling, you mustn't let this silly thing upset you so. Let me dig, show you that there's nothing there, and then we can put the whole thing to rest."

She pushed him away. Now she screamed, her voice rising in a shrill crescendo, "No, no, no! You mustn't do that. You mustn't dig." She became pleading. "Please, darling. I beg you. Please don't."

He held her against him. He felt her tears on the back of his hand. He leaned forward and kissed her brows. "Silly darling," he whispered. "If you really want to, we'll go up north for a couple of days. Crieff Hydro? I'll see if they have a room."

CRIEFF HYDRO WAS A large Highland hotel, built in the Scots Jacobean style, surrounded by the hills of Perthshire. Its history as a hydropathic institution gave it a sedate, rather old-fashioned atmosphere that still appealed not only to families but also to those who appreciated walks in the forests, healthy bouts of swimming, and gentle rounds of golf.

"I love this place," said Colin, as they came to a halt in the hotel car park. "I used to come here as a boy, you know. I had my first kiss over there." He pointed to a cluster of rhododendrons.

Rose glanced in the direction that he was pointing. She said nothing.

He turned to her. "Are you all right?"

She nodded mutely. How does it feel to have killed somebody, she asked herself. And then thought, It feels like this—just like this.

Colin looked concerned but tried to jolly her on. "Let's go and check in," he said. "Then we can go for a walk before dinner. I'm building up an appetite."

They were shown to their room, which overlooked a lawn on which a small group of people were playing croquet. They heard their laughter drift up from below. In the distance, the hills were an attenuated blue.

"This is such a beautiful country," said Colin, as he gazed out of the window. "Look at those blue hills. They're like watercolours."

She glanced; then she turned away.

"My darling," he said. "I can see that you're suffering. You mustn't, you know. You've done nothing wrong."

She stared at him. *Nothing wrong?* Did he even begin to understand what she had done? Did he have the slightest inkling of how she felt—under this great cloud of guilt and remorse? It was not his fault. Nobody could understand the anguish of accidental slayers, other than accidental slayers themselves.

They went out for a walk. Following a path that led into the trees, they found themselves gaining ground, looking down at the towers of the Hydro from above. The croquet players on the lawn were small black dots now; a dog ran across the grass, pursued by two children, the size of ants.

Suddenly, she stopped and grasped Colin's arm. Not far away, on a path that led in a different direction, she had spotted another couple. They were disappearing into the trees, and she did not get a good view of them, but the woman had a beehive hairstyle—she was sure of that.

"What is it?" asked Colin.

"Th-there," stuttered Rose. "Those people."

The other couple were just a flash of colour in the forest; now they were gone.

"What about them?"

Rose's voice was tiny. "I'm sure I saw Tiger."

He looked at her. "Where?"

She waved a hand. "Those people. The woman. That was Tiger."

He looked over his shoulder in the direction that she had pointed. "I can't see anybody."

"That's because they've gone."

He turned to look at her again, more searchingly now. "You saw somebody?"

She nodded. "A couple. A man and a woman. The woman was Tiger—or looked pretty much like her."

He sighed. "Looked like her . . . Lots of people look like other people, Rose. That man in the reception down there—at the Hydro—you know who he looked like? Andy Murray—the tennis player."

"Maybe it was."

"What would Andy Murray be doing working in the Crieff Hydro?"

She shrugged.

He tried to be patient. "All I'm saying is this: you're imagining things. You've had a shock. The human mind is . . ." He was not sure what he wanted to say. The human mind is susceptible? The human mind is suggestible?

"It was her," muttered Rose.

He looked again into the trees, to where the other path disappeared. "I don't think it can have been her," he said quietly.

"Because she's in that trench?"

He kept a level tone. "I didn't say that. You know I didn't say that."

He took her arm and led her back down the track towards the hotel. They returned to their room, where Colin ran a deep bath in the old-fashioned tub. "I feel like soaking," he said.

She lay down on the bed and closed her eyes. She saw the trench. She saw council workmen coming back and scratching their heads. Then, in her mind, they picked up their shovels and began to dig out the earth. She wanted to stop them, but they paid no attention to her, and very quickly the trench was empty again. She looked into it. Tiger was sitting on a small pile of soil. She looked up at Rose and smiled at her. Monty, at her feet, opened an eye, and then closed it again, as tired dogs may do, not wanting to raise themselves from their slumbers.

"There you are," said Tiger, and added, "I've been waiting for you."

Rose opened her eyes again. She wondered whether this was what madness was like. Perhaps it came upon you in exactly this way, leading you into increasingly troubled fantasies. And then, finally, unable to escape the torment, you lapsed into incoherence.

Colin had his bath. Then, when he had changed into fresh clothes—Rose did not bother to change—they went down to dinner.

A waitress came out of the swing doors that led into the kitchen. She stopped and looked in Rose's direction. Rose met her gaze and gave a little gasp.

"What is it?" asked Colin.

"That waitress . . ."

Colin glanced towards the waitress, who was making her way towards a table on the other side of the dining room. "What about her?"

"I know you'll be cross with me."

Colin frowned. "I won't. Of course I won't be cross with you."

"It's Tiger. I could swear it's Tiger."

Colin did not bother to look. He reached out across the table and took Rose's hand. "Darling, I don't think you're well."

"It's her," whispered Rose. "I'm sure it's her."

Colin sat back in his seat. "That's it," he said. "We're going home tomorrow morning. And I am going to excavate that trench and show you there's nothing there."

She opened her mouth to say something, but no words came.

"Understand?" said Colin. "That's what I'm going to do. This has gone far enough."

She found her voice, at last. "And then what? Are you going to turn me in to the police?"

"Oh, don't be so ridiculous. This is all in your imagination. There's nothing to hand you in over. Nothing at all." He paused. "We'll go home first thing tomorrow. I'm sorry, but that's what I want to do. Full stop."

ROSE FOUND IT DIFFICULT to get to sleep that night. Eventually she drifted off, but her night was fitful and disturbed. In the morning, she did not go down for breakfast with Colin, saying that she was not hungry. He had a quick meal and then came back to pick her up from the room. Once in the car, they set off in silence and did not speak until they reached the bridge over the Forth; she said something about the rail bridge in the distance, and he simply nodded and made a non-committal remark.

Once at the house, he helped her in with her case and then went off to fetch a shovel.

"I wish you wouldn't," she said.

"I have to," he answered. "We can't go on like this." He looked at her imploringly. "Are you going to come with me?"

She shook her head. "Oh, my God," she muttered. "I can't believe this is happening."

"Well, if you change your mind . . ." He went outside. He did not care who saw him. You were entitled to dig in your own garden if you so desired. He dug.

IT WAS HOT, uncomfortable work. The air was dank in the trench, and the earth got in his hair, his nose, his eyes. But he continued, tossing each spadeful up into the sky, not caring whether some of it rained down on him. He half believed that he would find nothing at the bottom of the trench—just a water main—but he also half believed that at any moment his shovel would dig into something soft—a leg, or the flank of a dog—and if that happened, he had no idea what he would do. He rehearsed possibilities: he could make a clean breast of things with the police. They would see that it was all an accident, and that Rose was innocent of any serious crime. But then again, they might not: they might disbelieve everything he said—they may even think that he was the one who had killed Tiger. Of course, it was always open to him to fill in the trench again. Then they could put the house on the market and get away altogether. They could go to live in Glasgow—it had been said to him often that there was a seat waiting for him in the company's branch over there. If they did that, then Tiger's disappearance would remain a mystery for all time. It would be no more than another unsolved cold case. That sort of thing was not uncommon, and eventually everybody forgot about them.

He heard a voice above him, and for a moment he thought that Rose had relented and come out to see how he was getting on.

"You look busy."

It was Tiger.

Colin dropped his shovel. He took a step backwards, bumping against the side of the trench. Small pebbles fell like rain.

"Sorry to give you a fright," Tiger said. "I just thought I'd check that everything was all right. I wasn't sure who might be digging up your garden."

There was a sudden bark, and Monty appeared beside his mistress. He looked down into the trench, a long line of saliva dribbling down from his fleshy jaws. The pungent-smelling saliva touched Colin's face. He retched.

"Careful, Monty," said Tiger. "You wouldn't want to fall into that." She looked sharply at Colin. "You wouldn't want him to do that, would you?"

Tiger looked at her watch. "I must dash, Colin," she said. "Ray is coming back from Aberdeen any moment. I must get his lunch ready. Good luck with . . . with whatever it is that you're doing."

OVER LUNCH, TIGER TOLD Ray what had happened. "Poor Monty fell into a trap that horrid woman had dug," she said. "I went out to rescue him. It was pitch dark. Horrible."

Ray picked a piece of ham out of his teeth. "Poor Tiger," he said. "Poor sweetie-pie."

"I know," said Tiger. "I almost fell in myself."

"Tut-tut," said Ray. "We're always very careful on the rigs."

"But I didn't," Tiger went on. "Then the next morning I saw her come out to see whether she'd caught poor Monty. I watched her with your binoculars. She was obviously dead worried. She wouldn't look into the trench, and I realised that she thought some dreadful thing had happened."

Ray frowned. "I'm not sure—"

Tiger interrupted him. "She came over here to look for us, so I hid in the spare bedroom with Monty. She searched the house and obviously thought I was in the trench she had just filled in. I could just imagine how she felt."

Ray now looked uncomfortable. He shifted in his seat. He took another piece of ham. "And then?" he said.

"I let her stew," said Tiger. "They went off somewhere, and I imagine that she had a sleepless night. Serves her right."

Ray put down his fork. "You shouldn't have done that," he said. "That was cruel."

"I was just getting even," Tiger protested. "She asked for it."

Ray stared at her, his eyes narrowed. He felt tired. It was hard—far too hard, and he had no further energy for the deception that it involved. "I may as well tell you," he said. "I've met somebody up in Aberdeen. I'm having an affair."

Tiger was silent. "You wouldn't," she whispered. Then she went on, "Tell me, Ray—tell me—you wouldn't, would you?"

"I would," he said. "And I'll tell you something else, Tiger—she would never do something like this. Never."

TIGER AND RAY SEPARATED three weeks later. She went off, with Monty, to spend a few months with a friend from school who had a house in the Borders. The friend introduced her to a local dairy farmer, Brian, who admired her greatly. "Never change your hair-style," he said earnestly. "Never." They married eight months later, after the divorce came through. Monty loved the Borders. He also loved Brian, who had a nice smell, from a dog's point of view.

Ray apologised to Rose and, separately and more freely, to Colin. "I'm ashamed of what Tiger did," he said.

"And I'm ashamed of what I did," said Rose. "But thank you so much for saying that you are ashamed."

"It's what you have to do," said Ray. "You have to say sorry."

He and Colin became good friends. They went bowling together with two other friends of Ray's—Eddie and Gordon. Sometimes they went to the pub after bowling. Gordon told them how he used to be a ballet dancer. Colin was not sure whether to believe him, and his incredulity showed. "I'm not making this up," said Gordon. "I was. I swear I was."

"He was," said Ray.

Dignity & Decency

OUR CELEBRITY CULTURE ENCOURAGES ALL THE WRONG VALUES. It creates a world of inflated egos, in which people behave with discourtesy to others and with scant regard to that old-fashioned virtue: modesty. That is one of the issues that occurs in this next story, set in the literary world—the world of editors and book festivals. There are two heroes here: one is a young man who carries with him the burden of unrequited love. For some, that is a sentence under which they serve their life. He does so with dignity and decency, as many do. Then there is a Mr. A. J. Canavan, an Irishman, whom we never meet, but about whose virtues we hear. The good that people do may be felt well after they have left us—and it may be felt in ways that we do not anticipate.

A central issue about revenge is addressed in this story, and sides are taken. Revenge may be entertaining, but ultimately, we must acknowledge that to exact revenge is the wrong thing to do. It just is. Mercy and forgiveness are important goods that we must stress at every opportunity. We have to forgive, rather than seek revenge. Remember Nelson Mandela, that gracious and good man, who embodied that so demonstrably. Forgiveness heals; it allows us to unclutter our lives with the business of the past; it makes room for human flourishing. It also facilitates the happy ending, which is what we want in most, if not all, the books we read, and in life too.

One, Two, Three

—•◆•—

ONE

"A DEGREE IN ENGLISH LITERATURE? ME?"

Yes, thought Sam. That is exactly what I want. Exactly. And it had been his ambition, right from his teenage years, when an inspirational English teacher interested him in the novels of Anthony Trollope and Charles Dickens. His favourite was *The Pickwick Papers*, which he read three times by the age of sixteen. But he also enjoyed *Barchester Towers*, because he thought Slope was such a vivid, detestable character—as was the bishop's wife. Hateful people, both of them. Slightly later, he went through a D. H. Lawrence phase, followed by a spell of reading Jack Kerouac. He also read the Fitzgerald translation of *The Odyssey*, and the poets of the First World War, especially Wilfred Owen, for whom he felt great sympathy.

His English teacher was a man called Mr. A. J. Canavan. He was an Irishman, a graduate of Trinity College, Dublin, and an enthusiast for the works of W. B. Yeats and Flann O'Brien. He said of Sam, "You know what makes teaching worthwhile? I'll tell you: it's when you get one pupil—just one is enough—who really responds to what you are trying to teach. Sam has been mine. He made it all worthwhile."

Mr. A. J. Canavan developed a respiratory complaint and died at the age of fifty-six. He lived to hear, though, that Sam won his place to study English at Durham, and that gave him great pleasure. In his will, he left the pick of his library to Sam, who selected thirty books from his collection and took them with him to university. In each of these books he wrote, *This book belonged to a great man, Mr. A. J. Canavan.*

Before he went to Durham, Sam's parents bought him two pairs of corduroy trousers, an Aran sweater, and a suit of thornproof tweed. This was in 1984, when people still wore suits and, for that matter, corduroy trousers. Sam did not particularly like jeans, anyway, although that was the uniform of most students by then. He rather hoped that he might look a bit like Dylan Thomas in his corduroy trousers, his old tweed jacket, and a wide tie he had bought at a church bazaar.

"Quite the literary gent," said his father. "Good for you, Sam."

They drove Sam to Durham and dropped him off at his university hostel. Sam's father helped him carry his possessions up to the study bedroom that was to be his home, while his mother went off to buy him some fruit and packets of biscuits. "You don't know what the food will be like," she said. "Best to be safe."

"It'll be fine, Mum," Sam assured her. She fussed so much, but then she was his mother, and that was what mothers did. They fussed. He went on to remind her about the arrangements. It had all been spelled out in the leaflet they had sent him. "They provide two meals a day. That's what we pay for. All I have to do is get my own lunch."

"Don't forget to do that," she said. "You have to have regular meals. It's really important."

"For the brain," said his father, smiling.

He said goodbye to them and waved as their car drove away. He saw his mother turn in the passenger seat of the car and blow him a kiss. She had been crying just before they left, the tears running freely down her cheeks, her mascara smudged like ink in the rain. Then they were gone, and he turned to go back inside to begin the next three years of his life. He felt a sudden rush of excitement. This was the end of a long childhood. This was the beginning of his own adult life. This was the start of an adventure.

He drew in his breath. He felt almost dizzy with excitement. It was a feeling of extraordinary richness—of exhilaration, really. He could start to make decisions.

FOR THE FIRST SIX months of his university career, Sam lived in the student hostel to which he had been assigned on first arrival in Durham. But then he was asked by a young woman in his Victorian literature class whether he would like a place in the student flat in which she and three other friends lived. This was in a Victorian terrace and was larger than most places of that sort, having been formed by the knocking together of two modest cottages. This meant that there were five bedrooms, as well as a sitting room. There was a postage stamp–sized garden at the back, looking down towards the river.

His friend was called Janie, and she came from Newcastle. The other students were Kate, who was studying music; Thomas, who was a mathematician; and Ben, who was studying philosophy and economics. "We get on well," said Janie. "You'll like it."

He hesitated. He was not sure what lay behind Janie's invitation. He looked at her enquiringly.

It was if she knew. "You may be wondering why I'm asking you," she said.

He looked away, embarrassed. "No. Not really."

But she did know. "Yes, you were. You were wondering whether I fancied you."

He blushed. "I wasn't." And then added, "That's ridiculous."

"I do like you," she said. "I wouldn't have asked you if I didn't like you. That wouldn't make sense, would it?"

"I suppose not."

"But I'm not sitting here hoping that you and I will be an item. I promise you I'm not doing that."

He nodded. "Of course you aren't."

"Good," she said. "I wanted to make that clear. We all have our own rooms. It works best like that."

He grinned. "Of course, it does. Flatmates are . . . well, flatmates."

"So?"

He made up his mind. "Yes. Why not?" He had made friends at university, but few close ones. To be part of a small group like this—even though he had yet to meet the others—seemed to him to be just what he was looking for.

He was the last in, and so he had the worst room—one with a small window and a view only of the neighbour's shed. It was sparsely furnished, with a rickety table, a chair, and a small wardrobe. He pinned up a poster above his bed, to cover the stains—somebody had thrown a cup of coffee at the wall. The poster was a picture of Edward Hopper's *Nighthawks*.

"That's so sad, that picture," remarked Janie. "Look at them. Urban alienation."

"I don't know," he said. "They don't look unhappy."

"Why that picture?" she asked.

He shrugged. "Because maybe that's the way I feel," he said.

"Detached? Is that how you feel?"

He shook his head. "No. I wouldn't say that. I think the people in that painting are waiting for something to happen. And that might be how I feel, I suppose."

She looked at him. "And do you know what you're waiting for?"

He said that he did not. Most people, he felt, had no real idea of what they wanted out of life.

"Love?" she said. And then added quickly, "Does that sound corny? I think it does."

"No, it's not corny. It's true."

"Something can be both corny *and* true," she said. She gave him an intense look. "Don't leave it too late."

"Leave what?"

"Love. Don't leave it too late."

He laughed. "But I'm nineteen—same as you. We both have plenty of time."

"Maybe. Maybe not."

He was not sure how you fell in love. He wanted it to happen to him, but he had not experienced it yet. There had been nobody. He had been ready for it to happen, but it simply had not. He had thought, when he read Lawrence, that he might learn something there. Lawrence's characters were passionate; they felt things deeply. He tried to cultivate that ability in himself, but it did not seem to work. There was an earthy current, it seemed, that Lawrence seemed able to tap into; he had no feeling for that at all. He would never succeed in being Lawrentian.

But then it happened to him, and it happened in a way that he had not anticipated. He walked past Ben in the kitchen one evening— Ben was at the stove, and Sam wanted to retrieve something from the fridge. He passed him and their arms touched. He gave a start.

"Not much room," said Ben. "Sorry."

He felt as if he had touched a live electric wire. He looked at Ben and swallowed hard. This was not the way he had imagined it would be, but then everybody said that love caught you unawares, and that you could never tell under what guise it would come to you.

Impulsively, he said, "Do you like this place?"

Ben frowned. He gave Sam a quizzical look. "Where? Here? The flat? Durham? The world?"

"Any of the above," said Sam, and laughed.

But Ben had found the question interesting. He said, "I thought it would be different, somehow. I thought that when I got to university, everything would be clear. But it wasn't. It was the opposite, really."

Sam waited for him to explain. Ben looked into the pot on top of the stove. He was heating tomato soup, taken from a can.

"What I found," Ben continued, "was that instead of being simpler, everything became more complicated."

"But isn't that how life is?"

"I suppose so." Ben shrugged. "It's just that I hadn't expected it to be that way."

They stood in silence for a few moments. Then Ben said, "Have you ever been skydiving? I have, you know."

Sam was surprised. It had never occurred to him that anybody he knew would go skydiving. Why would they? He said, "You haven't, have you? Really? From an actual plane?"

"That's the way you do it," said Ben. "They take you up, and then you jump out. Not with a line attached. You count the seconds and then you pull the ripcord."

Sam rolled his eyes. "I can't imagine . . ."

"No, you can't. Because it's like nothing else."

Sam looked at him. Why had this happened? And would it last? It could not. It could not, because . . . Because it was not how he had planned things to be—in so far as he had planned anything; and because it was not going to work. Ben liked him—he considered him a friend, he imagined, but that was all there was to it. He was seeing a girl called Anne—Sam had seen them together, and she came to the flat on occasions. They ate soup together, and she sometimes left chocolate chip cookies that she brought in a tin. Was she a sky-diver too?

He left the kitchen and returned to his room. He felt ashamed of himself. They said there was nothing wrong with feeling like that—and how could there be, if that was the way you felt? What was wrong with finding that somebody else made sense of the world for you? What was wrong with thinking that somebody else was that signifi-cant? Nothing, he thought, and yet it was not to be, just as it was not to be for anybody who found love unreciprocated, unreturned. It was just the way things were. You couldn't have everything you wanted in this life: there were plenty of people who loved the wrong person, who loved somebody unattainable because the other per-son was involved with somebody else, or who would not, could not, notice them.

He sat at his desk. There was a book in front of him; he had been reading it before he went through to the kitchen. It was one of the books he had inherited from Mr. A. J. Canavan, and he opened it now. It was a commentary on Shakespeare's sonnets, and he realised now that this is how Shakespeare felt. He had never understood that before; now he did. This is what the sonnets were about: a moment or two in a kitchen, a conversation about something that had nothing to do with anything; a feeling that the world was incomplete and would forever be incomplete, because of separation from somebody you just wanted to be with since you liked the way they looked at things, or what they said, or because they made you feel at one with whatever it was in the world that we needed to feel at one with. All of that. And Shakespeare had left us all those lines of pain and regret and beauty. He had left them there, to be misinterpreted by just about everybody, but to be understood by those who felt as he did about this, whatever *this* was.

· · ·

THREE YEARS WAS A much shorter time than he had imagined it would be. In the week before their graduation, Sam and Janie went for an Indian meal together. They were more or less alone in the restaurant, because it was a warm summer evening and people wanted to be outside. From where they sat, they could see the sky outside, and it was almost without colour, so pale in its blueness, and so sad, said Janie. He asked, "But how can the sky be sad? The sky is just . . . just air."

Janie said, "We project our feelings onto the things around us. A landscape is sad or threatening or even happy because that's how we happen to feel when we look at it. That's pretty elementary."

He looked at her and smiled. "Pretty elementary?"

"Yes. You don't need a degree to grasp that."

"Yes, but that's what we're about to get. A degree from this"—he gestured out into the street—"from this ancient university."

"Well, not so ancient," she corrected him, "unless you think of all those monks." She paused. "It could have been much earlier, of course. I suppose you know that. It could have been much earlier if Oxford and Cambridge hadn't deliberately stopped it in the sixteen hundreds."

"Ignore them," said Sam.

"I do."

She looked at him across the table. "And now, we go our separate ways. All of us."

He nodded. "Work. The world. Reality."

"Are you looking forward to it?" she asked.

Sam hesitated before replying. "I'll miss this place. Friends . . . I'll miss my friends."

"You'll make new ones. And it's not as if we're going off to different planets."

He said that she was right, but he added that in practice he thought it would be hard to stay in touch with everybody. It always was—in spite of best intentions.

"Best intentions," she mused. Then she looked at him and said, "Will you see Ben, do you think?"

He was casual. "Perhaps. He's not sure where he's going to be, of course. He was talking about going to McGill in Quebec for a master's."

She looked thoughtful. "I like Ben a lot. I didn't when he first moved in, you know. I thought he didn't like me all that much."

Sam assured her that she was wrong. Ben definitely liked her.

"I know that," she said. "It's just that he's one of these people whom everybody likes because he's good-looking and funny and . . . well, you know how it is."

She stopped. Sam thought about what she had said: you know how it is. What did that mean?

"I like him," he said.

She was watching him. "I know."

"But . . ." He shrugged.

She said, "I know, Sam. Yes."

He held her gaze. Then she said, "Is it that hard? Is it?"

He nodded. "Very hard. Sometimes. And then at other times, no, not at all."

"Which I suppose is what life is going to be like from now on—for all of us."

He smiled at her. "I like you too, of course. Even though you sometimes don't wash up all the plates you use. And you definitely use my milk from the fridge, without asking—I've seen you, you know. You think I haven't, but I have. I notice these things, Janie."

She made a show of mock contrition. "But have you forgiven me?"

"Of course I have."

TWO

B ROCK MAXWELL WAS A SUCCESSFUL AUTHOR. AT THE AGE OF fifty-four, he was one of the bestselling writers in the country and was published in eighteen languages. Three films had been made of his work, starring actors whom the public went to see irrespective of the film's plot, or lack of it. His memoir, *The View from the Top*, was the most extensively borrowed biography in the public library system, and it was followed by a book of essays, entitled *You're It*. He was often seen on television discussing matters of the day, on which he inevitably had firm views.

It was an open secret amongst publishers that Maxwell could not write.

"He's virtually illiterate," his principal publisher said to a friend. "Tell it not in Gath, and publish it not in the streets of Ashkelon, but Maxwell can't write for toffee."

"And yet," pointed out the friend, "and yet, you publish him, don't you? And people buy his books by the bucketload. What's the secret?"

The publisher grinned. Lowering his voice, although they were quite alone, he confided, "Look, he came to us out of the blue. Slush pile stuff. I've always made it a rule—rule number one, I call it— that you look at everything that comes in. And I mean, everything. Why? I'll tell you. Because there are a lot of stories—and few of them apocryphal—about how people turned down major bestsellers. Everybody has one of those stories. Somebody rejects something that goes next door and, wham, hits the jackpot. Sorry, Mr. Homer, your Trojan War story just won't sell. Yes, yes, the wooden horse is interesting, but that's not what readers these days are looking for. And look, Mr. Hemingway, I think you can write—I'm not saying you can't write—but nobody wants to read about deep sea fishing these days. And as for you Mrs. Christie—a body in the *library*, you say. Come on! Get real.

"Anyway, we had somebody going through the slush pile of unsolicited manuscripts—an unpaid intern, actually. She was a niece of one of our board members, and she was marking time before going on to something else. I think she was getting married to the son of some landed chap in the Cotswolds. In other words, she was about to *disappear*, but she wanted to have something on her CV. So, her job was to make tea and smile at everybody and go through the slush pile to see if there was anything in there that might need a second look by somebody who knew what they were doing. She liked it, she said. She said that it was an effort sometimes to tear herself away from some of the things she read. Ninety-nine point nine per cent of it was pure rubbish, but occasionally she stumbled on something readable.

"She told me about some of the things she read, and we had a good laugh. Some of them were outrageous—fantasies of one sort or another, by people one would obviously not want to meet. Others were unintelligible. Most needed no more than forty seconds before they could be discarded. So, if you came across a manuscript with the dedication *To the cats in my life,* you did not really have to spend much time reading any further. Nor did you have to bother too much with the romantic novels involving nurses and doctors. Those exist, you know. They exist in their hundreds. Or the sort of book that she mentioned to me one day—volume one of a proposed series, *Nudist Camp Romances.* I'm not making that up. Somebody actually submitted that.

"But she came to see me one morning and said that she had found something with a very exciting plot. 'It's not at all well written,' she said, 'but it's compelling. I don't know why—it's just a compelling story.'

"I took a look at it, and I had to agree. The writing was appalling—clearly the work of somebody who had been taught no grammar, but the ins and outs of the plot were riveting. We decided to call it in. I wrote to the author and asked him to drop in to see us.

"He turned up, and that was how I first met Brock Maxwell. He came to see me four days later, and that was how it all began.

"Would you like to know what he was like? All right. Arrogant. Really pleased with himself. He had made a modest success of a horse stud somewhere, and he thought he could repeat this elsewhere. In fact, he said to me, 'I've decided to move into literature.' Those were his exact words—I shall never forget them. I sat there, utterly astonished at his sheer nerve. But I had a feeling, you see, that this rubbish that he was writing would go down well with people who like rubbish, and there are an awful lot of those. Millions, in fact.

"So, we decided to publish that first novel of his. It was called *The Big Grab,* and it was about somebody who stole an airliner. That was the territory we were in. It transpired that it was an inside job, and the pilot was in on it. I suppose he had to be. Of course, every sentence needed to be rewritten—verbs added, and so on. We had a freelancer on our books, somebody who had spent years editing a *Letters to the Editor* column on a newspaper and who knew how to make rubbish intelligible. He did a good enough job, but then he went and died, and so we had to give the job of editing the next one to an in-house person. Fortunately, we had somebody who had been with us six years and was good with a blue pencil. An English graduate. He did the next one, and the one after that. He's on the fourth now.

"But let me tell you a bit about our friend Brock Maxwell. He's bought himself a house in the country. He mixes with the smartest company. He thinks he's the expert on everything. And all the time, he's completely ignorant, and he still can't write. All he does is invent his ridiculous stories and then write them in his irretrievably adolescent style. We do the rest—all of it. He makes a great deal of money and plays the *grand seigneur* as a result. And he treats people abominably. Our younger staff are terrified of him, as are junior booksellers. He makes people cry, you know. If anything is not exactly as he wants it to be, he sounds off and creates one heck of a stink.

"And yet, the readers love him. We go into reprints almost immediately, no matter how many copies we print. The public can't get enough of him, but then, the less said about the intelligence of the public, the better, I suppose. Does that sound condescending? I suppose it does. But it's true—it really is. We live in an age when people have been encouraged to be stupid. We've dumbed everything down more than anybody would have thought possible, but still there are further depths to be plumbed. Watch this space—just watch it."

SAM DROVE OUT FROM Oxford in a car he had hired for the day. He normally met Brock Maxwell in the office in London, but had, on occasion, taken proofs out to him at his house, or had a meeting there to discuss some queries that a copy editor had raised. He did not relish these meetings, because Brock Maxwell always seemed scornful of him in some indefinable way. He looks down on me, Sam thought. He doesn't like me.

On this occasion, he was taking a corrected draft for the author's approval. The manuscript had needed extensive rewriting—as it usually did—but Sam did not imagine that their meeting would take unduly long, as Brock Maxwell tended to accept his suggestions without demur. Whole pages could be rewritten—sometimes being changed out of all recognition—and simply approved with a cursory glance and a nod. He did not think that it would be any different this time.

Sam was now twenty-seven. He had been with the publishing firm since graduation, six years ago, and he enjoyed his job. He had progressed rapidly, as he had a good grasp of public tastes and a sound eye for editing. He found rewriting easy, and he felt proud of the way in which he could transform Maxwell's sloppy and ungrammatical prose—no more than ill-thought-out jottings, if one were to be brutally honest about it—into coherent prose.

He was happy. He had used an inheritance from an uncle to pay the deposit on a flat in Jericho, in the centre of Oxford, and he was able to do a lot of his work from home. He went into London twice a week, to show his face about the office, but his real work was done in his study, with its view of the canal and the tow-path that ran alongside it. The only drawback was a small pub at the end of his street. This attracted a particularly noisy breed of undergraduate, and they sometimes woke him up at midnight with their inconsiderate shouting. But that was a small thing: what counted was that Sam liked the place he lived in, enjoyed the work that he did, and had a circle of good friends in the area. One of these was Janie, who had ended up living just around the corner from him. They met three or four times a week and shared a meal, or coffee, or simply each other's company. He might be in love with her, he thought. Just. It was possible. He dreamed of her a lot; only the previous night he had dreamed that they were playing tennis together, which they had never done in their waking hours. Did exercise in your sleep count? he wondered—and smiled at the absurdity of the question.

He thought that he would invite Janie to move in with him, now that the lease on her minuscule flat had come to an end. They had lived together before—and he thought they might do so again. She had hinted at it—or, at least, he had thought she was hinting at it—and it made sense to split bills in this life, just as they had done when they were students in Durham. He thought of them—his flatmates of those days—and wondered what the others were doing: Ben, for instance. And for a few moments he imagined his friend tumbling through the sky, his arms spread wide, briefly a bird in flight.

Now, parking the car under one of the trees that lined Brock Maxwell's drive, he saw Beth Maxwell—"Long-suffering woman," their sales director had sighed—looking out of a window. And then she opened the front door, smiled weakly, as if to sympathise with him, before showing him into the drawing room. Brock Maxwell was sitting on a sofa, holding a newspaper, which he tossed down on the floor when Sam came in. He glanced at his watch. Even from a distance, Sam could tell that it was an expensive one.

"You're late," said the great man. "I've been waiting."

Sam looked down at his own watch. They had agreed that he would arrive at ten thirty. It was now ten thirty-four.

"I'm very sorry, sir." The "sir" slipped out; he was back at school for a moment, although this was no Mr. A. J. Canavan, who disapproved of rudeness, who never spoke harshly or unkindly.

The apology was ignored. "You've done the final chapters?"

Sam nodded. "What I've done is to—"

He was not allowed to finish. "Sit down. Here. Next to me. Coffee?" It was a series of commands—even the last one, which was nominally a question.

"That would be nice. Thank you."

He sat down on the sofa and extracted the sheaf of papers that constituted the final chapters of *Call at Midnight*.

"I must say that the action is very gripping," Sam began. And it was, he thought, although the writing was appalling, the characterisation one-dimensional, and the sub-text of selfishness repulsive.

"Naturally," said the great man. "That's what they expect."

The readers were always "they"; Sam had noticed that before. It was a universe of "I" and "they."

"And they get it," he muttered.

The great man gave him a sideways glance. "Let's get on with it," he said.

Sam watched as Brock Maxwell shuffled through the pages, hardly bothering to read the numerous sections that had been entirely re-written.

"You've been busy, young man."

Sam smiled. "I do my best. And I know that you don't mind my being . . . proactive."

Brock Maxwell said nothing. He turned over a page.

Then Sam said something that was to change everything. He said it without any thought as to the consequences; he did not mean it, really. It was another of those instances where something slips out—just as the "sir" had slipped out earlier on. "Don't worry: I don't think anybody will ever discover I've written half of this."

He laughed as he spoke, but the great man did not. The great man froze.

"What did you say?" Brock Maxwell's tone was icy.

"I was only joking."

There was complete silence. Then, very quietly, the great man flicked through the last of the pages and handed them to Sam. "Right," he said.

Sam had realised his mistake. "I'm sorry," he said. "I didn't mean—"

Brock Maxwell cut him short. "That's fine," he said. "Send me a proof once you have one."

"There'll be time for another meeting," Sam said. "If there's anything that needs sorting out. We're ahead of schedule here."

The great man stood up. He ignored what Sam had just said.

"My wife will show you out."

And with that he left the room. Sam looked glumly at the manuscript in his hand.

THREE DAYS LATER, the publisher called Sam into his office. He looked grave.

"Look, Sam," he said, "this is very awkward. You said something to Brock Maxwell."

Sam felt his knees go weak. "May I sit down?"

"Of course."

"I didn't mean to offend him," he said. "I really didn't."

"I'm sure you didn't," said the publisher. "I know you well enough to be aware of that." He shook his head. "Perhaps you should tell me what you did say."

Sam explained. The publisher listened and, when Sam had finished, he groaned. "I can just imagine it," he said.

"I apologised," said Sam. "I said sorry straight away."

The publisher made a despairing gesture. "He's put a gun to our head."

Sam closed his eyes.

"Yes," said the publisher. "He says either you go or he does. He says that if you're still on the staff in a month's time, his next title goes to somebody else. The works. Paperback. Audio. Everything." He paused. "And you know what that means, of course. Roughly twenty-three per cent of our net annual profit."

Sam stared down at his feet.

"I've spoken to the chairman," the publisher went on. "He's prepared to stand by you, as am I. However, we have come up with what we might call a compromise solution. Would you like to hear about it?"

Sam nodded.

"If you resign," the publisher continued, "I'll do everything I can to get you another job. In fact, I have already lined up something for you to consider. But, more than that, we've worked out a financial package. You'll get an *ex gratia* payment of a full year's salary. I've spoken to the lawyers, and they point out that if we were to dismiss you, and you took us to a tribunal, the whole business would cost us a lot of money anyway. So, this really should save everybody something in the long run."

The publisher stopped. He looked at his hands, folded together before him on the desk. "I feel wretched about this," he said. "But there are other jobs on the line, you know. If we lost Maxwell, we'd have to get rid of three members of staff, including Molly, whose husband, as you may know, is far from well."

Sam raised a hand to stop him. "I accept," he said. "It's my fault."

"I feel so embarrassed," said the publisher.

"You mustn't," said Sam. "You've been very decent about it."

"I can't stand that man," said the publisher.

"I suspect you're not alone."

They both laughed.

"And the job you mentioned?"

"Ah, yes. My brother-in-law, Chris, as you may know, runs a medium-sized literary festival in the Cotswolds. He's in charge, but they need an assistant director. The salary's not bad, and the work is very interesting. You could combine it with freelance editorial work. You'd be better off in the long run."

Sam did not have to think much about this. "Thank you," he said.

The publisher was relieved that what he had feared would be a very painful meeting had gone so smoothly. "That man," he said, shaking his head. "I wish that Nemesis would pick him up on her radar. One, two, three . . . bang."

THREE

POOR SAM," SAID JANIE. "POOR YOU. POOR, POOR SAMMY."

They were having dinner together, and Sam had cooked a beef stroganoff. Janie's expression of sympathy came after Sam had told her that one of the authors appearing at the festival was to be none other than Brock Maxwell. But, more immediately, he had to ask her not to call him Sammy.

"Look," he said, "you can call me Samuel—although nobody else does. You can call me You, or you can use my surname . . ."

"I can't call you Wallace."

"It's my surname." And, he remembered, it was what Mr. A. J. Canavan called him. "Don't forget Eliot, Wallace. Go back to the *Four Quartets*. Luxuriate in the language . . ."

"It may be your surname, but you're not Wallace to me." She paused. "It makes me think of Wallis Simpson."

"Well, don't call me *Sammy*, all right?"

She bowed her head in acceptance. "This stroganoff is fantastic. But are you going to have to deal with him?"

Sam shook his head. "No. William is."

William was the publicity director of the literary festival.

"He might have forgotten by now," said Janie. "How many years ago was it?"

"Four," said Sam.

"Well, a lot has happened since then. I suspect he'll have forgotten who you are. Characters like that only remember the people they meet if they're important. No disrespect to you, of course . . ."

Sam said that she was probably right. "But this is the interesting bit," he said. "You won't believe this."

She waited.

"William had planned a special event," Sam went on. "He's having a big marquee *Mastermind*-type event. A quiz for celebrities. They get up on stage and are asked general knowledge questions and a special subject. The usual sort of thing. We've got four people signed up for it, including that famous footballer who claims to have written a book. It was ghost-written, of course, but everybody's being polite and not mentioning that."

"And Brock Maxwell?"

"He agreed to participate, but . . ."

"He wants top billing?"

"No, he didn't say anything about that. What he wants is to see the questions in advance."

Janie gasped. "No!"

"Yes."

"What did William say? Did he tell him to get lost?"

Sam shook his head. "I was really surprised that William agreed. He said that it will make a real difference to the crowd that day, and that will have a knock-on effect on book sales—on everything, really. They'll come to hear the great Brock Maxwell."

"But that's so dishonest," protested Janie.

"That's what I told him," Sam said. "But he just smiled."

"That's all?"

"Yes. He just smiled."

"So, he's going to come across as being impressively well informed?" exclaimed Janie.

"That's very much in character," Sam said. "There's a massive ego there."

Janie looked thoughtful. "What are you going to do?"

Sam shrugged. "Nothing. It's William's event. I've told him I don't approve, but I can't throw my weight around."

Janie looked unhappy. "Sickening," she said.

Sam agreed. "Sometimes I think the world's a very flawed place," he said. "It's full of deception, of one sort or another. Falsity. Lies. Bullying behaviour."

"And boastfulness," added Janie.

"That too," said Sam.

They lapsed into silence. After they finished their meal, they turned on the television and watched an episode in a crime series. They knew the villain would get his just deserts—that always happened in the parallel world that was portrayed on screen, even if it only rarely happened in real life.

THEY NOTICED THE EFFECT of Brock Maxwell's appearance at the festival. Although they usually got better crowds on the third day of the festival—always a Saturday—on this occasion there were at least another two thousand people thronging into the grounds of the country park where the events took place. Sam was wary: he had no intention of bumping into Brock Maxwell, and so he asked one of his assistants to tell him when the great man arrived.

"Here now," the young man told him, just before lunch. "Big car—lots of fuss. He insisted on bringing the car into the grounds. What a . . ."

He did not complete the remark, just looked away. The volunteers who helped at the festival were all told not to be rude to the guests, whatever the provocation.

"It's all right," said Sam. "A commonly held opinion."

Shortly before the author *Mastermind* event was due to be held, Sam met William in the office tent.

"A big crowd, I see," Sam said. "Well done."

"Ten thousand pounds in ticket money," said William, smiling with pleasure. "How's that?"

"Not at all bad," said Sam.

William drew him aside. "I know you disapprove."

Sam said nothing.

"You do, don't you?" William persisted.

"Well," said Sam, "I think it's dishonest. He's deceiving his own fans. And we're letting him do it. That makes us . . ."

"Accomplices?" supplied William.

"In a word, yes."

William lowered his voice. "Actually, I have a score to settle with that man."

Sam stared at him. "With Maxwell?"

William looked about him. There was a general hustle and bustle in the tent, but nobody could overhear their conversation. "He humiliated me once," he said. "It was years ago. I was working in a large bookshop in Manchester. I was in charge of events. Maxwell came to do a talk and there were large crowds—really large crowds. We ran out of stock for the signing. I'd ordered plenty, but we hadn't anticipated quite as many people would come along to get a signed copy of his . . . of his rubbish. Anyway, they did. And then we ran out . . ."

Sam listened intently.

"When we ran out, Maxwell got hold of the microphone and announced to the whole shop that the organiser of the event—and he named me—was completely useless. He said, 'He calls himself a bookseller, but draw your own conclusions everyone.' And then he stormed off. My manager was furious—with me."

Sam shook his head. He was not surprised. "That's the way he treats people," he said. "No surprises there."

But he was surprised that William should so readily have fallen in with the author's outrageous insistence on seeing his quiz questions in advance.

But then William said, "Payback day today."

William took some papers from a file. "See these?" he said. "These are copies of the question sheets we gave to Maxwell. These are the questions he will be expecting and will have prepared the answers for." He held up a different set of sheets. "And these—these are the questions I'm going to give the quizmaster." He grinned. "Different, you see."

Sam gasped. "He doesn't know that?"

William was triumphant. "Of course not. He's going to go on stage thinking that he'll make a clean sweep and that everyone will be vastly impressed with the range of his knowledge. Big genius. Big genius. But"—he paused, savouring the moment—"but, in fact, he's going to get zero because he won't know any of the answers. His natural ignorance—which is fathomless, I believe—will be revealed."

William rolled his eyes with delight. He thrust a copy of each sheet into Sam's hand. "Watch from the wings. Watch it all unfold—every glorious moment of it."

Sam was silent. The event was now about to start, and one of the volunteers had brought the team of three authors, including Brock

Maxwell, to the back of the tent. It had been planned that they would walk down the aisle acknowledging the applause that would greet their arrival. Brock Maxwell's fans would be especially excited, as some of them were already sneaking photographs of their hero.

Sam stood well back out of sight of the audience. From where he was, at the side of the stage, he was partly obscured from view even by the participants—although if Brock Maxwell turned and craned his neck, he might see him.

The quizmaster came on stage and began proceedings. When he introduced Brock Maxwell, the applause was thunderous.

The other two authors went first. They were asked a range of general knowledge questions, and then questions around a special subject they had chosen themselves. Some of the questions were intended to be humorous, and they brought laughter from the crowd. Between each author, a musician came on stage and entertained the crowd for five minutes or so. The audience enjoyed itself.

Then it was Brock Maxwell's turn. He stood behind the contestants' podium, confident and smirking. The quizmaster reached for his sheet of questions and posed the first question. "Who was the first person to climb Mount Everest?"

There was complete silence. Brock Maxwell frowned. He stared at the quizmaster. "Could you repeat that?" he asked.

"The question is: who was the first person to climb Mount Everest?" And then, "I take it you've heard of Mount Everest, Mr. Maxwell?"

Brock Maxwell looked down at the floor. "Pass," he muttered.

The answer was given. "I would have accepted either Edmund Hillary or Tenzing Norgay," said the quizmaster.

The next question was asked: "Who wrote the novel *Brideshead Revisited?*"

The clock at the back of the stage ticked. The audience murmured. "Somerset Maugham?"

"No. Somerset Maugham did not write *Brideshead Revisited*. Nor did you, I believe, Mr. Maxwell!"

The audience loved the joke. Brock Maxwell smarted.

I am witnessing, thought Sam, a man's humiliation. That is what this is: a public humiliation. Then he said to himself, And it is exactly the same humiliation that he has inflicted on others. Exactly the same. Is this how it has to be?

Sam heard the voice of Mr. A. J. Canavan. He was sure he heard him.

And that is the point at which he stepped forward onto the stage. The quizmaster looked at him with surprise. He knew, though, that Sam was the assistant director, and so he did not challenge him as Sam gave him the other sheet of questions—the one that Brock Maxwell had already seen.

"A bit of a mix-up," Sam whispered to the quizmaster, taking from him the sheet of unseen questions. "Here. These are the right ones."

The quizmaster shrugged. He had not been told of William's agreement with Brock Maxwell. "Administrative error," he announced to the audience, who laughed appreciatively.

From the podium, Brock Maxwell watched Sam. His expression was impassive. The event continued.

"Now, Mr. Maxwell," the quizmaster continued, "after that brief mix-up: with which city in India was the production of jute particularly associated?"

Brock Maxwell smiled. "Calcutta. Or Kolkata, as it now is. It changed its name in 2001, to match the Bengali pronunciation."

"That's impressive," said the quizmaster.

The audience applauded.

And then, "Here's a tough one: can you name the three astronauts who took part in the Apollo 13 mission?"

Brock Maxwell put a hand to his brow, to give the impression of thinking. "I'll try," he said. "Let me see now: James Lovell, Fred Haise, and . . . and . . ." The audience held its breath. "And Jack Swigert."

The quizmaster was impressed. "Absolutely," he exclaimed.

"James Lovell had already flown three missions," Brock Maxwell continued. "He had clocked up five hundred and seventy-two space flight hours before the mission began."

There was an audible intake of breath from the audience. Everybody was astonished. "He's brilliant," whispered a woman in the front row to her friend beside her. The friend nodded. "Amazing," she whispered back.

． ． ．

IT WAS BROCK MAXWELL who sought out Sam afterwards. Sam had not intended to meet him, but the great man found him in the office tent. He drew him aside.

"I wanted to see you," he said. "We haven't seen one another for . . . for what? Five years?"

"Four," said Sam.

Brock Maxwell's gaze was unrelentless. "What happened back there?"

"A mix-up," said Sam.

"You saved me."

"Perhaps," said Sam.

Brock Maxwell was silent. He looked up at the roof of the tent. Then he lowered his eyes. "I think I might owe you an apology," he said.

Sam hesitated. "You might also owe an apology to William, you know."

It was a few moments before this drew a response. Then, "Perhaps. But you . . . Will you forgive me now?"

"I already had," said Sam.

JANIE COOKED DINNER that night. She said to Sam, "You're tired."

He said, "It's been a long day."

"Of course. And tomorrow's a big day too."

"Yes. But it's all going well. Really well."

They looked at one another and smiled. It was.

Alexander McCall Smith is the author of the No. 1 Ladies' Detective Agency novels and of a number of other series and stand-alone books. His works have been translated into more than forty languages and have been best sellers throughout the world. He lives in Scotland.

A NOTE ON THE TYPE

The text of this book was set in Ehrhardt, a typeface based on the specimens of "Dutch" types found at the Ehrhardt foundry in Leipzig. The original design of the face was the work of Nicholas Kis, a Hungarian punch cutter known to have worked in Amsterdam from 1680 to 1689. The modern version of Ehrhardt was cut by the Monotype Corporation of London in 1937.

Typeset by Scribe,
Philadelphia, Pennsylvania

Printed and bound by Berryville Graphics,
Berryville, Virginia

Designed by Betty Lew